OF MERCHANTS
& HEROES

PAUL
WATERS

OF MERCHANTS
& HEROES

MACMILLAN

First published 2008 by Macmillan
an imprint of Pan Macmillan Ltd
Pan Macmillan, 20 New Wharf Road, London N1 9RR
Basingstoke and Oxford
Associated companies throughout the world
www.panmacmillan.com

ISBN 978-0-230-53031-7 HB
ISBN 978-0-230-70398-8 TPB

1 3 5 7 9 8 6 4 2

A CIP catalogue record for this book is available from
the British Library.

Maps designed by Raymond Turvey

Typeset by SetSystems Ltd, Saffron Walden, Essex
Printed and bound in Great Britain by
Mackays of Chatham plc, Chatham, Kent

Visit **www.panmacmillan.com** to read more about all our books
and to buy them. You will also find features, author interviews and
news of any author events, and you can sign up for e-newsletters
so that you're always first to hear about our new releases.

ITALY

GREECE

THE AEGEAN BASIN

HOTSPUR: . . . the time of life is short;
To spend that shortness basely were too long . . .

Shakespeare, *King Henry IV*, Part 1, Act 5, Scene 2.

It is in the capacity to love, that is to see,
that the liberation of the soul from fantasy consists.

Iris Murdoch, *The Sovereignty of Good*

ONE

WHEN I WAS FOURTEEN I put aside my boy's tunic and assumed the plain mantle of adulthood. We held a ceremony at home on the farm, at the shrine of the Lares beside the olive grove. The slaves and the farmhands stood by while my father sacrificed a goat-kid, and afterwards poured wine and incense for the god.

I had supposed, without knowing how, that from that day everything would be different. But next morning, when the feast was over and my new white toga had been folded and packed away in the old bronze-bound clothes-chest in my room, I felt just as much a boy as before. It was only later that year that I learnt what it was to leave childish things behind, when I killed a man.

I daresay, if you are a Roman, this will not surprise you greatly, for at that time the remnants of Hannibal's army were still scattered all over Italy, raiding farms and setting upon unwary travellers. But the man I killed was not one of Hannibal's men, nor was I in Italy when it happened. And though I was glad he died, I had not intended to kill him.

My father was a quiet, pious, learned man. He could have gone to Rome and made a name for himself, and a fortune with it, as many men were doing then. But he used to say that fame among fools was no fame at all, and chose instead to stay on our farm in high Praeneste, reading his books and living with the steady turn of the seasons, as his ancestors had done before him. He was at that time about fifty, lean and grey-haired and old-looking. But for all his gentleness he had a core of iron.

When I grew up, and had learned a few things for myself, I came to realize that he was a good man, and his quiet came not from dullness but from wisdom. But at the time, like any boy of fourteen, I merely thought him distant and austere, and I longed for something new.

Change came soon enough. In that same year, the first of my manhood, he called me one day to his study and announced he intended to pay a visit to my uncle on the island of Kerkyra, where the Roman naval base was. Saying it was time I saw something of the world, he took me with him. And so it was, that spring, when the ewes had borne their lambs and the snows had melted from the high passes, that we took the coast-road south, and at Brundisium boarded a merchantman bound for Greece.

I remember on the prow was carved a fearsome gaping serpent's head, Carthaginian work with blood-red eyes and bared teeth. The Libyan crewman with the gold hoop earring and oiled black hair laughed when he saw me staring, and whispered in my ear that it was to ward off the evil spirits of the sea, of which there were many. So much for magic charms. I have never put my trust in them since.

The other passengers were businessmen mostly – traders and merchants on their way to Kerkyra and Greece, full of their affairs, and measuring their worth by their neighbour's. They sat about under the awning at the stern, or hung over the rail looking gravely at the water, mumbling prayers for luck, or talking loudly with false confidence. For a sea crossing is always uncertain.

And there was the girl.

She kept herself apart, standing at the far rail with her elderly, fussing Greek tutor. I smiled at her once, but she did not smile back. She was fine-boned, with a mantle of white silk pulled up over her hair. Even while her things were being carried on board, the Libyan had his eye on her. I saw him sitting on a coil of mooring line, picking at his glistening hair with his long nails and staring like a lizard. Once, she turned and caught him, and then he looked away. He had a strange expression on his face, like hunger. I have seen it many times since; but then I was young, and did not know it for what it was.

As for me, I liked the way she kept to herself and ignored the chattering merchants. She had a natural dignity, complete in what she was, like someone old caught in a child's body.

Little did I know, on that bright morning, that she would tear my life apart. Such is the blindness the gods grant to men, to spare them from madness. The Fates weave what they weave, and not even a god can undo their handiwork.

The pirates came on the afternoon of the second day.

We had already crossed the open water between Italy and Greece, and were sailing south, following the coast of Epeiros with its dark cliffs and pine-clad hills. Already, far ahead, the shadowy peak of Kerkyra island loomed on the horizon, and the passengers, anticipating the end of their journey, had begun to spread about the deck. I could see my father, his face serious, nodding as one of them bored him with some business talk.

I turned back to the sea. I was sitting by the anchor in the prow, with my legs dangling over the side, looking out for dolphins. The girl had come forward and was standing nearby, under the shade of the great square sail. Suddenly she stepped up and said, 'What is that?'

I looked up at her, then followed her gaze. At first I could see nothing except the still, rocky coastline, pink and purple in the slanting light. I shaded my eyes with my hand.

'No, there,' she said, pointing.

Off to one side was a small wooded islet. It was so close to the coast that I thought at first it was no more than a headland jutting out into the sea.

A low sleek craft had emerged, speeding out from under its lee, bearing down on us, its black oars thrashing on the water.

I stared stupidly out at it, not understanding, wondering why a fishing boat was in so much hurry, and why it needed so many men. A second craft raced out behind the first, and the first spiders of fear crept up my spine.

There was a silence. Then, from the stern-house, one of the passengers screamed, and suddenly there was shouting and running everywhere. The helmsman dropped the steering-pole; the ship began to veer towards the shore. Over the din the pilot was barking out orders; but no one took any notice.

From my place in the bow I stared back appalled, trying to see my father, and found myself looking into the face of the Libyan. He was sitting calmly to one side. I thought at first he was asleep, until I saw him turn and look at the girl with his cold, staring eyes.

There was no time to consider this. Her tutor came rushing, flailing his arms and pushing at the passengers who stumbled into his way. When he was close enough he began wailing that we were all about to die.

So far I thought the girl had not understood the danger. But now, in a sharp, clear voice, she said, 'Yes, Gryllos. I have seen. Can you swim?'

He looked at her, then gaped at the water with horror.

'No,' she said. 'Nor can I. So we shall have to see what these pirates want.' She cast her eye over the deck at the panic around her. Then she said, 'You are a man, and a slave, and I am a senator's daughter. So calm yourself. It is me they want most of all.'

She turned back to the rail, and her eyes met mine. She was older than I, but only by a year or two; yet all around us men three times her age were tearing their hair and crying out to the gods. It was not that she was not afraid; her face had turned ashen, and I saw, before she steadied it on the rail, that her small hand was trembling. But somehow she faced down her fear and mastered it, young though she was.

All this I comprehended in an instant; and I knew then that it was more than my life was worth to let her see me afraid. So I swallowed my rising terror and stood beside her, and solemnly said, in the voice my father used when he addressed the gods, 'I will not let them hurt you. I promise.'

She looked into my face with surprise. Her mantle had fallen back from her head. The breeze rippled in the folds, and stirred the wisps of her hair that strayed out from beneath. When I think of her, that is what I remember. 'Thank you,' she said after a moment, and she smiled, as a mother might smile at the innocence of a child.

Then, turning sharply to the whimpering slave, 'Be quiet, Gryllos! Shame on you.'

The pirates fell upon our ship like hounds on a wounded stag. The pilot protested and they killed him. They greeted the Libyan as an old friend, slapping him on the back and laughing and joking with him as they towed us ashore and marched us up the hillside. I listened to them. At home, I had learned enough Greek to know they spoke some version of it; but their accent was strange and uncouth. I asked my father who they were.

'Illyrians,' he said, casting a grim look at our laughing captors. 'A nation of pirates and thieves all of them.'

We were being led up a steep narrow path that rose between the cliffs, and could only talk when they were not close by, or they would slap and punch us, and threaten us with their knives. I could see the girl up ahead, being led by the Libyan, and presently I remarked under my breath, 'The girl said it was her they wanted.'

'What they want is gold,' said my father. 'They will demand a ransom, in exchange for her life.'

I tilted my head towards the Libyan. 'That man knew.' And then, as my mind worked, 'But what of us, Father?'

For a moment he did not answer. Then he said, 'We have no gold to give them.'

I looked up at him and considered what this meant. I was young, but I was not a fool. I closed my mouth on my next question.

Ahead I saw a sudden movement as the Libyan's arm went up and he snatched the veil of thin white silk from the girl's head. She had bound her hair at the back with a small enamelled brooch, white on gold; the delicate fili-gree work glinted in the sunlight. Now he tore it roughly from her head, not even troubling to undo the clasp. Even from so far back I saw the fair strands of her hair come away with the brooch; it must have hurt, but she did not flinch. She walked on, not lowering herself to notice.

But my father had noticed. His face was stiff and expressionless as carved wood, and his eyes glared with anger.

The pirates had made their camp in the ruins of some once-great city. Some ancient cataclysm must have made the citizens flee. It stood abandoned, crumbling white-washed houses and caved-in roofs spread out across the plateau to the edges of the pine forest. Their leader was waiting in what must once have been the marketplace, standing on the steps of a ruined temple, looking out to sea.

He was not like the others, who were dark and thickset and festooned with looted jewels. His face was broad and boyish, and he had a mass of flaxen hair that fell curling about his shoulders.

A charcoal fire was glowing in a bronze bowl on the altar. As we drew near he seized a fistful of incense from a casket and tossed it in. The incense spluttered and hissed, sending a plume of blue smoke up between the bleached columns. Then he turned and grinned at us. He seemed almost friendly, until you saw his eyes, which were dark and cunning.

From beside me someone spoke, in a voice charged with anger and disgust. 'You dare to do honour to the gods, who uphold order in the world?' It took me a moment to realize it was my father.

The other passengers stared at him. But the blond pirate threw his head back and laughed.

'Do you suppose,' he cried, 'I am honouring Zeus the Cloud-Gatherer, old man? Or Far-Shooting Apollo? Or Harmony? Or Justice?'

He swept his arm to and fro through the incense-smoke, scattering it. Then he leapt down the remaining steps.

Close up, I could see his boyish prettiness was flawed. Under his short beard his cheeks were pockmarked, and there were lines about his eyes, making them look oddly older than the rest of him, like an old man's eyes planted in a young face. With a sudden wild movement he gestured back at the temple. The roof had collapsed long ago; the faded columns pointed up to the empty sky, supporting nothing. Within, in the cella where the image of the god should have stood, were piled up glittering heaps of stolen treasure: strong dark-wood chests bound with brass and iron, tall amphoras of wine and oil, inlaid caskets of the kind men keep their savings in, and women their jewels; and, strewn all about, great piles of embroidered linen, silks, and fine dyed wool, cloaks and dresses spilling from open chests and tossed about on the flagstones like worthless rags. If their owners had been ransomed, they had left without their clothes.

'The gods are gone!' cried the blond pirate at my father. 'So I choose my own gods – what could be better? Shall I tell you their names? They are Lawlessness and Impiety! Great Lawlessness, who orders the world, and Impiety, who suckled me at her lush breast.'

He laughed, and slapped his thighs, greatly amused, and the other pirates joined in.

'Does that shock you, old man?' he went on, suddenly serious. 'But look at me!' He spread his arms out sideways like a man showing off a new tunic. 'I am rich and powerful; I have all I desire. And you? You are my prisoner, a broken crushed old fool like all the rest. I live and thrive, and you will soon be dead.' His face twisted in a parody of confusion and he thrust up a questioning finger. 'So, tell me, whose gods are greater, mine or yours?'

He began to turn away; I do not think he expected an answer. But my father pointed to the sheer edge of the plateau, where an ancient twisted olive tree was growing out of a fissure in the rock. The tree was half dead. On one of the fractured, leafless branches there was a lurid growth of fungus. With a bravery and a depth of anger I never knew he possessed he said in a cold, steady voice, 'There are some creatures that live by drawing their life-force from another. For a time they thrive, but when the host they feed upon dies, they die too, for they are nothing in themselves.' He nodded at the tree. 'Do you recognize it? It is a parasite. And so are you.'

There was a stunned, appalled silence. The passengers stared wide-eyed at my father. The only sound came from the harsh rasping of the cicadas.

The pirate's brow creased and the grin melted from his face. From behind, the other passengers began to protest, crying out to this barbarian that my father did not mean what he said, that he spoke only for himself, that fear had unhinged his mind and they would find money to pay for their ransoming. They went on and on, pressing forward, stretching out their arms in entreaty. But my father did not turn, or pay them any heed. His face was set in an expression of calm contempt.

Suddenly the pirate rounded on them. 'Shut up!' he yelled.

They ceased as if struck by a thunderbolt. All except the Greek slave, who was beyond controlling himself. He continued with a high-pitched quivering whine, like a keening woman, or a bitch's pup.

The pirate was still standing in front of my father, studying his face. There was a pause. Then he reached into his matted golden hair, searched around, and brought his hand forward once more with his thumb and forefinger pressed together. Between them he was holding a louse. He held it under my father's eyes.

'Look!' he said, grinning, 'a parasite; a brother of mine.' He crushed the creature and wiped his fingers on his leather tunic. Then he laughed, and after a moment the passengers, in an effort to ingratiate themselves, laughed with him.

All except my father and I. And the girl. We just looked at him in silence.

Eventually the laughter died limply away. It was forced and artificial enough; but no one, it seemed, wanted to be the first to stop. Then the Libyan stepped up.

'Well?' said the blond pirate.

The Libyan manhandled the girl roughly forward. With a flash of his white teeth he said, 'Already, Dikaiarchos, the message has been sent. I saw to it myself, before we left Brundisium. Her father will have it by now.'

The girl said, 'He will pay you nothing.'

The blond one, the one called Dikaiarchos, pouted at her. 'No? Oh, but I think he will. He is a very rich man, and you are his only daughter. He can spare me a ship-full of gold; but he cannot do without you.'

He gave her a sweet smile, and she glared back at him. Beside her the Greek slave was still whining, biting his hand in terror. Dikaiarchos frowned and sighed, and made a quick flicking gesture with his hand. At this the Libyan turned, and in one swift fluent relaxed movement, like a man describing an arc, he took a small curved blade from his belt and slit the slave's throat.

He fell and died, like a beast at sacrifice. We all stared

at the fallen corpse shuddering in its gathering pool of blood. I think it was then that I guessed what lay in store for the rest of us.

'Take them away,' said Dikaiarchos. He turned and started to walk up the temple steps. The Libyan called out his name. He looked back.

'You said I could have her. You promised.'

Dikaiarchos wrinkled his nose in distaste. 'Did I? Oh yes. Well, have her then. No marks though. No mess.'

At this the girl started forward. But the Libyan was ready, and he snatched her back to him, locking his blood-spattered hand around her wrist and holding her. For a moment she struggled; but she must have realized it was futile, and soon she ceased, and just stared ahead, still and soundless, like a snared bird.

We were led away, back through the empty town, up along the cliffside path between the ruined houses.

Once the girl glanced round. I saw the pleading in her face, and then the despair as the others looked away.

I had supposed, in as much as I was still capable of thought, that the Libyan would take her off to some private place; but halfway up the street, like a man taken short who cannot wait, he pulled her aside, pinned her against the wall with his forearm, and forced his bloody hand between her legs.

The passengers averted their eyes; but it was not to spare the girl, it was to spare themselves. Meanwhile the other pirates watched like dogs waiting to get at their dinner, and I realized the Libyan was only the first. My heart filled with shame, and disgust at all mankind. But I did not turn away.

The Libyan was grunting, and muttering in her ear. He shifted, and a shaft of the sinking afternoon light caught the bronze studs of his belt. I saw the girl's hand there, gently moving. It might have been an embrace; but it was not. Slowly she was feeling along the studs with her fingers, towards where his dagger lay in its sheath of leather.

Beside me my father noticed too. Almost imperceptibly his head shifted. Then, at the top of his voice, he shouted out, 'By God! Have you no shame at all?'

Immediately the other prisoners hushed him in a frenzy of loud reproachful whispers, hissing through their teeth that he had done enough already to get them all killed. The nearest pirate stepped up and smashed his fist into my father's face. He stumbled, and when he righted himself his face was bleeding from the nose and mouth. But it had given the girl the time she needed.

Her delicate fingers closed around the dagger's hilt. I see that dagger still. It was cream-white, ivory or bone, smeared still with her tutor's blood. Carefully she nudged it upwards, a little each time, moving with the Libyan's motion. Her hand paused; her fist locked around it, and with a sudden clear-voiced cry she plunged it into his heaving side.

He spun round with a great bellow, his lizard-eyes wide and bulging. She buried the knife again, somewhere in his belly; then, as he stumbled, she shoved him away from her and ran.

The street was on an incline, with steps of cracked

marble sprouting grass-tufts and overgrown with wild thyme. At the top, where the road turned, there was a low wall, knee high, and here she halted.

The Libyan was stumbling after her, clutching his wounded blood-oozing side with one hand and flailing at her with the other. I could not understand why she was waiting. In an instant he would be upon her.

'Run!' I cried. Then I saw what had stopped her.

The road did not turn, as I had thought; it ended there at the low wall, and beyond was nothing but a sheer drop down the cliff-face.

She looked, and hesitated. The Libyan, realizing she was trapped, was roaring out what he would do to her. She took one last look at him. Then she turned and stepped into the void, as easily as a person might step over the threshold of a house.

There was silence.

The Libyan reached where she had been. He peered down. Then he began to laugh. It was his laughter – chilling, cruel laughter from some foul place in his soul – that finally released the madness in me and made me do what I did.

Our captors, in their shock, had forgotten to hold us. I broke away, ducking past the nearest of them and running. The Libyan turned, and I slammed into his side with all my strength, in the place where the girl had stabbed him.

He yelled out in pain, and struck my head with his fist. But I must have caught him off balance, for then he teetered and stumbled backwards. His foot caught on the ledge, his arms went up, and with a look of amazement on his face he toppled over the low wall and was gone. There was a long-drawn-out terror-filled scream as he contemplated his death. The scream broke off, and then there was silence.

The other pirates came crowding up and gaped over the precipice. Then their eyes slewed round to me.

I heard my father's voice cry out in Latin, 'Go! Find your uncle. Caecilius is his name. Remember!' And then, switching into Greek, he waved his arms and shouted at the pirates, 'Your friend brought that upon himself, the animal, and his death was gentle compared with what you will suffer when the Romans come.'

I looked at him. For a moment, before he looked away, our eyes met and locked, and suddenly my mind was sharp and clear, and I understood what he was doing.

He continued shouting like a madman, calling down the curses of the gods, telling the pirates they were worse than beasts. Then I turned and ran. I ducked through a frameless window and scrambled through the saplings and twisted brambles, running for my life through the ruined interior of a house.

Twilight was falling fast. There were hurrying footsteps, and somewhere behind me one of the pirates shouted out. But then another said, 'Let him go. It will soon be dark. The wolves will have the brat before morning.'

I came out into what had once been the back yard of some grand house. There was the broken basin of a fountain, and a statue grown over with ivy. I scaled a crumbling brick wall at the back, and scrambled up a steep incline beyond it. At the top I came out onto a terrace of overgrown, tangled vines. Ahead was the dense pine forest. Only then did I pause and look back.

Out beyond the plateau the sun had sunk into a dazzling crimson glow across the sea. At first I could see nothing else. But then, in the ruined town below, a torch moved between the buildings, and I saw the pirates and prisoners assembled, and in their midst the blond one they called Dikaiarchos.

He held a sword in his hand. At his feet, prone in the dirt, lay my father.

I thought at first it was the twilight shadow, and the glare of the torch, that obscured his head. But then the torch-bearer drew nearer, and I saw what they had done to him.

A farmer will set light to a field. The field will burn, and afterwards there is nothing. That was how my mind felt. I could conceive of no future. My past seemed no more than a dream. My only reality was pain.

For days I wandered about the pine-clad ravines, expecting at any moment to be captured, or to be taken by wolves, as the pirates had predicted. For food I ate berries and roots and whatever else I came across, not caring whether or not they were deadly. Eventually I came to a long flat sea-strand, deserted but for an old fisherman who had paused there to sew his nets. He spoke Greek, or a version of it, and agreed to ferry me across the strait to Kerkyra.

It is a lesson every man should learn, to know how it feels to have nothing in a strange city. I had not considered, till then, how I must have looked. My hair and body were filthy, my tunic ripped open from where I had fallen down a slope of rocky scree; my hands and knees were grazed and bloody.

I wandered around the stalls of the quayside market, trying to stop one of the people to ask where the house of Caecilius was. But even before I spoke they shook their heads and turned away. And all the time, amid the smells of cooked fish, and stalls of fruit and honey-cakes, hunger gnawed at my innards like a sickness.

Reaching Kerkyra was the only thing that had kept me going. Now, after so many days of forcing myself onwards, something inside me collapsed and I gave in to despair.

I cast myself down by a wall on the edge of the market and sank my head in my hands. I would have wept, if I had been able to; but I had not wept once since the day I escaped from the pirates – the day my father died to save me. And then, as I sat staring at the ground, I heard through the babble of Greek and Epirot and Phoenician voices the steady familiar cadences of Latin.

They were two sailors from the Roman naval base. At first they looked at me with as much suspicion as the others. But when, in a torrent of words, I managed to say something of what had happened, and when they heard I spoke Latin, they paused and listened.

Yes, they said, they knew the name Caecilius – a man from Campania, who ran the trading station and supplied the fleet. Was that the man I wanted? Relieved beyond measure, I assured them it was, though in truth I did not know.

One of them knew where the house was; he was going that way and would take me there if I wished. And so they conducted me through the narrow, busy streets of Kerkyra town, up the hill to a high-walled, white-painted mansion overlooking the harbour.

The house-steward cast his eyes over me and told me to wait outside in the street, leaving me standing like some beggar at the closed iron gate while he ambled off to consult his master.

He returned after some little while. The master was busy at supper, entertaining important friends; but I was to come in and clean myself up, and my uncle would see me presently when he was free.

He led me to a bath-house at the back, ordered the attendant to find me something to wear, then left me.

I sat on the edge of the great marble bath and looked around. The room was decorated with tiles of lapis-blue and panelled frescoes of plump naked dryads bathing in a woodland pool. There was a marble towel-stand with gilt fittings, and in the corner a stone-topped table with little jars of scent in bottles of coloured glass. Nothing could have been more different from the spare simplicity of home, and as I scrubbed myself with a great soft sponge I wondered for the first time what had made my father want to come here.

No doubt all children begin with the tastes of their parents, until they think for themselves, and change, and take the trouble to school themselves in something better. But not all change is progress. I remembered how my father used to laugh at the new fashionable men of Rome, the thrusting ambitious knights who left their farms in the hands of bailiffs and went off to the city to make their fortunes. Taste and wisdom, he would say, does not change with the seasons. He used to say they were chasing their own shadows. And yet he had set out to come to this strange, rich man's house, leaving the home he loved. And it had cost him his life. I could not understand it.

The bath-attendant returned with a clean tunic of rough slave's homespun, and carried away my old clothes to the furnace, as a housewife might carry off a dead rat; and in due course the steward returned and said my uncle would see me.

I had supposed he would have sent his guests home and I should find him already grieving. But as the steward led me through the garden, I heard the sound of men's laughter echoing along the colonnade. They were still at their wine.

My uncle Caecilius was reclining on a dining-couch, propped up on one elbow in the Greek style, balancing a great embossed silver wine-cup in his hand. It was clear he was got up for some grand party. He wore a long robe of fine-combed wool dyed light green, scarlet doeskin sandals buckled with golden clasps, and, on his head, a great bushing wreath of spring flowers. His hair was jet-black, but his face was pale and going to fat. Beside him reclined a young woman, scantily dressed, with her hair bound up in elaborate plaits. She stared at me through painted eyes. Even I, with my country naivety, could see she was no wife.

'Ah, Marcus,' he cried, a little too loudly. 'We thought you were dead. If you had been a little earlier you could have joined us; but tell the slave to give you something from the kitchen. Still, I expect you will have a cup of wine?' He fluttered his hand at a slave in the corner, who began ladling wine into a cup from the krater.

I said, 'I am alive, sir, but my father is dead. We were taken by pirates.' I had already poured all this out to the steward, and had supposed he would have told my uncle.

And so he had. For then he said with an unsteady swing of his wine-cup, 'Yes, it really is very unfortunate, and it will be an unwelcome surprise for your mother. Still, we can discuss this another time . . . But tell me, how is she?'

I looked at him and thought, He is drunk; he does not comprehend. I glanced at the other guests. They were all middle-aged men like my uncle, each with a young female companion. They were gazing at me with shining eyes and expressions of frozen merriment, and I had the sudden sense that I was an embarrassment.

My uncle was still looking up at me, his mouth half open, and I realized he was waiting for me to answer. I managed to tell him something or other, but all the while I was thinking, as I had already reflected many times before, of what I should say to my mother, of how I could explain that I had brought about my father's death.

A wave of tiredness like nausea swept over me. I glanced down, at a loss, and my eyes rested on the girl. Her fingers and toes were painted bright red, and she was wearing a dress of thinnest silk, through which I could see her breasts and painted nipples. She was pouting and looking at me with bright vacant eyes.

I ignored her, and looked back at my uncle. 'Thank

you, sir, for your hospitality, and for these clean clothes,'
I said, pulling myself together. 'But I am very tired, and
should like to go and sleep.'

For a moment he frowned at me. But then, waving
away the boy who had come with the wine, he cried,
'Yes, yes, go and sleep then. The slave will show you a
room.'

Even before I had left the courtyard I heard the
laughter resume, and the clank of the wine ladle as
the cups were refilled.

I was given a room on the upper floor, with a window
that looked down the hill towards the harbour. I told
myself next day, when I had eaten and slept, that I must
have interrupted some important gathering of my uncle's,
that today his mood would be different.

It was not until nearly noon that the slave came to
fetch me.

Caecilius was in his workroom, seated behind a large
desk topped with green onyx, upon which were strewn
scrolls and tablets of accounts. His face looked puffy and
grey. A flask of wine and a half-empty cup stood by his
arm.

He motioned for me to sit, and, after a pause, he set
his papers aside and looked at me. Then he began to ask
questions about our farm – the crops and buildings, the
number of slaves, the yield, the livestock, and the arrangement of the land.

I answered as best I could, wondering what concern it
was of his. As I answered he nodded to himself, and now

and again made notes on a wax tablet. He seemed to be considering something; but whatever it was he did not say, and at length he changed the subject and began to talk of his own affairs – the supplies to the fleet which he sourced from Italy and Greece; the difficulties he had with employees and slaves, and other business to do with agents and cargoes. And then he dismissed me, saying he had an appointment at the naval yard, and we should speak again presently.

I waited for the rest of that day, but he did not send for me again. On the following morning he went out early, and did not return till night.

Three days passed. Then four. Each morning I expected he would tell me he had arranged my passage home. I thought, at first, he was leaving me to rest and recover, but on the fifth day, tired of waiting, I went unbidden to his workroom and asked him.

I had begun to wonder, indeed, whether it was a question of money, though he did not seem short of it, and so I began by saying, 'I realize, sir, I have nothing to pay my passage; but I am sure my mother, when she hears, will arrange—'

'Come now, Marcus,' he said, cutting me off with a wave of his hand. 'This is not a time to talk of money, not at all – though,' he added, his eye dwelling on mine, 'I am glad to see you are mindful of it and give it its proper value.' He sat back in his chair. 'But I was just about to come to this, for as it happens I have decided to make a trip to Italy myself. One of my own trading ships is due to sail for Brundisium with a cargo of Korinthian silver-work at month-end, and—'

'—Month-end?' I cried, shaken out of all politeness and staring at him. 'But sir, it is only just new moon.'

His fleshy mouth hardened.

'I do not need to be told what day it is.' He waited for me to apologize, then went on, 'You need not concern yourself with your mother: I have already sent her a letter; and, since you have wisely brought up the question of money, you must ask yourself why I should pay passage on another man's ship, when I can use my own.'

He raised his plump hand and made a money-counter's sign with his fingers. 'This,' he said, when he was sure I had understood the gesture, 'is how I have succeeded in life. Your father never thought in such terms – if he had, he might have made more of himself.'

I looked down at the inlaid floor, for I could not trust myself to meet his eye. I had crossed mountains and forests and ravines to get here; I told myself this was just one ordeal more in a season of pain, and then I should be home, and need never see this man again.

Two

I FOUND MY MOTHER sitting at her loom, in her
favourite room with the rowan-shaded window that
looked out towards the distant hills. The late sunlight,
shafting through the window, was on her face, and for a
moment I saw her expression of deep, hopeless sadness.
But then, hearing me enter, she looked round, and seemed
to drive it from her by an act of will. She stood, and
extended her arms to me, and at this all my carefully
prepared words left me.

Hurrying forward I cried, 'Mother!' and embraced
her. And then, at last, the tears came.

She held herself still and silent in my embrace. I said,
'He wrote to you.'

'Yes,' she said, 'he wrote. But I knew before that.
Priscus was in Rome when the news came. There was a
girl travelling with you; there was a ransom demand. She
was a senator's daughter. They wanted gold.'

'Yes,' I said, remembering.

She eased herself away from me. She was wearing her

hair tied up as she always did. Fine wisps of it spilled about her brow. There was more grey in it than I remembered.

'As soon as he heard, Priscus cut short his visit and hurried here to tell me. But at Rome there was no word of you. It was only when I received Caecilius's letter that I knew you were alive.'

I said, 'Has no one else come back?'

She shook her head and looked out at the sloping lawns. 'The consuls sent a warship to Epeiros. They found only bodies . . . or what the wolves and crows had left of them. You are the only survivor, Marcus.'

I drew my breath, and in my mind's eye I saw once again the girl struggling with the Libyan, and stepping calmly out into the void. The dreadful haunting thought returned that had clung to me like a sickness since that first day: that, but for my intervention, they might somehow have lived. Had I condemned them all? Was I the agent of their deaths? I furrowed my brow and tried to recall what had happened; but it was like trying to bring back the details of some demonic dream.

I sat down on the couch and put my head in my hands, and, struggling for the words, I stumbled through everything that had happened that day – the Libyan, the girl, the pirate-chief called Dikaiarchos who had killed my father. When at last I was done I looked up at her, smearing away my tears with my palms. Her eyes were dry. In a firm voice she said, 'If you had not done what you did, you too would be dead. That is all.'

She saw me shake my head, and after a moment went on, 'Before you were born, when I was little more than a

25

girl, I gave birth to a child. In the first week of his life he died.'

I jerked my head up and stared, shocked out of my self-pity. 'But . . . I never knew.'

'No. You did not. But I am telling you now. For a long time I blamed myself, thinking there was something I should have done, or not done. In the end I grew ill, and wished for death. But my own mother, seeing this, came to me and said, "That is enough. What happened is with the gods, who see more than men, and you must not presume to know more than they. So cease, and think to the future. You have a duty, to Rome, and to your husband. You must bear him another son." . . . And then,' she said, 'you were born.'

I stared at her. Her face was set. She seemed hard as stone. Through the window I could see the red and mauve furnace of the setting sun; and, from somewhere outside, I heard one of the farmhands calling.

'I remember Cannae,' she said, raising her head, 'when we thought all was lost. Carthage had defeated us, and there were those who gave up hope. Yet we survived, by our fortitude, and by believing that we should endure . . . There are times, Marcus, when courage is all you have.'

I looked down at the stone floor, chastened into silence by her cold, stern words. This was her way, as it had always been. It was the Roman way. Grief was an indulgence; and though she surely suffered, her suffering was for her alone. It seemed hard, but she had come from a hard family, brave men and brave women who through the generations had survived by facing down hardship and loss. Of all her long line of ancestors, she was not going to be the one to break.

And nor, I decided, was I.

Next day, I went around the hillside to see Priscus, our neighbour. He and my father had known one another since they were boys. He lived alone now in his old stone farmstead, his wife having died in childbirth long before. When I was three, his only son had fallen at Trasimene, fighting against Hannibal, in the war that had lasted a generation. Such is loss. All this I had always known. Now, for the first time, I felt it.

He was a man who knew the value of silence. During those first days he would invite me to eat with him on his terrace overlooking the valley, a simple meal of beans and cabbage seasoned with some bacon, and an earthenware cup of cool wine from his own hillside vineyard. He was a gentle, white-bearded man, who seemed at peace with himself in spite of his great losses, and I found his company a comfort. He never taxed me with questions or sought explanations. If he spoke, it was of commonplace, everyday things: the land and the crops, and the passage of the seasons. He would take me walking with him along the tracks beside the fields, reminding me, now that the farm was my concern alone, that this field ought to lie fallow for a year, or another be planted with greens; or that the vines were thickening out well, but he had noticed, when he had chanced to pass that way, that the elmwood supports needed attention, or the ditches needed clearing; and might he send his steward and some of his hands to help?

The days passed, and, after a fashion, I began to heal. I drove myself hard, but behind the activity, and the tiredness I felt at the end of each long day, there was a constant uneasiness I could not expel. It was like an itch I could not scratch, a greyness in my soul, an absence of I know not what.

It showed itself in ways I did not expect. The friends I had known since childhood, who lived in neighbouring farms, or in the town, seemed suddenly insipid and shallow. I had enough wit to know it was I, not they, that had changed; but I could not say what troubled me, for I did not know it myself. I felt like a man who has seen too much, like someone who has travelled down to the underworld and there beheld great horrors not fit for mortal men to see, which, returning, he can find no other who will understand.

Amidst this inner turmoil, which I could speak of to no one, I found I was happiest when I was alone. I rose each day at cock-light and worked till I was exhausted. Tiredness helped, and doing things. But then, in the deep of the night, I would wake with a start, naked and sweating, with the cover kicked from my bed.

As the water of a pool, stirred up at first, slowly clears, so my dreams began to resolve. What troubled me was my father, or his restless shade. It was when he came to me in a dream, whole at first, then headless, mouthing words I could not hear through his white, blood-smeared lips, that I knew. Next morning, in the first grey light, while the mist still clung to the hill-slopes, I went round to the yard behind the house and took a cock from the hen-coop. I put it in a withy basket and took the path that followed the edge of the oak forest, to the little plot where our ancestors had been buried, generation upon generation, time out of mind – all except my father. There was a shrine there, squat stone columns overgrown with ivy; and, beside it, an altar.

I took off my tunic and stood naked, and opening the basket I seized the bird and with my hunting knife cut its throat, letting the blood flow over the ancient stone. Then I touched the warm blood to my brow and breast, as I had seen done at a sacrifice, and extending my arms up to where the first red of dawn showed over the mountain tops, I prayed, 'Mars the Avenger, never before have I sought anything from you. But now, if this sacrifice is pleasing, grant what I ask. The man's name is Dikaiarchos. I do not know where he is, but gods see more than men and I need you to guide me to him. I have a debt to settle. Let me avenge my father's death and repay blood with blood. Guide my steps, and make me the killer I must be!'

I looked up. The first darts of golden sunlight were shafting over the ridge. A bird screamed, and I saw a great tawny eagle swoop over the treetops. It dropped, then surged upwards, its wings beating the air, holding in its talons a writhing snake. The breeze stirred up the valley, rustling the oaks, and in my breast I felt power course through my body like new blood, and I knew the god had heard me.

Afterwards I went down to the stream below the orchard to wash. I cleaned the blood away, and lay drying myself on a flat rock at the water's edge.

Presently, from along the path, came the sound of footfalls kicking through the leaves. I propped myself up on one elbow to look, and saw Priscus ambling along the path. He raised his arm in greeting and approached.

'Up with the dawn, I see, Marcus.' He sat down beside me and dipped his hand in the water. 'But isn't it cold for swimming?'

'It's warm enough; but I did not come to swim.' I fell into an awkward silence, dabbing with my foot at the chill mountain water.

He cast his eyes around. 'Well, it is a pleasant spot, even so . . . for whatever you were doing.' He made to stand. 'But I must go. I was on my way to inspect the beehives. The meadow is full of yellow flowers; the bees will like that. Perhaps, if you have finished, you would like to come along.'

I said yes, and took up my tunic from where it lay on the rock beside me. I saw his eyes move. My hunting knife was there, concealed by my clothes. I had forgotten to clean it.

'So you have been hunting,' he said, seeing the blood on the blade.

'No,' I said, 'not hunting.'

With a frown I took the dagger and started to wash it. I had meant to keep my morning's work to myself, but I would not lie to him. I sat back down and told him what I had done.

He listened without comment, and when I had finished

30

he was silent for a while. Then he said, 'And the god heard you, you say?'

'Why yes, Priscus, I know he did. And there was a great eagle, coming from the right. And in his claws he held his prey. It is a sure sign.'

He nodded slowly to himself, and pulled a face under his white beard. I was drying my knife on a clump of grass, but seeing this I set the knife down. 'What is it?' I asked. 'Do you think I did wrong?'

He shrugged. 'It is an honourable prayer,' he said eventually. 'But you must be careful what you pray for.'

This irked me, and I asked him what he meant, saying I knew well enough what it was I had prayed for. 'What is it?' I said. 'Do you suppose the god did not listen, or that I have offended him?'

He shook his head. 'No, not that. You saw the eagle, and you felt the truth of it in your heart. It is in such ways that gods speak to men. No, the god heard you. But sometimes, when they grant what a man asks, they also grant what he has not foreseen.'

'You talk in riddles,' I said crossly, turning and pulling on my tunic. For the first time I had felt whole again. My being pulsed with the knowledge of it, and I did not want to hear his doubts. 'Anyway, what is done is done. It is with the god now, for good or ill, so let us go and see your beehives.'

He said no more about it.

The warm weather came, and that year I turned fifteen.

I drove my body hard, and my body responded. Where

once I had needed the help of the farmhands in lifting a beam, or pulling a cart, now I could do it alone. I had been a slender child, but now I thickened out. My muscles knit to my bone, and I felt my strength as something pleasing.

Whatever Priscus thought, since the day of my sacrifice to Mars the Avenger my bad dreams had ceased. I had a purpose, and that purpose was Dikaiarchos the pirate. He filled my waking thoughts, and at night I dreamt dreams of revenge, of how I would find him and kill him, and let my father's shade drink his blood.

Soon I received another sign that the god had heard me. One day, when I happened to be searching for a tree-axe at the back of the old storeroom, I found a pile of javelins hidden behind a stack of farm tools, and, beside it, wrapped in oiled cloth, a warrior's sword. The sword was heavy antique work, with a fine pommel of worked bronze turned to verdigris with age. My father had never mentioned it, and I guessed from its look it must have belonged to my grandfather, who had died before I was born, kept from the days when each household was its own fortress and saw to its own defence.

I cleaned up the blade and waxed the ashwood shafts of the javelins; and when I was not working I taught myself to handle them, swinging and thrusting the sword, and casting the javelins at targets in the woods.

I discovered I had a sharp eye; soon I could hit a tree trunk no wider than a man at a leaping run. As for the sword, it was too heavy for me at first; but it grew lighter as I worked at it and the muscles firmed in my arms and sides and shoulders.

A hungry man will find food where a sated man does not. And so it is with anger. It disciplined me to rise each day before dawn; it gave me strength when my body was tired; it guided my spear to a leaping hare in the forest, or a fat dove on a tree bough. And when I returned home with my prey strung over my shoulders, that prey had a name: Dikaiarchos.

I grew taciturn, and solitary in my pursuits. When I came across my old friends in the town I thought them soft and aimless; and they, no doubt, found me strange and withdrawn. But I served the god. We had made a pact. When they asked me why I was so much alone, I gave them vague excuses about work on the farm. They did not believe me, and soon ceased to ask. But I knew they would not understand.

One late afternoon, I was sitting on the grass terrace outside the house, sharpening my hunting knife on a whetstone, when my mother came to me.

'You were singing,' she said with a smile.

I shrugged and smiled back. 'I had a good day. I caught a hare.'

She sat down on the stone bench and asked about the work on the farm. I answered, sharpening my knife blade as I talked, telling her how the corn in the lower fields was growing good and strong, and the livestock was thriving, and how I was pleased with the new draining ditches I had dug in the vineyard. I had been laughing, recounting some nonsense of how our old bad-tempered goat in the yard had butted the swineherd into the water-trough; but now, all of a sudden, like an unexpected chill on a warm day, it came to me that there was something she had not yet come to, something she was waiting to say. I called to mind that she never came looking for me just to make conversation, and breaking off I looked up at her and said, 'Mother, tell me what has happened.'

I had guessed right. At this the brightness faded from her face and she made a small sad dismissive gesture. Immediately I cast aside the sharpening-stone and leapt up. Only then, when I was standing, did I see she was clutching a letter in her hand.

'Your uncle Caecilius has written,' she said, raising up the letter with its broken seal. 'Let us go inside, Marcus. There are things we need to speak of.'

We went to my father's old study. I had scarcely entered here since my return, and now I glanced round in surprise. His book-scrolls with their carefully written labels were stacked neatly on the shelves, just as he had left them, but on the desk, among the coloured stone paperweights he liked to collect, his papers lay open and strewn about. It looked as if someone had been going over the accounts.

But that could wait. My mother had closed the door, something she seldom did.

I said, 'What does *he* want?' I spoke more sharply than I intended. I was remembering Kerkyra. I had not given a thought to my uncle Caecilius until now.

She crossed the floor and sat down in the old cross-backed pearwood chair beside the window before she answered. The letter was still in her hand. For a moment, before she stilled it on her lap, I thought I saw it shaking. She sighed and looked at me. It was not like her to put off what needed to be said.

'You may as well hear it now as any time. Your uncle Caecilius intends to marry me.'

I jumped back as if something had bitten me. '*Marry* you?' I cried. 'What is he talking about? Has he lost his mind?'

'Listen to me, Marcus, and stop gaping like some peasant at market—'

'But Mother, you know nothing of him, nor he you . . . You would not like him . . . I know you wouldn't.'

'Liking does not come into it,' she said flatly.

'But Mother!' I cried, pleading now. 'You do not know what you do. What madness is this? What has he told you?'

As I was speaking she had crossed to my father's desk. She pushed at the papers there. 'Did your father tell you why he was going to Kerkyra?'

This caught me by surprise and I broke off. 'No,' I said, narrowing my eyes. 'What of it?'

'No. Well he would not have troubled you with such things; that was his way. Your father was a good man, Marcus; but he was not a man of business. He was content to let the farm run just as it always had. Why should he make changes, he used to say, when all was as he liked? But the world has changed. We cannot go on as we were.'

I looked at her face, trying to work out what it was that stirred my memory. And then, with a surge of anger, I knew. These were not her words I was hearing. They were Caecilius's.

'Let the world change!' I cried at her. 'We have the farm. We can manage, you and I.' I began to talk about the coming harvest, which showed promise; and the olives; and the vines. She let me go on for a while, but then I saw her gently shake her head. 'What then, Mother?' I said, gesturing angrily. 'Is it not enough?'

She gave a thin, sad smile. 'If it were a case of hard work, we should be wealthy beyond measure. Do you think I have not seen you? But all this comes from long ago, when Hannibal's army was ravaging Italy. Times were hard then; your father fell into difficulties, and Caecilius gave us help. He was generous when no one else would be, and now he is calling in his debt.'

I stared at her. 'His *debt*?' I cried. 'And what are you? The payment? By all the gods, what does he take you for?'

'That is enough!' she said sharply. She walked to the window and looked out. Without turning she said, 'I will not lose the farm. That is what matters.'

It was no use. I sat down heavily in my father's chair and pushed my hands through my hair. My mind burned with anger. I drew my breath to rage against her, and against cruel Fate that had brought us to this. But then the words she had spoken pierced my consciousness, like light through stormclouds, and I nearly cried out with the pain of it. I stared at the papers strewn on the desk in front of me. The accounts. She must have been through them many times before she came to me. What was I doing except making it worse? She would not lose the farm. That was what she had said. Caecilius had made a request – a demand – and she was doing this to keep our home . . . and I, for all my effort, was no more than a useless child who could not help her.

My anger drained from me, replaced by something worse. I looked up. She was still looking out through the window. Her back was straight, her face fixed and grave and full of pain. But for a moment I saw what she kept hidden best of all: her weakness, and my eyes stung with tears of impotent rage. She was like some great noble bird – a mighty she-eagle – old at last, broken by time, but proud to the end.

I swallowed and blinked down at the floor. It was all I could do not to weep out loud, for the great injustice of the world. But I knew what she would have said: Tears do not stop the sun from rising, or make rivers run uphill. So I set my mouth firm as hers, and peered at the accounts spread out upon the desk, as if they meant something to me, and after a moment I said, 'Whatever you do, Mother, you will always have my love.'

An older man – or a wiser one – would have spared her such words at such a time. But I was young, and thought that feelings were all. I heard her catch her breath and saw her clutch at the window frame.

'My dear, only son,' she said, in a voice that cracked my heart.

Later we talked of details, as, after a death, the members of a family might talk of arrangements for the funeral, concerning themselves with invitations and what to eat, while the body lies in the next room unmentioned.

Caecilius was still in Rome, where his business, he said, had taken some months to complete. If his offer was acceptable, he had written that he would make the journey to Praeneste. She showed me the letter. I did not tell her it was not even in his own hand. He had got a secretary to write it.

When all had been said, I went off into the hillside forest, up through the firs and stone-pines to a place I knew, a bare rock ledge that jutted out over the valley, where I could be alone.

For a long time I stood, listening to the shifting wind stirring the branches, and the echoing cries of the mountain birds. I do not know what I had intended, other than to be away from people, and away from the house. But now, seized by rage, I punched my fist into the nearest tree trunk, and cried out long and loud, calling on Mars the Avenger to see me and remember.

My lone voice echoed down the valley. The startled birds scrambled from the trees. And then the only sound was my breathing, and the beating of my heart.

Caecilius arrived half a month later, in a lavish painted carriage with curtains of scarlet-dyed leather, drawn by two Gaulish mares with decorated harnesses, attended by liveried outriders.

I waited outside the house to greet him, as my mother had asked, and beside me stood the assembled house-slaves and the farmhands, washed and got up in their best, standing primly with their hands folded in front of them, as they did at the shrine on the festival days when my father offered something to the gods. We had had plenty of time to arrange ourselves there, having seen an hour before the gaudy vehicle lumbering up the steep winding track from the plain. It might have been suitable for the easy roads close to Rome. It did not suit Praeneste.

But in time the carriage drew up, and my uncle clambered out. He was wearing an expensive fine-combed woollen tunic, cream-white, bordered with leaping stags picked out in red; and on his feet new calfskin boots. He had put on weight, and his hair was blacker than I remembered, stark against his puffy white face, like a blackbird's wing against marble.

He looked along the line of waiting farmhands, passing over me until I remembered to step up and speak the formal words of greeting.

He peered at me. I had pulled on a clean tunic, but otherwise I looked no different from the slaves and farmhands. But then he seemed to know me.

'Why, Marcus,' he cried in a booming voice, 'look at you. Brown as a nut, and surely you have grown. I was expecting the same timid child, not a handsome youth.' He laughed and glanced around. 'But where is your mother?'

I told him she was in the house, waiting to greet him.

'Then let us go inside,' he said. He snapped his fingers at one of the liveried outriders and said, 'See to my things,' and then, as we took the short path to the house, 'I have done much useful business in Rome, and soon I hope—' He broke off with a curse and swatted a dragonfly aside with an irritated swipe. From the corner of my eye I saw one of the young farmhands suppress a smile. Even they could see my uncle did not belong in the country. 'Well,' he continued, looking warily to where the hovering insect had relocated itself, 'we can talk of all that in due course. And,' he added, taking me confidentially by the elbow and pulling me to him, 'you must learn to start calling me father now, not uncle.'

I do not know what decency dictated, or what passed for right behaviour in Rome. I had assumed he was only paying a short visit, for the sake of form. But next day wagons loaded with his possessions came labouring up the hill-track: caskets, chests of clothing, even ornaments and furniture. I realized he had come to stay.

The marriage took place before month end. There was a brief ceremony. No guests came. I was glad of that, for in my mind it was no marriage, just a contract, and a sordid one at that.

That night I lay in bed and pictured him with my mother. I drove the thoughts away, fearing madness. I rose before dawn, and went climbing on the hillside. I sat on the rock ledge, and watched the sun rise over the mountains.

The formal adoption happened soon after. The words were spoken, and I became, as far as the law was concerned, Caecilius's son and he gained the power of a father over me.

How true it is, that one perceives what one has only by losing it. At once he began to make changes. The little festivals and banquets we held for the farmhands and their families to signify the motions of the seasons and to honour the local gods – the field-spirits, the guardians of the boundaries, the nymphs and dryads and gods of the spring – he cancelled, saying, when I asked him, that too much time was spent on superstitious foolery when there was a farm to run. He employed the men to work; if they would not, he would find others.

I listened as he discoursed on such things and said nothing, not out of fear of him, for I felt none, but because I knew no words of mine would sway him, and because the farmhands, whatever he said, would no more ignore the gods of the place than they would cease to breathe the air. The sacred spirits were as real to them as the trees and streams.

Quickly enough I began to understand that to Caecilius everything was merely a question of good or bad business. He talked of it with reverence, as a philosopher might talk of truth. He had a conception in his head, and expected the world to conform to it. Yet I never quite understood what it was that he did. When I asked him, he told me he traded; or, at other times, that he bought and later sold, and knowing how and when and where was the key. He was fortunate, he said, for he had a nose for a good deal. This was a favourite saying of his, and he would tap his nose with his finger, and peer at me with his small eyes as if he were imparting to me something of great significance.

Despite his vagueness, I soon came to understand, though, that he had profited, in ways he never quite explained, from the war against Carthage, which at that time was nearing its end. I had lived with the war since my first breath. But now, little by little, town by town, our great general Scipio was at last driving Hannibal out of Italy. I think Caecilius was the only person who spoke of the war's end with regret.

Though my father had distrusted the city, he had always talked of sending me to Rome when I was old enough, to be educated by one of the new professors from Greece, who were setting up schools in the city. At the time I did not like the idea of leaving home, and had asked him, if he did not care for the city, why he wanted to send me there. To this he had answered that the city was one thing, and knowledge was another. It was not for him to withhold knowledge from me, without which there could be no wisdom. I must make my own choices, and to do that I must know something of the world and what wise men said about it. Besides, he had said, it did a man good to know the life of the city, even if he later rejected it.

But Caecilius had no time for such things. 'What is it you want to know?' he would say, and when I could not answer he would wag his fat finger and say, 'There! If you cannot tell me, then you have no need of it. Better to learn business than waste your time – and my money – on those talking heads in Rome.'

So Rome was forgotten.

It was soon after this, one hot day in high summer, when I was working with a group of farmhands in the orchard, that the swineherd came running from the house.

He was a hulking boy called Milo, rather simple, who had a habit of blurting out whatever came into his head, however indiscreet. Usually he made the others laugh with his observations, but now he came bounding down the terraces to where I was standing halfway up a ladder and cried at the top of his voice, 'Marcus, sir, you must do something: he is sending old Postumus away!'

I climbed down from the ladder and set aside my basket, and told Milo to sit down and tell me all he had heard. He spilled out his words in his usual rambling way and I listened, though I scarcely needed to, for I had guessed already. But at least the pause allowed me to master my rising anger. Postumus was the oldest of the hands on our farm. He had grown slow of late, and forgetful, and already I had had to intervene with Caecilius, who thought him inefficient and a waste of money, though Postumus was old enough to be his father.

I heard Milo out, then left him in the orchard and went up to the house.

I found Caecilius in my father's old study, which he had made his own. I avoided the room if I could. He had removed my father's books, replacing them with a matching set of painted vases he had imported from Greece, of rampant satyrs chasing nymphs. He looked up sharply when I entered. He expected people to knock, even me and my mother. I was dusty from the orchard. In the cool interior I could smell my sweat.

'Yes?' he snapped. 'What is it?'

'You are sending away old Postumus,' I said.

He set aside his papers and sat back, as if he had been waiting for this. 'Yes, I am. He is a hired hand, not a slave, and I have no more use for him.'

'No one has thought to tell you, sir, with all that has happened lately, but Postumus has been with us all his life, and his father before him. He has nowhere else to go.'

'And I have a farm to run.'

'But sir!' I cried. 'What else will he do? He is part of

the family almost, not some old shoe to cast out on the midden.'

He stared at me and there was an awkward pause. No doubt I had gone too far. But I was angry.

'Is this the way your father taught you to speak to your elders?' he said pompously.

'My father would never have dismissed a man like Postumus.'

His thick lips tightened into a harsh line. 'I will not speak ill of the dead, Marcus. Your father had his merits, I daresay. But he was too indulgent by far, and such men are taken advantage of. These workers' – with an angry wave towards the window – 'are paid to work. One day they will *all* be old and useless. What then? In my opinion you are much too close to the farmhands; it is bad for discipline to think of them as 'family' as you call this man. And now I see they have you dancing to their tune. I suppose they put you up to this, or do you deny it?'

I began an indignant answer, but he silenced me. 'No, do not speak. Listen. Out of consideration for your mother I will find something else for this old man to do, though God knows what. But do not come to me again with such a request, unless you intend to pay for it with your own funds. I hope that is clear.' He reached out and pulled a letter from a pile of scrolls, saying, 'And while you are here there is something else. I have decided to appoint a bailiff here: there are useful men all over Italy – discharged servicemen, landowners down on their luck – who will accept what they are offered. My business will soon take me away, and it is clear to me I cannot leave things to run themselves.'

This was his revenge. The expression on his face told me so. He was not a man to be crossed, even in the smallest thing. Everything was a battle, and every battle had to be won.

I said, 'But sir, I can manage.'

'Oh? I do not think you can. But either way I do not intend to leave you here, wasting your time picking apples and threshing corn like some land peasant. You are more useful to me elsewhere; I need help, and now you are my adopted son it is time you earned your way.'

He paused – a significant, self-satisfied pause to let me know who had triumphed and who had lost in this exchange. For a few moments our eyes locked, mine full of anger; his challenging me to say more. Eventually I looked down at the grey-stone floor; I was powerless, and he knew it, and he wanted to make sure I knew it too. Then with a contented grunt he went on, 'So. I am awaiting news from Rome that will determine my future plans. When I am ready you will be told.' He fluttered his hand. 'Now you may go and tell old-man Postumus of his good fortune.'

Before long my new stepfather had another surprise for me. I knew he had been married once. But I did not know, until the day before a carriage arrived bearing her, that he had a daughter.

She was twelve years old. Her name was Caecilia, but her father called her Mouse. It was not a term of endearment. It was his way of mocking the way she looked.

He spoke to her like a servant, ordering her to fetch things, telling her to pull her chin up, and not to drag her feet, and not to whisper, and not to sulk. She had flat brown hair, hacked short with no care for how she looked; she had a pale, round face, and dull eyes that never met yours. I might have hated her, for being his daughter, and for moving in to the house I still thought of as mine. But she was too pitiful to hate. Seeing his bullying, and how he put her down, I felt sorry for her.

She mooned about the house, or sat with my mother, or alone under the shade of the rowans on the sloping lawn outside.

At first she was so shy of me as almost to be mute, and if I was around she would keep her eyes downcast like a slave. But one afternoon I had occasion to speak to her. It was some days after she arrived, when, returning from some business on the farm, I found her sitting alone on the terrace, peering intently at a scroll which lay open on her lap. Seeing me she set it quickly aside. 'Hello Mouse,' I said. 'What is it you're reading? Has he set you to work on his accounts?'

Her big round face flushed to the ears. Reluctantly she picked up the book and proffered it, as if I had caught her doing something forbidden. I looked at the edge of the scroll and immediately recognized it. It was a book of Homer, which recently I had rescued from its exile in the outhouse. I was trying to master the Greek, having decided I must educate myself as my father would have wished. I had left it lying in the house.

'Homer, is it?' I said, somewhat dryly. 'I suppose you read Greek then?'

To tell the truth, I had intended this as something of a putdown. It irked me that she had helped herself to my

46

book. Who did she think she was, to come to my house and take my private things without asking?

But in her hesitant voice she replied, 'I can read a little of it, but I am not really very good at all.' She flushed once more and looked down. 'You are cross with me. Here, take it; I should have asked you first, but Father said you had gone to the fields, and I was going to put it back before you noticed.'

I had a sharp reply ready. I was still smarting from the dressing-down Caecilius had given me, and Mouse was an easy target. But each of us has the power to pass pain on, or let it stop with us. I thought of Caecilius. That was enough to make me swallow my harsh words.

'Well never mind,' I said instead. 'Read it if you like. Anyway, you are right, I have work to do.'

She looked up then. I saw the beginnings of tears in her eyes, and for the first time since she had arrived she smiled. She reminded me of the timid little birds I used to coax to my hand in winter with the promise of food, when the snow was on the ground and they were hungry. I said, 'There are other books too, you know. They're hidden away at the back of the barn there, but I can show you, if you want.'

'Oh would you!' she cried.

I laughed. 'Why not? Anyway,' I added, kicking at the grass, 'I shan't have time to read them. Your father is taking me away.'

At this her face fell once more. 'Yes, Marcus, I heard. That is what he is like, always moving, never still. It's like a sickness. But I wish you were staying.'

From that day we were friends.

Next morning, before work, I took her up to the barn. On the way I said, 'I suppose, if you can read, you must have books at home.'

'I have no home,' she answered straight away.

'Well you must have somewhere. Where were you before you came here? Rome, wasn't it?'

'Oh, Rome for a while. And before that Cales in Campania. Then Sicily; then Cales again. And now I am here.'

'Doesn't he keep you with him?'

She shrugged. 'He does sometimes, when it suits him. But business comes first.'

'Ah yes,' I said. I was beginning to learn that for myself.

We clambered through the bales and casks and assorted implements to the dark corner at the back of the barn where Caecilius had dumped my father's library. When I had first found them there, the books were cast into a heap, piled up with no care for the order of the volumes, food for the rats. Knowing what they had meant to him I had picked them up and placed them out of reach of the damp, thinking thereby to preserve some part of his memory.

Now, seeing them, Mouse reached out and touched them reverentially one by one with her stubby fingers, turning the fluttering labels and whispering, 'Oh, oh,' to herself. In the dusty halflight the happiness shone in her face. It touched my heart. Her unselfconscious joy made her seem almost beautiful.

Presently, after we had spent some time picking

through the scrolls, I said I must go; the farmhands would be waiting. But before I left I said, 'Mouse?'

She turned from the books and looked at me with her big eyes.

'I just wanted to say ... I am glad you are here. Everyone needs a home, so this is yours, for as long as ever you want. Don't forget.'

Priscus our neighbour stopped calling at the house. But about a month after the marriage, when I had gone up to the town on some farm matter, I ran into him at the market.

For a little while we spoke inconsequentially. Then there was a pause and he said lightly, as if carrying on from what had gone before, 'I met your stepfather the other day, while I was walking in the orchard.'

'Oh?' I said, catching his eye. 'Then you are fortunate. He seldom ventures from the house.'

He paused and coughed, and pretended to look over a stall selling knives and hooks. 'He called me over ... I think, actually, he thought I was one of the farmhands. He was looking up at a tree and wanted to know what was wrong with the apples. I told him there was nothing wrong with the apples, if I was any judge, but that he was looking at a plumtree.'

I laughed out loud.

'Still,' went on Priscus, frowning, 'it is an easy enough mistake, after all, and I suppose he grew up in the city, where one does not learn such things.'

'The city? Not at all. He's from Campania, where the

people take in farming with their mother's milk. But not Caecilius, it seems. He despises farming. He is a man of business, so he says.'

Priscus raised his grey brows and walked on, and when I caught his eye he said, 'Ah, a man of business. Well, indeed.'

We carried on down the narrow cobbled street in silence. Then I could restrain myself no longer and I burst out, 'I tell you, Priscus, Father would have hated such a man. Everything has a price, and he makes it his business to know it. He thinks all things may be bought and sold. He calls it "business", and now he says I must learn it.'

Priscus nodded into his beard. One never quite knew, with Priscus, whether he was amused or not. 'Well,' he said, 'there's no harm in learning the value of things, or how else will you learn judgement? What price, I wonder, does he buy friendship at?'

I laughed. 'Friendship?'

'Or love?'

I shook my head.

'Then, it seems, he does not know the price of every-thing, after all. But what of you, Marcus, who know so much less than he about "business"? What price, would you say, do these things fetch?'

'Why, no price at all, Priscus!' I cried. 'A man cannot buy and sell such things!'

'And yet,' he said, 'they have a value.'

We had come out at a small, paved square. I had often played here as a child, and knew it well. On one side, shaded by a spreading lime, there was a stone bench beside a fountain. Here we sat, and looked out over the valley. The sound of goat-clappers came tinkling across the terraced fields, and, from somewhere beyond my view, the voice of a herdboy singing.

Priscus said, 'You see, Marcus, some things have value yet have no price, and a wise man learns them and their worth. So do not let the standard of the marketplace be your guide. A man goes there for flour and greens, but not for virtue.'

I drew down my brows and gazed out at the distant hills, the oak groves and the descending rows of cypresses, and was seized suddenly by the beauty of the place, and by Priscus's gentle wisdom, which, in my youthful hurry, I seldom heeded. My father had said to me once that it was the burden of the wise never to be listened to. I remembered his words now, though I could not recall why he had spoken them. I said, 'He is going to take me away from here.'

'You will be back. In the meantime, think of it this way: there are things you can learn from your stepfather; though not the things, I suspect, that he imagines. But you will draw what you need nevertheless, and leave what you do not. Remember, it is in your power to fashion yourself into what you will be. And your stepfather is right in this at least, that you cannot stay here for ever. The world is stirring, and you serve nobody's good by hiding from it, least of all your own.'

I turned to him. 'Is that my fate, then, Priscus, to be some merchant?'

'I doubt it. But that is for you to decide. Besides, you made a vow, as I recall. Have you told your stepfather of it?'

'I have told no one,' I said, 'least of all him. He would not understand.'

'No, perhaps he would not. And such things are best kept between you and the god. But you have not forgotten it, I see.'

'I will never forget,' I said, in a voice of iron.

THREE

SOON AFTER, WHEN THE grapes were ripening on the vines, and the upland mornings were cool with the first hint of autumn, Caecilius summoned me to his study.

He had set old Postumus to repaint the walls, and had hung veils of pink and saffron about the windows. It looked more like a bridal chamber than a study. My father's furniture had gone, all except his broad topped desk of polished oak. Caecilius sat behind it, looking pleased with himself.

'How is your Greek?' he said, slapping his palms down on the table.

I told him I could manage it well enough.

'Then good. Since I have gained a son, I may as well make use of him.' This, for Caecilius, passed for humour, and he broke into a loud barking laugh, his small eyes narrowing in his plump face. Then he went on, 'I have received the news I was waiting for. You had better get the slave to pack your things; we leave the day after tomorrow. For Tarentum.'

He returned his eyes to his papers – a sign that I was dismissed.

I said, 'Why are we going to Tarentum?'

He pretended not to hear – this was a habit of his – but when I waited standing before the desk he finally huffed and jerked his head up. 'You will find out soon enough, since you are coming with me. For now, all you need to know is that I have been granted a contract by the censors in Rome, a great opportunity and a sign of their favour. Now, as you can see, I am a busy man, and you have preparations to make.'

I said no more. This was how he was. He liked to hoard knowledge as a miser hoards gold, not for any good it did him, but merely for the pleasure of knowing he had something another man lacked. And when he shared it, it was done grudgingly, passed out in small irritating useless gobbets. He liked to pretend it was that he did not care to be questioned. But, in truth, it was merely that knowledge was a form of power over others. He knew I was curious, so it pleased him not to tell me.

In the meantime I prepared to leave home. Tarentum was one of the great Greek cities in the south of Italy, colonized by settlers from Greece when they first began to venture westwards. It had been a great metropolis when Rome was no more than a village of mud-and-wattle huts on a hill. I remembered, for it had been much spoken of when I was a young boy, that there had been a great siege there, one of the many battles in the long war with Carthage.

But this was all I knew. Eager to find out more, I went off across the fields to visit Priscus.

'Ah yes,' he said, 'it was in the dark days after Cannae. Hannibal's army were crawling all over Italy, and our allies, sensing how the wind was blowing, were turning against us one by one.'

He paused as the serving-girl brought a dish of figs and honey-cakes and set them down on the terrace where we were sitting. He poured me a cup of watered wine, and then went on, 'There was a faction at Tarentum that declared for Hannibal and Carthage; but we had a garrison in the citadel, and though the city turned against us, the garrison held out. Do you remember the year my hay barn caught fire, and you all came to help, and afterwards your father gave me half his fodder to see me through the winter? You must have been – what? – ten, at the time.'

'Eleven,' I said, remembering the day of the fire; it had almost spread up the hillside, through the dry oaks and pines. Half the town had gone to help. We had stayed up all night, passing buckets and beating back the flames.

'Ah yes. Well, that was the year General Fabius was consul. He marched to Tarentum and laid siege, and before Hannibal and his army could come to its defence the city fell.' He took a fig from the bowl, bit into it and frowned. 'But what business has your stepfather there?'

I told him what I had got from Caecilius. When I mentioned the censors in Rome he said, 'Ah, the censors, so that's it. Fabius confiscated a great deal of land after the siege, and the censors were given the task of allotting it to our citizens. They have been trying to give it away to colonists ever since; but no one wants it. Indeed, last time I was in Rome, one of their agents even offered an estate to me – for nothing, if I would farm it. But I told him

I had land enough of my own, and was not interested in taking another man's. There is too much trouble in it . . . Here, take another fig, they're here to be eaten.'

We paused, and ate, and looked out across the land.

It had rained that morning. The air was cool and damp, and fragrant with the smell of woodsmoke from the vineyards. I recalled that I should have been out on the slopes, helping with the grape harvest, if I had not been going away.

'And yet,' said Priscus, meeting my eye, 'I really can't suppose your stepfather has decided to take up farming.'

I thought of how, that morning, I had seen Caecilius picking his way across the muddy yard in his expensive shoes, his mantle hitched up, a look of distaste on his face.

'No,' I said smiling. 'Nor can I.'

We exchanged a look, and talked of something else.

And so, soon after, I came to Tarentum, with its great enclosed harbour, and mighty citadel overlooking the bay. From the carriage I stared in wonder at the long, colonnaded walkways with their shops and crowds, and the bright-painted gilded temples in their tree-filled enclosures. For the first time in my life I thought: This, surely, is civilization, many men coming together to build what no man could build alone. And, with that feeling of awe, I felt for the first time my own great ignorance. This was a whole new world, and I knew nothing of it.

Caecilius had taken a lease on a house – an imposing

mansion on a slope overlooking the inner harbour, between the temple of Apollo and the marketplace.

He went strutting into the high, marbled, light-filled entrance hall, and then looked out to the fine garden beyond. 'Ah, yes,' he declared with satisfaction, 'this will suit me. You can see the house once belonged to a nobleman. Whatever else these Greeks lack, they know how to build for comfort.'

I ran my fingers over the delicate fluted columns. Everywhere was space and brightness. It made our home in Praeneste seem rough and dark and ancient. Then I asked what had happened to the nobleman.

'Oh, I don't know. Really, Marcus, why do you ask such foolish questions? I daresay he perished when the city was taken, or went away. Who can say? Not there you fools!' – suddenly shouting at the slaves who were struggling with his luggage – 'Can't you see it belongs in my study? Marcus, see to all this, will you? I need to go and rest.'

Later, two men arrived, agents whom Caecilius had sent ahead of him from Rome to arrange his affairs. One was fat and full of self-consequence. The other had a pinched, failed-looking face.

The old Greek slave who should have admitted them at the door was in the house unpacking; there being no one to see them in, they had come wandering through the entrance hall and onto the garden terrace.

'You, boy!' the fat one shouted. 'Don't stand idling. Go and fetch your master.'

He had taken me for one of the slaves.

Before I could answer, Caecilius, who must have heard, stuck his head out from the upper balcony. It was pleasant to see their faces when I was introduced. But these, Caecilius said, were the men I had to work with. It was a bad start.

When I had time to myself, I explored the city, and wandered along the wide boulevards and shaded alleyways, looking in at the shops and temples and gardens. I had never seen so many people all in one place. Like all visitors, I climbed the steep path up to the citadel – which the Greeks call the akropolis – the fortified hill with the squat-columned temple of Poseidon on top. From there, looking out from the walls, I could survey all of Tarentum laid out below me on its narrow peninsula, with the sea and curving coastline on one side, and the great lagoon–harbour on the other. But most of those first weeks were taken up with work.

I began to learn something of Caecilius's business; and something of him, too.

In Praeneste, there were pigs that could smell out fungi that were good to eat, even when they lay hidden beneath the earth. In just the same way, I found, Caecilius could sense where profit was to be made, where other men saw nothing but waste and emptiness.

Priscus had been partly right. Caecilius was in Tarentum because of the confiscated land. But he was not there to farm it himself. He was hiring bailiffs – failed stewards from elsewhere, or men from Rome without work – who would oversee the farming estates until the censors found colonists who would take them over. They were not farmers; they knew as little of husbandry as he did.

'But that does not matter,' he told me. Their job was to manage the bands of slaves – Carthaginians captured in the wars; Sicilians; Libyans for the most part – and it was these who would plough and harvest and see to the animals. 'And you shall be my eyes and ears, making sure they do not rob me.' For he knew the type of men he had hired well enough. They would deceive him as soon as his back was turned.

I daresay, if I had discovered all this at once, I should have contrived a way to leave, with no thought for the consequences. But, in the way he had, Caecilius told me only a little at a time, and what he told me he dressed up as something other than it was.

It was ugly, sordid, boring work. The agents – Florus and Virilis – resented me; the land-bailiffs, who were little more than criminals, were bristling and suspicious.

And as well as this spying dressed up as supervision, there were other tasks too. He had not abandoned his shipping business, or his contract to supply the fleet in Kerkyra. And, Tarentum being a great port, there were ships to meet, cargoes to inspect, and manifests to check.

One morning, Caecilius called me to his study and gave me a note to take to the praetor's residence. The praetor, he explained, was a man called Caeso, a politician of some importance in Rome, who had been sent to govern Tarentum after the siege. I was to take the note and wait for a reply. Such relationships, he told me with the air of one imparting a mystery, must be cultivated. Indeed, he said, he was surprised he had not yet been invited. 'But no doubt the praetor is a busy man, and his good-for-nothing clerks have overlooked it.'

I went off. The praetor's residence was not far from ours, a large walled house on the edge of the sanctuary of Aphrodite. Returning, I heard the loud self-satisfied voice of the fat agent in my stepfather's study, so I decided to wait in the garden, among the palms and oleanders.

But Caecilius must have seen me pass the door. He called, 'Come here, Marcus, please.' I went in. Florus and Virilis were there.

'Well?' he asked. 'Did you take the note as I instructed?' He inclined his head at Florus, and addressing him in his listen-and-learn tone went on, 'As I was telling you, significant men are always useful to one another. The praetor will know my name from Rome, of course, and he will want to meet me as soon as possible.'

He returned his gaze to me and there was a pause. They all looked at me expectantly. This was just what I had hoped to avoid.

'Well?' said Caecilius again, tapping the desktop with his ring.

In a hesitating voice I said, 'I took the note, sir, but—'

I tried to signal with my eyes that it would be better for us to speak alone, but Caecilius burst out impatiently, 'But what? Come along, boy, pull yourself together, what was the reply? When does the praetor wish to see me?'

'There was no reply,' I said.

'No reply?' he repeated, the colour rising in his plump cheeks. Now, finally, I had his attention. I could see his mind working. Quickly he said, 'Of course, you saw the praetor *himself*?'

He could hardly have supposed this. Even Caecilius did not see messengers himself. He left it to the steward, or one of the slaves. But I knew what he was doing. He was saving face, at my expense.

Awkwardly I explained what he must have known very well, that it was one of the praetor's staff who took the note.

'Some idiot clerk,' he said, nodding at Florus and Virilis. 'And did he read it? I don't suppose he did. I don't suppose he could read Latin at all.'

'Yes, sir. He read it while I waited. He was Roman. He spoke Latin to me.'

There was a silence. Florus had developed a sudden interest in the oleander beyond the window. Virilis was looking at his boots.

My stepfather cleared his throat. 'Well, Caeso is a busy man. He has a whole city of Greeks to take care of, after all. But really, Marcus, you might have waited for an answer . . . No!' – raising his hand as I drew my breath – 'do not attempt to answer me back! Let me finish. Must I always see to a job myself, if I want it done properly? I suppose you went hurrying off to waste your time in the market, or were gaping at the shops. I have told you before. Work comes first!'

In fact I had come straight back. I did not tell him this now. Nor did I say that I had pressed the man at the praetor's residence for an answer. He had been no mere clerk, but a quaestor or some other senior official: a Roman, dressed in a white tunic bordered with red. He had been courteous, and, when I asked, he had looked over the note again, and repeated that there was no reply, adding, 'Who is this Aulus Caecilius, anyway, some sort of merchant?'

61

None of this I mentioned now to my stepfather. Instead I said, 'Do you want me to go back again, sir?'

'Oh, no; leave it, leave it.' He fluttered his thick hand at me in a gesture of irritated dismissal. 'I expect I shall hear something during the course of the day.'

In fact he heard nothing. It was I who met the praetor first. And in circumstances neither of us could have foreseen.

Tarentum interested me well enough, for there was always something new to see. But I had not grown up with city life, and there were times when I was glad to escape to the hinterland, where the great farming estates were. Though I disliked the sour mistrustful bailiffs on the farms, who had grown hard and brutal as the slaves they oversaw, yet it was pleasant to ride out among the horse-farms and orchards and vineyards, and to be away from Caecilius for a while.

It was a fine day of warm winter sun and clear skies, with a fresh breeze blowing in from the sea. Both agents – Florus and Virilis – were with me, riding beside me along a grassy track, chattering to one another over my head. We had already called on half a dozen farms, and had two more to visit before turning back.

All of a sudden, from beyond a low ridge, there came the sound of men shouting. Florus, who just then was talking, broke off and stared. I jumped off my horse and scrambled up the ridge, keeping low.

From the top, where the track joined the main route to Tarentum, I saw a troop of soldiers in Roman uniform.

They were fighting off a band of wild, dishevelled bandits who had set upon them.

The Romans were cavalrymen, dressed in short mail tunics and scarlet riding cloaks. They had dismounted, and were formed into a tight defensive circle. They were outnumbered by at least three to one; but they held their formation, while their attackers came at them like a pack of dogs.

As I watched, a great rage surged up within me. For a moment, I could hardly breathe. And then I understood: I had seen such men before, and they had torn the heart out of my life. These were not Dikaiarchos's men – but they were the same creatures, and I needed no more prompting than that. I had no armour, but we were all riding with short swords. I do not know what I intended; all I knew was that I would not stand by and do nothing while other men died.

I looked back, to call one of the agents to bring my sword from my saddle. My horse was where I had left him, chewing at the grass. But the agents were no more than specks in the distance, flogging their mules for all they were worth. They had deserted me.

I ran down and snatched my sword, then raced up over the summit of the ridge, yelling out a battle-cry at the top of my voice.

The bandits, remnants of Hannibal's army by the look of them, were facing away from me. At the sound of my voice they started, and jumped round in surprise.

The first man I killed outright, with a blow to the chest. The next, who came running, I wounded, making him fall, and one of the Roman cavalrymen finished him off. I had never been in battle before. I was an untrained youth against bitter defeated veterans. They had their soldier's training, and the sharp taste of defeat in their mouths. But I had my anger. It coursed through my veins like fire.

Time slowed. I moved and ducked as swiftly as a darting swallow, yet my mind was cool and clear. There are things a man knows in his bones, and in his soul, before ever he has time to reflect on how or why. In such a way I knew the hand of Mars the Avenger was guiding mine. Not for nothing do the poets call battle a dance. That was how it felt, each movement and turn following on from what went before, a flowing sequence whose end was life or death.

Yet soon the fighting was over. The man I killed must have been some sort of leader. When the others saw him dead they cried out to one another in their strange guttural tongue and fled. I paused. Near me an elderly man in Roman uniform had fallen. His horse was half on top of him, whinnying in pain. Two of the others dragged the creature off. I helped to sit the man up against a rock. His breath was laboured. Blood spilled out from under his corselet.

Beside me one of the soldiers said, 'Who are you, youth? Where are you from?'

I gave some reply. I was coming to myself, feeling light-headed and somehow detached. Everyone was crowding round the old man. Between his breaths he hissed, 'Stop fussing! Can't you see the boy is about to collapse?'

And then, just before I fell, I saw the welling blood, and the sword-gash in my thigh.

They bound my wound, and took me back to Tarentum on a withy stretcher. The old man, who had grey cropped hair and a firm-boned, soldier's face, was borne back next to me. I do not think I was properly conscious, but I remember him saying, 'Those Carthaginians thought you'd brought the army with you. So did I. I have seldom heard such a battle-cry.'

I should not have said it; but in my dazed state I turned my head and with a grin said, 'You should mind yourselves. You are lucky I found you.' And at this they all laughed.

I must have passed out shortly after. The next thing I remember is waking on a bed in a strange room. The shutters were closed. Brilliant bars of sunlight shone through the slits.

I lay still, staring up at the ceiling. It was wooden – dark wood, oak or cedar. I must have slept again. When next I opened my eyes, a young man was looking down at me.

'Here, drink this,' he said smiling. And as I drank, 'You bled white, but the wound is clean and will heal now.'

I drank. The water made me feel better. 'Where is this place?' I asked.

'You're at the praetor's house, in Tarentum. You are quite a hero here, you know.' I suppose he saw my look of surprise, for then he said, 'Did you not know, then? You saved the praetor's life.'

His hair was light-brown, carelessly unkempt, and curling at the brow. He had a frowning, sensitive mouth, but when he smiled his teeth showed broad and white. His beard was still a youth's, thin and wispy on his cheeks. But what struck you most was the intense blue of his eyes.

'Who are you?' I said, propping myself on my elbow and rubbing my eyes.

He laughed and gave me his hand.

'I am Titus. The praetor is my uncle.'

When I was well enough, I was taken back to my step-father, and for a few days I rested. When the bandage was off, I saw the wound in my thigh healed cleanly, as Titus said it would; but it left a long pitted scar, which showed when I wore a short tunic. I examined it in private whenever I was naked, wishing it away, for it made me feel ugly and self-conscious.

I needed no one to remind me of it. But when I was on my feet once more, and able to undertake some dreary paperwork for my stepfather, he would pull up my tunic and show my wound to the various business associates who came and went all day, saying with a shake of his head, 'You see? The boy will have it till the day he dies. But he got it saving the praetor's life – I imagine you have heard? – so perhaps some use will come of it.' And thus, for Caecilius, my pain had value.

In time the soreness and limping passed. But the shame

of having my body exposed and prodded by uncaring strangers stayed much longer. I have often wondered, since, whether he knew quite how much he humiliated me, hauling up my tunic-hem so that he could show his ogling friends.

The two agents, Florus and Virilis, had told him they had ridden off in pursuit of other bandits, whom they had seen bearing down on us. 'Is that so?' I said wryly when Caecilius told me this. But I remembered something my father used to say: Never demean yourself to argue with a liar. I said nothing more.

One day soon after, when I was back on my feet and had been set to work at the makeshift trestle table in Caecilius's workroom, the old Greek house-steward came hurrying. 'Sir,' he cried, 'you have a visitor. It is the praetor's nephew himself, Titus Quinctius.'

'Ah!' said Caecilius, pushing back his chair and straightening his tunic. He tossed a writing-tablet on my desk. 'Finish these manifests, will you, Marcus. I may be some time and they must be completed by tomorrow's sailing.'

The old slave – a quiet, cultured man called Telamon – coughed and looked vexed. 'Forgive me, sir,' he said, 'but it was the *young* master he was asking for.'

Caecilius was already on his way to the door. He halted, then turned, doing his best to fix his face.

'Why yes. How not? Well come along, Marcus, get to your feet. He is not a man to keep waiting.'

I stood, and for a moment old Telamon met my eye, and we exchanged a private look of intelligence and humour. Then, assuming once more his dutiful mask, he conducted us to where Titus was waiting in the high light-filled entrance hall.

'Greetings, sir,' said Titus, turning from the balustrade as Caecilius came bustling.

'We are most honoured,' cried my stepfather. He made a shooing gesture at Telamon. 'Hurry along now, don't just stand there, send to the kitchen for refreshments.' And back to Titus, 'Wine, perhaps, and some small thing to eat? I have a good Campanian vintage . . . Or perhaps something lighter, from Sicily, ah yes now, I have a shipment from Etna—'

'Nothing, thank you,' said Titus, cutting him off. 'Your good steward has already asked me.' There was a pause. Titus looked beyond Caecilius's bulk and grinned at me. 'In fact I have come to show your son a little of Tarentum, now that he has recovered. He has spent long enough cooped up with his honourable wound; I think he could do with some air.'

I waited for Caecilius to object; but he pressed his hands together and cried, 'Why yes! An excellent idea! Come along, Marcus, don't keep the man waiting, when he has so generously put himself to such inconvenience for your sake.' And to Titus, 'It will do the boy good to venture out a little more often. Do you notice his limp? Show him, Marcus. Exercise will help it along, though of course I fear it will never be gone entirely.'

Titus looked with concern. 'Why I shouldn't have noticed it at all . . . But Marcus, if you had rather not . . .?'

Before I could answer, Caecilius cried, 'Nonsense! Nothing would suit him better.'

'Then good. Let us go then. We need not wander far. Tell me, have you seen the library and the gardens?'

Winter in Tarentum was warm compared with high Praeneste. The sky was a deep, cobalt blue, and the sharp sunlight glittered on the bay. As we walked – with me slightly limping – along the colonnade beside the marketplace, I asked how Titus's uncle Caeso was recovering from his own wound.

'Oh, he is well enough,' Titus answered with a shrug. 'He has an excellent Greek doctor from Syracuse; but he would be better still if he would only take the man's advice and rest a little. But he shouts at him to stop fussing. He says he has lived fifty years without doctors, and does not need them bothering him now . . . Ah, this way.'

We came out in the precinct in front of the library and climbed the smooth marble steps. Inside were row upon row of scroll-niches, rising up among tiered columns. Here and there men were reading, sitting at tables or standing by the racks. Sunlight shafted in from high windows.

'You smell that?' said Titus, sniffing the air. 'It's cedar. They use it to preserve the books.' I sniffed. I remembered the smell from my father's small library at home, which Caecilius had cast away. I looked about. I had never imagined there could be so many books.

We walked about for a while, and greeted the librarian. Then went into the courtyard garden behind. The street outside had been busy – as, it seemed to me, all streets in Tarentum were – but the garden, high-walled, with a long shaded pathway and urns of lavender, was a haven of peace. We found a sunny alcove and sat down on a bench.

Titus stretched, drew in his breath, and considered the great building with its sculpted, painted pediment and coloured marble.

'Beautiful, isn't it?' he said, 'and all this was made by men. How I long to see Athens, or Pergamon, or Alexandria! We have so much to learn from them.'

His blue eyes shone. Touched by his enthusiasm, and by the grandeur, and wanting to show him what I felt, I said, 'My father would have loved this place. I wish you could have met him.'

'But what do you mean?' he said, looking at me. 'Surely I met him no more than an hour ago.'

'What, him?' I cried, jolted out of my shyness and staring. 'Oh, no! *He* is not my father; you must not think it.'

And then I explained.

He listened in silence, occasionally nodding and frowning. When I had finished he said, 'Truly that is a hard thing to bear. It would have been an honour to meet such a man. And, now I think of it, Caecilius did not have your look at all.'

He smiled, and I knew he was trying to put me at my ease.

'You know, Marcus, there is something about you that sets you apart from the common run of men. I can see it in your eyes, like fire.'

At this I blushed and looked down. The memory of Epeiros had stirred my anger, and it is a strange thing when a man can see your private thoughts in your face.

'But now I am embarrassing you,' he said with a pleasant laugh. 'Come on, let's walk some more.'

He stood, and pausing met my eye. 'One thing though. Don't let anyone quench that fire. It is the forge of your soul.'

We left the library gardens and walked on, down past the theatre, pausing for a while at the sanctuary of Persephone, with its porch of tall columns, and its row of painted terracotta statues on the roof. He told me how, before he had come to Tarentum, he had served as a tribune under the consul Claudius Marcellus. He had fought, he said, against Hannibal in Italy, and had been nearby on the day that Marcellus was ambushed and killed by Hannibal's cavalry.

'That was a dark day,' he said. 'It is easy to forget how it felt, now Scipio has driven them out of Italy.'

He paused and shook his head.

'Too many have died – at Cannae, and Baecula, and Metaurus; a whole generation lost, and we must not let any nation do this to us again. Soon Scipio will have chased them all the way back to Carthage – if the gods are willing, and his enemies in the Senate do not thwart him first. The world is only safe for those who make it so. There are men always and everywhere who will enslave the weak and the unwary. A man must make himself strong: without that there can be no other freedom.'

I gazed up at the temple with its sculpted pediment, but in my mind I saw the rocky crags of Epeiros, and my anger stirred within me. 'But who are these traitors,' I said, 'who work against Scipio even as he fights for our safety?'

He smiled. 'You are not the only one who is frustrated by them. But they are not traitors. They are leading men in Rome – senators, even ex-consuls some of them. But they are wrong. They suppose that if only we remove the Carthaginians from Italy, we will be left in peace. "Let us stay secure within our own borders as before!" That is what they say. They are old men, and they yearn for the past, when things were simpler – or seemed so. But there is no going back. Twice Carthage has made war on us. That is enough. There must not be a next time.'

Before we parted he took my hand and said, 'Well, Marcus, I am glad to see you healed – and don't worry about that limp' (he had spotted my frustration with it as I walked), 'it is nothing, it will be gone in a few days.' He paused, considering, then went on, 'But listen, I am holding a small dinner-party – just a few friends – why don't you come? I'm sure your stepfather is too busy to do much entertaining. I will show you a side to Tarentum you have not seen.'

Caecilius was waiting with a host of questions when I returned. Had I seen the praetor? Had I been to the residence? What had we talked about?

My answers did not satisfy him.

'Always think, boy,' he said, 'in everything you do, what there is to be gained. A conversation with important people is never a conversation merely.' He tapped his temple with his little finger. 'Gain, gain, gain. Always look for gain.'

Two days later, I returned from the harbour, where I

had seen off a cargo of Tarentine pots and ironware, and was passing through the entrance hall, when old Telamon beckoned me aside with a quick worried wave of his hand.

'Oh, Marcus sir,' he said, keeping his voice down, 'while you were out a note came from the praetor's residence, and a box with it. Your name was written on it. Really, it could not have been clearer.'

I glanced at the cypresswood table in the corner, where such things were usually left. But except for the tall vase of green glass that always stood there, which Telamon kept stocked with herbs and flowers from the garden, the table was empty.

'Then where is it?' I said. But even as I spoke I had guessed.

Poor Telamon. Whoever the previous master of the house had been – and he was too discreet to speak of him to me – he had clearly been a man of breeding and fine manners. With Caecilius, he was at a loss. Seeing this I thanked him, and said, 'No matter; I understand.' And then we both looked round as Caecilius's summoning voice came from his workroom.

The note, as I had already guessed, was from Titus. It lay open on the desk, an elegant papyrus scroll with the name 'Marcus' in a bold hand in black ink.

'It seems, after all, that you have made a favourable impression,' said my stepfather, looking up. 'Now Caeso the praetor is sure to be at this gathering: you must do your best to persuade him to grant me the supply-contract for the garrison. At the moment that fool Mummius has it; but I can offer a better price. Make sure you tell him so. Shall I write it down, with the figures? Or will you keep them in your head? And don't forget to tell him I am already supplying the fleet in Kerkyra – though I expect he has heard that already . . .'

He talked on, but he must have seen my eyes stray to the note, for he broke off and said, 'What now? I receive many messages each day, and of course I did not notice your name till I had opened it.'

'No, sir.'

He peered at me and sniffed. 'Anyway, you are my son by adoption. You are under my authority and I may do as I please. Here, read it yourself.'

He pushed the note across the desk at me.

It said: 'Titus to Marcus, greetings. Come the day after tomorrow, at sunset. Meanwhile here is a small token, from uncle Caeso, who fares well, and from me. Something Greek. If you like it, wear it.'

The box – a small, painted gift-box – sat on the desk. The seal was broken and the cord had been undone. Caecilius must have been busy at it when I arrived.

I lifted the lid, and pulled out a fine white tunic with a border worked in green and scarlet, and held it up to look at it. It was better than anything else I possessed.

'Fine work,' nodded Caecilius, rubbing it with his short, thick fingers. 'Milesian wool. It would be hard to find such quality even at the best shops in Rome.' And then, glancing up and giving me a sharp look, 'This Titus, it is said, likes all things Greek. You are not a bad-looking lad, despite your scarred leg. Make sure you watch yourself at this party of his.'

Thus, in his expert way, he added vinegar to the wine.

I pretended I did not know what he meant, but no doubt my reddening face betrayed my understanding. I had received a gift from a friend, nothing more. But all things, for him, had to have a base motive; and until he had uncovered it he was not content.

Titus's dinner-party was indeed very Greek – elegant supper-couches of polished wood and striped, silk cushions; a flautist in the corner, playing a Lydian air; a dinner service of antique silverware, and, upon it, a varied meal of small exquisite portions – Sicilian sucking kid, honeyed fowl scattered with sesame, spiced fish wrapped in delicate pastries – all perfectly prepared and served by well-trained staff.

When I arrived I asked after Caeso the praetor.

'He is in bed, and will not be joining us,' said Titus. 'His wound is troubling him. At last he is heeding his doctor's advice and resting.'

He led me in among the couches, introducing me to his friends. There were two Romans about Titus's age, called Villius and Terentius; there was a young tribune from the garrison; and there were two Greeks from Tarentum, who were something to do with the city government.

I greeted all these people. But the person who drew my eye was seated on the couch of honour next to Titus's place. It was all I could do not to stare at her in wonder. She must have been well over forty, but she held herself like some exquisite work of art, and was as graceful as the haunting, gentle music coming from the alcove. She wore a silk robe of the darkest blue, worked around the edges with gold filigree; her chestnut hair was bound up and plaited, and held in place with a gilded brooch fashioned in the shape of a swallow. I knew enough by now to realize that she was a courtesan. But from her presence, you might have supposed she was a queen among her subjects.

She had been speaking to one of the other guests, but as Titus led me to her couch her dark eyes flashed up. They were painted with just a hint of colour. Her look was deep and intelligent and appraising. Titus said, 'This is my friend Pasithea. I have set you beside her.'

She smiled up at me.

'So you are the brave young man who fought off the Carthaginians. I have been looking forward to meeting you.'

I made some shy answer. I felt like some rustic lout, who finds himself in the presence of a goddess.

But she had made it her business and her art to know how to put a man at his ease; and soon, with a few words, a look, a gesture – I could not tell quite how she did it – she made me forget my awkwardness and think only of her.

I relaxed, and began to enjoy myself.

Titus, that evening, was sharing his supper-couch with a girl called Xanthe. She too was a courtesan, as were all the women there; but I could see they were also firm friends, who enjoyed each other's conversation as much as each other's bodies. Now and then, with a scarcely conscious movement, she would touch his arm or hand or leg as she talked, or turn her blue-painted eyes to him and smile. She was aware of her body, and its effect. But there was nothing crude or distasteful or grasping. Her laughter was like dewdrops, her manners faultless. She was an artist, and one look at Pasithea showed who had been her teacher.

Titus's friend Villius was on the couch nearest mine, and while we ate he told me he had recently come from Rome, and had known Titus since they were both boys. He praised my home town of Praeneste, saying he had visited the shrine of Fortuna there; and for a while we talked of home, and places we knew in common.

Later, Titus spoke of Tarentum. It was his uncle's wish to restore self-government to the city; he was trying to persuade the Senate in Rome to agree. The good people – the aristocrats, the men of education – had never supported Hannibal, and in his view many men had been unfairly dispossessed in the chaos following the siege. The time had come, he said, to put right this injustice and make Tarentines not subjects of Rome, but friends and allies.

As I listened I thought of Caecilius, and how little this would please him. I was glad the praetor was not there, for it spared me from putting to him Caecilius's embarrassing requests for business, which, in such company, would have shamed me beyond reason.

Later, when the guests stood and mingled, Pasithea asked me how I was enjoying the city and what I had seen.

I had assumed, up to now, that she was Tarentine

herself, but she said that, though she had been in the city for some time, and had a number of friends here, she had come from Greece.

'From Athens?' I asked, imagining her home in some such great and sophisticated city.

She laughed pleasantly and dipped her eyes. 'No, my dear. I grew up in a little place called Abydos. I don't suppose you've heard of it.'

In fact I had, and told her so, for it was a city Caecilius often mentioned, lying as it did on the shipping route from Greece to the Black Sea, where his ships sometimes put in. I asked her why she had left.

'Oh, it was so *dull*.' She leant over and laid a hand on my arm. Her touch was light, yet full of feeling. I caught a hint of the scent she wore; it was delicate and bright, like springtime air, with a hidden depth that lured the senses. 'You know, when I was a girl, I used to think it was just that I was easily bored. Have you ever felt that way, Marcus? But after I had visited Korinth and Athens, I realized it was not me, it was Abydos.'

She rolled her eyes, and I laughed, as she had intended. She laughed with me, and her gold earrings flickered in the lamplight.

'And so,' she continued, 'I left, and went to Korinth, that most delightful of cities. Have you been? Oh, how I adored it after Abydos! I still do. Parties, friends, theatre, music; and always something new to stimulate the mind. I have a little house there on the Kenchreai road, with a pretty garden. But I like to travel, and of course I have friends everywhere.'

She talked on, telling me about places in Tarentum I

should visit, asking about my fight with the Carthaginians, and a little about my life before I came (though not much of that – I think Titus had warned her). She made me laugh; she made me wish to know her better; she drew me out of my shell and made me feel alive.

As I sat, my tunic hem had ridden up a little, as tunics do. Without thinking I eased it back down, to hide my scar. It had become something I did.

No one noticed, or so I thought.

But a little later Pasithea placed her hand to my thigh and with a gentle tap said, 'It is a mark of honour. No decent person could think otherwise. Do not cheapen it by being ashamed.'

She was full of such acts of attentive kindness. This one, when I was young and vulnerable, I have never forgotten.

I had heard talk, even in quiet, backward Praeneste, of these famous Greek courtesans, for the boys who had been my childhood friends used to whisper about them, and speculate. Knowing no better, I had assumed they must be like the rough whores that lived in the alleyways behind the market there, who catered for the goatherds and cattlemen when they brought their livestock up from the hills to be sold.

I realized now how wrong I was. Pasithea had a mind as sharp as a barber's blade, and wit to go with it. So did Xanthe. The Greeks called them hetairas, which means companion; and that is what they were. Whatever they gave, they gave freely. They did not demean themselves by asking for payment, or announcing a fee. They merely accepted a gift, offered freely by those they counted as their friends. They were women who had chosen to be their own masters, and if there was a cost to such freedom, they were prepared to pay it.

I returned my attention to the conversation around me. Titus was asking Villius about the elections in Rome, which had recently taken place.

'Scipio was there,' said Villius. 'He was canvassing, and putting himself about among the people. Fabius spoke against him, of course. So did—' and here he named a number of senior men in Rome, men from ancient and powerful families.

'What did they say?' asked Titus.

Villius shrugged. 'The same as always. They say Scipio should make peace, if peace is offered. They are tired of war.'

Titus turned to me. 'You see, Marcus; it is as I was telling you.' And then, to Villius, 'By the gods, we are all tired of war. But being tired of war will not turn away our enemies. Now, at last, after so many years, Carthage is at the point of defeat, and these old men want to pull back, like dogs that bark but will not bite. We made the mistake once before, and they came back, even stronger, and many men have died. No,' he said, with an angry gesture, 'if we ignore them now, they will be back when our attention is elsewhere, and next time we may not be so fortunate. The gods do not grant luck to fools. It is not so long ago that Hannibal was camped at the very gates of Rome. Do they forget so soon?'

Villius laughed. Something of a silence had fallen, and he broke it saying, 'Well I see you haven't changed. But you know what your father would say.'

'Oh, him!' said Titus with a dismissive wave. He drew his breath, and I thought he was going to say more. But in the end he just shook his head and took up his wine-cup. Beside him Xanthe made some light comment. He turned to her, and for a while the conversation changed.

But presently Villius said, 'While I was in Rome I saw Lucius. They have quarrelled again, he and your father.'

Titus paused. For an instant, such a look of anger clouded his features that Xanthe, who had been resting her hand on his, took it hurriedly away.

With a quick apologetic smile he took it back and held it in his own broad hand. 'No,' he said. 'It's not your fault.' And then, to Villius, 'They always quarrel. That is what Father does best. Lucius needs to get away. I shall write to him again and ask him to come. He is my brother, after all, whatever his faults, and I must do what I can.'

The tables were cleared. A dancer came on, a lithe dark-skinned Greek boy from Tyre, who danced to the accompaniment of pan-pipes and a lute. Xanthe, who was sitting on the other side of me, was asking in wide-eyed curious tones about Rome, which she seemed to regard as a fearsome barbarous place, far distant and never to be visited, like the lands of the painted Kelts, or the Hyper-boreans. We were speaking lightly, and laughing. The dancer, naked but for his loincloth, moved in the lamp-light; the pipes played their prancing melody. Then, like a sudden ice-wind on a summer's day, from across the room I heard a name that made me jerk my head around and stare.

One of Titus's friends, one of the Greeks, was talking about King Philip, king of the Macedonians. But it was not the sound of Philip's name that jolted me. It was Dikaiarchos's.

Titus saw me stiffen and look.

'What is it?' he said. 'Do you know this man?'

I said, 'I shall never forget, and one day I shall kill him.'

I had not intended to say this. But now the words were out, and so, with everyone's eyes on me, I explained why.

When I had finished, Titus's friend – his name was Mimas – said, 'Well I am sorry. If you ask me, we are all going to hear a lot more of him.'

I asked him why.

'He has been seizing Roman grain ships, and nothing is more likely to draw the Senate's attention than that. Everyone says Philip is behind it, though he denies it of course. But he and Dikaiarchos are guest-friends.' He raised his black brows, and with a smiling glance about the room added, 'There are some, indeed, who say they were once lovers . . . But however that may be, they are certainly thick as thieves. You should keep your eye on them, Titus. Scipio won glory by driving Hannibal from Italy. What could be nobler than freeing Greece from under the heel of that bully Philip?'

Titus stroked the soft boyish beard on his chin. He took up his cup, and his blue eyes shone. I remember that moment, not only for my own sake, but because I saw the end, and what became of it. I have often wondered, after, whether this was the beginning.

The party broke up soon after.

While I stood on the porch outside, waiting for the torch-bearers, Pasithea came up and kissed my brow.

'Be sure to come and visit me,' she said, as if it were only me that had made the whole evening worthwhile. 'Anyone knows where I live. I'll send my boy with a note.'

Then the torch-bearer came, and she went off across the garden and under the arch, the goldwork in her long sweeping dress catching in the light from the cressets as she moved.

FOUR

SPRING CAME. PRIMROSES SHOWED on the slopes among the cypresses, and the port, which had been quiet for the winter, grew busy once more.

My stepfather had gone out early, down to the harbour with Florus and Virilis. I was in the garden when I heard from within a great commotion of shouting and rushing of feet. Then Caecilius appeared on the step. He looked as if he had run all the way up the hill from the marketplace. His face was red and blotchy, his breath labouring.

'He's dead!' he cried, throwing up his hands. 'He's dead!'

Florus appeared beside him in the doorway, and then Virilis, both of them eager-faced and full of moment.

'Who is dead?'

'Why, the praetor!' cried Caecilius, staring at me as if I were an idiot. 'Caeso! He died less than an hour ago, with the dawn. It's all over the market.'

'But his wounds were healing.'

'Maybe he caught a chill – who can say? But anyway he is dead. You must go with your condolences . . . Make sure it is noticed. Go and change those clothes – hurry! Go now, while the news is fresh, before the crowds arrive.'

I changed my clothes and made my way to the praetor's house.

The crowds were already there – flatterers, opportunists, sycophants, men on the make, all of them full of eager showy grief. I left again without speaking to anyone.

The next we heard was that Titus had stepped in, assuming the imperium from his uncle. He had been doing the governor's work already; and in due course the Senate, with its eyes fixed elsewhere on the war with Carthage, approved it.

During this time, Titus was much occupied with the affairs of government, and I with my stepfather's business. I had not seen him for a while. But one morning I was returning from some errand, and was passing by the gardens of the sanctuary of the Dioskouroi, which, just then, were heavy with almond blossom, when I saw him, standing with his back to me, close to the gateway that leads out to the marketplace.

It was early, and the stallholders were still setting up. I was rather surprised to see Titus there. It was not his habit to dawdle around the market, and, though he did not go about town with a formal retinue, which he said the Tarentines would resent, nevertheless he would usually have two or three friends with him.

I crossed along the portico to greet him. As I drew

85

near I sensed there was something about him not quite right. His hair was the same, falling in brown tufts about his neck. But he held himself oddly, as if he were tired or ill. Or – it came to me even as I spoke his name – drunk. But that could not be. Titus never allowed himself to get stumbling drunk anywhere, let alone in the public market-place.

He turned and stared into my face with cold unfocused eyes. I felt a chill down my spine. It is a strange unsettling thing not to be recognized by a man you count as a friend.

'Do I know you?' he said harshly.

And then realization dawned.

'What is wrong with you?' he said. 'Do you lack eyes to see?'

I spluttered out an apology.

'Then look and remember,' he said, unforgiving. 'I am not Titus. I am Lucius.'

So Lucius has come then, I thought to myself as I hurried away. And then it came to me where he had emerged from. It was the alley behind the portico, where the rough taverns were, the ones that open at dawn to cater for the market traders, and for men who cannot get through the morning without a cup of wine.

I regretted my mistake. I hoped, when I next saw him, I would be able to make a better apology. But I did not dwell on it, for just then something closer to home had begun to trouble me.

It had started towards the end of winter, and at first I did not credit what I saw. It was a habit from my childhood to rise each day with first light. One morning

I was in the garden alone, sitting on the bench beside the wall, when I saw a girl flitting along the portico. She paused by a column, ran her fingers through her hair and straightened her mantle, then, with a quick look about her, darted up the steps and into the inner hall. She had not seen me. There was a spreading jasmine that grew up the side of the house. It had concealed me from her view.

I sat back and smiled to myself, and at the time thought little of it, supposing she was some friend of one of the slaves. My stepfather forbade such visits. She was leaving before he awoke.

But when one looks, one notices. A few mornings later I saw her again. She was less discreet this time, more sure of herself. Once again she paused to arrange her clothes, and this time I took a better look at her. She had thick black hair, and wore a cheap necklace of copper and glass beads. The strap of her shoe was troubling her, and as she snatched at it with her fingers a sharp shrewish expression passed across her features. She had the look of a Phoenician or Sicilian, a thin face with a pointed chin; one saw many of them in Tarentum, especially at the port.

When she disappeared inside I followed, and from the porch saw her exit through the main gateway and hurry off down the street, keeping to the side, out of the light. I returned to the inner garden, and this time followed the direction from which she had first emerged. At the far end of the portico, concealed behind a clump of oleander, was a doorway in the wall, and beyond an open passageway which ran along the back of the house, strewn with dead leaves. At the far end, at the top of a flight of stone steps, was a back door to my stepfather's sleeping-suite. The girl's footprints showed in the dust.

I returned to the bench beneath the jasmine and considered. I shall not pretend I was greatly surprised. I told myself what one hears everywhere: that a man's pleasures are his own. Yet I found myself filled with distaste. This was not just any man; he was the man who had chosen to marry my mother.

Nothing of the varied diversions of Tarentum had seemed to interest him. I recalled with an ironic smile how he had declared, primly, that he did not have time for such frivolity as the theatre or the concerts at the odeion, or the pleasant garden walks. I reflected too that, for all his money, he had chosen only this harsh-faced trull as a companion. Yet how could it be otherwise? He would never have picked a woman with the charm and refinement of Xanthe or Pasithea. They would have shown him up for what he was.

When, later, he finally emerged from his rooms, dull-eyed and irritable, for my mother's sake I did not mention the girl. But when, later in the day, he snapped that he was tired, I allowed myself to say, 'You should do your best to sleep more, sir, in spite of all this work. You are getting no younger, after all, and look what happened to Caeso.'

When Titus next invited me to one of his dinner-parties, his brother Lucius was there. As soon as I could do so discreetly, I made my apologies for my mistake. He seemed to accept them; but he looked at me oddly, as if he did not know what I was talking about. Perhaps this was how he showed I was forgiven. It was disconcerting, in one who looked so like Titus, to find his manner so different. From a distance they looked identical. The same chin and brow and falling brown hair, the same regular features. But there was a sullenness about his mouth and eyes, like an ill-bred child's deprived of what it wants.

There was always a studied Greekness to these gatherings. A youth or a girl would gently sing to the accompaniment of a lyre or flute; or, at other times, Titus would arrange for some well-known rhapsode from Tarentum or other of the Greek cities in Italy to recite tales of heroes and ancient love. There was style in everything, and careful good manners.

All this I noticed, because it was new, and diverting, and exotic. I noticed too that it seemed to irk Lucius. He talked over the music; he complained that the service at dinner, with its carefully chosen, exquisitely prepared portions, was too slow; but most of all he complained about the wine, for he was a man who liked to drink at his own pace, which was faster than anyone else's. To make his point, he would drain his cup no sooner than the serving-boy had filled it, then indicate it was empty by setting it down loudly on the little olivewood table in front of his couch and gesturing with a snap of his finger for the boy to refill it.

Not surprisingly, after the way we had met, I seldom found cause to speak to him, nor he to me. But at one such party he came striding across the room and, interrupting my conversation with Villius and Pasithea, asked abruptly, 'Where do you live? Is it the house above the harbour? The one with the white walls and tall palms?'

I answered that it was, and at this he nodded and walked off, and I thought no more about it.

But then, next morning, Telamon came to me and said, 'Marcus, sir. There is a man to see you.'

It was Lucius.

'I am going to the palaistra,' he said. 'I do not like to go alone, and thought you might come.'

I must have looked at him with surprise. I have never been good at hiding my feelings. I blush when I am angry, and I gape like an idiot when I am shocked. This time, though, I had self-command enough to hide my astonishment with a cough. I knew that Titus, with his liking for Greek things, would occasionally go to the palaistra, with its wrestling-ground and running-tracks and ball courts. But even he went only when his Greek friends invited him.

If you are Roman, you will understand this reticence. At home I had certainly hardened my body, in the normal work of the farm, in hunting, or, more recently, in teaching myself to run and throw the javelin and swing the ancient heavy sword I had found in the outhouse. To all these there was purpose. But to work one's body as an end in itself, as a sculptor might work clay into a statue, or a potter a fine pot, was still a thing strange to Romans.

But I thought to myself: Titus has set the fashion in Greek manners, and Lucius is following it. It came to me too that this was some sort of peace-offering by Lucius. It would be churlish to refuse, when he had made a special point of coming to my house.

So I called for my cloak and we set off.

The palaistra in Tarentum lay not far from the library. It was a complex of colonnaded courts, some laid with turf, others paved, and shaded by plane trees and tall cypresses. The entrance was through an archway, off the street behind the library gardens.

We passed through the gate and into the small fountain-court where the changing rooms and bath-house were. From somewhere I could hear the laughter of youths and the splash of water; and, further off, the barking orders of the wrestling-trainer.

'This way,' said Lucius.

I began to wonder what he had in mind. I hoped it was not boxing or wrestling. I had never wrestled in my life, and the boxers I had seen about the streets of Tarentum were fearsome creatures, bruised and cauliflower-eared. But, stealing a quick glace at Lucius, I reminded myself that these sports would suit him even less than me. He was biting his lip and glancing about. No doubt, I thought, his friends would be waiting somewhere, though he had not mentioned any friends on the way. Perhaps, I thought, Titus was here, and this was Lucius's little joke.

We came out in a grassy colonnaded square with a running-track. In the shadow of the covered walkway, he halted.

I glanced about. I could see no one I recognized, no friends approaching to greet us.

Beside the track the running-trainer, a lean greying man in a homespun tunic, stood leaning on his cane, chatting with a group of youths. By the look of it, he had just finished a session. Around the court the youths were scattering, ambling off in twos and threes in the direction of the bath-house.

I looked at Lucius. His lips were slightly parted; his eyes were fixed on the middle distance, where a youth about my age was standing with his friends.

Just then the youth laughed, and laughing glanced round. His hair was golden-bronze, short-cropped, and dark about his brow, where his sweat had made it damp. Standing naked as he was, dusty from the track, he might have been some god's statue, perfect in proportion.

As he turned, he saw Lucius staring at him. For an instant he paused, and his smile turned to a frown. He looked quickly away, and made some comment to his friends. At this, one or two of them looked our way.

The youth said something else, and then with purpose they all walked off in the direction of the bath-house.

Beside me, Lucius let out his breath. I had not realized, till then, that he had been holding it in.

'That,' he said, following the youth with hungry eyes, 'is Menexenos.'

Afterwards he wandered on, but listlessly, seemingly without purpose, through the spreading complex of the palaistra, along colonnades, across lawns, through gardens. We came to the swimming-pool. Three or four swimmers were ploughing strongly through the glittering sun-reflecting water. Lucius narrowed his eyes and peered at them, and I had the sense he was looking to see if one of them was the youth we had seen on the running-track.

I was tempted to say, 'I think your friend went to the bath-house.' But he had begun to grow sulky and irritable; and besides, I had the sense that this beautiful strong-boned youth was no more Lucius's friend than the hare is friend to the hound. It made me feel awkward, and I held my tongue.

Eventually we passed under a stone arch and came out once more at the fountain-court where we had entered. He gave a languid sigh, like a man who is sickening for something.

'Are your friends not here?' I said, looking about. 'Where did you arrange to meet them?'

'What friends?' he snapped, rounding on me. 'You are here, aren't you? What are you talking about?'

I was about to say, 'Then why did you come at all?' But I did not. I was beginning to understand.

There was a spreading plane tree beside the gateway to the street, and a marble seat beneath. Here he sat down.

'Well you may leave now,' he said, with the tone of one dismissing a slave. 'I think I shall wait here for a while, and see who comes and goes.'

I left him. I remembered he had said he did not like to go alone to the palaistra. He had asked me only because there was no one else to ask. I felt angry and ashamed, for it seemed to me the only purpose of the morning had been his pursuit of the youth he had called Menexenos. Indeed, I should have considered it altogether a wasted morning, if, at that time, so many of my days working for my stepfather had not seemed no more than wasted time.

When next I saw Lucius, a few days later, it was at a large gathering that Titus was holding at the praetor's residence. He showed no sign of friendliness; he made no mention of the morning at the palaistra; indeed he scarcely spoke to me at all. All this I shrugged off; but there was worse to come, which I could not ignore.

That evening, Titus was entertaining important men visiting from Rome: two influential senators and their friends, acquaintances of Scipio, who that year was consul. He had brought in extra couches, and turned the long entrance hall with its frescoed walls and fine fluted columns into a banqueting room. The food, as usual, was exquisite, and from Syracuse he had hired a famous bard he knew, sending a boat specially to Sicily to fetch him. He wanted, he had said to me, to show these men from Rome some of the fine things Greece could offer.

And there was more on offer that night than food alone.

If, up to now, I have not mentioned love, there is a reason. There had been girls enough at Praeneste to be courted, and to be had. But after Epeiros something had changed. I knew the urgings of my growing body; but something – a deep-seated reluctance I was aware of only partly – held me back, like the worm in the apple that keeps one from biting.

Whatever it was, my instinct shied from it, and if ever some pretty girl smiled at me, I was civil, and cool, and would walk on.

Once, before one of his banquets, Titus had said privately to me, 'Xanthe has many friends, you know . . . You need only say the word.'

I had thanked him, but answered that I was happy with the company as it was, and he had said no more.

Yet I had answered with only half the truth, for in my deepest heart I yearned for love, though in my imagination it had no form. It became something I thought about. Why, when other men seemed content, was I not? Had Epeiros changed me for ever? It seemed to me that it was so, but I did not understand it. I began to think that I was not capable of love at all.

That evening, while the other guests were still arriving, Titus took my elbow, and leading me discreetly to an alcove said, 'Xanthe has brought a friend of hers tonight. Her name is Myrtilla. I was going to put her next to Terentius, but his sister has come from Rome and they will sit together. So I have put her with you. I hope you don't mind.' He grinned and added, 'Anyway, she is good company. I think you will like her.'

After this I looked out for her, as you may suppose, and noticed straightaway when she walked in with Pasithea.

She was dressed in a short white dress of fine linen, with a bronze clasp in the shape of a dolphin. I guessed she was a little older than I, perhaps seventeen or eighteen. Her hair was black, like mine, and she wore it short.

The slave took her mantle, and she paused to scan the room with dark intelligent eyes. Her body – or as much of it as one saw – was lithe and smooth, like a dancer's.

Lucius was sitting a few couches away from me, in the corner under the lamp-standard. As she passed I noticed his eyes go up from his wine-cup and follow her. He seemed about to say something; but Pasithea, walking tall and stately beside her, immediately turned to him and said, 'Greetings, Lucius. I hope I find you well,' and at this he grunted and returned to his wine.

The dinner passed as Titus had planned. There was a good deal of political talk, of Rome, of the war and the defeat of Carthage, which could only be a matter of time now. The bard and the kitharist who accompanied him were politely applauded, and when he had done, and the tables had been cleared away, the guests left their couches, joining friends, or wandering about the torchlit garden.

Myrtilla, as Titus had promised, had been a faultless companion. I suppose I had drunk more than usual, and I daresay the wine helped; but by the time the meal was over my initial shyness had gone and she and I were talking easily.

Pasithea, who had been sitting elsewhere, came and sat beside us. 'I think,' she said smiling at us both, 'that Titus is in love.'

'Well that is no surprise,' I said laughing and glancing down the long room to where Titus was standing with his arm about Xanthe on the steps of the terrace.

'Oh, everyone loves Xanthe,' she said, 'but after tonight I realized that Titus has another love affair as well.' She gave a teasing laugh and flashed her brown eyes at me; and then, to the slave-boy who came offering wine, 'No, my dear, no more.'

I watched the boy hurry off to the corner, where Lucius was angrily beckoning.

'Another love affair?' I asked, half joking. I knew Titus was fond of Xanthe, and they were as much friends as lovers. But there was no other that I knew of.

'Why yes, something far more serious,' she said. 'He is in love with Greece – or, at least, with the idea of Greece. Did you see his face when the bard was singing? He was lost in it. Unreachable upon the plain of Troy.'

The bard had ended by singing of how old white-bearded Priam had ridden out from Troy to ransom his dead son Hektor, falling at Achilles' knees and begging him to accept the gifts he brought in exchange for the body of his child. I had never heard it done better. Even the old senators had ceased their talking and fallen silent. I had even seen one of them wipe a tear from his eye – discreetly, for, being Roman, he would not have cared to have it noticed.

'Well the song was beautiful,' I said.

'Yes,' she said, 'and Titus is infatuated and he is a dreamer. He is in love with an image.'

I looked at her. She was wearing, that night, a sumptuous gown of shimmering green, woven with tiny white roses. Her hair, bound up with a jewelled fillet, fell in little sculpted curls beside her ears. Smiling I said, 'Any man can love from afar. Surely, Pasithea, you know that more than anyone.'

She laughed her pleasant laugh and rested her hand on my knee. 'Well you are a charming, delightful, handsome boy,' she said, 'and if I were fifteen years younger, I should take you home and eat you up. But nowadays my bed is big enough only for one, and I am not going to let you turn my head with your flattery.'

I laughed.

'But mark my words,' she went on, 'every coin has two faces. One day Titus will wake from his dream, and then he will see the other, and he will be disappointed.' Someone called her name and she glanced round. 'But I am being far too serious. So I shall leave you two alone, and go and talk to my other friends, before they start to think I am neglecting them.'

We watched her drift off through the crowd, pausing here and there to talk as she went. I turned to Myrtilla and smiled.

'Come on,' she said, taking my arm in hers. 'Let us go and walk in the garden for a while. It is a beautiful night, and I am tired of all these people.'

We made our way outside. There had been a rain shower, and the night air was cool and pleasant. Through the streaks of cloud, over the light of the cressets, the Milky Way glittered like a silver belt. The air smelled of grass, and the delicate fragrance of night-scented flowers.

At the end of the terrace, where the vine grew up between the columns and cascaded down, broad-leaved, from the stonework, she turned and kissed me on the lips. 'That,' she said smiling, 'is for being such a good companion. I have enjoyed myself. I thought I was going to have to spend the evening with one of those grim old senators.'

We laughed; and then I remembered to kiss her in return.

She met my eye. 'I have a little house close by, and a bed large enough for two.'

I frowned and looked out into the darkness. Along the meandering paths, the torches flickered, burning low. The shrubs beyond the terrace rustled with a breeze blowing in from the bay.

It is not in my nature to force myself on anyone. But, during the course of the evening, she had made it discreetly clear what was on offer, if I chose to take it. I had enjoyed myself, though I had not thought I should. We had laughed and talked. In the end it seemed churlish to refuse, and somehow weak. Besides, after her pleasant company I did not want her to think I did not like her.

I smiled, and was about to answer, when the bushes at my side rustled and cracked, and from the overgrown path a dark figure emerged into the light.

Myrtilla stifled a cry and jumped back.

'Hello, Lucius,' I said, startled.

He did not answer, but looked straight past me with unfocused eyes at Myrtilla. He must have been watching us. 'Who is the girl?' he said in Latin, as if she were some goat at market.

In Greek I answered, 'This is Myrtilla, my friend.'

All of a sudden he lunged forward and groped her roughly with his spread hand. With a cry she pulled away. He snatched at her and with a tear the top of her thin tunic came away. The little dolphin brooch that had held it fell clattering on the floor at her feet.

'Come in with me,' he said, trying to hold her by the arm.

In a quick, deft movement she slid from his grip and stood away, holding up her tunic with one arm and extending the other, ready to fend him off. In a slow, clear voice she said, 'I choose my friends, sir, and whoever you are, you are not one of them.'

All this had happened so quickly, and so unexpectedly, that it had taken me by surprise. But now I remembered myself and stepped up in front of Lucius.

He was a little taller than I, but I was broader. And, now that I had recovered my wits, my anger was rising.

'Leave her,' I said, stepping up to him. 'She is my friend and my guest. Leave her alone. You are drunk, Lucius. You will be sorry in the morning.'

I saw his fists clench and rise. Behind me, Myrtilla caught her breath. 'Sorry?' he cried. 'So you're suddenly the little gentleman, are you? Will you have her then, eh? If not, then make way for someone who will.'

He tried to step around me. I stepped to block him. My muscles tensed. But I thought to myself: I will not hit him first, for Titus's sake. But if he strikes me, he will regret it.

Then, from the far end of the terrace, a voice barked out.

Lucius swung round startled. It was Titus.

'That is enough,' he said, his voice as hard as crystal.

Lucius paused, bit his lip, hesitated, then uttered a curse and went stumbling off into the shadows of the garden.

Titus strode up. He looked at me, and then at Myrtilla's torn dress.

'This will never happen again,' he said, 'you have my word.' Then he stepped briskly down the terrace steps, following his brother.

There was a silence.

Myrtilla said under her breath, 'Who was that?'

I told her. I crouched down to pick up her brooch.

She took it from me, and when she did I saw her hand was shaking. 'Then,' she said, turning and looking out into the torchlit garden, 'I owe something to Aphrodite that you were my companion tonight, and not a beast like him.' She pinned the little dolphin back in place and arranged her clothes. And then, darting her small head forward, she kissed my cheek.

'That is to say thank you,' she said. 'I'm glad we met, Marcus. But now, I think, I shall go home.'

And then she hurried off down the steps. She did not even call the slave to fetch her mantle.

For some time after this, I was occupied with my stepfather's affairs. With the spring, the sea routes were open once more, and there was much to do at the harbour.

Fat, self-important Florus had left during the winter. No one told me why. With him gone, Caecilius handed to me Florus's duties of overseeing the arrival and departure of his trading vessels, negotiating with the warehousemen, and paying the shippers. He made a good deal of this; but in truth it was simple, dull, repetitive work.

Even so, I was glad of it, for it kept me from my own thoughts, which, after the incident with Myrtilla, had started to oppress me.

One morning, after seeing off a cargo of purple-dyed Tarentine wool bound for Asia, I had an hour to myself and decided to walk up to the akropolis to watch the merchantman as it departed across the bay.

It was a pleasant spring day. The sky was streaked with high cirrus clouds, and a clean fresh breeze was blowing off the mountains. I stood at the wall, feeling the sun on my back, and watched the ship as it passed through the narrows. It unfurled its blue and white striped sail, and pressed out east, passing the brightly coloured fishing smacks as they returned home from their morning trawl.

Caecilius would soon be grumbling. It was time I returned.

But before I left I paused to look at the great temple of Neptune, whom the Greeks call Poseidon. I gazed up at the decorated pediment, where Lord Poseidon stands holding his trident in one hand, spreading the other in a calming gesture out over the sea.

Stepping back, I knocked into someone and stumbled on the steps. I turned, apologizing, and found myself looking into a face I knew. It was the youth called Menexenos. It was not a face one forgot.

'Forgive me,' we both said, speaking at once. Then we both laughed. His hair was damp still; he must have come from the palaistra.

I said, 'No, it is I who should watch where I am going. I was looking at Poseidon.'

Beside me he glanced up. 'Yes,' he said, considering. 'It is old work. But there is something in it that touches the soul.' He smiled, his clear grey eyes studying mine. 'And the carvings of the horsemen on the east side are better still. Have you seen them—? But forgive me, perhaps you need to be elsewhere.'

'No,' I said.

'Then come and look,' he said, touching my elbow and leading me back up the steps.

He was right. The sculpture-work was beautiful. A painted frieze, running above the columns: Poseidon in majesty; horses and riders; a sacrifice at an altar. Though, in truth, I had noticed it before, for some reason I did not tell him so.

As I stood looking, I felt his eyes on me.

'But I have seen you before,' he said, drawing down his brow. 'You were at the running-track, with the Roman. And you are Roman too, I can tell from your accent.' He paused, and his expression hardened. Then he asked, 'Is that man your friend?'

I thought of the night at Titus's, and shook my head.

'Not my friend,' I said. 'I know him; that is all. He is the praetor's brother. His name is Lucius.'

'Yes,' he said, frowning.

'You know him then?'

He shrugged. 'I have seen him at the palaistra. He stands and watches.'

I had the sense there was more to be said. But he seemed to think better of it, and instead he turned his head and looked out across the bay.

He was wearing a simple tunic, held at the waist with

a belt of brown leather. He stood a little formally, with his arms at his sides, and his well-shaped feet planted firmly on the ground. But there was nothing self-conscious or affected about him.

I could see what must have drawn Lucius; no man alive could not. He had an austere beauty one wished to reach out and touch. And yet, for all his fine athletic form, it was a beauty that shone from within, like light from a window.

'Well,' he said, turning back and smiling, 'I am on my way to meet my friend Eumastas. Why don't you walk with me?'

We made our way down the path from the citadel to the town. As we went, he told me he was not from Tarentum, but from Athens, and was here as Eumastas's guest-friend. Their families, he said, had known each other for generations, and he had travelled to Tarentum on his father's behalf, partly to visit, partly on a matter between his father and Eumastas's. Then he said, 'He owns a horse-farm in the valley . . . or he used to.'

I knew the valley well. It was pleasant open country, with paddocks and chestnut groves, and vineyards on the terraces. 'Oh?' I said. 'What happened?' But even before the words were out I realized. I bit my lip, and cursed inwardly at my thoughtlessness.

Menexenos frowned. I said, 'I am sorry.'

'No, it was tactless of me to mention it. I forgot, for a moment, who you are. The Romans took his farm, after the siege, and since then his family has fallen on difficult times. That is why my father sent me here, to bring them something to tide them over.'

I thought of Caecilius and his agents and the slave-driving stewards. 'I am sorry,' I said again.

'Well it is not your fault. It is war. But the injustice of it is that Eumastas's father was one of those who supported Rome all along – it was the city mob who cast their vote for Hannibal. But when the call came to defend the city, he obeyed. He is from an old Tarentine family. It was a matter of honour.'

We had passed through the market and were almost at the stone gateway of the palaistra. Up ahead I saw a youth waiting at the entrance. He was one of those I had seen with Menexenos before; thickset and dark-haired, with a heavy brow and square jaw; a wrestler, not a runner. He had none of Menexenos's beauty; but when he looked up and saw his friend, his hard face brightened, and there was affection in his dark eyes.

He greeted me with perfect manners; but somewhat stiffly. I could hardly blame him.

Menexenos explained they were on their way to the lyre-teacher for a lesson. This was something Titus had told me about. It seemed wellborn Greeks not only trained their bodies, but learnt harmony and music also. He had also told me such an education was thought rather old-fashioned nowadays among Greeks, and was the preserve of the old families, the aristocrats who had once ruled the cities.

'Why don't you come with us?' he said.

I thanked him, but said I ought to be going. It seemed an insult for me to impose myself on Eumastas, who was clearly too well bred to say what he must have thought of me.

I suppose I must have paused as I was taking my leave. For, even now, somewhere in my heart, I knew I wanted this beautiful youth as my friend. My hesitation could have been no more than a moment, but I sensed that Menexenos noticed it.

He paused, frowning at the ground, as if considering something. Then, looking up, he said, 'I'll be here tomorrow, training in the palaistra. Why don't you stop by, if you have the time—? I'll look out for you.'

For an instant then our eyes met, and some other knowledge passed between us; unspoken, like the touch of fire. Perhaps it was a trick of the light sifting through the plane trees, but before he turned to go, I thought I saw his cheeks redden.

Next day, I made the mistake of mentioning to Caecilius that I wanted to go out. 'We would all like to go idling round the town, Marcus,' he said, 'but this paperwork needs attention, and then you can go down to the harbour-master's office for me, and see what has happened to that cargo of Egyptian unguents I have been waiting for.'

'Yes, sir,' I said. But returning from the port I took the long route back. Only when I reached the main gate of the palaistra did it come to me that we had not fixed a place to meet.

He was not in the courtyard by the entrance, with its shading tree and lion-head fountain. I sat there for a while, in the place where Lucius had sat. Then, somewhat hesitantly, I wandered on, through the courts and ante-rooms and covered walkways.

I did not know the rules of the place, where one should go or not go, and did not want to fall foul of one of the sharp-voiced trainers, or the gymnasiarch. And, more importantly for me, I did not wish to appear that I was searching. For it had already crossed my mind that Menexenos might not have meant me to come. If a Roman, at home in Praeneste, had said do this or that, he would have meant it and there the matter ended. But with Greeks I was not sure. Perhaps, after all, he had merely intended to be polite.

After a time of desultory wandering, trying to look casual, I came out at the gardens behind, and sat down on a bench beneath a great spreading cedar. Then I saw him, coming from one of the inner rooms.

'Why, there you are, Marcus!' he cried, taking my hand. His hair was damp; he smelled of fresh oil, with some hint of pine in it. As if he needed to explain it, he said, 'Eumastas had to go home. He needs to run some errands for his mother.'

We walked, and he showed me around the great complex: the ball-courts, jumping-ground, and different running-tracks with their starting-stones and turning-post, engraved with the initials of runners long dead. We looked at the grassy courts behind, where older men played ball, or sat talking under the porticoes. There were meeting-rooms, lecture-halls, rooms for painting, for music, and for washing and changing and massage.

As we walked, we talked. He said he had been in

Tarentum since early spring, and I guessed he could not have been long in the city that day when I had come to the palaistra with Lucius. His father, he said, had a house in Athens, and a farm in the Attic countryside, which had been in the family since before Solon's day. They grew corn and olives and wine, and kept goats and sheep. He owned a young horse, a grey colt, and had ridden in the mounted javelin contest in the Athenian games. But now, he said, he was training for the pentathlon, which was his father's wish.

Something in the way he said this made me glance at him, and he added with a rueful look, 'Father was a pentathlete himself in his time; and his father before him won the crown. He wants me to do the same. That is his great hope.'

'But not yours?' I said.

He shrugged.

'I like the running, and the javelin, and the diskos. But as for wrestling and boxing ... Well, you can see for yourself what it has become.'

As we had been talking we had passed under the arch that leads into the wrestling courts. Menexenos stopped at the pillar. 'You cannot win in the pentathlon without wrestling. And you cannot win in wrestling unless you make yourself like *that*.'

He nodded into the sunlight. In the ground ahead the fighters were at their training, grunting and heaving like oxen in the dust.

'They do not serve in the army and protect the city, because their bodies will not stand it. They cannot sit a horse. They can scarcely walk, so bound are they in muscle. From childhood they are torn from their mothers' breasts and bred for one purpose – to win at the games. It is said they are fed five pounds of meat every day, if you can believe it.' He shook his head. 'They cannot play the lyre; they scarcely know how to read. What kind of life is that for a free man? A slave's destiny is not his own and you can forgive him for what he cannot change. But for a freeman to choose such a life is madness – or worse, it is a deliberate insult to the gods. Yet the common people think these men heroes.'

I looked at them. I tried to think of something good to say of them, but it just seemed to me ugly and pointless. 'But how does one compete against such men?' I asked. 'What contest is there?'

He shrugged. 'Can a man compete with an ox? To match them, one must make oneself like them. Better to go and plough the fields on my father's farm. At least there is honesty in that.'

He let out his breath and caught my eye, in case he had talked too much. 'Well, anyway, we take the world as we find it, I suppose. But it was not thus when my grandfather won his crown. Such things are made by men, and men can change them.'

Like the first shoot of an oak growing up from an acorn, tender at first, easily broken, but stronger with each day, so our friendship grew. Each time we met, we found some excuse to fix a place to meet again, until it came to be something expected between us.

It was about a month after this, however, that the

thing happened which I had dreaded, for it was then that I ran into Lucius at the palaistra.

He had been away in Rome, on some business of Titus's, and had recently returned. I was passing along the colonnade behind the running-track, and had already spotted Menexenos up ahead, standing with Eumastas and a group of other athletes, clustered round the trainer. They had just finished their session, and the trainer was explaining something to them, pointing now and then with his cane at the track as he talked. I was about to step out from the shadow when, up ahead, I caught sight of Lucius.

He was slouching against one of the columns, half concealed. Just as before, he was watching Menexenos with all his attention. He had not seen me.

Before he had departed for Rome, I had run into him once or twice at the praetor's residence. We had been civil to each other, but he had not mentioned the night of Titus's banquet, either to apologize or for any other reason.

There are men, it is true, whose greatness of soul causes them to forget petty disagreements, or affect to. Yet I do not think Lucius was such a man. I think he felt he had done nothing to apologize for. Either that, or he simply did not remember. Certainly he had been drunk enough.

Either way, I had enough sense to know it would be best if he did not see me at the palaistra as Menexenos's friend. I stepped back under the deep shade of the walkway.

Beside the running-track the trainer had finished whatever it was he was saying. The youths around him began to drift off towards the bath-house.

As soon as the trainer was gone, Lucius made his move. Eumastas was talking to Menexenos. I saw his head go up. Then Menexenos turned.

Lucius, who normally walked around with an expression of aggressive sullenness on his face, was attempting to smile. It showed as a nervous, alarming grimace. It was clear, even from where I stood, that he was very tense. Then I noticed that he was clutching something in his hand, some sort of leather pouch. He went up to Menexenos, spoke a few words, then held it up, proffering it.

Menexenos glanced at this thing, and then at Lucius's flushed uneasy face. He said something, and then Lucius began fiddling hurriedly with the cord that held the pouch closed, and from it he pulled a pretty silver strigil, and a small pear-shaped flask of oil, tied at the neck with a white ribbon.

I saw Eumastas's brows go up. Menexenos spoke, made a polite gesture with his hand, and then, when Lucius answered, he shook his head. He made to turn, but suddenly Lucius caught him back by the arm.

I do not think, to tell the truth, he had intended to snatch at him. But his uneasiness must have made him clumsy.

Menexenos turned, his expression hardening. He spoke again and shook his head; then he turned away, and he and Eumastas strode off towards the bath-house, leaving Lucius standing on the grass beside the track, pathetically holding the strigil and flask in his hand.

I saw no more. People were beginning to stare, and this was not a scene I wanted Lucius to know I had witnessed. But a little later, when he had washed and dressed, Menexenos came to me in the gardens, to the place we had appointed. His flint eyes looked troubled. But it was Eumastas who said, 'Your Roman friend was here again. I thought he had gone away.'

I said, 'He did. He was in Rome.'

'Well now he's back.'

Menexenos turned. 'Leave it, Eumastas. I told you, he is of no importance. Let us forget it.'

Though I had grown up in Praeneste, I was not wholly naïve. I had eyes to see, and I knew that Lucius was not the only suitor in the palaistra. There was a certain ritual to it, and often it was done with style and grace. I had noticed for myself how, in the courts and walkways, beside the running-track, or the wrestling-ground, or the pool, men would stand and watch, seemingly with nothing better to do. There were always lectures going on, and music classes, and games of different sorts; and with all this activity there was a constant traffic of people.

But these men did not come to play, or to be with their friends, or to improve themselves. They came for no other purpose than to gaze upon the naked youths.

I had at first been taken aback by this. But in time I perceived that the young men, stripped for exercise, took no notice, and I began to understand that it was of no concern to them if others chose to look at their bodies. They were what they were, as God had made them, and that was that.

Besides, there was something else I had begun to

understand. Not all the onlookers were unwelcome. Some of the youths had lovers, and were pleased when they came to support them. But these men behaved with honour. Never before had I seen anyone there accost a youth in front of his friends and try to press a costly gift on him. Little wonder Menexenos had not wished to speak of it. It would be thought shameful, and people would suppose Lucius had been given encouragement.

I had wondered, too, about Eumastas. I had seen how, when he watched his friend on the track, his stolid features would soften into a rugged beauty, and his dark eyes shine with tenderness. Whether they were lovers or not I could not tell. They were both well bred, with an aristocratic formality, and, whatever they felt for each other, such people did not make a show of their emotions in public.

There was something else too, that lay behind all the rest. I can say it now.

Like sunlight breaking through mist, my own clouded feelings had started to resolve. No one with eyes to see cannot be touched by beauty; and beauty changes us, like the purifying fire. I was drawn to Menexenos, with a need I only half understood, and it made me uneasy. He had a poise and confidence I lacked; he seemed self-contained, entire, perfect; like light, or the memory of childhood. I grew conscious of his expressions, his movements, his very smell. But what moved me most was what was deepest. Sometimes, when he thought no one was looking, I would see it in his face, like a cloud passing over water, a profound melancholy, kept in check, hidden from public view, that melted my heart and touched my soul.

All my life, I had never thought of myself as handsome. I had been a slight boy when I was young; after my father's death, when I had driven myself hard, I had broadened and gained muscle, and took on the appearance of a man. But there was always the darkness within. The sword-wound in my thigh, which Caecilius never ceased to remind me of, seemed to me a mark of all my imperfection. It confronted me every time I stripped, reminding me of my ugliness.

I knew I was not like other men. I was alone. Not one day went by that I did not remember my vow to the god, and the murderous purpose I had given myself. At night, as I lay in my bed, I would whisper to the darkness, 'Dikaiarchos, you cannot hide; I am coming for you.' My promise of vengeance lay behind every waking moment, and haunted my dreams. It gave meaning to my solitude.

My only respite from this was when I was with Menexenos. I glimpsed, in some inexplicable way I could not fully grasp, a light that led out of the pathless dark, a chink of sunlight beyond the cave. It made me yearn to be more than I was; but if anyone had asked me what, I could not have told him.

Yet I sensed it as clearly as the day. And to see Lucius make a fool of himself troubled me deeply, not for his sake, but for my own. For I had an inkling that, but for my pride, and my sense of dignity, and my wanting Menexenos to respect me, I was capable of just the same. It sent a cold trail of fear down my spine, as when a man stares into an abyss. I yearned to be whole; I knew I was not. I yearned for Menexenos.

All these thoughts I kept to myself. I had no words to express them, even had I dared.

And thus matters stood, when, one day soon after, when Menexenos, Eumastas and I had gone swimming in the bay, he suggested I should train with them at the palaistra.

The summer heat had recently come on. The hillsides were loud with the sound of cicadas. We were basking on a flat, warm rock beside the water, drying off in the afternoon sun. Menexenos, looking at my body, said, 'You know, Marcus, you are no weakling, and yet I never see you train.'

I told him, somewhat shyly, how I had worked on the land at home.

'But what of athletics? Is there no gymnasion at Praeneste then?'

I laughed out loud, thinking how shocked the simple townsfolk at home would be at such a thing. 'No,' I said. 'There is nothing like that.'

'Then why not come with me and Eumastas?' he said. 'We can do some diskos and javelin and perhaps some running too. But we can start with the diskos, eh Eumastas—? But Marcus, why are you frowning?'

'But Menexenos,' I cried, 'I am a Roman!'

'What of it? You are in Tarentum now; and, Roman or not, you are still a man.'

I thought of what Caecilius would have to say if he knew, and smiled inwardly. 'Then yes,' I said. 'Why not?'

There is movement in the diskos-thrower which, when it is done at its best, combines purpose with grace, like the dance of a warrior, or the flight of an eagle. Menexenos was a master of it, so much so that other youths at the palaistra would pause and watch, and the trainer, if he was around, would lean on his staff and say to the younger boys, 'Observe, and learn.'

He was also a good teacher: calm and patient and exacting. When he taught me, as with everything else he did, his whole mind was on it. I wish I could have said the same for myself.

He would stand close, turning my shoulders and guiding my left leg into position with his foot. 'No, like this, just as I showed you,' he would say, placing his hand over mine, and forming my fingers around the rim of the disk.

Close up, he smelled of sweet male sweat, and pine and dust and oil; and where our flesh touched I could feel the heat of his body like the touch of fire.

'Now swing your arm back, here, like this . . . You're not concentrating, Marcus! Well, no matter. Let's try again.'

And we would try again.

FIVE

'HE IS A DANGEROUS PIRATE, raiding and plundering the cities of the Aegean, and Lucius says . . .' Titus broke off. It took me a moment to realize.

I had been looking out of the window into the garden as he talked, my eyes on the fronds of the pear tree; but my mind was elsewhere, ranging along the cliff paths on the wild coast of Epeiros. He had been talking about Dikaiarchos.

He said, 'You look as if you have seen some underworld spirit.'

And that was how it felt. But I said, 'Forgive me, Titus. I was remembering.'

'Well,' he went on, 'he is playing a dangerous game. King Philip thinks we are too exhausted by war, and too afraid of another, to heed what he does. He is backing every pirate from here to Asia. And he is rearming, building another fleet, in secret. But one cannot spend money like that and not have it known.'

'Yet surely,' I said, pulling my mind together and

forcing myself to concentrate once more on the conversation, 'he would not dare cross to Italy. He knows what happened to Pyrrhus.'

'Pyrrhus was defeated, but only by a whisker. It was a close thing then; and this time Scipio has taken the flower of our army to Africa. Philip knows that. What better time to strike?'

Mimas, Titus's Greek friend, who was there, said, 'Would he be so brazen? Does he suppose the Greek cities here would back him?'

Titus shrugged. 'He may not care, if he is strong enough. The trouble is, no one can predict him. If he means us no harm, why is he being so careful to hide his intentions? Some say he is building this fleet to attack Antiochos in Asia. Philip, meanwhile, declares that he is Antiochos's friend.'

'He claims he is everybody's friend, when it suits him,' said Mimas.

'Exactly. And if he is everybody's friend, why does he need a fleet so urgently?' He made a frustrated gesture. 'And then there is Egypt—'

That year King Ptolemy of Egypt had died. His son, also called Ptolemy, was still a child, and in the chaos of the succession there had been rebellion in Upper Egypt. 'Perhaps,' said Titus, 'he has his eyes on Egypt. If it fell into his hands, he would have Antiochos like this' – he pressed his thumb and forefinger in a pincer – 'and he would control the grain trade from Alexandria as well.'

Mimas whistled through his teeth. 'What do your friends in Rome say?'

'They say do one thing at a time: let us deal with Hannibal first.'

'Do you agree?'

'Up to a point. But we must watch Philip. Whatever he is up to, it will not be to Rome's benefit. He is waiting to see if we have the stomach to stand up to him.'

My stepfather had asked me to find out what was afoot in Greece. Now, when I told him what I had heard, he was impatient with me, for it was not what he wanted to hear.

'Oh, Titus is talking nonsense,' he said, dismissing my words. 'There is no threat from Philip.'

Like many middle-aged men, he had ceased to challenge himself years ago. He had grown complacent in his views, and because he surrounded himself with men who dared not contradict him, he had come to believe he was right in everything. He saw only what he wanted to see, and just now he did not want anything to disrupt a trade deal he was working towards with his new contacts in Greece, importing silk from Kos and Syria, and glassware from Phoenicia.

Lately, too, he had begun to collect valuables, having been told by one of his merchant friends that there would soon be money to be made in it, especially in Rome, where there was growing interest in such things. So he instructed his agents in the East to pick up what they could, from cities impoverished by war or want, and send them with his regular cargoes, without enquiring too deeply into their provenance. He would show them to me when they arrived, and indeed they were fine work. I recall a cup of banded sardonyx embossed in white, of a young man holding two horses; an embossed glass bowl from Egypt, with a tint of green, which looked like deep sea-water when the sun caught it; Adonis surrounded by hovering cupids, with the mourning Aphrodite beside him in a bower of flowers. This last – which struck me as voluptuous and overripe – he particularly liked, and kept for himself. The rest he put away, intending to sell them later.

'There will be a rich trade in such things one day, mark my words,' he told me, peering at his Aphrodite and touching her smooth marble body with his thick fingers.

During that summer, I had begun to reflect on many things I had hitherto taken for granted. I asked myself how a man perceives good, and how he works out for himself what makes one thing, or one man, worse or better than another.

In part, this had come from my conversations with Menexenos, who seemed able to discern, by looking, what was genuine and what was fake. It was not a thing he made much of. But now and then he would pass some comment that would make me look again at a statue, or a sculpture, or a painting, and see some new depth to it.

I wondered where he found such knowledge. It was more than a skill. It seemed to me he saw such things as part of some living whole, and could judge them and how they fitted.

In such small ways as this, over the past weeks, Menexenos had come to fill my thoughts. One day, during this time, Caecilius had complained, 'What has happened to you lately? You never concentrate on what matters. You grow less like me every day.' It had made me aware that I was changing.

When I was a boy at home, on days when the sky was clear and cloudless, and as blue as cornflower or a stone of sapphire, I used to go climbing on the mountainside, high up, to the crags where the ash trees clung to the rock and even the nimble goats trod carefully. The climb was hard, and would leave me panting. But then I would turn and stand between earth and sky, looking out to where the river glittered like a thread of silver in the valley far below. And at that moment the world was changed, and my petty cares would fall away, and I would know the effort of the climb had been worthwhile.

So it was with my young soul. In dwelling upon the good things I saw in Menexenos, it seemed I had grown more aware of everything, and of myself in particular. It was hard, just as the climb up the hillside had been hard, because most times it was my own failings that I saw more clearly. But if ever I wondered if it was worth it, I needed only to look at Caecilius. He had been right. Like a ship departing the shore, the distance between us was growing. I was changing; he was not – or not in the same way.

Sometimes, now, there would be not one girl creeping out of the house in the early morning, but two; and not always the same two either. On one such day, appearing at mid-morning with a great purple bite on his neck, and dark shadows under his eyes, he marched into the work-room and declared crossly, 'You have been out too much of late.'

He was always in a bad mood after these night-time sessions. That day, I had been up since the dawn, working to clear a heap of pointless work he had assigned to me. I had almost finished, and had planned, later, to meet Menexenos. Now, stung by the injustice of his words, I replied, 'Is there anything I have left undone, sir?'

'I daresay there is,' he huffed, 'if I bothered myself to look. But I have better things to do.' He sat down at his desk and began pushing irritably through the tablets and scrolls. 'But what I wanted to say to you, Marcus, is this. I am planning a gathering at month-end for my friends. I expect you to attend.'

He ran through the names of several of his business associates, adding at the end, 'It is time I showed them how a man of means can entertain. It is not only the praetor who can hold a banquet. Oh, and there are some female friends of mine who will be there as well.'

I said nothing. Just then the door sounded. It was Telamon, carrying a tray with a cup and flask – my step-father's morning wine.

'Set it there, and leave,' snapped Caecilius.

Telamon, who knew the danger signs as well as I, hurriedly set down the tray and left, pulling the door shut behind him. There was a tense silence, like the quiet before a storm. The only sounds were the rattle of the wooden writing-tablets as Caecilius shuffled them, and his occasional snorts of displeasure.

Then it came. With a loud crack he slapped the tablets down on the desktop and cried, 'I suppose you are waiting to take yourself off to the palaistra again, is that it? Do you think I don't know how you spend your time? Virilis saw you only the other day, loitering there.'

'Loitering, sir?' I felt my colour rising. As usual he had found the weak spot in my armour. 'I make no secret of where I go. You need only ask, if you wish to know. And I do not loiter. I go for exercise, and to meet my friends.'

I was tempted to ask what pallid round-shouldered Virilis was doing at the palaistra, but it did no good to goad him.

'Exercise!' he shouted, gesturing so violently that he hit his wine-cup, spilling black wine in an arc across his papers. 'You are not so young that you do not know the reputation of those places.'

I cursed inwardly, knowing I had reddened to my ears. 'I have nothing to be ashamed of,' I said.

'No? Virilis has seen you there stripped naked, as bare as the day you were born . . . I see you do not even try to deny it.'

'But sir!' I cried. 'Everyone strips. That is how it is.'

'I dare say. Greeks, after all, are capable of any vice. But remember, boy, you are a Roman, and think of your mother's honour, even if you forget your own.'

He glared at me, daring me to reply. There was spittle on his lips. The vein in his temple throbbed, and his face had turned as dark as the wine in the flask.

This, I knew, was a place I did not wish to venture. Somehow – for I was now very angry myself – I managed to collect myself. I told myself this outburst had nothing to do with me, or with the palaistra. I recalled the two girls I had seen leaving with the dawn: coarse, pale, overpainted, bitter-faced creatures, whispering harshly to each other as they went, clearly dissatisfied. So much, I thought, for my mother's honour. And as for Caecilius's paternal guiding hand, I reflected that he was all for discipline, except when it came to himself.

Month-end came, and with it Caecilius's banquet. It was everything that a symposion of Titus's was not. It was like the screech of an untuned fiddle after the harmonious lyre. There was a great bonfire in the garden, roaring into the night beside the palms and cypresses. There was raucous, drunken conversation. There were torches of flaring pitch, and piles of seared meat. And later, when the tables were at last cleared, a dancing girl came on, with a painted belly and castanets on her fingers, who cavorted and leered between the couches, and pressed the laughing guests' faces towards her crotch.

'Buy in bulk' was one of my stepfather's precepts, one of the lessons of trade he said I should learn. This he had done with the girls. They had not been brought to converse, even if they could have made themselves heard. But in any case the noise was a relief; it spared me having to make small talk with my neighbours, whose conversation was limited to shipping costs, the price of slaves, and the prospects for the corn harvest.

Later, when the fire had burned low, one of the girls threw herself on my couch, and without any pretence of talk shoved her hand up under my tunic. I recognized her. She was one of those I had seen creeping through the garden. I pulled her hand away.

'What?' she cried indignantly, slurring her words. She smelled of Lydian oil, and female sweat. She snatched down the low front of her dress, exposing a drooping breast. 'See! There is a feast here. Why don't you eat?'

She was speaking almost at the top of her voice. From across the courtyard I saw Caecilius's eyes slew round.

'I find,' I answered, as she lolled before me, 'that I am not hungry.'

She shrugged and went off muttering, leaving her breast exposed, and settled on another couch, where, I saw, she was eagerly welcomed.

In such ways as this the evening passed, as slowly as a sickness. It left me feeling bleak and empty and without hope.

Indeed, in the days that followed, it began to seem to me that there was corruption everywhere, not just at home. For, just then, Lucius's advances towards Menexenos had resumed, and were becoming harder to ignore.

I came one day to the palaistra to find a commotion in the inner court, with the boxing-master talking angrily to one of the other trainers, and a group of youths standing about listening with grave faces.

As I approached I saw Eumastas coming my way. I asked him what had happened.

'What else?' he said, frowning at me. 'It's that Roman again.' And then he told me.

There were limits, which even the most besotted suitors observed, and one of them was that the youths were left to scrape and sluice down without disturbance. Lucius, ignoring this, had followed Menexenos into the bath-house, and had proceeded to pester him there in front of all the others.

I shook my head. 'But what did Menexenos do?'

'He ignored him, of course. He would have handled it. But just then the boxing-master came in, and found the man sidling up to him. He called the slaves to throw him out. You can imagine how it looked.'

I stared at him, appalled.

'Yes,' said Eumastas. 'I know. It was terrible. And it gets worse. Lucius asked the boxing-master if he realized who he was.

' "Yes I do," answered the master, "and that makes it more shameful still. Now get out, or must I go to the praetor myself?" '

I blew the air through my teeth, imagining the scene. That Lucius could bear such humiliation was hard to credit.

But it did not end there. Next thing I heard, he had discovered the house where Menexenos was staying with Eumastas.

Though he had lost his farm, Eumastas's father still kept a house in the city, in a leafy neighbourhood beyond the theatre, with a view out to the sea. I never went calling there. It embarrassed me to impose on his civility, after what had happened to his farm.

But one day, after we had been out walking in the city and were about to part outside the walled doorway of Eumastas's house, Menexenos said, 'Come in for a moment. I want to show you something.'

I followed him into the tree-shaded outer courtyard. There on the ledge was a small bronze statue of Zeus carrying off a squirming Ganymede, done in the new style, all soft lines and gross emotion.

'What do you think?' asked Menexenos.

'It's horrible.'

'Yes,' he said, scowling at it. 'Nasty and overdone. It was delivered this morning, along with this note.' He showed me a corner of papyrus tied with ribbon, upon which was written, 'To the beautiful Menexenos, from a secret friend.'

'I shouldn't mind,' he went on, tossing the note aside, 'if it were just for my own sake. But I am only a guest, and no one here could afford such a piece. It insults my hosts, especially when you think where it comes from.'

'What will you do?' I asked.

'I thought of putting it up for sale, but that would not do. So I am sending it back to the praetor's residence.'

I nodded, and looked down gravely at the bronze god with the grinning naked child in his arm. Then, looking up again, my eyes met his, and we laughed.

There were other gifts after that. A crown of gold olive-sprays; a belt-clasp set with lapis; a handsome arm-band of twisted silver, fine Keltic work from Gaul. He sent them all back.

If we had smiled at these follies, there was soon something it was harder to smile at.

Lucius must have been making enquiries. One day, waylaying Eumastas in the street, he told him he could ensure his father's farm was restored to him. He did not waste his time with hints, but added, with a long, significant look, 'However, there is something you must deliver to me in return.'

'In that case,' replied Eumastas immediately, 'the price is too high.' And with that he turned his back on him and walked off.

He related all this to me later, adding at the end, 'I have not mentioned it to Menexenos, and I don't intend to. I am telling you, Marcus, only because it is time someone put a stop to this madness.'

'Yes,' I said, racked with shame. I had already wondered many times what I could do. Speaking to Lucius was no good. And the idea of going to Titus on such a matter appalled me. Yet Eumastas was right. I was a friend of Titus, and I was a Roman. I, if anyone, should intervene.

I resolved to seek a private meeting with Titus and speak to him.

Before I could do so, however, on a hot afternoon shortly after, when the stormclouds were looming and the air was close and still, the whole business came to a head.

The festival of Poseidon was coming up, which in Tarentum is quite an affair, with concerts and games, and plays in the theatre. Menexenos had been asked by the trainer to help out at the palaistra, training the young lads who would run in the sacred torch-race.

Not wishing to throw oil on fire, I always did my best to make sure I was absent when Lucius was in sight. But he had not been back to the palaistra since the day he was ejected; and, believing, naturally enough, that he would not come again, I had grown careless.

I was standing with Eumastas and some others at the side of the track, watching Menexenos preparing his troop of boys. Suddenly Lucius strode out from the shadow of the colonnade. He went straight up to where Menexenos was waiting at the starting line, having calculated, no doubt, that he could hardly walk away and leave the boys standing.

I stared, appalled.

'By God,' muttered Eumastas beside me. 'Has he no shame at all?'

Lucius was speaking. I saw Menexenos glance round once, shake his head, then turn away. At this Lucius went closer, and began whispering into his ear, and plucking at the sleeve of his tunic. The young runners, who were standing about waiting to line up, looked at one another and began to titter.

Suddenly Lucius cried out furiously, so that his voice echoed round the court, 'Ha! Look at your godlike looks! But beware! Good looks fade, and you will not always eclipse the sun.'

There was a stillness like death. Menexenos looked at him, but said nothing; or not, at least, in words; his expression was eloquent enough. I saw him draw in his breath, and then, turning back to the wide-eyed gaping boys he said, 'Come on, now, line up, and have your torches ready.'

Lucius had gone white. For a moment he did not move. Then, all of a sudden, he swung round, and his eyes settled on my face. He started. I do not think, until that moment, he knew I was there.

And then he lost all control.

At the top of his voice, in front of everyone, he accused me of every sort of baseness, saying I was trying to steal his quarry after he had chased it to its covert, and that I was a thief who snatches the trophy without running the race. 'Oh yes!' he shouted, jabbing his finger, he knew what I was about. 'But have you stripped for him yet? Has he seen your ugly white-scarred thigh?' He spat in the dust. 'He is haughty and superior, this conquered Greekling, and I am not good enough for him. Do you suppose, then, he will look at a runt like you? You would disgust him.'

He ceased. Everyone stared. Even the boxing trainer, coming in from the next court, had paused in the archway, his mouth fallen open.

At some point in his tirade, Lucius's Greek had failed him, and he had used the Latin terms. I imagine most people there did not know them. It was little comfort. It did not take a seer to guess what they meant.

Lucius seemed suddenly to grow conscious of where he was. He looked wildly about him at the gathering, silent crowd and bit his lip. I think even he realized he had gone too far. Then, with a cry, he turned on his heels and ran out under the archway.

I had never felt more ashamed in my life. Wounds in battle were nothing compared with this. I wished only that the earth would open up and swallow me. The last thing I wanted to do, that day, was go to the praetor's residence. But when, at length, I returned home, there was a message from Titus, asking me to call on him that afternoon.

Titus's steward, Sextus, who knew me, said when I arrived, 'Ah yes, Marcus sir, he is expecting you. You'll find him in the gardens, on the bench at the end of the walkway. Verginius has just finished with him; I expect you'll pass him on his way out.'

As he predicted, I ran into Verginius on the terrace. He was a military tribune of the Roman garrison, and we had always got on well. He paused and greeted me, and we exchanged a few words. He was something of a talker, which was just as well, for I had not recovered from the morning, and could scarcely string my words together.

He spoke, as I recall, of the campaign in Africa, which was coming to a head, and would bring, so everyone hoped, an end to the war. Finishing off, he said, 'Well, it's time I got back to barracks. You'll find Titus down there near the herb-beds, but I'd wait a while if I were you. Lucius has just arrived. He seemed rather agitated . . . Why Marcus, you've gone grey as a corpse; is something wrong?'

'No, Verginius,' I managed to say. 'Thank you for telling me. I think I'll wait here then, until he's finished.'

He left me, and I sat down on the stone bench behind me, and held my head in my hands, wishing I were anywhere else but here. Then I jerked my head up and stared in horror. From somewhere beyond the tall myrtle bush which divided the terrace from the garden came the sound of Lucius's voice, approaching along the path.

I leapt up. I think I should have run off, and thought of an excuse after. But the only way out was back the way I had come, which meant crossing the corner of the garden. To walk straight into them as I tried to flee would be even worse.

So I waited. The voices drew closer. Titus was saying, 'But Lucius, it is in your own hands. Do you not see that?'

Then came Lucius's voice, answering in a wailing tone, 'But he is so noble and so beautiful! I need him!'

I stared into the myrtle flowers, scarcely daring to breathe. A song thrush, sitting among the leaves, stared back at me, its head cocked to one side.

Then I heard Titus say sharply, 'You have been at the wine again. I can smell it on you.'

'Well wouldn't you?' Lucius flared back. 'You are beginning to sound like Father.'

'Don't bring him into this. But he was right at least in one thing: the world will not fashion itself to your wishes, no matter how much you rail at it.'

'But I want him!' moaned Lucius. 'He *must* love me! I have given him gifts . . . everything . . . I have given him everything.'

There was a whimpering sound.

I looked about, thinking: I must not be found here. *I must not!*

There was a pause, and the sound of sniffling.

And then, 'Oh Titus, my desires frighten me so. What am I to do?'

More gently, Titus said, 'This is wine talking, not my brother. Wipe your eyes, Lucius, and try to remember yourself. A man cannot buy love; no, not even you. If the boy is not interested, then that is that. Come now, there will be others. But no one will love a drunkard. You must govern yourself, little brother. What else will you have me do? Put the wine under lock and key?'

This set him off again. But at least I could allow myself to breathe once more: the voices were receding back down the garden.

When, eventually, Titus saw me, he gave me a brief, searching look, and I wondered what else Lucius had said. But it may just have been that, by then, I must have looked as though I was sickening for something. We spoke of whatever business it was that had brought me there, though it was clear that both our minds were elsewhere. Afterwards, when we were walking back to the house, he said, half to himself, 'You know, if you beat a colt long enough, and hard enough, and often enough, it will shy even from its own shadow. A creature can be broken . . . and so can a man. . . . My father has a lot to answer for.' He drew in his breath in a long melancholy sigh. 'But forgive me, Marcus. I am talking of my own concerns. Come, you look as if a cup of wine would do you good. Now that I think of it, I could do with one myself.'

We returned to the terrace, where the steward had left wine, and a dish of honey-cakes. He must have brought it out while I was with Titus. I noticed that one of the cups had already been used. Titus, I saw, noticed it too. He raised his brow; but to me, at least, he made no comment.

The summer weather remained close and airless, and my bleak mood stayed with me like a cloud that will not move.

After that terrible morning at the palaistra, I had done my best to apologize to Menexenos.

'For what?' he had said. 'It's not your fault.'

Yet I could not dispel the thought that I had brought

shame on him, and that, but for me, the appalling scene at the palaistra would not have taken place. Lucius had said I would disgust him, and in my melancholy state it seemed that it could be no other. I felt all my ugliness, and was sure he must perceive it too.

Bad as this was, it was only part of what troubled me. I began to ask myself what he must now suppose of my own motives, which he had heard described in such detail by Lucius. For all I felt for him, I could not bear to have him think I was some suitor in Lucius's mould. Since I felt unable to explain any of this, I began to grow quiet and withdrawn with him, and took less trouble to seek him out.

I knew he noticed it. Once or twice he said, 'I looked for you at the palaistra today, Marcus,' or, 'Where have you been these past days? I have missed you.'

I would make some bland excuse, blaming work, or whatever came into my head. Perhaps he sensed I was lying. Before long he ceased to ask, and I left him to think what he wished. It seemed better that way.

But I suffered. I had been touched by light. The return to night came twice as hard.

When next I saw Pasithea she fixed me with her wise brown eyes and said, 'You have scarcely spoken two words this evening, Marcus. I think it is time you and I had a talk. Come and see me, the day after tomorrow. I shall send my slave Niko to fetch you.'

Two days later, at the time of lamp lighting, Niko came to fetch me, a black-skinned slave-boy from Memphis in Egypt, with shining eyes and large gold earrings. Though he was a slave, he was clearly learned, and I guessed he had been schooled by Pasithea, of whom he spoke with great fondness.

In due course we came to a pink-washed house built on a terrace on a slope, shaded by a hanging vine.

Pasithea was waiting for me at the back, sitting in the little private high-walled courtyard, beside a pool of water lilies fed by a tinkling fountain. She had dressed carefully, as always, and tonight she was wearing a light dress of sky-blue silk, woven with flying and sitting swallows picked out in gold. Her hair was loose, adorned with a garland of roses.

Niko brought a jar of cool honey-coloured wine, and a bowl of bread and black olives, and a little yellow-glazed plate of goat's cheese, and while he was busy with this, Pasithea chatted, telling me of her plans to travel to Greece in the autumn, where she planned to visit her home in Korinth, and stay with friends elsewhere. Then she paused and looked me in the eye, and said, 'I hear your stepfather has been entertaining his friends.'

'You heard about that then?' I said miserably, supposing his grossness must be the talk of the whole city.

She smiled. 'Don't be so surprised. I am one of the first to know of such things. After all, my friends talk to me; and I have many friends.' She caught my eye and winked. 'I suspect, though, that your stepfather's little gathering was not quite to your own taste. Is that what has cast you down, or will you carry on suffering alone and not tell me?'

And then the words came.

I had not realized how much I needed to talk to someone. I do not know if was the wine, or her gentle comprehending smile, or the peaceful courtyard under the stars. But all of a sudden, like a dammed-up torrent, out rushed all my pent-up feeling. I told her Caecilius was a brute, that he humiliated me for his sport, that he brought dishonour on my mother, who was good and honest and true. I lamented the day he had married her, and supposed I must have displeased some god to suffer so much ill luck. It seemed to me, I said bitterly, that there was no beauty in the world, that the only truth was baseness and self-seeking.

I went on for far too long; I spoke in anger, resenting the world and my place in it.

But when, at last, I had finished, she placed a comforting hand on my forearm and said gently, 'All this I understand, Marcus my dear. You are not the first to think this, nor will you be the last. And it is true that a man who is intent on finding ugliness will not need to search for long. But is that really the only truth?'

I shrugged. 'I look about me and that is what I see: men who are no better than beasts, who walk on two feet instead of four, and snatch at what they desire like starvelings at a feast.'

'You are talking to me of man's place in the world, yet you tell me he is the worst you can conceive. Is all else a dream then?'

'What else is there?' I said sulkily.

She sat back and regarded me with irony in her eyes.

'What then?' I said.

'Look to what you love.'

Our eyes met.

'Yes, indeed, my dear. That is your guide. It is there

you will find your proof that man is more than you describe.'

She paused, and with her finger stirred the bubbling water of the pond. The spreading lilies bobbed their petalled flowers at me. Then she smiled softly; not mockingly, but wise and knowing.

Lightly she said, 'I hear, too, that our friend Lucius has been making something of a scene.'

I sank my head in my hands. 'Truly, Pasithea, nothing escapes you. Do you have eyes even in the palaistra, where no women go?'

She laughed. 'Nothing so mysterious. The boxing-master is a friend.'

'Even you have heard about it then?'

'Who has not? It is all round the city.'

It was worse than I thought. I shuddered, remembering the things Lucius had called me. 'It is a great humiliation,' I said, blushing to my ears.

'For Lucius, yes. But you have no reason to be ashamed. Nor does Menexenos. Every person with a shred of taste knows the truth, that he would not concern himself with an uncouth sot like that. Lucius thinks he is free, because he takes what he wants. But now he has found something he cannot take – not for money, nor persuasion, nor threats. I doubt he has ever experienced such a thing before.'

I sat forward and pressed my knuckles to my eyes. 'I should go away. Menexenos is disgusted at me. I know it. You did not hear what Lucius said.'

'It does not matter. Anyway, the boxing-master gave me a good enough report, and, believe me, I have heard worse . . . But why are you so troubled? Is it that it is a lie, or that it is true?'

I jerked my head up. 'It is a lie of course! How can you think otherwise?'

She smiled. 'Menexenos has beauty enough to draw husbands from their wives. There is many a young hetaira who would be only too pleased to entertain him, if only he would have her.' She raised her cup and glanced at me over the rim, adding, 'And many a youth too, I daresay, though you would know more about that than I.'

'Oh no, Pasithea!' I cried. 'You do not understand. It is not like that. It is true that I have seen him, and he has been kind enough to show me something of Tarentum, and made me feel at home. But there is no more than that.'

She sat back, regarding me.

'You fear your desires,' she said eventually.

I knew I was blushing. My ears were burning. I wanted to hide my face. But I owed her more than that, so I looked back at her. 'I have seen what desire does to a man,' I said.

'If you despise the glutton, do you therefore turn away from food? No, Marcus, you do not. And nor can you banish desire: it is part of your very soul. So you must learn to know it, and master it, and let your reason guide it. There are many good things that the young have, but always they lack one thing . . .'

She paused, until I said, 'What thing?'

'The god says, "Know yourself".'

'Easy to say,' I answered frowning. 'But hard to do.'

'I did not say it was easy. But it is necessary. Come

now, Marcus. The truth is written all over you. There is something in our souls that knows when it has found what it seeks. You know it, but you will not acknowledge it. Must you let it slip away?' She raised her hand and continued, 'But I shall say no more, or you will be cross with me. One thing though. I am old; I have seen a great deal of life, and if there is one thing I know it is this: never allow yourself to forget how to love. That most of all.'

I looked down at my feet, wondering what sight she possessed that allowed her to see so much of me. I thought of her trade. 'Do you love, Pasithea?' I said.

I looked up, and her blue-painted laughing eyes met mine.

'Oh, yes, my dear,' she answered. 'Always.'

The day of Poseidon's festival came. I watched the games with Menexenos and Eumastas. Lucius was nowhere to be seen.

The boys' torch-race was held at twilight in the sanctuary below the temple. It went without a fault, and the crowds cheered.

Afterwards, a group of friends came up with the trainer, congratulating Menexenos and taking him off to celebrate. 'Come, Marcus,' he said smiling. But I declined; for earlier, looking at me across the torchlit crowd, I had seen a face I knew. It was Myrtilla.

I had not seen her since the night at Titus's, when Lucius had set upon her. Now, amid the flaring torches and laughing crowds and the heat of the night, I do not know what drew me; but when the others had led Menexenos away I edged off through the crowd, pausing here and there to watch the prancing sword-swallowers; the jugglers with their flying torches; the knife-dancers; the bare-chested glistening acrobats with their oiled bound-up hair. And by the time I came upon her, I might almost have supposed it was by accident.

'Hello, Marcus,' she said. 'I wondered when we would meet again.'

There are some things we know, even before they happen. Perhaps some god guides us, or perhaps we see more than our conscious minds tell. But I knew, from that moment, what was to come.

We drank some wine at a stall, and watched a dark-skinned Sicilian as he danced a leaping jig to the accompaniment of pan-pipes and a tambourine. Later, without words, we took ourselves off from the crowd, to a quiet garden behind the sanctuary, a place of shadowy trees filtering blue moonlight.

There were others there, on the benches in the alcoves, or seated on the lawns, lovers from the festival, quietly talking, looking up at the stars.

Presently Myrtilla said, 'My house is not far.'

We climbed the narrow street, our hands touching. Higher up the hill, the warm summer air was heavy with the smell of pines, and all about us the cicadas called into the night.

Her bedchamber looked out over the steep hillside behind. Incense glowed in a fretted bronze censer, and a little shaded lamp burned beside it.

There was pleasure in our lovemaking, I will not deny

it. But when the moment came, all I could think of was the girl in Epeiros, and the Libyan with his probing, bloodstained hand.

Afterwards, silent and naked beside her, I stared up at the black shapes of the rafters, feeling solitude envelop me. I had asked Mars the Avenger to single me out, to grant what my angry heart burned for. Be careful what you pray for; that was what Priscus had said. The words came to me now, calling through the silence. Was this, too, part of it?

The gods, in their wisdom, deny men foresight. What destiny in its closed hand held for me I could not tell. But I understood now what I had sought this night. I had sought an escape from myself; I had sought to be like other men, who tumble a girl and wake up next day with a wine-sore head, and think to themselves, 'This is life; I am content.'

Know yourself says the god. I had chosen my own hard purpose. There was no place for tears. Fear touched me. And emptiness. And then, for some reason I could not fathom, I thought of Menexenos.

Next morning, returning home with the dawn, I saw Eumastas buying vegetables in the market. He was speaking to the stallholder, his face stern and intent; and beside him waited a slave, holding a basket.

I remembered Menexenos had once told me how, since the family had fallen on hard times, these chores were something Eumastas took upon himself, to spare his father. With this in mind, I moved on discreetly under the far colonnade, intending to pass by unseen.

The market was still quiet. Just then the slave happened

to glance round and recognizing me, he raised his hand in greeting.

At this Eumastas turned, and thereafter there was no avoiding him without rudeness.

'Hello, Marcus,' he said, a little awkwardly, when I came up. He paused, frowning, and glanced about at the stalls and early shoppers.

I made some comment about the morning, and after that a silence fell between us. I was about to excuse myself and leave him, when to the slave he said, 'Take these home, will you.' And then, turning back to me, 'Come, Marcus, let us walk a while. There is something I want to say.'

In all the time I had known him, he had never been anything less than civil. But nor had he gone out of his way to spend time with me when Menexenos was not around. I wondered what he wanted.

The slave went off with his basket. We left the market-place and set off up the steep path that led up to the citadel. Near the top Eumastas paused, at the place where the terrace looks out across the bay.

He was never one for words, but he had not spoken all the way up the path. When he reached the terrace he turned, leaning against the low wall. He narrowed his eyes against the morning light, studying my face.

I looked back at him. My head was hurting. I had drunk too much wine the night before.

'Is something wrong, Eumastas?' I asked.

He paused before he answered. Then he said, 'You do not know Menexenos as I do.'

'You are his oldest friend. Everyone knows that.'

'Yes, I am.' He turned and frowned out across the

wide sweep of the bay. Low sunlight glittered in a shining path over the water.

'People are drawn to him,' he went on after a moment. 'Not all of them good. It makes him wary.'

So this is it, I thought. I had wondered when Lucius would become too much for our friendship to bear. 'Truly, Eumastas, I am sorry about what happened with Lucius. It fills me with shame when I think of it. I should have spoken to you before, but—'

He looked at me oddly, making me break off. 'Lucius?' he said.

'But isn't that what this is about?'

He frowned deeply.

'Menexenos is my friend, Marcus,' he said, with the air of one beginning again, 'and I will not let any man hurt him. Do not suppose, just because he does not make a show of his feelings, that he does not feel.'

I had not slept much that night. My mind was slow, and I could not grasp what he was trying to tell me. I thought to myself: They are lovers then, as I first supposed; and he is trying to warn me off. I thought of Lucius and his ill-bred pestering. I would rather die than have Eumastas think the same of me. I said, 'You need not fear, Eumastas. I will never do anything to come between you.'

I thought this would have been enough. But instead he frowned even more deeply. The sun flashed in his brown eyes, like fire in brushwood, and he made an impatient gesture with his arm. 'What are you talking about?' he cried.

I was feeling awkward enough as it was. Now I was beginning to feel foolish. I said, 'Are you not lovers then?'

'We, lovers?' He laughed – a rare thing in Eumastas.

But then, seeing in my face that I was serious, he stopped. 'Oh, I love him well enough. More than I love any man except my father. But no, we are not lovers. Did you suppose it?'

'Yes.'

He shook his head. 'Then you are wrong. Perhaps I have known him too long; or perhaps, as I fear, it is just that I am not capable of the love of men.'

For a moment we looked at each other without speaking. I said, 'Then what is this about, if not Lucius or you?'

He tossed his head. 'You Romans! I like you, Marcus; but your people are not my people, and I cannot understand you as I should a Greek. Do you truly not know, then?'

I looked at him with a mixture of surprise and understanding. My mind began to clear. Pasithea's words came back to me.

'It may be,' continued Eumastas, shaking his head, 'as is said, that you Romans have no feeling for these matters. Or is it just that you care only for girls?'

I looked down, and scuffed my toe in the dust to hide my confusion. Up on the citadel, the priest of the temple was ringing the morning bell, a gentle ping, ping, ping, like the sound of the goat-clappers on the hillside at Praeneste. I thought of Myrtilla, and the girl in Epeiros; and then I thought of the touch of Menexenos's skin when he drew against me at the palaistra.

Looking up I said, 'No, it is not that.'

I could feel my colour rising. I had never spoken of such things before.

Know yourself, said the god. Yet this I did not know. Or, perhaps, I had known it for ever. I thought of my ugly scarred leg, and all my imperfection. What he was telling me seemed hardly possible. I shook my head. 'But surely Menexenos has— Is there no one in Athens, then?'

'That is what everyone thinks – that there must be someone somewhere. But there is not.' He shrugged. 'It is not that he does not wish it otherwise. I think he believes that what he seeks is not to be found. He is in love with honour, Marcus; and a thing beyond honour, which he sees, but I cannot explain. When I ask him, he tells me it is the light behind the sun, whatever that is . . . But whatever it is, I know he had rather have no one than choose a base lover.'

There was a long silence. I think he felt as embarrassed as I.

Eventually I said, 'I did not know – I never guessed that—' I broke off, and stared out at the bay.

'I thought you were toying with his feelings,' he said. 'It made me angry.'

I shook my head. 'No. Never that.' And then, looking at his face, 'I would never do that.'

'In that case,' he said, 'I hope you will forgive me.'

'There is nothing to forgive. Nor can I conceive of being his friend and not yours.'

He nodded. I think I even saw the hint of a blush on the sides of his broad neck.

'Then let us make it so,' he said, in the formal way he had.

And he took my right hand, like a man sealing a bond.

SIX

IN LATE SUMMER, BEFORE the first gales of autumn began, Pasithea sailed for Greece.

Menexenos and I saw her off from the quayside. To my surprise, the two of them had become firm friends. I had wondered, at first, whether they would get on at all, for they were, it had seemed to me, creatures from different worlds, breathing different air. Only afterwards did it come to me that this was not quite true. They were both, in their different ways, above convention. They saw things with their own eyes, not the eyes of others; and what they found in each other, they liked.

As for me and Menexenos, to the onlooker, it might have seemed that nothing had changed, and that was how we both wished it. I know what my stepfather would have asked, if he had known. I made sure he did not; not out of shame, but to protect what was beautiful from his clumsy hands.

Any man's kiss was strange to me. For the rest, I began to realize he was as hesitant as I.

He said, one day, bringing up his hand and drawing my forehead to his, so that our skin touched, 'There will be a time. We will know.' He explained he wanted our love to be a love of the soul, because, in the end, there was no other.

I thought of Lucius, and I understood.

There was a change within me, like spring after winter. It showed itself in small things. For the first time, music spoke to me, echoing the deep harmony of the world. At the palaistra, my diskos-throw flew true, and I came to understand what Menexenos had tried to teach me from the start, that it was my heart that made the disk fly, not the muscles in my arm and shoulder. Even, at times, my stepfather seemed to have some buried good in him.

But though I walked in light, Mars the Avenger stayed at my shoulder. It was not long before I heard Dikaiarchos's name again.

With my work at the harbour, I had come to know the port-master, and the sea captains who regularly put in. One day I would hear that Dikaiarchos was in Krete, leading the pirates there; another, that he was terrorizing the islands of the Kyklades, stealing the crops and burning the cities; and on another that he was harrying the Rhodian traders, or on the coast of Asia.

There were those who said he was no more than a clever thief, exploiting the lack of authority in the Aegean Sea. But Titus, to whom I took these reports, disagreed. 'They believe what they want to believe; they have their eyes on Africa still. But we shall soon see what he is about.'

I was often up at the praetor's residence, now that

Lucius was not there. Titus had said one day, shortly after his outburst at the palaistra, 'He has gone away. He has business in Rome to attend to.' He said no more than that, and I did not ask.

The captains and the crews at the harbour were hard men. Each voyage, they knew, might be their last; and perhaps it was because they walked in step with death that they loved life as they did, or perhaps they were the kind of men who would have loved life anyway. When I got to know them they told me their tales – for all seafaring men are full of wonders to tell. I felt a kinship with them. They had a nobility of their own, not like the criminals my stepfather had hired to manage the farm-estates, who were greedy and vicious and bitter, even though they lived like kings among their wretched slaves.

One of my friends at the harbour was a young Greek by the name of Theramon, from Italian Heraklea. His father had been a potter there, and his father before him. But Theramon wanted to go to sea, and against his father's wish he had done so.

He had begun with nothing, but had found investors in Tarentum who believed in him enough to finance a ship and make him captain. His ship had a red sail with the first letter of his name picked out in white. He was proud of it, and of what he had made for himself.

Shortly before Pasithea left for Greece, I had seen him off on a voyage to Mytilene, carrying a cargo of purple-dyed Tarentine wool. Afterwards he was sailing on to Pergamon, on a commission my stepfather had given him. I did not know the details; Caecilius, unusually, had dealt with Theramon himself.

That voyage, he was carrying passengers too: a father and mother, and two small fair-haired girls who grinned and waved to me as the ship put out to sea, loving the adventure, oblivious of fear. Their smiling faces stirred my memory, but I put the dark thought from my mind. I grinned back at them, and waved till they were lost from view. Only afterwards, when Theramon's ship had vanished through the narrows that led from the harbour to the open sea, did I allow myself to frown. My life was full of such sudden remembrances, though mostly they came at night, or in my dreams. But on my way home, I made sure to pause at the shrine of Poseidon, and offered a pinch of incense.

About a month later, I was standing on the quayside, tallying a cargo of wine-filled amphoras bound for Rome, when one of the stevedores tapped me on the shoulder and with a grin said, 'Look, there's old Caecilius.'

I looked. He seldom came down to the port, considering it beneath his dignity. He was standing at the end of the quay, beside a newly arrived merchantman, remonstrating with the captain.

I set down the wax tablet I was holding and went to him, supposing he had come looking for me.

'There you are!' he cried, turning his back on the man he was talking to. 'What, by the dog, is all this about Theramon? Did you not think to come and tell me?'

I looked from him to the captain behind him. His name was Phylakos. He sailed the run from Kos and Rhodes to the Greek cities in Italy. We got on well, but he was not a man to be spoken down to, which my stepfather was a master of, and now he gave Caecilius a prod in the back and said, 'The youth does not know yet; that is why he hasn't told you.' And then, meeting my eye, 'I was going to come when I was done with the harbour-master. I heard it in Rhodes, from a man just in from Khios . . .'

'Drowned?' I asked, my belly tightening.

'Butchered, even the two little girls, after the pirates had had their pleasure with them. It was that vaunting corsair bastard Dikaiarchos again. He left his altar to Lawlessness and Impiety on the seastrand. They say it is his sign.'

There was little to be said. Presently Phylakos went off. As soon as he had gone Caecilius cursed out loud. 'It is a heavy loss.'

'Yes,' I agreed.

'Oh, you don't know the half of it. I don't mean the cargo of wool. That can be made up. But he was carrying a small fortune of my silver.'

I stared at him in disbelief. Misreading my expression, he took my arm and went on in a confidential tone, 'I did not tell you at the time: that captain – what was his name again? – was engaged in a private mission for me – something I did not want talked of – taking funds for arms to a contact of mine in Pergamon.' He tapped his nose. 'They were to be shipped to Antiochos in Syria. It had to be kept discreet.'

In a flat voice I said, 'Now Dikaiarchos has your silver, or King Philip does, who everyone says is his ally.'

'Well, perhaps,' said Caecilius, not listening. 'All I know is I have lost my money. Curses on this pirate – what did you say his name was?'

'Dikaiarchos, sir. He was the one who killed my father.'

'Was he? It is time you put all that behind you. What's done is done.' And then, rubbing his chin and frowning, 'If only I had divided that cargo.'

I said nothing. I did not trust myself to speak.

Titus was right. It was not long before we heard of King Philip again, and Dikaiarchos with him. News came that he had launched an attack on the cities of coastal Asia, and with the treasure he had seized he was arming his fleet. He took Lysimacheia, then Thasos; he harried the cities of the Hellespont.

When I told Menexenos this he said straight away, 'He means to threaten Athens.'

I asked him how he was so sure.

'It is the strategy of every enemy of Athens. He who controls the Hellespont controls Athens, for it is our grain-route from the Black Sea. It is our food supply.'

When Titus next held one of his suppers, he said beforehand, 'It would be an honour if your friend Menexenos could come as well. Should I send an invitation? – yes, I think so,' he mused to himself, 'but ask him as well, when you see him, and tell him from me that I should be very glad if he would come.'

I wondered who had told him. Xanthe, probably. I smiled to myself. I had supposed I had been a picture of discretion; but love shines out, and, looking back, I daresay it would have taken a blind man not to have seen it.

It was the sort of kindness Titus always strove for. The easier course, after what had happened with Lucius, would have been for him to say nothing. But that was not his way.

At Titus's supper-party, his friend Villius was present, on a visit from Rome. He visited often, for he acted as a confidential go-between between Titus and his friends in the Senate. Mimas the Greek was with him; and Titus had invited Verginius from the garrison, and one or two others I knew less well.

Everyone felt Pasithea's absence; but pretty fair-haired Xanthe was there, sharing Titus's couch as always, bright and full of conversation. I was greeting her when Verginius arrived late, having been detained by some business with the garrison. I looked up with something of a start, not at him, but at the girl on his arm. It was Myrtilla.

She was a professional, of course. Yet I feared, in my innocence of such things, that she would feel slighted, for I had not seen her since the night of Poseidon's festival. I need not have been concerned. She greeted everyone pleasantly, and when she came to me she caught me with her intelligent eye, as if to say, 'What happened between us is ours alone.' Then she turned to Menexenos. 'You have chosen a good friend, Menexenos son of Kleinias. I see you can tell gold from dross. Many cannot.'

'Then,' he said, smiling back at her, 'you have the greater skill, who saw the gold before me.'

This pleased her, as he had meant. She said, 'I am not sure whom to envy most, him or you.'

Menexenos laughed. 'Why, me of course, just as the rest of the city does.'

I shook my head and blushed at this flattery, and with a happy laugh Myrtilla went skipping off to sit with Verginius.

Except for me, who was a few months younger still, Menexenos was the youngest there that evening. But he could be placed in any gathering and shine. Whether the subject was the city or the soul, he spoke with grace and humanity and wit.

That evening the talk was all of Carthage and King Philip. Old Quintus Fabius, the Roman general who had retaken Tarentum in the siege seven years before, had recently died. He had been five times consul, and was one of those who opposed Scipio. The Senate had already agreed to allow Scipio to carry the war to the enemy in Africa; but later, to thwart his rival, Fabius had persuaded the senators to refuse Scipio a levy of troops: the only men he was permitted to take were volunteers, if he could find them.

Fabius thought, by this ruse, he had blocked his rival. But when Scipio called for volunteers there was a clamour of men who wished to follow him, so greatly was he loved. Now they were at the gates of Carthage, preparing to face Hannibal in the final battle.

Though Fabius was dead, Scipio's enemies still grumbled on – among them, it seemed, Titus's own father – saying that to fight Hannibal in Italy was one thing, but to fight him on his own soil, on the very threshold of his home, was another. They warned of defeat, and of tempting the gods.

All this we talked about. Then the conversation turned to King Philip and the growing chaos in the Aegean. Titus asked Menexenos what he made of the raids along the Hellespont, and Menexenos replied with what he had already told me, that Philip meant to threaten Athens.

Titus listened, nodding slowly in agreement. When Menexenos had finished he turned to Villius. 'What are they saying in Rome?' he asked.

'They avert their eyes like superstitious women. Your father says the Aegean is none of our concern. Let Philip do what he wishes, so long as he leaves us alone.'

'Is that what he says? Did you hear what Philip did to Thasos?'

The citizens of Thasos, he said, facing defeat, had agreed to surrender, on Philip's promise that he would spare them. 'So they opened the gates, and as soon as Philip was in possession of the city he sold them into slavery.' He shook his head. 'But why am I telling you? You know what a monster he is. My anger is for that blustering fool my father, who will not see it.'

A silence fell. We had all come to know what Titus thought of his father; but it was not something anyone wished to comment on, only to have it remembered later, when father and son became reconciled.

After a moment Villius went on, 'There is a rumour in Rome that Antiochos has made a pact with Philip.'

Titus set down his cup and looked at him. 'To what purpose?' he asked.

'Egypt,' nodded Villius. 'Antiochos has coveted Egypt for years, just as his father did. He wants to conquer all the lands Alexander once held, and now is his chance, while it is in chaos after the succession.'

'And,' said Titus, 'he doesn't want Philip to stand in his way.'

'So it seems.'

Titus rubbed his downy beard. 'And what, I wonder, will Philip want in return? What can Antiochos offer him?'

'What else but a free hand in Greece, and control of the Hellespont, and the chance to bring King Attalos low in Pergamon? He has already ravaged his kingdom, and there is an old feud between them.'

'No one will support him, when he breaks his word and sells whole cities into slavery. Does he wish to rule a wasteland?'

'I don't think he cares, so long as he rules it.'

Titus frowned. 'There are limits even to kingship,' he said. 'Tyrants ignore justice at their peril.'

There was a pause as everyone considered this. The only entertainment that night was a single lute-player. In the sudden silence I could hear him quietly picking out a slow echoing Phrygian melody, a tune laden with melancholy.

It was Mimas the Greek who spoke next. 'Those two,' he cried, 'Philip and Antiochos, are like wolves that fight over a carcass.'

And then, to everyone's surprise, Xanthe, who usually had little to say on such matters, said, 'In that case they had best beware. For sometimes, when the wolves are busy, the lion steals up unheard, and snatches the carcass from them both.'

Titus, who had been frowning at his wine-cup, turned

and looked at her with raised brows. 'Why Xanthe, you little minx! And who, then, is the lion?'

She popped an olive into her mouth. 'Rome is the lion,' she said.

Titus burst into a laugh. 'Well, wise strategist, I can see we'll make a general of you yet. But that, I think, is a feast which even Rome has no stomach for.'

Caecilius, too, who seldom heeded the world beyond his own interests, had his eyes set on the East that year.

The loss of his money on Theramon's ship was not, it seemed, the great financial disaster he first made out. In two months he was ready to send more money for his Asian venture. He kept the fine details from me, but I knew he was up to something. He would say, with unconvincing casualness, 'Ah, I think, today, I shall go to the harbour myself and deal with Phrikias; the walk will be pleasant.' Or he would cough and enquire, 'Tell me, Marcus, has news come yet of Hamilcar's ship?' Or Chares's. Or Mellon's.

He liked to keep his absurd little secrets; but he liked even more to let me know he had them. I took no notice of his half-spoken sentences and heavy hints, and certainly did not descend to questioning him, which was what he wanted. If he did not wish to tell me, that was his affair. His evasions merely reminded me how he did not trust anyone, not even me, whom he called, when it suited him, his son.

The East, being at that time a place of trouble and uncertainty, was, for Caecilius, a place of promise. Where honest men saw ugliness in chaos, he saw opportunity. He would quiz me for whatever news I had heard on the quayside; and, at times, if some tale particularly interested him, he would hurry down to the dock himself and question the captain who brought it.

I knew my friends – Menexenos, Eumastas, Titus – despised him. How could they not? Who, after all, can respect a man who treats the acquisition of money as an end in itself, and has no care for the fortunes of others except what he may make out of them?

A good man, Menexenos said to me one day, needs wealth as a means to the good life. 'Yes,' I said straight away in answer. 'But if he does not trouble himself to know what the good life is, how then does all his money serve him? He becomes its slave, not its master.'

That summer, for the first time, I had begun to dwell on such questions. I asked myself what it was that makes a man good, what steps he must follow, what lessons he must learn. The answers still eluded me. And yet, for all my uncertainty, I knew that Caecilius was everything I did not want to be.

During that year, he had forged links with a certain Kritolaus of Patrai, a politician and an orator of accomplishment.

Kritolaus, he told me, had persuaded the people of Patrai to elect him to supreme power, and, upon gaining it, had driven out the landowners and put the wealthy aristocrats to death, seizing their property, which he had promised to share out among the poor.

'Of course,' explained Caecilius, 'he has taken his cut, as is only natural. But now, it seems, some of the rabble have complained, saying he has helped himself to what is not his.' He nodded wisely and added, 'It goes to show . . .'

I do not know what it went to show, but, of late, Kritolaus had decided he was in need of an armed body-guard to protect himself from his own citizens; he had come to Caecilius for weapons.

When I happened to mention this business to Menex-enos he said, 'Oh yes, Kritolaus. He is a demagogue. The very worst sort.'

By now, my Greek was very good, but this word was new to me. 'Is a demagogue not an orator, then?' I asked.

'Not quite; though it is true that both men use their voices to persuade others. But an orator is a man who is guided by the common good, and uses his skills to persuade others to it. But a demagogue will say whatever is necessary to gain power, and to enrich himself.'

We had left the city that day, and were walking beside the water along the great curve of the bay. I said, 'Yet Caecilius said the man is well liked.'

'Perhaps so. He steals from the few, and gives to the many. It is the way to easy popularity. Yet you say he now needs an armed guard to protect him from his own people. Well I suppose the money has run out. And as for the men whose property he has stolen, he can hardly suppose they will forget it. He must live every day in fear.'

He fell silent. Presently, coming to a great rock, we climbed and sat, and looked out at the sea, and the distant ships. It was a beautiful day. The high-summer humidity had gone, and the air was fresh and clean.

I had intended to go on and mention something that had been weighing on my mind. Caecilius had been hinting that it might suit him to send me to this Kritolaus in Patrai as his agent there. As usual it had all been conveyed in half-completed sentences and indirect comments; and I knew, if I questioned him on it, and let on that I did not want to go, it would only strengthen his resolve to send me. So I had said nothing. And now, with Menexenos too, I decided my fears could wait for another time, when there was something more definite to tell him. So instead of speaking I jumped to my feet, pulled off my clothes, and dived from the rock into the bright cool water, and he jumped in after me.

Later we returned by the inland path. On the far terraces, men were moving with baskets, gathering the harvest. In the distance, beside a spreading farmstead, a sleek herd of horses stood grazing in the golden sunlight of the late afternoon. I knew the place well. How could I not? It was one of the farms my stepfather was contracted to manage. It was the farm of Eumastas's father.

The man Caecilius had put in charge there was not as bad as most; he was a smallholder from Campania who had a love of horses. But I seldom went that way, even so. I had tried to speak to Caecilius about the farm, telling him it had been seized unjustly, and that Eumastas was my friend. In answer he had said, 'Then you had better spend less time with Greeks, as I have told you before.'

I was remembering this, when Menexenos, who had been silent for a while, broke into my thoughts and said, 'I have had a letter from my father.'

Our eyes met. We both knew what this meant, for we had spoken of it.

'So soon?' I said.

He frowned out across the valley. 'He says, with the future so uncertain, it is time I was home.'

I walked on a few paces before I answered. I had already resolved, many times, that when this moment came I should steel myself to bear it like a man. As Menexenos had once said, there is no disputing with necessity. I said, 'Is it so bad, then?'

'He says there will be war. He does not know when, not exactly. But the motions have begun. Philip is a great vaunting bully, just like the Athenian Demos, but at least he has intelligence with it, which is more than you can say for the Demos. When it comes to matters of war, they are like the glutton at the overladen table, impatient to begin, but with no idea of how they will finish.'

'When must you go?' I asked.

He crooked his arm around my neck and drew me to him. Close up I could smell the faint tang of sea-salt on his body.

'It must be before the shipping lanes close for winter,' he said.

'Not long then.'

'No. Not long.'

I nodded, reflecting that there is pain even in love. Not for the first time I thought of how I was Roman, he Athenian; and in the natural course of things we walked different paths. Thus the Fates had woven our destiny, before we were born. And yet I knew I would not have it

160

different. That summer had been like day after a long night.

As if reading my thoughts he said gently, 'This we always knew. For the rest, it is what we decide to make it. There is a power in longing, Marcus. Always remember that.'

We had reached the top of the low ridge. A breeze had picked up, stirring the leaves in the olive groves and ruffling our tunics. Ahead, in the near distance, Tarentum lay before us, red roofs and white houses, and, on the citadel, Poseidon's temple with its golden trident.

I thought, at first, the noise I heard was the breeze whistling in the valley. But now I realized it was the sound of many men's voices, rising and falling, carried on the wind. It was not the sound of battle; it was something else. It seemed to be coming from within the city, or from the garrison fort beside it.

Beside me Menexenos's head went up. He had heard it too. We looked at each other.

'Something is wrong,' I said. 'We had better get back.'

We quickened our pace. I saw, ahead in the distance, outside the city wall in the place where the wagons and carriages wait, a small crowd was gathering. Then I noticed a Roman legionary on mule-back, striking out along the path, urging the creature on with a switch on its rump. He was an old, lean, grizzled centurion. His face under his beard was flushed, and his mouth was moving, as if he were shouting, or singing. But he was too distant for me to make out his words.

We cut across the downward slope to intercept him.

When he was near enough for me to hail, I called out in Latin, asking what had happened.

'Zama!' he cried back, breaking into a grinning laugh and waving the withy switch in the air so wildly that he nearly fell off the mule.

'What does he say?' asked Menexenos.

I shook my head. ' "Zama' . . . But I don't know what he means . . . I think he's drunk.'

We sprinted down the track and caught him up.

'Zama!' he cried again when I asked him. And then, after a long belch, 'Have you not heard? It's over boy, though I don't think you were born when it began . . . How old are you? Sixteen?'

'Seventeen. What is over?'

'General Scipio has hammered those Carthaginian bastards, right outside their own city. It is finished at last. The war is over!'

Then he slapped the mule's side and rode off, singing drunkenly to himself.

Everyone has their own tale of how they heard the news. That is mine. Later I heard more.

Scipio had done battle with Hannibal. He had entirely defeated the Carthaginian army and their allies, outside a village by the name of Zama. Hannibal had fled the field, and the elders of Carthage had sued for peace.

When I got home I found Caecilius in his workroom, holding forth to his friends. He was a man who liked to have his say, even on matters he knew nothing about, and now he was telling them, 'Of course I foresaw this long ago; that is why I have diversified my business. Well there is peace, and there will be consequences, I daresay; but we must press on as best we can. I met Scipio once, you know. An able man, though rather full of himself . . . Ah, Marcus, there you are. Where have you been? I hope you are not thinking of going off to join the foolish merriment.'

Autumn drew on. It seemed to me I was aware of every turning leaf. The tang of woodsmoke hung in the air, and at the harbour the long-haul merchantmen put out for their final voyages before the winter gales began.

Now, when Menexenos was leaving, I refused to be cast down. One day Eumastas came to me and said, 'My father is having a dinner-party, a farewell – just a few friends – will you come?'

I looked at him. This was the first time he had invited me to his house. I understood. He had his father's honour to think of.

Perhaps he read these thoughts in my face, for then he said, 'If we have suffered misfortune, it is as much the fault of the Tarentine mob, who supported Hannibal, as it is of Rome. You are my friend. That is enough.'

I thanked him, and accepted.

Eumastas's father, Aristippos, was a decent country gentleman. He behaved as if he did not deign to notice his straitened circumstances; but it was clear he had never managed to adjust to them. He had salvaged, I saw, his old furniture from the farm: great carved antique chests, heavy tables, and dark-wood couches with silver feet. Anyone could see it did not belong in that cramped town house. But, then again, neither did he.

Seeing him constricted in his little prison like a caged bear I felt for him. He reminded me of Priscus, and of my own father; he was a man used to space, to walking out over the fields, tending to his animals, and regulating his life with the seasons. He never mentioned it. But one saw the loss in his eyes.

Later a linkboy lit me home through the dark streets. I was almost at the gate, and was just about to pay off the boy, when I noticed the postern move and a girl slip discreetly out. She flashed her eyes angrily at the dazzling torchlight, pulled up her veil, and hurried away. But I had seen enough to recognize her. She was one of Caecilius's night-time visitors, one of the most regular, a raddled shrew with a voice like a crow's. Something must have happened, for her to be leaving before the dawn.

I gave the boy his coin and went inside. The entrance hall was dark, after the light of the torch-flame, and I paused for a moment, waiting for my eyes to adjust. Then I heard the boards creak on the upstairs landing; and, from above, Caecilius's voice called out, 'Marcus, come here. I wish to speak to you.'

He was waiting in his private sitting room upstairs. On the table a single lamp-flame glimmered dimly under a fretted cover. Beside it stood a wine-flask, and, I noticed, two cups.

He sat down heavily on the couch and took up his drink. In the dim light his jowly face looked blotched and puffy. 'I want to know,' he snapped, 'who this youth called Menexenos is.'

I paused. It was late, and I was tired. I had not been prepared for this.

'He is my friend, sir,' I answered.

He lolled his head and guffawed. I realized he was very drunk. '*Friend?*' he drawled. 'Is that what you call it? I hear he is more than that . . . or less.'

He brought up his cup and drank, like a parched man who has found water. Then, all of a sudden, he thrust his head forward and barked out, 'Does he make love to you?' He used the crude Latin barrack-term; deliberately, laying heavy emphasis on it, savouring it, rolling it with his tongue, investing it with as much filth and ugliness as he could.

There was a silence. The word hung in the air between us, like some creature. Just then, a chance breeze from the window caught the lamp-flame, making it flicker and spit, casting wild shapes on the wall, and illuminating the bed through the double-doors beyond.

The sheets were undisturbed still. I thought of the girl in the street. The subdued lighting was intended for an occasion different from this.

My anger surged in me then, coursing through my veins, making my head throb with the beating of my heart.

I took a step forward. Slowly, with a voice of steel, I said, 'No sir, he does not. But if he asked me, I should do it gladly. Now is there anything else you wish to know? If not, then I shall go to my bed. I am tired; and, from the look of your state, you too need your sleep.'

And then I turned and strode out of the room.

Next day I went with Eumastas to the harbour to see Menexenos off. We stood near the gangboard, talking of this and that, while around us the stevedores finished the loading. Finally, all too soon, the captain called down from the deck that he was ready to put to sea.

'Well, it is time,' said Menexenos. He embraced Eumastas. Then he turned to me.

As we held each other close I whispered in his ear, 'There is power in longing . . . I have not forgotten.'

'Make sure you believe it,' he said, his breath warm on my neck. 'There is no distance between us, however far apart we are, unless you make it so.'

And then he drew me back, and kissed me.

In the days and weeks that followed, I set myself to training hard at the palaistra, either with Eumastas or alone, not caring what others made of it. Once or twice, turning from my exercise, I caught sight of my stepfather's agent, sly rat-faced Virilis, lurking in the shadows. I had already guessed it was he who had been spying on me. But let him spy. I had nothing of which I was ashamed, either before Caecilius or before the gods themselves, who see everything.

I worked my body hard, using reason to perfect what, on the farm, I had acquired by chance.

In part, this work at the palaistra was for Menexenos; for I missed him even more than I had supposed, and to run where he had run, and strive where he had striven, put me in mind of him.

I asked Eumastas to tell me about Athens. He had been there once, when he was a boy; but mostly, he said, he had stayed out in the country, on the farm of Menexenos's father Kleinias.

Eumastas was never one to chatter, or to use many words when few would do. He would speak, answering one's question, and then fall silent. When first I met him, I had taken his heavy-browed expression for brooding, or dislike. But it was not that. I think, in the end, it was just that he did not have much to say, and, being conscious of it, it made him awkward.

The port was quiet, but eventually a late-season cargo ship put in. The captain asked for me, and when I came he handed me a letter from Menexenos. He had arrived safely. Athens was full of war-talk. He missed me.

Then the winter gales set in, and there was nothing more.

It was a time of changes. The war, which had gone on since before I was born, was over; and now, Caecilius announced to me one day, his business in Tarentum was drawing to an end. Soon all could be left to his agents and managers. There were officials he had to see at the praetor's residence, and, in one of the petty humiliations he inflicted on others to confirm his sense of self, he took me with him as a porter for his piles of documents, as if I were a slave.

The residence was not only Titus's dwelling, but also a large complex of offices and outhouses where officials worked. I had no reason to suppose, that day, that I should see Titus himself. But as I laboured with the burden of papers, following my stepfather, he emerged from a doorway at the far side of the wide square courtyard, attended by the tribune Verginius and a group of clerks.

'Why Marcus, you look weighed down like a mule!

Let me find someone to carry that . . . what is it all, any-way . . . was there no slave to help you?'

He took some of the tablets and books and scrolls himself, and passed others to the clerks. 'By God,' he said laughing, 'there is enough for two men here. What are you doing, training for the pankration?' Then he looked up and saw Caecilius, some twenty paces ahead, under the portico by the offices, wagging his finger at one of the officials. 'Ah,' he said frowning. 'Your stepfather.'

Just then Caecilius turned with a cross look, to see where I was. As soon as he saw Titus his face changed, and he came hurrying across the cobbles, all smiles, his mantle swishing to and fro about his bulk. 'My dear Praetor, what an honour, why I was just saying to my son here . . .'

He talked on – flattering nonsense – until Titus eventu-ally cut in with, 'I believe you are leaving us, Aulus Caecilius? Have you decided yet where you will be going?'

'Back to my estate in Praeneste,' he answered. 'At least for the winter . . . As for afterwards, who can say? I have interests in Greece, as, indeed, you may have heard; and elsewhere too. But as I often say, the world is full of opportunity, and—'

'Quite. Then I wish you success.' And then, turning to me, 'I hear a ship put in from Athens last week. Is there word from Menexenos?'

Before I could answer, Caecilius burst in with, 'Ah Menexenos! An excellent young man, for a Greek.' He paused and frowned to himself, perhaps remembering that Titus had a reputation for being a friend of Greece.

Titus looked at him. 'Yes, excellent indeed; and a

person I count as a particular friend . . . But you must have a great deal to do, Aulus Caecilius, and I am keeping you from your business . . . Marcus, why don't you give all this rubbish to the clerk' – stubbing his thumb at the pile of documents – 'I want to show you something – if, Caecilius, you can spare him?'

'Oh yes, yes, of course; yes, certainly,' blustered my stepfather, giving me what he supposed was a private conspiratorial nod.

'Good. Come then, Marcus. And good day to you, sir.' He put his arm through my elbow, and led me off towards the main house.

'I shall miss you,' he said as we walked. 'Verginius says you have been practising sword-work at the barracks. What is it? Will you be enlisting next?'

I laughed. 'A man ought to know how to defend himself. He must know how to fight.'

'Indeed. Well, if Verginius is any judge, you already fight better than many men. You move well, he says; and you are fast.'

We passed under the long colonnade beside the gardens. Further off, slaves were busy raking the lawns, or tending the low ornamental hedges. 'We shall meet again,' he said, 'but mind you come for one last dinner before you leave . . . just some close friends, Xanthe, Mimas, perhaps Verginius too . . .' We came to the table that stood on the terrace, and here he paused. 'Now,' he said, 'to business. That friend of yours you told me about, the one with the horse-farm. What was his name?'

I said, 'Eumastas.'

'Ah yes, Eumastas.' He picked up a scroll from the

table. 'I wanted to do this long ago. It has all taken far more time than it needed. But I had some unexpected opposition to overcome.' He frowned at the scroll, then handed it to me, adding, '. . . not least from your stepfather, who insisted I went through the formal channels at Rome. Still, it is done at last, and here is the deed to show it. You may tell Eumastas his farm is restored to him.'

I stared at the document, written in the broad clear hand of hieratic Roman officialdom. I swallowed, then remembered to thank him.

He waved my thanks aside. 'It is justice,' he said. Then, seeing my hesitation, 'But what is it?'

'Just this, Titus: I'd rather not tell him myself. You see, his farm was never my gift to give, and I should not want him to think it was, after so long.'

He nodded. 'I understand. I'll send Sextus. He will handle it well.'

'And my stepfather?' I said, thinking how he had mentioned none of this to me.

His blue eyes flashed, and with a grin he replied, 'The clerks will be informing him, even as we speak.'

SEVEN

PRAENESTE IN WINTER. MIST hung in the valley
like a silk veil; but when we mounted the track that led
up into the foothills and started to climb, we left the mist
beneath us, and the morning air was sharp, and clear as
crystal.

My mother was waiting on the step, proud and straight-
backed, and at her side stood Mouse, my stepsister. A
group of the farmhands had gathered; and, with them, but
carefully apart, the new bailiff my stepfather had brought
in – a black-haired, staring, uneasy-looking man.

I stepped up, and my mother greeted me and took my
hands in hers. 'Why, you are a man now,' she said
smiling. 'I see the reflection of my own father in you . . .
You see, Caecilia' – to Mouse – 'how broad and strong
he has become.'

Mouse smiled, and when I embraced her she whispered, 'Welcome home, Marcus.'

Her hounded look had gone; her modest, attentive
face showed a new confidence.

In the days that followed, I wandered about my old familiar haunts – the tracks among the oak trees; the stream and apple orchard and the high grove with its ancient grey-stone shrine where my ancestors lay. I saw straight away that the bailiff had made changes.

He was a fussy, garrulous man, ingratiating with my stepfather and me, but sharp with everyone else. The reason for his nervousness became clear after a morning touring the meadows and terraces with him. He had learned whatever knowledge of farming he possessed in the fertile lowlands of Campania. It could not have taken him long to discover that his methods did not suit high Praeneste, where the conditions were different. But he was not the kind of man to take advice, and when the farmhands tried to set him right, he had rebuffed them with anger.

So he had sown too late; he had planted new vines on north-facing terraces where they would not grow; he had left the water conduits until they had silted up, and, ignoring the farmhands' warnings, he had neglected the hay harvest so that there was not enough winter fodder for the livestock.

I do not think Caecilius noticed any of this. But one thing he could not fail to notice, and shortly after our return I was passing the door of my father's old study when I heard his snappish complaining voice coming from within. He had been reviewing the accounts. I could hear his abrupt questions, and the bailiff's complicated evasive replies, blaming the land, and the farmhands, and the weather.

It seemed unjust, and I was on the point of bursting in

to put him right, and, indeed, I had already put my hand onto the great iron latch, when from behind me I heard my mother's voice say sharply, 'Marcus!' and when I turned in surprise, for I had not known she was there, 'Please come; I should like to speak to you.'

She led me to her sitting room before she spoke again. She asked me to close the door. Then sat down and looked at me. 'You have taken a look at the farm, I suppose?'

I said, 'Yes,' and was about to go on, but she raised her hand, silencing me. 'Then you have realized,' she said, 'that this bailiff' – his name was Retius – 'is a fool.'

'Indeed, Mother!' I cried, and began detailing the chaos on the farm.

She listened for a short while, but when I paused she said, 'All this I know, Marcus; or do you think I learnt nothing from my own father, and from yours? But what do you think will happen if you tell Caecilius?'

'Happen?' I said staring. 'Why, I hope he sends him away. What else?'

She nodded. 'And then,' she said, 'he will bring in some other hireling, and I shall have to begin again with him. At least this man Retius perceives in some dim way that he has failed. And that,' she said, pausing and meeting my eye, 'is where I want him.'

I began to understand. Caecilius had seen nothing wrong with the farm, other than the accounts, which was the only thing he understood about farming. He had misjudged Retius, and if he were to seek another he might find an even greater fool. My mother, in her way, had found the lever that enabled her to manage him herself.

I could not but smile. My mother, seeing I had understood, nodded once, then turned away.

Soon after I arrived, Mouse said coyly that she had
something to show me, and led me through to the back
of the house, where her own small room was.

'Why Mouse!' I cried laughing, 'you have built yourself a library!'

There were carefully fashioned shelves against every
wall; indeed there was scarcely room for the bed any
more.

She looked at me with big eyes. 'You are not angry
then?'

'Angry? How could you think so? Why, this is wonderful.'

Immediately her nervousness left her. She sat down on
the bed and happily explained how she had rescued my
father's old books from the damp outhouse, and had
asked Milo the farmhand to help her build the shelves.

I went over and cast my eye over the books. Each
volume had been sorted, labelled with new tags written in
her careful hand, and stacked. I asked her how many she
had managed to read.

'Why, all of them,' she answered, her eyes bright. She
looked so proud, and so happy, that I crossed the room –
no more than a pace or two in that little space – and
hugged her.

When I stood back I saw she had blushed. But she did
not avert her eyes, as she would have done before; and
now, being sure of my reaction, she told me more. She

had discovered, she said, that some of the books were old and worn, so she had begun to make her own copies. Shyly she took a scroll from a casket beneath the bed and showed me. She wrote in a fine, clear hand. I nodded and smiled, and told her so, and could see that she was pleased.

She said, 'But I have a favour to ask.'

'Then ask it,' I said smiling.

'It is said that there are books in Greece beyond counting. When you go, if you happen to see any, will you send me one, or maybe two, if you can manage it?'

'Why yes, Mouse, of course.' This was something Caecilius could easily have done for her, if he had been minded. Then I said, 'But who told you I was going to Greece? No one told me.'

She tipped her head towards the door. '*He* did. Patrai, he said . . . Didn't he tell you then?'

I set the book aside.

'I half knew, for he has business there. But he did not tell me, not properly.'

'He never does.' She looked at me. 'Don't you want to go?'

I shrugged. There was much I could have told her, but I did not want to muddy the clear water of her happiness. So I only said, 'I should have preferred it if he had asked me, that's all.' But to myself I thought: Kritolaus and Patrai. I wonder what that will bring. And then I thought of Menexenos.

Shortly after the winter solstice, a messenger came with a letter from Titus, saying that his friends in Rome had secured him a new position. He would be leaving

Tarentum, and, since he was passing close by, he proposed to pay a visit, if it was convenient with my stepfather.

'Why of course, of course,' cried Caecilius when I mentioned this, and to my mother and Mouse, 'it is a great honour for a man like Titus to single me out for a personal visit; I expect you to do everything to accommodate him. It is an opportunity.'

He arrived a month later, when the first blossoms were showing in the apple orchard, accompanied by a mounted escort, which he billeted in the town.

That evening we ate a meal my mother had prepared. I shall not mention all my stepfather had to say. He talked a succession of tedious, irrelevant, superficial pleasantries, mingled with heavy-handed enquiries about how he might benefit from Titus's affairs. He kept apologizing for the food, which my mother had taken much care with, saying, 'Of course you are used to far better than this peasant fare,' or, 'Leave it, I'm sure you must find it dull.' He was sharp with the serving-girl, calling her clumsy and mulish, and making her worse. And Mouse, who would have enjoyed Titus's company, was banished to the kitchen and told to eat with the servants.

Next morning Titus caught my eye and said, 'Come, Marcus, let us get some air.'

We took the track through the high forest, and while we walked, he told me his news.

At Rome, he said, there had been something of a dilemma about what to do with him. He had gone to Tarentum with the rank of quaestor, and in the normal course of political advance, he could have expected an aedileship next. But then his uncle Caeso had died, and he had been made praetor, missing out the rank of aedile completely. It had seemed pointless and wrong to everyone to reward him now with an aedileship, which would in effect be a demotion. 'So they have appointed me to a land commission, which will distribute land to Scipio's veterans back from the war in Africa. Oh, it is not so great in itself,' he said, 'but it will get me noticed, and I will get to know the veterans. They will be useful allies, when election time comes round.'

I congratulated him. I knew he hoped for a consulship one day, and the votes of these old soldiers would count. I asked if there was more news of Philip and Greece.

At this he looked serious. 'Indeed there is; and it has caused quite a scandal at Rome.'

After Hannibal's defeat at Zama, he explained, when the prisoners were being rounded up, four thousand Macedonian infantrymen had been found among the Carthaginian troops.

I looked at him in surprise.

He nodded. 'Yes. Four thousand. No one thought Philip was truly neutral when he claimed it; but no one thought a Macedonian army would be fighting with our enemies.'

The Senate, he said, was furious, and their anger was heightened when Philip had sent envoys to Rome, arrogantly demanding the release of his men.

'What did the Senate say?' I asked.

'They told them these men were enemies of Rome. If Philip now found them in chains he had only himself to blame.'

I whistled through my teeth.

'What will the Senate do now?' I asked.

'Nothing,' he said, and the impatience showed in his voice. 'Still nothing. They will watch and wait. Perhaps, now, they will watch more carefully. But there are still too many who think the problem will go away if they ignore it for long enough.'

As we talked we had been climbing the wooded path that led past the old ashlar walls of Praeneste, and we emerged now onto a wide rocky ledge that looked out over the valley. It was the place where I often used to come as a boy, when I wanted to be alone. Below us, the land fell steeply away. The chill air smelled of pine and morning dew.

Titus walked to the edge and looked out at the distant snow-tipped peaks. He drew a deep breath, and after a pause mentioned the name of a man, and asked if I had heard of him.

I had not.

'He is a senator; one of those who have been supporting me. But that is not important. He had a daughter once. He lost her four years ago – in Epeiros.'

I had been leaning against a pine trunk with my arms folded. But now I stood up straight and looked at him.

'About a year ago,' he went on, 'one of our triremes captured a pirate ship, not far from Kerkyra. Most of the pirates were killed in the fighting. But not all. The survivors were questioned, and one of them admitted to being there on the day the girl died. You tried to save her . . . I never knew.'

I drew my breath and gazed out across the valley, remembering. Far away, a flock of swans was moving across the sky, white against blue. The memories of the past came closing in upon me. I said, 'I tried, but I could not save anyone at all. She died, and so did my father. But for me, they might have lived.'

I heard Titus shift and turn, and felt his eyes on me. Eventually I looked up. He said, 'Is it for this that you pursue Dikaiarchos?'

I scuffed at the ground with my toe and shrugged. 'In part. Sometimes I think he has made me what I am. It is a kind of curse.'

His blue eyes were intent upon me, but how could I explain? It seemed to me that Dikaiarchos had burned himself into the very core of my being. Great hatred changes men, as does great love. I knew that now. Dikaiarchos dwelt within me. How could I tell that to any man? Eventually I said, 'It is with the gods. I made a vow.'

He nodded at this, and for a short while he was silent. Then he said, 'I think it's time I told you why I have come.'

We resumed our walking, and he explained that since Philip's Macedonian troops had been captured in Africa, he was more sure than ever that war would come. What he did not know was how, and where. 'I shall be tied up with business in Italy for some time; I need someone in Greece, someone I can trust, to be my eyes and ears there. Your stepfather's business would be a perfect cover. You can come and go without drawing suspicion, and you will be in the right place for—' He paused, and swept his hand impatiently at the air, '—for whatever happens. Will you do it?'

I did not hesitate even for an instant. 'You know I will.'

He laughed. 'Yes. I knew. Well then, let us go and speak to your stepfather.'

Caecilius, when he heard, could talk of nothing else. To him, influence at Rome was all, and now I was clearly in favour at the highest level. Titus let him talk on for a while, and then reminded him of the need for discretion. He did not want it put about in Greece that I was his agent, not yet.

'You can rely on it,' Caecilius told him. 'Discretion is why I have been so successful. Anyone can tell you.'

That spring, I sailed for the second time from Brundisium to Greece.

We put in at Kerkyra, and once again I walked the quayside – not, this time, as a destitute boy who had just lost his father, but as the well-dressed son of an important Roman merchant. We stayed just long enough to load a cargo of unmarked crates, and then put out southwards, bound for Patrai.

Before I left, Caecilius had said with a pointed look, 'There is no need to concern yourself with the cargo for my friend Kritolaus; when you get to Patrai he will take care of things. I should have liked you to spend more time there. Never mind, though. Serving Titus is far more valuable to me.' He tapped his nose in the irritating way he had. 'Word at Rome is that Titus is a rising star; we must cling to him like a burdock seed.'

I believe he trotted out these words to me as much out of habit as anything, as a man might chant the words of a litany he does not understand.

Since the night in Tarentum when he had questioned me about Menexenos, certain things had changed between us. He had not once questioned me about Menexenos again. Nor did he refer to what had happened that night. But afterwards I noticed he grew more careful with me, lecturing me less, and ceasing to demand to know what I did with my time. I guessed that it had been long since anyone had stood up to him on any matter at all. I sensed, too, that he was glad to be rid of me.

I sailed via Patrai, delaying there for a month, long enough to maintain the pretence that I was travelling on my stepfather's business. But soon the ship put in that was to take me east, and the journey to Athens passed without incident.

The harbour front at Piraeus was busy with all the usual port traffic – handcarts; mule-wagons; bare-chested stevedores working the cranes or passing bales, their rhythmic work-chants sounding across the water; shipping agents; passengers waiting beside their luggage; crewmen; soldiers; and all the traders and stallholders that served them. There were men of every race: olive-skinned Phoenicians; tawny Egyptians in their bright silks; chattering black Nubians with skin like polished ebony; Persians with their ringlet-beards and fine headgear; tall, muscled Kelts; and, of course, Greeks – rich, poor, slaves, freemen, dark, fair, bearded, clean-shaven, all calling and talking and moving about.

But amidst all this bustle, even from afar, I spied Menexenos, standing at the harbour entrance, apart from the crowd, under the tall cast-iron cresset, where the young boys stand fishing off the harbour wall. I waved, and our eyes met, and my heart surged with joy. His hair was a little longer. He was dressed in a short tunic, which showed the fine contours of his legs and arms. He looked like a god in repose.

The ship berthed. I leapt down, and we fell into a laughing embrace. And presently, when we were done with our greetings, he said, 'Come, Father is waiting to meet you.'

We left Piraeus and took the road up to the city. It was a bright clear morning, early still, and full of promise. As we walked I could see, ahead in the distance, the high-city rising up like a great boulder cast by Titans into the plain, wooded on its lower slopes, with Athena's temple on the top, and the other temples clustered round, brilliant in the slanting sunlight, a perfect jewel of blue and white and gold against a cobalt sky.

Menexenos's house stood on the rising ground behind the agora, set back from the street behind a high white-washed wall, in an enclosure planted with a great shading fig tree. A lean, grey-haired man emerged from within, and I knew straight away it was Kleinias, Menexenos's father.

He had his son's flint eyes, and the same look of calm intelligence; and though he must have been nearing sixty, yet he possessed an austere powerful beauty still, and a presence that needed no fine clothes to advertise itself. I think, then, for the first time, I understood what it was to be an aristocrat.

'You are welcome, Marcus,' he said, taking my hand in his own strong grip. He led me inside, to a pleasant sparsely decorated room where wine and sweet-cakes had been set out on a low table. He hoped, he said, that I had had a pleasant journey; he asked a little of Tarentum and Praeneste, and listened courteously while I answered, taking in every word and movement.

I shall not say that he put me at my ease. That was not what he was about. I wondered what he made of me, and realized, with something of an inner start, that not only was he aware of our love affair, but he approved it. It was not that I had anything to be ashamed of; but such things did not happen in Praeneste. Here, so it seemed, such things were as familiar, and as well regarded, as the few tasteful objects that adorned the room – a polished plate; a vase; a marquetry table.

He spoke in precise, clear Greek; not with affectation, but with the unconscious confidence of a man who knows his tools and uses them to their best. But I quickly sensed that light conversation did not come easily to him, and as soon as enough time had passed for good manners he said that he had some business to attend to, and hoped I would forgive him if he left us.

When he had gone, Menexenos rested his hand on my shoulder and said, 'Well that is done. He can be rather stern at times.'

I smiled up at him. 'He's magnificent, like some perfect thing; like that vase in the corner there.'

He laughed. 'Yes, well perfection isn't always easy to live with. But come, I'll show you your room.'

Next day, after a breakfast of bread and cheese and watered wine, Kleinias bade us farewell, saying he was going to the family farm in the country, where he preferred to spend his time. 'I tire,' he said, 'of the city's noise and madness: each day a scandal and a crisis, which, by the time I return, will all be forgotten as if it never happened. But I daresay you two will prefer it here for a while. Well you are young. But come out to the farm when you are ready.'

In the days that followed, Menexenos took me about the city, and I marvelled, as every man who goes there marvels. I had never seen so much marble and gold and fine statuary collected in one place. And if one could ever tire of the painted temples, hidden shrines, monuments and sacred gardens, there were artisans and merchants for every trade – armourers, carpenters, jewellers, tailors; makers of caskets and vases and fine instruments; sellers of spice and wine and perfume; and more booksellers than I had ever seen before. We passed schools where boys learnt letters, geometry and music; we went up the Pnyx, where the Athenians meet in assembly; we climbed the steep pine-shrouded hill to the high-city and gazed at the image of the virgin goddess in her temple, a figure of ivory and gold as tall as the temple roof, with incense burning in censers around her and curling up to the rafters.

Emerging from here, we paused at the ramparts, and Menexenos pointed out a complex of red-roofed buildings beyond the city wall, in a grove of plane trees and cypresses, with a running-track beside.

'That's the Lykeion,' he said. 'I go training there when I'm not out at the farm . . . And out that way' – placing his hand on my shoulder and turning me – 'is the Akademy.'

I looked. This other place was further off, about a mile from the walls, in a suburb of smallholdings, set in a garden of tall trees beside a river. 'Is that a gymnasion too?' I asked.

'Well, yes, though it's better known now for its philosophers . . . See there' – pointing out a walled building beside it, half-obscured by tall trees – 'that's the school Plato founded. His tomb is there, in the gardens among the myrtles, and that building – the white one – is where he lived.'

He had been training, he said, for the pentathlon, having been chosen for the Panathenaic games, which would take place that summer. If it went well he might try for the Isthmia, as his father wanted. But that was still two years away. He had been working on his javelin-throw. He was confident with the stade-long sprint, and pleased with his diskos.

'Well you were always good at that,' I said.

He laughed. 'Yes, it is my best.'

'And the wrestling?' I said.

He shrugged, and frowned up at Athena's temple. Below the roof, in painted relief, was a scene of men in battle with centaurs – half man and half beast. For a moment his eyes dwelt on it.

After a short pause he said, 'My grandfather won the crown in the pentathlon, and his father before him. It goes back beyond memory. Father still has the prize-vases out at the farm.'

'But no crown for your father? Did he not compete?'

He met my eye. 'He did not win.'

I nodded, and thought of lean, austere, strict Kleinias. Defeat must have come hard to him. I said, 'Things have changed since your grandfather's time . . . the games have changed. We've both seen that.'

He made a gesture with his hand. 'You are right, Marcus. But it is tradition, and we do it because of that, and because there is still an excellence to the games – something that touches the gods – however much ignorant men may forget it.' He paused, frowning, and began toying with a pebble on the ledge. He grew conscious of it and set it aside. 'Well I ought to tell you: I had a brother once, you see.'

I had been gazing at a bronze Apollo which stood opposite the temple. But now I looked at him. 'A brother? You never said. What happened?'

He shrugged. 'We do not speak of it at home. He was a great athlete, and Father had great hopes for him. A horse threw him, out on the farm one day. The first we knew of it, the horse came home without him; and then we went looking. His neck was broken. Father said it was swift. His name was Autolykos.'

'I am sorry,' I said.

'You spoke yesterday of perfection. He was five years older than me, and *he* was perfect.' He nodded towards the temple. 'He might have been the model for that Apollo there, if they still did such work nowadays. Beautiful and virtuous, just as the poets say. If he had lived, he would have won the games, whatever it took. That was how he was. And when he died, I promised to myself I should win for him.'

The shadows were lengthening as the sun sank over the distant hills. Already, far below, the lower city was in shade.

I remembered how, at Tarentum, I had spied the deep private sadness in his face, how it had illuminated his features with such fine beauty. I saw it again now, and wondered if this was the cause.

In my self-centred unhappiness, in my preoccupation with my failings, I had not considered that he too had his own demons to conquer, and his own pain. It seemed now that I saw him anew, with new knowledge. Love stirred within me; not like fire, though I knew that well enough, but like a perfect solitary note of music that encompasses all the world in its wholeness.

We stood in silence, each communing with his thoughts, watching as the sun dipped behind Mount Parnes, and the evening star glinted on the horizon, presaging the night. I felt a new closeness to him, a loss of folly, a clarity of vision; until, surrounded as I was by shrines and temples, I even wondered if some god had touched me on the shoulder, and whispered, 'See now what I see, if only for a moment; for here is truth, present among men.'

Next morning Menexenos said, 'Let's go out to the Akademy, I'd like to show you something.'

So we walked out through the great crenellated double

gateway that the Athenians call the Dipylon, past old memorials of the war-dead, and took the path through the gardens and smallholdings, until we came to the shaded grove of the Akademy gardens.

It was early still. Here and there people ambled along the wandering paths. We came to the gateway that was the entrance to the school of Plato. A small group was gathered there. I supposed from their serious manner and carefully nurtured young beards that they must be the philosophers Menexenos had spoken of, and asked him.

'Oh yes,' he said, casting them an attentive look, 'or they imagine themselves philosophers anyway. That is why they dress like that, and don't smile. But if wisdom came from such easy conceits, then every actor would be a better philosopher than any of them.' He grinned at me, and we walked on.

Presently we turned off the path and crossed the lawn, and came to a myrtle-shaded altar set in a clearing. Yellow and white wild flowers grew all about. Some had been plucked, and lay drying on the altar-stone, as one does when one wants to offer something to the gods. Menexenos paused, and so I asked what sacred place this was.

He gazed round at the shading myrtles before he answered. I think he even blushed.

'It is sacred to Eros,' he then said. 'It is a place for lovers. I used to come here, when I was a boy, and offer something.'

'Alone?' I said.

He smiled at my question, then nodded. 'Always alone.'

I considered the little sprigs of flowers on the altar. 'And did the god hear you?'

'For a long time I thought not, and I started to believe that what I longed for was not to be found anywhere. And yet,' he said smiling, 'it seems he was listening after all.'

He flicked shyly at an overhanging branch. 'There,' he said. 'I have told you. I promised the god I should bring you here if I ever found you – and now I have done it. But I think Eros spied you long ago.'

I looked at him smiling, then took his arm and pulled him after me into the thicket of old trees behind. 'In that case,' I said, drawing him close, 'I think we owe something to the god in return.'

And then we kissed.

The rest of the day we spent walking alone, out beyond the Akademy, along the banks of the Kephissos. When we got back to the city there was a message waiting for me. It was from Pomponius, the head of the Roman legation to Athens, requiring me to call on him.

'One hears when a Roman arrives,' said Pomponius, casing himself back into his padded couch beside the window. He was a smooth portentous man of about fifty, with a paunch and a large self-satisfied face. 'And I believe,' he went on, smoothing down the folds of his mantle of fine-woven wool, with an embroidered border of prancing horsemen, 'that you are a friend of Titus Flamininus.'

'Yes sir,' I said. 'Do you know him?'

'I am a friend of his father.'

I nodded.

'You know his father?'

'No, sir. We have not met.'

'A pity. He is a good solid Roman – none of your foreign Greek habits – it is a shame his sons have not learnt more from him, instead of taking after that fire-brand philosophical type Scipio . . . Still, I have not asked you here to talk about that. Crispus' – nodding at the pallid young clerk who was standing in the corner by the desk – 'tells me you were in Tarentum.'

'Yes, sir.' I told him my stepfather had business there.

'I dare say. So you were not part of Titus's staff?'

'No, sir.'

He gave me a long stern searching look, and after a moment went on, 'It is said you are on private business in Athens. *Private* business,' he repeated with emphasis, 'and that is all very well, but if I know anything of Titus and his friends, he will have asked you to keep your finger to the wind . . .' Another pause. And then, 'What I am saying is, whatever else you are doing here, I don't want you meddling in political matters.'

'I shall not meddle, sir.'

'Good. Make sure you don't. There is enough trouble brewing here already. I imagine you have heard.'

I told him I had heard nothing, having only recently arrived.

He had been picking without interest at a bowl of sweets beside him. But now he sat back, pursed his lips, and considered me. I stood and looked at him. He had not invited me to sit.

'Well,' he said after a moment, 'since it is common knowledge, you may as well know. The Athenians have got themselves involved in a foolish pointless quarrel with a nation of nobodies called the Akarnanians – from west Greece somewhere, I don't even know quite where, but it is not important. What is important is that the Akarnanians are allies of King Philip, and now they have asked him for help . . . and *that* is something we do not need. Really' – he returned to the sweet bowl – 'I don't know why these Greeks must always be so touchy and quarrelsome. It was all caused by some nonsense to do with the Mysteries at Eleusis apparently. Outrage and offence, insults thrown, and now the Athenian Demos thinks it must teach the Akarnanians a lesson.' He shook his head. 'I tell you this, young man: whatever your friend Titus thinks, the last thing Rome wants is to get involved in this particular nest of hornets. Whatever we do, the Greeks will not thank us for it . . . So mind your step.'

'Yes, sir,' I said. 'I shall.'

And as I left the house I meant it, for I could not conceive how I might become involved in such a quarrel.

Not long after this, Menexenos took me out to visit his farm. It was small after the great estates of Tarentum, but it was neat and well kept, in good fertile land below Mount Paneion. There were barley fields, an ancient olive grove, and vines planted on the terraces that rose up the hillside behind the house. There were pastures with goats and sheep, and in the paddock a fine prancing grey colt that came nuzzling up to greet us.

The house was old, and as simply furnished as the house in Athens. But what there was was of fine understated quality – chairs of smooth polished olivewood, a low table inlaid with ivory, and an old tapestry showing the Kaledonian boar-hunt. All this I took in. But what caught my eye most was the vase on the ledge. It stood alone, with nothing near; and painted on it, red on black, was a diskos-thrower, his arms tied with victory-ribbons, his head bowed, being crowned with a wreath of olive leaves by Athena.

In honour of my coming, Kleinias ordered the steward to slaughter a kid, and that evening we feasted in the open courtyard on roasted meat, and sat late over cups of pink estate wine, with the single lamp-flame flickering on the surrounding columns, and the great sweep of the Milky Way overhead.

Kleinias asked what I had made of the city, and I told him I had never seen so much of interest and beauty in one place. I mentioned too, a little later, that Pomponius had sent for me, and had told me of a quarrel between Athens and Akarnania, which seemed to concern him.

'Well he is right to be concerned. The whole affair is a great example of foolishness.'

I asked him what had happened.

'It was the smallest of matters, and so it should have remained.'

Two young men from Akarnania, he said, rich men's sons who had come to Athens to take in the sights and enjoy themselves, had followed the crowd that was on its way to celebrate the rites at Eleusis. When the crowd entered the temple of Demeter where the secret rites were held, the two Akarnanians had followed, not realizing that entry was forbidden to all but initiates. They had carried on chatting innocently to each other, asking those around them the sort of questions tourists ask, and soon they were noticed. Then there was fury. The initiates dragged the youths to the priests of the temple, and before anyone could stop them they had put the two to death for sacrilege.

'It was a needless, hysterical reaction: all false, assumed outrage. Those boys should have been given a beating and sent home, not murdered. The mob at Eleusis, in its frenzy, did not reflect that Akarnania is allied with Philip, and Philip is waiting for an excuse to make war on us.'

He shook his head. 'I do not know a great deal of Rome, but I understand that there the best men rule, men who have learned to set aside their passions and private interests for the good of the city.'

I answered that I had heard that this was so, and he continued, 'It was the same here once, and then good sense and moderation prevailed. But now the city mob – the wretched vaunting Demos – are supreme; and politicians, whose task it is to lead, merely follow, pandering to them like a soft parent who gives sweets and gifts to an overindulged child, and offers them no correction.' He paused, and sighed. 'Well, I am talking on. The foolish will always be more numerous than the wise, and so to be ruled by the many is to be ruled by fools.'

He said no more on the subject, and, soon after, made his excuses and took himself off to bed.

But I thought about what he had said, and next day,

when Menexenos and I had gone out to inspect the vines, I asked, 'Why is it, Menexenos, that the common people – the Demos – rule, if they are so foolish?'

'There are those,' he said, 'who think that, by ruling, they will make themselves better, just as a horseman or a runner grows better with practice.'

'But your father does not agree?'

'He has seen a good deal of the people's fickleness. He says you do not teach a drunkard sobriety by leaving him alone in the wine store. Nor do the people have the right to do wrong and injustice, just because they are many. If they are not willing, or able, to school themselves in virtue, then they should leave the affairs of the city to others.'

We had come out at the summit above the vine-terraces. The upland was spread with a patchwork of delicate springtime flowers. On a far headland a temple overlooked the turquoise sea, and in the distance a mer-chantman, its great russet sail swollen in the breeze, glided towards Piraeus.

I said, 'And you, Menexenos, what do you think?'

He walked over to the ledge, where the land fell away, and, shading his eyes with his hand, looked out to the sea. The breeze stirred his hair, and the edges of his tunic. 'This I believe,' he said, 'that a man does not find himself in a crowd, but in his solitude. The Demos is a figure, nothing more; and yet men worship Demos as a god, and by doing so stumble into error. There is nothing sacred in a crowd. If men know good, it is because each one has found it for himself. I learnt that on the running-track, and on the diskos-field. No man is born excellent, Marcus. And if some demagogue tells him he need not work at it, there are too many in the city who will believe him.' He shrugged and turned. 'And yet, for all that, Father is too severe. There is good in most men, if one only looks. He has ceased to look, having been let down too often. And who am I to judge him?'

Before we returned to the city, Menexenos took me to the women's quarters to meet his mother.

She was a frail-looking woman, soft-spoken and fine-boned, proud and precise. An air of melancholy hung about her, like shadow on a bright day; and afterwards, though he did not speak of it, Menexenos was quiet for a while. I thought of the prize-vase of the diskos-thrower, and of his brother who had died. It seemed to lie behind everything, though it was never mentioned.

Back in Athens, I went to one of the booksellers in the street behind the agora and bought something for Mouse, as I had promised. The bookseller made a great fuss of me, assuring me he employed only the very best copyists, and showing me the Egyptian papyrus he used. 'The very finest quality,' he said, nodding and inviting me to finger the paper, 'and with careful handling it will last generations. Ask anyone at the Akademy, or at the Painted Stoa.'

I spent half a morning there, browsing among the scrolls, trying to decide, among such riches, what Mouse should like best, knowing that what would delight her most would be to be here with me, browsing for herself. In the end I bought some volumes of Herodotos, a play by Agathon, and a dialogue about love by Plato, which Menexenos had once mentioned.

Afterwards, pleased as a child, I paused outside the shop to look over my purchases. Through the window I overheard the bookseller's voice say in a tone of hushed mock-horror to his friend, 'A Roman buying books! Whatever next? Do you suppose he can read?'

I was tempted to cough, to let him know I was there. But in the end I just smiled to myself, took up the parcel, and walked off. What mattered was what I made of myself; not what this fussing bookseller thought of me, or of Mouse, or of any Roman.

It was two days later, while I was arranging to send the books to Italy, that the trouble began.

I was on my own that day, Menexenos having been summoned to the gymnasion for athletics practice prior to the games. I had gone down to Piraeus to meet a sea captain I knew from my days in Tarentum, an old Syracusan by the name of Kratos, who owned his own ship and plied the route between Greece and Sicily. He had agreed to deliver my package for Mouse, and to take a letter for Titus.

We met at the appointed time, beside the sanctuary of Aphrodite on the sea front. I gave him my parcels, and we paused to talk.

There was a good deal of noise all about us – stevedores shouting and chanting; street-sellers; crewmen calling; the sound of wood on wood as crates were piled up, or loaded onto carts – but like a dog that catches a scent in the air, Kratos discerned among all this something that made him break off in mid-speech and cock his head. He listened, and under his beard his face hardened.

'What is it?' I said.

He looked from side to side, and then behind him. 'Trouble, that's what.'

And then I heard it. From the south harbour, which lay on the other side of Piraeus a few streets away, there came shouts of alarm echoing between the buildings.

Kratos peered down the quay to where his own ship lay moored beyond a row of four Athenian triremes. It was secured to the quay only by a single line, ready to cast off.

On the deck the crew were waiting, craning their necks and looking about with serious faces. They too had heard the commotion.

Kratos scanned the water and the mole, then gave a quick signal to his helmsman. From the stern the helmsman raised his hand in acknowledgement. Then he turned back to me.

'I'm off, and I suggest you do the same. I've seen harbour riots before. I'm not going to wait around for my ship to be looted or burned.'

He briefly shook my hand, assured me my parcel would be delivered, then hurried off to his waiting ship, throwing the mooring-line off the bollard as he passed it. The crew shoved off, and the short manoeuvring oars began to beat the water.

A sailor had appeared on the deck of the nearest trireme. He was calling, waving his arms and gesturing to someone at the far end of the quay beyond my view, asking what was afoot. Two workmen came up from below to see. But otherwise the triremes were unmanned. Beyond, I saw Kratos's ship at the harbour entrance. The great striped sail dropped and filled out in the breeze; the crew busied themselves with the rigging.

All about me on the quay, men were leaving off what they were doing. I turned to go. And then I saw the first of the great painted Macedonian war-galleys rounding the sea wall, its deck bristling with armed soldiers.

But it was not the soldiers bearing down on me that made me gape and stare.

He was standing in the prow, with one arm slung around the carved painted figurehead. He had tied back his flaxen hair, and in his hand he brandished a sword.

He turned, smiling and laughing to those behind him. A chill went through me. My hands went cold, and my breath stopped in my throat. It was Dikaiarchos.

I don't know what my first thought was. All along the quay people were crying out and running towards the back streets. My ears rang with the sound of my own heart beating, and it seemed the world moved slowly, and the sounds came from a great distance. It was as if some dark inner part of me, some creature of my nightmares, had appeared before my eyes, and the rest of the world had dimmed. I glanced round. But I knew I should not run.

I turned back. Two more warships had appeared, entering the harbour at full speed, their oars thrashing the water. I saw Kratos's ship pass the end of the mole, where the lighthouse is, moving the other way. The Macedonians took no notice. Whatever they had come for, Kratos was no part of it.

I forced my thoughts into order. I was unarmed. I did not even have a hunting knife (something I always used to carry in Praeneste).

I cast my eyes about for something to use as a weapon. One of the workmen from the moored trireme shoved past me. 'Hey!' I cried. But he ran on, not heeding, his face a mask of terror.

The sailor who had been calling was staring now across the water at the approaching Macedonians. I could not tell if it was bravery that stopped him running, or fear. Then, as I looked, I saw a stack of javelins, stowed on the deck, not far from where he was standing.

I scrambled up the gangboard. The weapons had been strapped down. I began tugging at the leather binding. From the poop-deck the sailor shouted, 'You there! What are you doing?'

The binding came away and I pulled a spear from the top of the pile. 'I am going to fight,' I answered. 'And you?'

For a moment he stared at me as if it had occurred to him only now that there might be a battle. He was a young sea-cadet, an ephebe on military training. His first beard showed like fine down on his cheeks.

But whatever was going through his head took only a moment. He leapt down beside me, and seized a javelin from the pile. 'I fight,' he said, looking at me squarely.

And then we turned to face the enemy.

The first of the Macedonian warships had come

alongside. Troops were leaping down and forming a defensive circle. Then, seeing they were unopposed, they began swarming along the quay. The leading ship stood out. From the prow Dikaiarchos was shouting out orders, pointing and waving his arms. The harbour front was deserted, the ground strewn with abandoned carts and crates and baskets. The Athenians had clearly been taken by surprise. There was no sign of defenders anywhere.

The young Athenian beside me saw all this and met my eye. He had a gentle, expressive face. I could see his mind working in his features, summoning up his courage. His jaw firmed, and he gave an almost imperceptible nod, as if to say: If today is the day, then so be it – I shall die a credit to my people, and to myself. Then his muscles tensed, he balanced his spear in his hand, aimed it, and threw.

He had aimed well. The shaft sliced through the air and impaled a running soldier, catching him in the throat, where his cuirass did not protect him. Then I threw too, and hit the man behind him. We grabbed fresh spears from the stack and took aim for a second time.

All of a sudden, just as I was in the middle of my throw, the deck under me lurched, making me stumble and causing my spear-throw to falter. I swung round to look, thinking we had been rammed. Behind, on the side facing the water, the warship bearing Dikaiarchos had come alongside us. The Macedonians were struggling with ropes and hooks, preparing to board.

I ducked down and grabbed two more spears, tossing one to the Athenian. He caught it expertly with one hand

and we advanced together. The Macedonian troops were boarding now – warily at first, in case we had reinforcements waiting below. It would not take them long to realize we were alone.

But my mind was not on that: I was watching Dikaiarchos. From the Macedonian ship he was calling, 'Cut the lines – quickly now.' His fox's eyes were bright and darting; he wore a cuirass embossed with a bursting sun, and where his bare skin showed from under it, it was deep-tanned, brown as walnut. All the while, as he shouted out orders, he was smiling and laughing. He was enjoying himself, like some wild child let out to play.

I took careful aim.

Running feet sounded on the deck behind me. I should not get another chance. I inserted my finger in the javelin-thong, bent my knees, and balanced the shaft in my palm.

Dikaiarchos had been looking away. Just then, someone shouted up to him. He broke off what he was saying and began to turn. I drew the air into my lungs, and with a great cry and twist of my body I let the spear fly, just as his eyes met mine.

His brows went up. A look of surprise crossed his face. Then the javelin was home.

I had aimed for his throat. I do not know if my aim was bad, or whether the ships moved. The spear came to a jarring halt in the neck of the carved figurehead, at the place where his hand held it.

I stared, appalled, knowing I had no other chance. Then his hand moved, and I saw the smear of his blood on the painted wood.

There was no more time. The Macedonians were upon us. The young Athenian ephebe leapt down to the lower deck. Three of them rushed at him.

The first one he killed. I leapt across the deck, snatched up another javelin, and took aim. But even as I did so, someone seized me from behind, jerking my arm back, twisting the weapon from my hand.

I heard the Athenian cry out and turned my head. A group of Macedonians had closed around him. The steel of their swords flashed in the sun, crimson with his life-blood. He did not cry out again.

My other arm was pinned back. I could feel the heat of the man's body behind me. I held my breath and waited for the deathblow.

There was a pause. The blow did not come. Then I heard a voice saying, 'Leave him; leave him for me,' and Dikaiarchos stepped into view.

But he did not turn his attention to me straight away. For a while he was occupied with directing the men, calling to the ships, shouting orders across the quay. Men began to scramble below deck. Only then did I realize what was happening: the Macedonians were manning the triremes.

I turned my head. Already the mooring lines had been cut. They hung limply from their bollards. The ship was yawing, parting from the quay. Down below I could hear men taking their places on the rowing-benches, and the clatter of the oarlocks. Dikaiarchos was stealing the Athenian warships.

Order returned. The oars began to beat the water. The ship moved out into the middle of the harbour, gaining speed. I saw two troopers carry off the corpse of the young Athenian and sling him over the side. Then Dikaiarchos crossed the deck and stood before me.

I wondered whether he would know me; but he showed no signs of it.

He raised his left hand, holding it in front of my eyes. Blood oozed from a wound, where my javelin had pierced him. He glanced aside, and held out his arm, and at this the soldier beside him handed him his sword. I noticed, as he gripped it, his eyes narrowed momentarily in pain. Then he took a pace forward, and levelled the point at my throat.

The sunlight glanced off the flat of the blade, dazzling me. I waited for the final thrust. But with a sudden swift movement he drew the sword aside, and I felt the sting of the blade as it cut into my forearm.

'Like for like,' he said with a grim smile, and I realized he did not intend a swift death for me; he was going to torture me first.

'Kill me!' I yelled at him.

He stepped up close, and gripped my chin hard in his bloody hand. I could feel his breath, and smell the rank smell of his sweat and his blood. All the time his eyes were locked on mine; I felt the power of his life force like something surging and living within me.

He paused, then drew back grinning. 'Not now; there will be another time for us, my beautiful black-haired friend.'

Then his arm shifted, and he stood back.

He glanced to one side. We were far from the quay now, nearing the harbour entrance.

'It's a shame to cast you away,' he said. 'I could have enjoyed you; but I cannot have Romans here. Now let us see if you can swim.'

He turned to the Macedonian trooper beside him and said, 'Throw him off!'

EIGHT

'HOLD STILL, WILL YOU?'

'I am holding still.'

'It's as well you can swim.'

'Well I can. You know I can.'

'Even so, you shouldn't fight without the right weapon. It's madness. What did you think you were doing? Taking on the whole of Macedon yourself?'

'You're angry.'

He frowned at the bandage he was fixing on my arm and gave it another tug.

'Menexenos, listen. It was him. It was Dikaiarchos. I already told you.'

'I know; I know.'

'But you are angry all the same.'

'If he hadn't realized you were Roman, I'd be dressing your corpse, just as poor Eudoxos's father is doing.'

I fell silent, remembering the Athenian ephebe who had fought with me. I had seen his father's face, when he came to claim the body.

I said, 'Well I am here.'

'Yes. Some god is watching over you.' He paused and sighed. 'I don't want to lose you. Not yet. I have only just found you.'

We were sitting on the edge of the bed, side by side. Using my good arm I gently turned his face to mine, and kissed his mouth. 'You will never lose me, Menexenos.'

'I said keep still,' he said grumpily, pushing me away. But I could tell from his voice that he was softened.

I sat still, and he finished the last knot on the bandage.

'There, that should do it. Be careful not to knock it; it's your sword-arm, after all.'

He looked up towards the window. From outside, rising up from the agora and the street, came the angry buzz of many men's voices. The Council had called the people to assembly. They were waiting for the signal trumpet to sound, summoning them to the Pnyx. In the courtyard I could hear Kleinias talking to a group of his friends. Everywhere there was outrage.

'I'd better go,' said Menexenos. 'Lie down. Get some sleep.'

I lay on the bed and closed my eyes, and listened to the passing crowd. I wished I could go myself, to hear what the people said; but the assembly was only for citizens.

I must have drifted into sleep. I was woken by the sound of someone beating on the main outer-courtyard door. I heard the slave go hurrying. Then came the voice of Pomponius, demanding in his heavily accented Greek to see me.

'What did I tell you?' he cried, as soon as the slave brought him in. 'Not only have you not kept out of trouble, you have got yourself involved single-handedly in a war with Macedon. I should not have thought such a thing possible. The last thing I want, with matters as they are, is a diplomatic incident with King Philip.'

I began to explain how I had been in Piraeus by chance, how I had been caught by circumstance.

'Yes, yes,' he said, interrupting. 'Every fool blames Fate when it suits him. And I suppose it was Fate that prevented you running off, was it? The Athenians managed to flee successfully enough. But not you. What happened to your arm?'

I told him about my arm, and then asked if he had heard any more news.

'Well I was not there,' he said, giving me a pointed look, 'but I did hear that the pirate commander – what was his name . . .?'

'Dikaiarchos.'

'Ah yes; Dikaiarchos. I heard he tried to attack the military harbour first. He must have intended to set fire to the ship-sheds and burn the fleet while it was on the stocks. But the harbour entrance was chained and blocked. So he sailed round to the north side instead.'

In the end, he said, the Athenians had lost only four warships. 'Of course, they don't like it; but it would have been much worse if he had got at the main fleet. It is the effrontery of it that angers them most. They still like to think of themselves as the chief city in Greece, and to have some brigand come sailing into their great harbour as if it were the anchorage of some island pleasure resort and help himself to their warships is more than they can bear.'

I said, 'But where is Philip? He cannot be far away.'

Pomponius had crossed to the wall and was peering at the tapestry – a fine woven image of a crouching youth, fishing beside a stream. He dabbed at the threadbare material and frowned at it, wondering, I suppose, why something so old and dull should be in the house of a man like Kleinias.

'No one knows where he is,' he said, turning. 'Some say he is in Boiotia; others say he is in Euboia; others again that he has sailed round to Korinth, where he has a garrison.'

'Then could it not be, sir,' I asked, propping myself on my elbow and looking at him, 'that he might be preparing to attack? Or what was this morning's raid about?'

'Oh no,' he said, smiling tolerantly. 'You forget, Marcus, I am here. He would not dare attack while a Roman legation is in Athens. It would cause a scandal. Not even Philip would be so reckless.'

He chuckled, the expert diplomat amused at the fool. 'Oh no,' he said again. 'It will all blow over in a few days. For all their bluster and talk of war, even the Athenian Demos knows there is nothing they can do. Taking on Akarnania was one thing, an easy little war without pain – or so they thought. But now Philip has given them a warning, and they will heed it. They will not dare rouse the lion from his den.'

'So what will they do?'

'Talk. That is what they are good at. They will bark for a while, and then slink off back to their kennel.' He crossed to the window and looked out. 'Ah, at last. It sounds as if they're finished. Then I must go; I have arranged to meet the magistrates straight after the assembly.'

He wished me a brief good day, then said, 'Next time, use your legs and run, as everyone else did. You are not here to get involved in someone else's war.'

And then he left me.

The wound on my arm healed. When the bandage was off there was a long diagonal scar across my forearm: a memento, just as Dikaiarchos had intended.

Menexenos was training every day for the games, which were drawing near. As soon as I was up, I ran with him, out beyond the Akademy, along the banks of the Kephissos.

It was my first day out of the house since the raid on Piraeus, and I felt the mood of the city straight away. In the Street of the Tripods, on the way to the Dipylon Gate, people had left off their business and were gathered in small groups, grave-faced, nodding and talking.

'Are they afraid?' I said.

Menexenos tossed his head. 'Probably; but that is not what they are gossiping about. They are unhappy, because they have not yet found someone to blame. Eventually they'll settle on one of the port officials, or someone in the Council too weak to fight his corner. He will be punished, and then they will feel better.'

We passed out of the Gate, and took the track past the orchards and smallholdings, increasing our pace.

Menexenos, who was faster, could always beat me in a contest; but today he was going slowly, keeping beside me, breathing easily. We passed the Akademy gardens, then joined the path beside the Kephissos. It was a fine morning. Red poppies and clumps of white hemlock grew on the bank. Little brown fishes, startled by our shadows, darted in the clear water among the reeds.

Presently we left the suburbs behind and ran on beside green meadows.

'See there,' said Menexenos presently. 'It is just what I was talking of. Every day the people walk past it, yet they do nothing.'

In the distance, across the flower-studded fields, was the line of the Long Walls, which once had run all the way from Athens to Piraeus, linking the city with its harbour in an impregnable defence. Now sheep grazed among the neglected masonry. The grassy stones looked pretty in the morning light; pretty, but useless.

I said, 'Yet once they had the foresight to build such a thing. Why leave it now to crumble? Does no one tell them?'

'Yes,' he said. 'But when it comes to deciding how the treasury funds are spent, they vote not for defence of the city, but for festivals and the public dole. They are like the man who banquets every night, but neglects to fix the roof. The truth is, they have grown complacent, and soft with pleasure.'

'Well they can't have it both ways.'

'They think they can, because when the elections come, they choose the man who tells them so. In the end, good men stay silent, and tend their own gardens, and the walls crumble.'

I shook my head, and was about to draw my breath

to say more, when, up ahead, coming from the direction of Piraeus and the sea, I heard a din.

We looked at each other with the same thought, and turning off the path made for the Piraeus Gate. We were still perhaps two furlongs distant. But as we drew closer the noise resolved. It was not cries of battle, as I had supposed. It was the sound of men cheering.

As soon as we were inside the gateway Menexenos called to a stallholder who was hurriedly packing away his wares and asked what the fuss was. The man shook his head and carried on what he was doing. But then another, rushing up from the harbour, cried, 'Rejoice! They have brought back our ships!'

'What are you talking about, man? Who has brought them?'

He was already hurrying away, to be first at the city with the news. 'The Rhodians!' he cried over his shoulder. 'The Rhodians and King Attalos.'

We pushed through the crowd and emerged onto the waterfront. At the quayside, making fast, were the four Athenian triremes that Dikaiarchos had stolen; and all about them an escort of other warships, flying on their masts the standards of Rhodes and Pergamon. From the decks the sailors, dressed in their liveried uniforms, were waving and grinning and calling out to the crowd on the quay; and the crowd, wild with joy, were waving and cheering back at them.

Close by, a captain from the Pergamene fleet was telling those around him what had happened. We pushed up to listen.

They had been trying to engage the Macedonians, he

211

was saying, ever since Philip had raided the territory of Pergamon the previous year. As soon as they heard rumours that he was in the area, King Attalos had ordered them to put to sea. And so it was they were nearby, out in the gulf off Aigina, when Dikaiarchos launched his raid. They saw the Macedonians making off with the stolen Athenian triremes and gave chase, and, since the triremes were undermanned, they proved no match for the Rhodian and Pergamene ships with a full complement of rowers. Before long the Macedonians, seeing they could not escape, had abandoned their prizes and fled on their own ships.

'And Dikaiarchos?' I asked.

One of the Athenians in the crowd turned and said crossly to me, 'What does he matter, Roman? We have our warships back. Our honour is restored.'

The others loudly agreed, and I said no more. Dikaiarchos was my concern, not theirs.

Later that day the people met on the Pnyx, and passed a resolution inviting King Attalos to come from Aigina, which at that time he was visiting, and address the assembly. When he arrived, soon after, it seemed the whole body of citizens came out into the streets to cheer him, lining the route that led from the Dipylon Gate to the agora. At the head of the procession, basking in the adulation, was the chief Archon, and clustered around him the other magistrates of the city. People threw flowers. Everyone cheered and waved. It was like a festival.

I watched with Menexenos from the steps of the temple of Demeter. The potters' workshops and masons' yards and all the shops of the Kerameikos had closed for the day. The long colonnade was lined with people. Fires were kindled in bronze tripods on the altars, and not far from us, on the temple steps, a choir of boys, clad in white and garlanded with oak-crowns, sang a paean.

King Attalos was mounted on a fine chestnut mare with a scarlet saddlecloth fringed with bullion. The gold flashed and glittered in the sunlight as he moved. At the Dipylon Gate he dismounted; and the archons and leading men escorted him into the city among the exultant crowds.

From my vantage point on the temple steps I saw him pass. He was crowned with a gilded olive-spray, and wore a long mantle of brilliant white bordered with purple. I had never seen a king before. This man, measured and stately, wearing authority like an old familiar garment, seemed bred to it, and I said so to Menexenos.

'Oh no,' he replied. 'He is the first king of Pergamon, and before that he was no more than a general.' Whatever he seemed now, he said, was what he had made himself.

I looked again. He was closer now, and to my surprise I saw he was not some man of middle age, as I had first supposed. Even though he held himself well, with a soldier's straight-backed poise, he must have been well over sixty. His hair was as white as his mantle.

'How old is he?' I said to Menexenos.

'More than seventy,' he said, and laughed when he saw my face. He was at an age when most men, if they were alive at all, would be at home, sipping at a warm posset, fussed over by granddaughters and great-granddaughters.

Instead he was waging war against the mightiest power in Greece, and roaming the ocean in pursuit of Philip. I gazed at him with respect and awe.

Later the citizens were called to assembly and a letter from Attalos was read out, for he had told the archons he had rather not address the assembly himself. He reminded the Athenians of their friendship with Pergamon, and urged them now to join him in the struggle against Philip. Then the Rhodians spoke, urging the same, and when the vote came, it was for war.

It was Kleinias who recounted to me what had happened up on the Pnyx. I do not know what prompted me – perhaps something in his tone – but when he had finished I asked, 'Did anyone speak against?'

We were back at the house, in the enclosure behind the street, seated on the stone benches beneath the fig tree. By now evening was coming on, and the shadows were deepening around us. But I saw Kleinias stiffen, and knew then what had made me ask, and what his answer would be. In his brisk, formal voice he said, 'I spoke against.'

'But why, sir?' I asked, taken aback. For I too had been caught up in the general mood of joy, and it seemed right for the city to repay King Attalos and the Rhodians for what they had done.

He turned his head and looked me in the face. 'I reminded the assembly that Attalos's army is far away in Asia; and that the Rhodians are a sea power. If Philip moves against us he will come not by sea but by land, and neither of them will be able to help us. We shall be alone.'

214

He gave a weary gesture. 'The chief Archon responded that the Roman ambassador had told him Rome would come to our aid if Philip attacked. I asked him then if he had received a formal assurance, for I had not heard of it. To this he did not answer . . . I hope you will forgive me for saying this Marcus, when you are our guest, but if my own conversations with your ambassador Pomponius are anything to go by, the Roman Senate is in no mood for war, and even if that were not so, there is no Roman army anywhere in Greece.'

I nodded slowly, thinking how sure Pomponius had been that the Athenians would not dare rouse the lion from his den.

I asked what had happened next.

'My words were greeted with all the sullen displeasure against the sober man at the party, who, when the krater is still half full and the dancing-girls are coming on, reminds his guests of the sore heads they will have in the morning.' He gave a wan smile at his little joke. 'It is said the Persians have a wise custom. When a momentous decision is to be made, they consider it twice, once drunk, and once sober. That is a piece of good sense our citizens would benefit by. They are drunk on war. When their heads finally clear, it will be too late.'

He stood, but paused before he went inside and, looking up at the darkening evening sky, added, 'There is something that terrifies me in the spectacle of foolish people exercising power.'

When he had left I said to Menexenos, 'He looks ill.'

'It is no surprise: it was far worse than he told it. In the assembly he was shouted down, and afterwards, as he made his way out, he was jostled by the rabble. It was shameful. All he asked was for the people to consider, before they declared war, how they intended to fight it.'

Attalos left a token garrison at Piraeus and sailed away. Philip and the Macedonians were forgotten, and, with the games drawing near, Menexenos turned his mind to his training.

When he was not running out beyond the city, he went practising at the Lykeion. He had the ability, which came of discipline, to close his mind to his daily cares and focus his whole being upon his task. It was like watching a man engaged in some act of solitary worship. His face was calm, his body poised and graceful, his grey eyes lit by some inner light. At such times his beauty took my breath away, as much as when I had first seen him that day in Tarentum. Even now I could scarcely credit that, out of the entire world, he had chosen me as his friend. It seemed I could hope for no greater gift.

I went to watch when I could. But that summer I was taken up with a labour of my own.

I had brooded on my encounter with Dikaiarchos. The god had brought him to me, and I had failed. Questioning myself on this, I had decided I lacked fighting skill, and though I sensed the lack, I did not know how to remedy it.

One day, at the Lykeion, I asked Menexenos's trainer.

He listened, regarded me with an appraising eye, rubbed his chin, then said eventually, 'I know the man you need, but he will refuse to teach you.'

This answer made me all the more determined, and after some talk the trainer agreed to take me to the man's house. He was, he explained as we walked, a retired sword-master. His name was Antikles; and he was difficult.

I asked the trainer what he meant, and he replied, 'He takes some pupils, and refuses others. It is not a question of money. I have seen the sons of rich men beg him, but he will not have them at any price. He despises modern fashion; nor does he spare the rod. He is feared by many.'

But, he said, if I was determined, then it was up to me to persuade him, for there was no one better.

We came to his modest house, and found him in the courtyard, sitting beneath the awning, burnishing the wrought pommel of a sword.

He listened to what the trainer wanted. Then, without even looking at me, he said, 'I do not take new pupils. Goodbye.'

I looked at him. He had a short grey beard and was dressed in a simple homespun tunic. His body was tanned and lean. He must have been nearing sixty.

I remembered the trainer's words to me, and now, stepping up under the awning, I said, 'Sir, I have been told I have no more to learn of sword-work, and perhaps it is so. All I ask is that you grant me half a morning. If I see you have nothing to teach me, as I suppose, then I shall trouble you no further.'

At this, as I had hoped, he slowly turned. He placed the sword to one side, and from where it stood propped against the wall he took up his osier cane.

I remained where I was in front of him. If he intended

to strike me for my insolence I had already determined I should take it without flinching.

But he did not strike. For a long time he looked into my face. Then he said, 'How old are you, boy?'

'Eighteen, sir.'

'Eighteen, and you suppose you have nothing to learn? What kind of fool are you?'

'I have trained hard. I know what I know. But I do not know enough for what I need.'

He considered me carefully, tapping the cane on the flags as he did so. Then, after a long pause, he said, 'I shall be at the grove of Wolf-Apollo at first light tomorrow. If you do not know where it is, find out. Be on time. I shall not wait.'

It was still dark when, next day, I made my way out to the Lykeion gardens, to the sacred grove where the marble statue of Apollo stands on a stone plinth, his hand stretched out, a lyre at his side, and a she-wolf at his feet.

I waited, shuffling about at the foot of the statue in the cool dawn, glancing out at the path from the city along which Antikles would come.

Suddenly, so close that it made me start, there was a stirring in the dark shadows, and he stepped out. I had not even seen him.

'What is that?' he said, scowling at the sword in my hand.

'My sword,' I said defensively. It was the old warrior's sword from Praeneste.

He took it from me and looked at it, holding it up to the brightening horizon, then balancing it in his hand.

After some little time of this he said, 'It is well made. A noble sword. But too heavy for you. You will need to build your arms and shoulders. Have you fought with it?'

'No, sir.'

He nodded, and then gave the sword back to me. 'No, I can see you haven't. Well, you have set yourself a hard task. Now strip, and we shall see what you can do.'

By the time the gymnasion started to fill in mid-morning I was bruised and sore and sweating. Antikles had not even taken off his tunic. It was as clean as when he had arrived.

In all the time we sparred he had hardly spoken. And yet, by his movements, he had conversed more eloquently than any words, showing me my errors, bringing forward my weak points so that it seemed I saw them clearly for the first time.

At the end, when I lay panting in the dirt after yet another fall, he stood over me, pressed me down with his foot on my chest, pointed the blade at my throat, and said, 'You are dead. Do you know why?'

'No,' I said, lying splayed beneath him.

He removed his foot.

'Get up.'

I got up.

'Now do you think I have nothing to teach you?'

I shook my head. 'I know nothing at all,' I said bitterly. And though, before, I had exaggerated in order to persuade him, now truly it seemed to me that all the skill I had prided myself in was no more than a conceit of knowledge, if this old man three times my age could crush me so easily.

I hung my head, then yelped and jumped back as he struck me suddenly with his cane.

'Do not tell me what you know is false. You fight better than many, and you know it. But do you know why?'

I shook my head, and then said, 'No, sir.'

'Because you are angry, that's why. It shines in your eyes like fire. It gives you something others lack. But beware, young man, of anger. It drives you, but it may also kill you.'

He struck me again, hard.

'That is for remembrance. Now go and wash the dust from your mouth, and be here tomorrow at dawn.'

When I returned to the house, the slave looked with alarm at my grazed arms and legs, sent for warmed water, healing herbs and a sponge; and then, while he helped me clean my wounds, told me a sailor had called that morning with a letter.

He brought the letter. It was from Caecilius, and was a catalogue of his own concerns as dreary as if I had never gone away. He had been in Rome; he had met some rich senator who could help him; he had his eye on a new military contract in Gaul; he was planning to visit Kerkyra once more, and perhaps Patrai. At the end he reminded me to keep my eye out for opportunity: with Philip striking fear into all of Greece there would be something of advantage, and he relied on me to tell him.

All this I read with little interest. But as I unfurled the last of the scroll a separate note dropped on the ground at my feet. I picked it up, and saw it was written in Mouse's careful hand.

She wrote: 'Caecilia to her brother Marcus, my special greetings. The books you sent arrived. Thank you; thank you. You cannot know what joy they bring me. They sit on my table, and when I look at them I think of you so far away. Your mother is well, and sends her good wishes. The farm is as it was. So is my father. We are sad to say he will soon be leaving us once more on business. But we are confident we shall cope without him. We have assured him he must look to his business interests above all else. He says he will be in Greece. If so you may see him. Be well. Do not forget me.'

I set the note aside. Caecilius would have read her letter before enclosing it with his, and she had written with that knowledge in mind. I smiled to myself. Her true thoughts, disguised from him, were clear enough to me, as she intended.

Later, returning from the Lykeion, Menexenos exclaimed, 'By Zeus, look at you! Were you set upon in the street?'

'Don't joke. It was Antikles.'

'Well he knows what he's about. I've been asking at the gymnasion, and everyone says so. And now I see the proof.'

I threw him a grim smile, and rubbed at my bruises.

In the days that followed I received many sound beatings from Antikles. Each day, when he had finished, he would say, 'Have you had enough yet?' and stubbornly I would say, 'No.'

Everything I thought I knew he managed to unravel.

And yet, for all the humiliation I felt, I knew I had found the man I needed. I clung to him like a limpet, and he would have had to kill me before I admitted defeat.

One early morning a few days later, when I arrived at our meeting place beside Wolf-Apollo, he said, 'Let us go for a walk.'

We took the country path out along the bubbling Eridanos, past the orchards and fields, and up the wooded slopes of Lykabettos hill.

Antikles said, 'Are you hurting?'

My pride wanted to tell him no. But I had learned he had no tolerance for dishonesty of any sort, and so I answered, 'Yes I am.'

'Then good. That is as it should be. Better these bruises than death on the battlefield. Or do you disagree?'

'No, sir.'

We walked on. He had not told me where we were going, and I had not asked. But after some time we came out at a clearing, and here Antikles said we should pause.

I glanced about. One of his lessons was that I must always be aware of what was around me. I knew by now that everything he did had purpose. I did not intend to be caught off guard.

Beneath a twisted wild olive, half hidden in the dappled shade, was an old stone altar, crudely hewn, and behind it a little shrine to Artemis the Huntress, overgrown with honeysuckle and ivy.

Already we had climbed a long way, and looking out over the plain I could see Athens spread below us: the agora and streets, the high-city with its temples, the Lykeion, and, further off, within the glittering stream of the Kephissos, the red tiles of the Akademy hidden among its dense-growing gardens.

Antikles sat down, holding his cane before him. 'We have reached a fork in the road,' he said.

I looked at him puzzled, wondering what I had missed; but he went on, 'You have made yourself strong, and I commend you for it. You fight well, with determination and skill. I commend you for that too.'

'Yet it is not enough,' I said flatly.

'For a man like you, who wants to put his hand into the fire, no. You cannot rely on your strength alone . . . or your anger. That path does not lead where you want to go.'

I cried out in frustration. 'What more is there? I have given everything I have!'

He regarded me silently from under his heavy brows, with a calm patient expression, as if he had expected this outburst. Eventually, realizing this, I let out my breath and sat down on the grass at his feet, and waited.

'I do not ask you to give,' he said quietly. 'I ask you to see.' He paused, then went on. 'You are full of rage and desire. You think you can crush it, but no man has that power.'

'What then?' I said, looking up at him.

'You must tame it, as the rider tames the wild horse. You must make yourself its master. You must search out what is dearest in your soul; and when you find it you must lay it bare . . . No, do not shake your head. I can see in your face that you understand. I saw it at the first. That is why I took you on.'

I drew a long breath. Somewhere on the mountain,

over the sound of the chirping cicadas, a kite screamed, lone and piercing. It screamed for me, calling from some other world. I was warm from the climb; yet I shivered.

'You see into my soul,' I said. 'But what has this to do with sword-fighting?'

He shifted, and looked me in the eyes. 'Everything. It has to do with being the best. And for that you must first be master of yourself.'

The days passed.

When I was not occupied with Antikles, I went to the Lykeion and watched Menexenos as he trained, standing in the long colonnade with the usual crowd of spectators and suitors and passers-by.

His diskos throw had come on well, and his running too. As for the wrestling, he said little about it. It depended, he told me, on whom he was pitted against in the contest. 'And that,' he said, 'lies with the gods, if the gods concern themselves with such things.'

It was a strange, restless time in the city, and I was glad I had my own business to concentrate upon. In the streets and the agora, everyone talked of war. Yet the days were calm, and life went on unchanged.

Pomponius, after his initial surprise, said it would come to nothing, that Philip had taken fright and would not dare give offence to Rome. When I mentioned this to Kleinias he frowned and said, 'Yes, yes, so everyone says; but where, then, is Philip?' And he was right, for no one, it seemed, was able to say.

One afternoon, when we had both finished with our

training for the day, Menexenos and I went out walking, and at length we found ourselves in the Outer Kerameikos, where the old tombs are. Passing one, I paused and looked, for something about it had caught my eye.

It was a weathered old stele with a tall white oleander growing in front, half obscuring it from the path. The paint on the sculpture was faded almost to stone, but the tale the carving told was clear. It showed two friends, their hands clasped in farewell, with a dog grieving at their feet.

I stepped up, and rubbed away the lichen from the carved inscription. Below the frieze were the words, 'Passing stranger, tell your friends that in this tomb rest Krates and Polemon, great-spirited men who lived a life of wisdom and now share bright immortality.'

I looked at it, and all of a sudden I was seized by grief, so much so that I blinked and wiped my eyes.

'Why so sad?' said Menexenos, stepping up beside me and touching my shoulder.

I shook my head. 'I was thinking,' I said, gazing at this forgotten monument to friendship, 'that life is short. No sooner does summer come than winter is in the air. Who remembers these two friends now? Even their tomb will soon be dust.'

He closed his hand gently on the back of my neck, kneading the muscles there. 'They had what they had. This stone was placed here so men might remember them for a short while. You are right; even stone crumbles. Yet what they had was real, and it lives still, for it has the power to touch your soul. So why be sad, when you have seen beauty?'

I nodded and smiled, and put away my grief. I often think he had the power to see further than I. For he saw light, where I saw only darkness. He saw the good in everything.

Half a month later, in the middle of the night, I was roused from a deep sleep by the sound of shouting in the street outside.

At first I turned over, thinking it was drunken revellers. But then what I heard made me leap up, for a man in the street was crying out, 'The Macedonians! The Macedonians are coming!'

I leapt from my bed and threw open the shutters. Already, up on the hill, lights were kindling. One moment, it seemed, there was this one man's voice. Then, all over Athens, there was shouting, dogs barking, and lamps appearing in windows and doorways.

A night-time watchman, up in the high pass at Dekeleia, had been the first to catch sight of Philip's troops. It was a dark night with no moon, and he would not have noticed them at all except, by chance, he heard the distant stumbling of a baggage-mule. Then, looking more carefully, he had seen them on the ridge, their torches extinguished, a faint moving shadow against the backdrop of the stars.

Immediately the captain of the fort dispatched his fastest runner, a victor in the long-race who knew the goat-tracks and secret paths. He ran through the night. But for him, the city would have been taken with the citizens still in their beds.

The alarm sounded on the high-city, summoning the reserves to the walls. In the house, Menexenos and Kleinias strapped on their armour, and Lamos the slave-boy counted the javelins in the holsters, and readied their swords. Then they were gone, and the room was still.

I turned to Lamos and said, 'What now?'

He shrugged. He was a stocky Thracian with a square, serious face and a mass of unruly red hair. He said, 'We wait.'

I sat down on the couch, and immediately stood up again. 'I cannot wait and do nothing. I'm going to fetch my sword.'

'But Marcus, sir. You are Roman, not Athenian. Besides, you have no armour.'

'The mercenaries have been called out; they are not Athenian either. And what difference one more?'

I hurried upstairs and fetched my sword from the chest in my room. It felt as familiar to me now as my own limbs. During my time with Antikles the muscles in my arms and sides had grown and hardened. The sword moved with my thoughts. I no longer sensed its weight.

I found Menexenos up on the high walkway above the Dipylon Gate. Seeing me he frowned, and opened his mouth to speak. But in the end only nodded.

I peered out through the crenels into the darkness. 'What news?' I said.

'Nothing yet.' He pointed northwestward. 'They will come from that way, down from Parnes.'

I stared out. Everything was still. Stars glimmered in a clear sky. In the distance was a deeper blackness, where the mountains rose up from the plain. It seemed a night like any other. It was hard to believe that Philip's army was somewhere out there, bearing down on us.

Menexenos called to a youth standing near. 'Lysandros, run down to Hippokrates' training ground and ask for one of their spare cuirasses, and see what else they can give you.'

'Yes, Menexenos,' said the boy adoringly, glad to be of use, his young face full of moment. He hurried off down the ladder. Under his breath Menexenos said, 'Curse you, Marcus; I knew you would come. But this is not your battle.'

I said, 'Remember what you said after Piraeus. I am here beside you. There is nowhere else I belong.'

He frowned at me, and tried to look disapproving.

The night wore on. Some time before dawn, scouts reported that Philip's army was on the plain. By now the city was lit up like a beacon. The lights must have told him his attempt at surprise had failed.

Presently someone said he had slowed his advance. There was no more need for hurry. Now he would wait for daylight.

At the time when the black of night begins to grey we saw them, a long line of men like a moving shadow, with the baggage-train coming up behind.

They halted a mile from the walls, and spread out along the bank of the Kephissos, and around the Akademy gardens. A band of red showed over the distant ridge of Hymettos; the birds began to chatter, and along the wall the order went out to douse the torches.

Down below in the street, on the city side of the

towered gateway, came the rustle and whisper of assembling men.

'What are they doing?' asked the youth called Lysandros, peering down.

Just then Kleinias appeared. He acknowledged me without much surprise, and cast a quick frown at the old cuirass and greaves I had strapped on. Menexenos said, 'Father, what's happening down there?'

'The Strategos,' answered Kleinias, in a flat weary voice, 'has given the order to attack. He proposes to rush out at first light and surprise the Macedonians.'

Menexenos glanced over his shoulder to see who was listening. Apart from me, no one else was in close earshot.

'What?' he said. 'Has he lost his mind?'

'He thinks it a clever ruse. He is gathering all the men he can find.'

'But it will be a slaughter!'

Kleinias paused. 'Pray God it is not; for we are ordered down there.' He looked at me. 'Not you, Marcus. There is no need.'

'Forgive me, sir,' I said straight away. 'But I am coming too.'

He sighed and shook his head. 'In that case, somebody had better find you a shield.'

We gathered in the wide-open space behind the gateway. As I took my position, some of the men around me patted my back and mumbled thanks. But mostly they just stared ahead, tense and silent, their hands clenching and unclenching on their sword-hilts as they dwelt upon their private thoughts. I saw old grandfathers there, white-haired gentlemen dressed in antique armour that could not have seen service for a generation. Further up the line, under the gatepost, the youth Lysandros was standing with some older men, doing his best to look brave. Menexenos saw him too, and with a squeeze of my arm went off to speak to him. I could not hear what he said, but the boy's face lit up and he nodded, and he came back with Menexenos to stand between us.

Above the gate towers the sky showed in long ragged strands of pink. From somewhere behind, the Strategos barked out an order. The bolts grated in their courses, and the gates swung slowly open. Then a man's voice sounded the long note of the paean, and all around the others took it up, until it was an echoing roar that fired the blood. Then we surged forward, out into the dawn.

Even in those first moments I sensed a faltering, just as a running man, seeing some unseen obstacle in his path, will try to alter his course, though he knows it is too late. It was little wonder. Most of the men had not been up on the walls: they had not seen the extent of Philip's army.

Ahead, all along the Macedonian line, orders rang out and trumpets sounded. The Strategos had been right in one thing: they had not expected us. But if they were surprised, it was the surprise of the lion that wakes to find the antelope has wandered into his den.

But it was too late for questioning. We fought among the orchards and paddocks and farmsteads, backing against walls, racing through barns, stumbling through pens among outraged geese and chickens. The Macedonians were slow to meet us, but when they did they converged from all sides, using their long pikes when they could, fighting hand to hand when there was no space.

Our line, such as it was, quickly broke and scattered. I found myself fighting around a wooden barn on the edge of an olive grove. The boy Lysandros had kept at my side, and there were some others with us I did not know. I looked round for Menexenos but could not see him. I guessed he had stayed with Kleinias, but there was no time to consider this, for just then, ahead and to the side of us, a troop of Macedonians came through the trees at the double.

We engaged them on the edge of the olive plantation, where a shallow ditch ran. For a while we held them back, and I was just starting to think they might withdraw when another troop came advancing from the other side, along the path beside the barn.

As he passed, one of the Macedonians cast a torch into the dust-dry hay inside. It caught immediately with a roar, and the flames leapt up. I turned my back on the fire and faced the advancing men. Then, behind me, from within the barn, I heard a scream – a woman's voice. She must have hidden there when the city gates were closed.

Someone rushed past me, in among the hay bales. It was Lysandros.

'Wait!' I cried, but he ran on.

By now Macedonians were coming at us from all sides. We were hopelessly outnumbered. Quickly I glanced round.

Dense smoke was curling from the high doorway of the barn. Already flames were licking at the straw beneath the tiles. I could not see Lysandros. I called his name. Then the woman screamed again, her voice full of terror. I beat back the man I was fighting, then ducked under the fiery lintel and ran inside.

Immediately I saw what had delayed Lysandros. A wall of flame divided one side of the barn from the other. On the far side of it a woman was crouching in an empty stall. Lysandros, his forearm over his face, was doing his best to beat down the fire with the flat of his sword; but as soon as he scattered the burning hay it settled and caught elsewhere.

I paused, stepped back three paces, then took a run and leapt through the flames. I ran to the woman, seized her by the arm, and pulled her up. At first she followed; then, seeing I was pulling her into the fire, she began to fight me, beating at my cuirass with her free hand.

'Stop!' I yelled. Then she just went limp and trembled, like a caught bird.

I half-heaved, half-threw her back the way I had come. The air seared my lungs. I could smell the hairs on my legs and forearms as they singed in the heat. And then we were through to the other side. I threw the whimpering girl into Lysandros's arms. 'Get her back to the city!' I cried. Then we both turned as four Macedonians darkened the only exit.

They were grinning, and I saw my death in their faces. The flames were closing on us. They could see we had nowhere to run. They began to advance, side by side.

I stilled my mind, as Antikles had taught me. Silently I said a prayer to Mars, God of War, and to Wolf-Apollo. And then I sprang.

One of the Macedonians, thinking I was as good as dead, was already casting hungry eyes at the woman. I knew the look. I had seen it in the Libyan, years before.

It was he I killed first. The other I took on my backward swing, while he was still staring in surprise at his dying comrade. Then Lysandros came at the third, driving him back, and I took the fourth.

'Now go!' I shouted, pushing him and the woman out through the burning doorway.

There is victory to be found even in the midst of defeat, and this was mine. As soon as I was outside once more I could hear the cries of the scattered Athenians, calling on each other to retreat. I covered Lysandros's path long enough for him to get away, then drew back towards the road.

It was there I saw Menexenos.

He was surrounded by three Macedonians, and a line of others was approaching from the orchard behind. I let out a yell and ran at them, killing one and wounding another. This gave the others pause. They hesitated and drew back, suspecting, I think, that I was the vanguard of some new force that was coming at them. It gave us enough time to withdraw.

From everywhere the Macedonians were surging forward to the walls.

As we fell back I noticed, at the head of their line, a man with a cropped black beard and gold-embossed armour, decorated with the sunburst emblem of Macedon. No one needed to tell me who he was. Even in the midst of battle, where he could easily be struck down, King Philip was wearing the royal diadem. He advanced with his men, leading from the front, and in that moment it came to me that not once had I set eyes on the Athenian Strategos. All I had heard was his disembodied voice, from somewhere behind, giving the order to attack.

The last defensive lines collapsed. The air was full of smoke, and the cries of the wounded. As I retreated I tripped on a corpse. It was one of many, and I took no notice. But then I saw something that made me pause and look again.

It was the simple wrought pommel that lay in the man's outstretched hand. I knew the sword. I had seen it many times, held over me, poised for the deathblow. It belonged to Antikles.

He was lying on his side, in a pool of his own blood, and I saw he had been run through from behind. His mouth and eyes were open still, but his spirit had left him.

By now the others were calling urgently to me. The gates were closing. But still I waited.

I knelt down and closed his eyes, and straightened his spattered tunic, and thanked him for all he had taught me, in case, perhaps, from some place where the dead go, he might hear me.

As I stood to leave my eyes fell on the sword again. I took it up. I knew he would have wished it.

Thereafter, the Athenians did not venture from behind their walls. The Macedonians, who could not storm them, fell back and made camp.

That day the city streets echoed with the wailing of

women. Later, the Strategos, the Archon, and the leading magistrates met in council, and put out after that it was a great victory that Philip had been repulsed from the walls.

Some – those who will cling to any delusion of good news rather than face the truth – were taken in by this. But, as Kleinias said to me later, all that had been achieved was that men were dead who, but for this pointless action, would be taking bread that night with their friends and wives and children.

I washed the filth from my body, went to bed, and slept. At dawn the slave roused me from a deep sleep. A messenger had called: Pomponius wished to see me at once.

I went angrily. No doubt someone had told him I had fought with the Athenians, and he would have a lecture to deliver. I was in no mood for it. My body was sore, and it had taken me a long time to get to sleep. Antikles's death had hit me hard. As I lay staring into the darkness, words of his had come back to me. He had said, only a few days before, that the man who lives each day fearing death dies a thousand times. Now he was gone. I had been his last pupil.

Pomponius's opulent residence lay on the far side of the city, in the fashionable quarter near the precinct of Olympian Zeus.

It was still only first light when I arrived, but already there was a crowd of clients waiting in the courtyard. I recognized the chief Archon, standing with a group of magistrates from the Council, talking urgently with members of the Roman legation.

'Ah, Marcus, there you are,' cried Pomponius, emerging from under the portico.

He beckoned to the Archon – a thin bony-cheeked man with quick, prominent eyes. I remembered how Kleinias, who did not like him, had said he was a clever speaker in the assembly, with the common touch. Now he merely looked pale and startled.

Pomponius turned to me, and declaimed in a booming voice intended for everyone, 'Well I imagine you have heard of yesterday's battle. Philip knows a Roman legation is here. And yet he dares to attack, even while we are in the city. It is an outrage!'

'It is contempt,' chimed the Archon.

'A deliberate insult,' said the man next to him.

'Deliberate,' agreed Pomponius, whose vanity had clearly been stoked with a good deal of this before I arrived. 'An affront to the whole legation . . . and to the Senate and People of Rome.'

All about us, voices rose in indignant complaint.

I said, 'You sent for me, sir? The messenger said it was urgent.'

'It is! I am going to speak to Philip myself. I am going to demand an explanation.'

'You, sir?'

'Well, all of us; not just me. You are a Roman, and a friend of Titus: I should like you to be with us. The more Romans the better . . . and it would do no harm if Titus were to hear of this.'

I asked what he proposed to tell Philip.

'Tell him? Why, that this must stop. What else? It

must stop *immediately*. He must withdraw out of Attika. He must pay reparations.'

He puffed out his cheeks and searched the faces crowding round; and at this everyone began speaking at once, encouraging him, praising his wisdom.

When I could be heard again I said, 'But what if he does not listen? It was Athens, after all, that declared war; not Philip.'

I had raised my voice to be heard over the din. Now, all of a sudden, there was silence.

I glanced round. The Archon, and magistrates, and clerks, and members of the legation, were staring at me. One might have supposed I had committed the grossest impropriety, or that they had not considered this question at all.

'Not listen?' exclaimed Pomponius, his heavy chin shaking as the words rolled off his tongue. And then – for the silence had continued, and everyone's eyes were upon him – 'Why, he would not dare – But if he does, then he may consider himself at war not only with Athens, but with Rome as well.'

He had spoken, uttering these words before half the government of the city. His large, jowly mouth set firm; but for a moment I saw a flash of doubt in his eyes. It was too late. The words were out. Everyone had heard them, and even now those at the back were repeating them to the others. No retraction was possible.

I saw the beginnings of a smile form on the Archon's thin lips. He glanced aside, and coughed, bringing up a concealing hand. I realized he had got what he wanted:

he had roused Pomponius into a frenzy of grandiose booming anger. He had led him on, like a muleteer dangling a carrot.

There was no more time to urge him to reconsider. He intended to march out of the city and confront Philip at his camp. When I tried to speak again he waved me silent, and hurried off to his rooms, saying he must dress for the meeting.

I waited in the courtyard with the others. Presently he emerged, got up in a heavy, embroidered woollen robe edged with purple, clasped with an elaborate brooch of gold torque-work studded with lapis, with a gilded olive-spray perched upon his large balding head.

I noticed one or two of the Greeks exchange glances. Athenians, as a rule, do not care for ostentation, thinking it vulgar. I stared at him. He looked like some rich Sicilian merchant on his way to a late-night drinking party.

Soon after, we set out, taking the street towards Dipylon Gate.

The Archon, who had been rather silent, came up, and in a lowered voice said perhaps, after all, it would be better if he himself were not present at this meeting with Philip: there was, he felt, too much bad feeling between Macedonians and Athenians . . . he should have thought of it earlier . . . he did not wish to jeopardize success . . .

'—Yes, yes, as you wish,' said Pomponius, not really listening.

The Archon dropped back, leaving Pomponius, and a few members of the Roman legation – and me – to exit through the city gate.

We took the path to the complex of buildings known

as the gymnasion of Kynosarges. I knew it well, having walked there often with Menexenos. There was a dense shading wood of cypresses and low pines, and, in the middle, a temple of Herakles. It was here the Macedonians had made their camp.

As we approached, I could see the troops' bivouacs suspended among the trees. Smoke from cooking fires curled up into a clear sky. They had raided the smallholdings, and the air was pungent with the tang of roasting meat.

When we were perhaps two-thirds of the way to the camp there arose a stirring, and moments later a band of uniformed men rode out on horseback.

'Let them approach,' said Pomponius, extending his arm in a gesture for us to halt.

We waited.

The front rider was a middle-aged man clad in a short cavalryman's tunic and a gilded cuirass. He dismounted a few paces off, removed his plumed helmet of scarlet horsehair, and strode the rest of the way on foot. He had a proud, handsome face, and dark, intelligent eyes. I knew it had been a sign of respect for him to dismount and remove his headgear. He could easily have ridden right up to us and addressed us from his horse.

Pomponius peered at him, narrowing his eyes against the sharp sunlight. Then he proceeded to make an embarrassing show of looking this way and that across the empty open ground, like a buffoon at the theatre who has lost his mule, before he said, 'Where is Philip? I do not see Philip.'

The Macedonian officer stiffened.

'The King is elsewhere,' he replied. 'I am here in his place. My name is Philokles. I am senior commander here.'

'—I don't care who you are,' Pomponius interrupted. 'I am the Roman ambassador to Athens, and I sent word that I wished to speak to Philip. Now go and summon him.'

If I had been anywhere else, I think I should have turned and gaped. Instead I stood rigid, like a soldier on parade. Pomponius never took much trouble with his Greek, and I believe, at first, the Macedonian thought he had misheard. For a brief moment he looked into the ambassador's face with a searching look of surprise, and his eyes strayed up to the large gilded olive-spray perched upon his head. Then his face set firm, and in a different, harder voice he said, 'King Philip is elsewhere, as I have told you. So say what you wish to say, or go back to the city.'

Pomponius glared. By now the sun was well up in the sky, and on the dusty road where we stood there was no shade. His fleshy face was growing crimson, and little beads of black-coloured sweat had begun to form where his dyed, carefully arranged hair met his neck and ears.

He glanced behind him at the junior legates and at me, with a face that said, 'What now?' Then he turned back, and in a voice quivering with outrage he spluttered, 'This is wholly unacceptable. I demand that you withdraw.'

Philokles looked him square in the face. 'Why are you here, Roman? Our business is with the Athenians, who declared war on us. Are they too afraid even to venture from behind their walls? What are you? Their herald? Have you come to tell us they surrender?'

Pomponius hesitated. I think only then did it occur to him that the Archon had pushed him into an impossible position. By now he was sweating heavily. His face was blood-red, though I could not tell whether this was from the heat or his anger. Beside me the junior legates exchanged glances, wondering whether to interrupt. If Philip was not there, Pomponius had an excuse to withdraw and reconsider. But before anyone could step up and whisper in his ear, urging him to do this, he had resumed speaking.

'Well if Philip will not come, then you can tell him this: in the name of the Senate and People of Rome, I forbid him to make war on Athens or any Greek city. I order him to withdraw immediately from Attika; and I demand compensation for the injuries done to the Athenians.'

Then he swung round, said 'Come along' to the rest of us, and strode off ahead, back to the Dipylon Gate, where the Athenians were watching from the walls, his heavy purple-edged cloak billowing behind him.

We did not have long to wait before Philip gave us his answer.

NINE

FIRST THE GROVE AROUND Kynosarges and the temple of Herakles went up in flames. Next was the turn of the Lykeion. We watched from the walls as the pines flared against the sky, engulfing everything – the colonnades from where I had watched Menexenos and his friends practise for the games; the bath-house, the public rooms with their lecture rooms and sculptures and fine paintings; even the sacred grove around Wolf-Apollo, which everyone thought would be spared out of reverence for the gods.

But the Lykeion was only the beginning. Next the Macedonians turned their attention to the Akademy, a place renowned throughout all Greece for its learning and excellence. I saw grown men with tears streaming down their faces as they watched helpless as fire raged through the school and library and tended gardens. There was nothing of military advantage to be gained by such destruction. It was, they said, the accumulated wisdom of all humanity they were destroying.

Next, Philip divided his army, leaving Philokles outside the walls of Athens to keep us penned in there, while
he marched on Piraeus.

I thought of the neglected Long Walls, by which the
Athenians might have moved in safety between the city
and the port. Now they stood in ruins. Piraeus, though so
close, had to look to its own defence as best it could.

Yet, by the favour of some god, and the stubbornness
of its small garrison, Piraeus held. Frustrated, Philip took
out his anger on the surrounding countryside, setting fire
to everything that would burn, and tearing down every
temple and shrine and object of beauty or veneration he
found. From the walls we watched the smoke rise all over
Attika as fields and farms were put to the torch.

When, finally, there was nothing left to destroy or
steal, and nothing for the army to feed on, the Macedonians withdrew, back the way they had come, northwards
over the passes to Boiotia. On the day afterwards, I rode
out with Menexenos and his father to see what had
become of the farm.

The road beyond the city was strewn with shards.
Even the dead had not been spared Philip's wrath. The
shards were the remains of funeral vases, which had stood
over the tombs that lined the road. The tombs, too, had
been smashed; human bones lay over the scorched earth,
spilled from their broken sarcophagi. In the rural demes
the little rustic temples with their wooden posts and straw
roofs had been set alight. The images of the gods lay
toppled.

Kleinias was not a man to make a display of his
emotion. But as we came upon some new piece of wanton

destruction he would shake his head, or comment on whose wasted land we were passing.

At one point, when we were beyond Hymettos, Menexenos said, 'Father, go back to the city. We can do this another day.'

'No,' he said. 'It must be faced.'

Mount Paneion appeared in the distance, and we turned down the track that led to the farmstead. Even from here I could see the blackened terraces on the slopes, where the vineyard had been.

Presently we began to pass grotesque, charred stumps in the fire-scorched fields. They were the carcasses of sheep. What the Macedonians had not eaten, or carried off, they had slaughtered, then burnt along with the crops.

Near the house the olive grove, the patient work of generations, had been hacked down and set alight. But by then we could see what they had done to the house itself. The walls still stood. But the roof was gone, and the windows were like eyeless sockets, black with soot.

For a while Kleinias just sat on his horse and stared, like a man who has fallen into a waking dream. Then he dismounted. I thought he would fall, but he leant on the horse to steady himself.

'They have taken your grey colt,' he said in a strange, slow voice, as if that were the only thing amiss among the devastation.

'Yes, Father, the colt is gone; but we shall get another.'

He nodded, and repeated, 'We shall get another.'

Menexenos caught my eye, with a look that said, 'We must get him away from this.' But already, with sudden purpose, Kleinias had struck out towards the house.

The antique tables with their delicate marquetry, the fine chests, the couches inlaid with ivory and silver, were burned to dust. Here and there in the charcoal I saw the stump of a fluted chair-leg, or some scrap of cushion that the fire had somehow missed. Through the soles of my boots I could feel the heat still, coming up from the flags.

When I looked up, Kleinias was staring at the ledge. It took me a moment to realize what had been there. Then, with an odd cry, he went stumbling across the room and fell to his knees, and began rummaging in the debris.

'Leave it Father,' said Menexenos, stepping up. 'Let us go.'

But Kleinias did not seem to hear. He raised his hand and stared at what he held there. It was a shard of pot, red on black. Even from where I stood, I could see the painted image. It was the head of a diskos-thrower, crowned with a victory wreath.

Then Kleinias spoke, and his voice was strange and weak and distant. 'It is enough,' he whispered. 'A man can endure only so many defeats.'

It seemed then that his strength left him, and he would have fallen prone in the black dust if Menexenos had not rushed forward and caught him.

'No, Father,' he cried, stricken, 'it will be well again; I will make it well again. Come now, back to the city. There is nothing for us here.'

Between us we got him outside once more. His arm was shaking. He blinked at the sunlight with empty eyes. A cold finger of fear and horror crept down my backbone, at the sight of such nobility brought low. It was as if his very soul had been extinguished.

We got him back to the city, but he was not the same man who had left it earlier that day.

All the way back, Menexenos kept talking to him: simple reassuring words. But his father did not respond, or even seem to hear. He just stared into the distance, swaying with the movement of the horse.

I could have wept to see their pain, but weeping would do no good, and so I just spoke occasionally, and took care of small things, and made sure Kleinias did not fall.

I had no words that would do justice to his grief, and eventually I gave myself up to my own thoughts, recalling to mind what Titus had once said, that a man has nothing unless he can defend it; that without that, no precious or beautiful or beloved thing is secure, for there are always men who will destroy what some other man has built.

Athens had once been the proud leader of all Greece. Now she had let herself fall to this. And it was not by fate; nor was it by the passing of time. It was by listening too long to the voices of fools. And here was the true taste of defeat, bitter to the tongue, like the tang of the acrid smoke that hung over the blackened fields.

When at last the high-city showed in the distance through the haze, untouched by the destruction, Kleinias seemed to draw himself together by some act of will. I remembered that his wife, Menexenos's mother, would be waiting at home for the news. He had to face her.

By the time we walked back through the courtyard door and she came hurrying from the women's rooms – a thing I had never seen her do before – he had regained a semblance of his old composure. He took her delicate hand and said, 'We shall make good, Menexenos is sure of it. And in the meantime we have the town-house, where we can stay until the farm is right again.'

I saw her eyes dart to his face. She must have realized. She was, after all, no fool. But she said nothing, at least in my hearing, and quickly led him inside.

In the city, the mood turned from shock to rage. Up on the Pnyx, the people complained of what they had lost, and cried with one furious voice that someone should have warned them.

The chief Archon, who knew his way with crowds, put forward a motion to have the Strategos impeached. This was done to raucous acclaim. Then decrees were passed, one after another, repealing every honour ever granted to any Macedonian, whatever his virtues. In the agora and streets, and on the high-city, honorific statues were torn down, and grateful inscriptions chiselled off. The Archon, with a politician's skill, knew that so long as the Demos's fury was directed at Philip, it was directed away from him.

One day, returning from the Pnyx, Kleinias found me stripped to the waist in the outer courtyard, practising my sword-work. He sat down on the bench beneath the fig tree, and watched me. I finished off, and setting my sword aside asked him if he was well, and if I could send for the slave, or fetch him something.

All this he declined with a shake of his head. Then he said, 'Listen now to what we have descended to. Today our wise rulers have decreed that if any citizen by word or deed honours King Philip, then anyone may lawfully

247

put that man to death, without trial or recourse to law.'
He gave a sudden, harsh laugh. 'Thus the brave Demos
wages war – with their tongues.'

It was a relief of sorts when, soon after, the time of
the Panathenaia came, for it seemed to me that a frenzy
of anger and hatred had taken hold in the city.

It was the hot summer month the Athenians call
Hekatombaion. Up on the high-city the sacrifices were
made, and the prayers were spoken, according to the
ancient rituals. Then the men and boys who had been
selected to compete processed down from the hill and
through the agora; and the citizens, distracted for a while
from their futile revenge, watched and cheered.

The stadium, which lay outside the walls, on the banks
of the Ilissos, had been spared by the Macedonians. This
was not from piety or shame however, but because the
massive close-laid ashlars could not easily be broken, nor
was there anything that would burn or could be carried
off.

I went each day, and from the terraces watched the
contests, with Kleinias at my side.

I had thought, at first, that he would not come. I had
even heard his wife's voice from the women's quarters,
trying to persuade him to stay at home. But he seemed
driven by a fierce determination, and insisted on seeing
everything.

As I expected, Menexenos came first in the diskos-
throw, outstripping his nearest rival by fifteen paces.
When the judges announced the winner, he smiled up to
us, and raised his hand. Naked against the backdrop of
white marble and fire-scorched earth, he reminded me

of the depiction on the black-glazed trophy vase. But this was something I kept to myself.

I glanced at Kleinias. His face was absent and immobile. He had said nothing to me, and I could not tell what he was thinking.

After the javelin-throw the judges spent some time measuring the places where the spears had fallen. Finally they announced that Menexenos had won by a handspan. But he stumbled in the long jump, and though he did his best to right himself as he leapt, the weights were off balance, and in the end a heavily built black-haired youth from the deme of Acharnai came first.

Next day came the foot races: the short sprint for the pentathlon, and the separate running races – the long-race and the two-stade sprint around the post. Of these, Menexenos ran only in the sprint, and this he won.

One finds, as a rule, that there is a type who takes best to running, another to boxing, and another still to wrestling. But in the pentathlon, where strength as well as speed count, there is no one type: one year it may be a runner who wins; another year a wrestler who has excelled at the javelin and diskos. It was not, in short, a contest where one could tell the victor by looking – though this did not silence the touts behind the stadium, who claimed to have a hundred ways to predict the outcome.

Last of all was the contest I cared least for: the wrestling. Why this should be, when I had made such a study of war and killing, I cannot tell. Perhaps it was because of what I had seen in the palaistra at Tarentum. But there seemed to me something brutish and unnecessary about it; and though Menexenos had said there once had been a particular excellence to it, I found it hard to see.

I had hoped he would be up against one of the lighter-built runners; but I think, already, I had guessed who it would be, and was not surprised, after the lots had been drawn, when the thickset youth from Acharnai stepped out.

He was not wholly unknown to me. I had seen him once or twice at the Lykeion, passing through with friends. But I had never seen him training there, and supposed he must have used one of the other gymnasions in the city. But when I mentioned this to Menexenos he said, 'No, he spends all his time out in the country – or he used to, before he lost his farm along with the rest of us. Now I don't know what he does.'

The wrestling was next day. We had not spoken of it, but now I asked Menexenos what his chances were.

He shrugged.

'He is strong, and determined – but, then, so am I.'

On the morning of the contest, I went early with Kleinias to the open ground beside the stadium, where the contest was to take place.

All along the bank of the Ilissos the crowds were starting to gather, and already the air buzzed with excitement and expectation. Food-sellers and wine-sellers had set up their stalls; there were touts taking bets, there were dice games and knucklebone-players; there were quacks full of portentous mystery, with cures for every illness;

250

there were sophists promising quick riches to the improvident; there were well-dressed courtesans, bright and stylish in costly Asiatic silks, standing under parasols held up by their slaves, laughing and talking with their friends; there were rough grim-faced whores from the city taverns, sprawled splay-legged beside the stream, cursing at the boys who splashed them from the water; there was a troop of dancers from Ionia; there were acrobats, jugglers, fire-eaters and rhapsodists.

I found Menexenos's friends waiting at the wrestling-ground. They greeted Kleinias respectfully, and made way for him at the front. Though it was early still, the sun was hot, and would soon be hotter still. The air smelled of trampled grass, and men's bodies, and athletes' oil.

In due course the judges arrived in procession and took their places under the striped canopy. The signal was given; the pipes sounded; and the competitors, naked and oiled, filed out before them. Menexenos's friends cheered, and so did I.

Beside me, Kleinias was quiet. He peered at the bulky youth from Acharnai, as if he were there in the sand-strewn ring himself, about to fight him. He had his walking staff in his hand. His fingers had clenched hard around it; and now and then, unconsciously, he jabbed it into the dusty earth.

I, too, had been appraising Menexenos's opponent. I had decided, with little evidence to justify it, that he must be some sort of brute.

But now, close up, and viewing him at his best, I could see intelligence in his stolid face. He had bound up his hair with a fillet. The broad muscles in his back and legs glistened in the sunlight. I had to admit there was a big-boned rustic beauty to him.

The umpire gave the order to prepare. Menexenos, his bronze hair bleached by the sun, and with a band around his forehead, planted his feet and waited. The umpire's hand descended, and the contest began.

Straight away the youth from Acharnai caught Menexenos, throwing him off his guard with a clever feint. They locked, twisting and struggling; then Menexenos fell. The youth sprang forward, about to leap upon him, but Menexenos rolled with the fall, bunched himself up, and jumped to his feet again, all in one movement.

At this the youth paused and waited, gauging him, watching carefully, his body tense and ready. They locked again, and struggled, and parted, and locked, in a series of inconclusive bouts.

As I looked on, I saw where his strength lay. No one could doubt that he was physically powerful, and at first glance it was easy to take him as brutish and stupid. But his appearance was misleading, and, knowing this, he used it to his advantage, allowing others to misjudge him as a fighter, as I had done. I began to realize that he had thought carefully about the structure and tactics of his fight, and for all he tried to conceal this from his opponent, yet he fought with an almost poetic skill.

Menexenos fell again; then a third time. The last was hard, and for a moment the youth had him pinned.

All around me the crowd were shouting out with cheers of encouragement or advice. But Kleinias was silent, his face set in a deep frown that looked almost like anger.

Menexenos went limp. Then, with a sudden twist and curl, like a snake under a stone, he was free once more. He sprang to his feet, and the fight continued. But, round by round, the Acharnaian was wearing him down, getting the better of him. At one time he played by physical force; at another, just when Menexenos was getting the feel of his tactics, he changed, and fought like someone else: darting, ducking, wheeling, pausing and appraising.

Menexenos fell again. The youth had thrown him with an arm-twist. He held Menexenos prone, pressing his face into the dust, and twisted his arm up behind him. Many men, at such a time, would have switched his arm up just a little too far, tearing the muscles, inflicting pain, and weakening his opponent before the umpire could intervene. But the Acharnaian, to his credit, did not stoop to this. Beside me Kleinias said, 'He must pull himself together, or he will lose.'

I said, 'Yes sir,' and scowled out at the fighting-ground, suddenly full of resentment at him. At first, indeed, I did not understand it; but then the truth came to me. His was not the support of a father for his son. It was no support at all. Rather, he had set upon Menexenos's shoulders the burden of his every setback and failure and unfulfilled hope; it was the loss of the farm, it was the dead older son who had fallen from his horse and died, it was the victory crown he had never won. Kleinias had forced him to become not one excellent son, but two; and Menexenos was like Atlas, supporting upon his shoulders his father's dreams. There were too many reasons why he could not permit himself to lose this fight; and Kleinias, standing there grim-faced, silent, judging, directing his will through his eyes like a beam of fire, was the greatest reason of all.

Kleinias spoke again, breaking into my thoughts, asking me whose son Menexenos's opponent was. I answered that I did not know, but that he lived outside the city, at Acharnai, on a farm there.

At this he grunted and nodded, and tapped his stick in the ground. Just then, Menexenos happened to glance my way. I raised my fist and cried out his name, and beside me Kleinias called out, 'Win, my son, for me, and for Autolykos.' I saw Menexenos's face set firm. With his forearm he wiped the sweat from his brow. Then he turned once more to face his opponent.

I saw, that day, that there can be honour and decency in every act of a man, if he so chooses. Both fought with grace, and style, and skill. When the end came, it was because Menexenos had managed to read the poetry of the youth's movements and discern the intention behind it. He began to predict whether he was about to play the bout heavily or lightly; he began to match him, meeting strength with strength, feint with feint, and clever twisting holds with clever twisting holds of his own. He brought the Acharnaian down and held him there.

Sweat ran down his body, forming runnels in the dust that caked his back and chest. The Acharnaian twisted; but Menexenos held him fast, in a lock which, for all its strength, looked as light as a handshake.

And then, after what had seemed an eternity, it was over, and the youth's arm went up in the sign of submission.

I yelled and whistled and stamped the earth with all

the rest. Menexenos turned, raised his fist, and grinned. From the podium the judge came forward, and proclaimed the winner.

Then we all surged forward to tie the victory-ribbons on his arms and thighs and around his head.

Kleinias cried, 'My son!' and there were tears streaming down the old man's face.

'I won, Father. I won.'

Then he turned to me, smiling into my eyes; and without a thought for my clothes, or what was proper, I embraced and kissed him, covering myself in oil and sweat and dust; and all about us the people cheered.

Later, I walked with him towards the wash-house. From everywhere people were calling out their congratulations and good wishes. We came to the arch that leads to the baths and changing-rooms. A crowd had gathered there, to see the athletes as they went in.

As we passed, a man pushed suddenly to the front and jabbing his finger shouted, 'You would not have won if you were not the son of an aristocrat.'

Menexenos looked round. The man had a thin, pallid face, and milk-white bandy legs. Seeing himself now singled out, he drew back a step. He looked as if he had just come from a workshop. Stone-dust clung to his sandy untrimmed hair, and the front of his tunic was stained with food.

'And you,' replied Menexenos after a considering moment, 'would not have won, even if you were.'

People laughed, and Menexenos strode off to the wash-house, where the other pentathletes were waiting at the door to congratulate him.

I let him go.

The pale-faced man, who had remained silent, now spoke again, addressing whoever would listen.

'People like that make me sick. They want for nothing, and spend their time putting down honest working folk like me.'

His bitter face was full of hate, and pride in his lowly state. I thought of the years of effort that had brought Menexenos to this day of victory, and saw again in my mind's eye the burnt-out farm, and Kleinias collapsed in the wreckage of his life.

I ought to have ignored him. He was a mean, petty man who was below contempt. But suddenly my heart filled with anger.

'Have I seen you at the Lykeion, sir?' I said, rounding on him. 'Or perhaps at Kynosarges' gymnasion, or the Akademy?'

He laughed harshly, catching the eyes of those who stood around.

'What, me? I am Mikkos the stonecutter, a working man. I don't have money to waste at the gymnasion, like the haughty oligarchs and mincing pretty-boys.'

'And yet,' I said, 'the entrance is free to all, is it not?'

At this he narrowed his eyes and looked suspicious.

'What if it is? I do as I please. I am a free citizen.'

'And in your freedom,' I flared back at him, 'you have pleased to make yourself what you are. So do not complain of it when a better man wins.'

I had said enough, and made to go. But he cried, 'Better? No man is better than me! In this city we are all equal!'

'Oh?' I said, raising my brow. 'Is that what you think? Little wonder, then, that you are content to be no more than you are. My friend is right. Even if you had the wealth of Kroisos, you would still be standing here, complaining about another man's excellence, instead of striving for it yourself.'

The bystanders laughed. I turned and walked away.

When I had gone a few paces I heard him shout, 'Roman dog!'

I paused in my step and glanced round. At this he let out a yelp and fled, pushing his way into the depth of the crowd.

The Panathenaia ended with the torch-race, and later Menexenos's friends held a party to celebrate.

He wore, that night, a simple white chiton bordered with a pattern of meandering squares, and on his head a wreath of oak leaves. It was an evening charged with all the power of youthful victory.

Everyone discussed the games – who had run or thrown well, who had been noticed; the successes of friends. But later, when the tables had been cleared, the talk turned to other matters.

The company that night were only athletes and their guests, but the range of their conversation was not limited to the diskos, the long jump, or the javelin-throw. They could speak with knowledge about husbandry, warfare, history or philosophy; and when the lyre was brought out, everyone could play, and sing a skolion.

One of the party, a friend of Menexenos's I knew from

the Lykeion, began talking of beauty, asking whether, as he had heard some sophist say recently, all beauty was no more than an illusion, an empty fancy of each man's taste.

He was lately in love, and when he brought the subject up everyone laughed.

'Really, Ismenios,' said one, 'you have been turning the conversation to Theodoros all night, and now you think you can get us all to praise him again by talking of his beauty.'

'Well,' said Ismenios, laughing with the rest, 'you can talk about Theodoros if you wish. I shan't stop you.'

There was a good deal of joking at this. But presently, when the laughter had died down, one of the others said, 'Then let us hear it from you first, Ismenios. Is your Theodoros beautiful to one, and ugly to another? And would both be right in thinking so?'

At this there was more laughter, but afterwards Ismenios said, 'Actually it is meeting Theodoros that made me consider all this properly for the first time. I am sure I have never been in love before. But now is different, and when I heard the sophist's words, I knew in my bones he was wrong, but could not tell why. And so I thought about it.'

'And what did you decide?' asked Menexenos, smiling.

'It seems to me now that truly there is beauty, or something beyond beauty, that is the same for all. I did not see it until now, not for myself; and because I did not see it myself, I did not think it was there. But now I understand. A man must look, and look in the right place, and, most of all, he must look with the eye of love.'

'All this,' said another, 'just from loving Theodoros?'

258

'How not? It is as though, for the first time, my eyes are opened ... Well Marcus agrees anyway; see, he is nodding.'

At this the friend who had come with Ismenios, a thickset pankratiast called Pandion, declared grinning, 'He says Theodoros is the first; let us hope he is the last as well. I don't think I can bear another month like this one, Theodoros-this and Theodoros-that, all while I'm trying to concentrate on my training.'

'Huh,' said Ismenios. 'Well you wouldn't understand; everyone knows you care only for girls.'

'Not true,' replied Pandion, winking, 'I would be Menexenos's lover any day, if only he asked me. But he never asks.'

There was more joking at this. Then Ismenios turned to me. 'You have been quiet, Marcus. What do you say?'

I shrugged. I had been hoping he would not ask.

But now, gathering my thoughts, I said, 'It seems to me there are many paths to the same summit. Some men take one path, some another. The paths seem different, but from the top, the view is the same. I think if every man could see clearly, he would see that what is most perfect is what is most beautiful.'

'Well said!' cried Ismenios, slapping his thigh, 'and that, surely, is Theodoros ... or perhaps' – drawing down his brow – 'it is Menexenos?'

'You see?' said Pandion, laughing and filling my cup, 'Ismenios is very confused. Now come, bring more wine, and let us sing another song.'

At length the party ended and the guests began to drift off. When Menexenos had bidden the last of them goodbye he returned to the room, and sat down beside me on the edge of the couch.

I saw him stifle a yawn.

'It is late,' I said, 'and you are tired. I shall go to bed.'

I made to move. But smiling he put his hand out, saying, 'But I am not tired. Are you?'

I was going to reply that he had been up since the dawn, and I know not what else. But then I met his eyes.

Eros gives men understanding at such times. I nodded and smiled; and after that there was no more need for words.

I woke to the dappled morning sun, filtering through the broad leaves of the fig tree outside his bedroom window. The light moved in dancing filigrees across the wooden floor and tousled sheets, and on Menexenos's arm where it lay across my chest.

He stirred, but did not wake, and I turned to look at his sleeping face beautiful in repose, and his naked body sprawled out across the bed.

His ribs and back moved gently with his steady breathing. He was bruised and grazed still from the wrestling. I might have kissed those wounds of his; but it would have woken him.

I thought of the long night, of how I had shared his body, drunk from the well of his being, locked my mouth hard on his; how I had been closer to him than any other, striving, as far as two men can, to make one body out of two.

Now, as he lay dozing, I knew with an aching sadness that his deepest being, his truest beauty, lay somewhere for ever beyond, for ever unreachable.

My heart filled with love and longing; and, with it, a deep soul-grief, like loneliness, like loss.

Later, when we were up and dressed, we went out in the city, and as we walked, we talked tenderly of love and friendship, and I realized with a little jolt of private surprise that, for all his self-assurance, this had been something new for him as well.

He was reticent and thoughtful, even bashful. 'A true friend,' he said at one point, 'is the greatest good a man can find in another.' He shyly explained that he had had many admirers, but had tired of their insincere flattery and silly gifts, and in the end had decided it best to offer up to the gods what he yearned for, thinking it was not to be found among men. He caught my eye, and gave a small, self-conscious shrug. 'I used to think all that was for the poets, just well-sounding empty words.'

'And now?' I said smiling.

'You know more than anyone.'

Just then, we happened to be passing behind the theatre, where we had been sitting on the hillside. He was not one for displays of emotion any more than his father. But now, as if to seal his words, he drew me to the wall, took my shoulders and kissed me hard on the mouth.

'There,' he said, his cool grey eyes kindling with passion. 'That is my answer.'

Pomponius sent a message asking me to call on him.

When I arrived, I found Titus's friend Villius there, in the cool high-ceilinged study beyond the courtyard.

We greeted each other warmly, not having seen each

other since Tarentum. Then Pomponius, never one for easy informality or lack of conceit, cleared his throat.

'Villius is here on a commission from the consuls and the Senate. We wish to discuss a matter of some gravity with you.'

He sat down behind the huge barrier of his desk and continued, 'A few days ago news came of Philip. He is in Thrace, it seems, causing havoc all over the Hellespont. Maroneia has fallen; and Ainos, Kypsela, Doriskos . . . Well, I shan't go on; I don't suppose you know these places anyway.'

'What matters,' said Villius, sitting forward, 'is that these cities are on the route between Europe and Asia. If Philip succeeds in taking them all, he will link up with King Antiochos in Asia, and will be in a position to hold all of Greece to ransom. The Senate has finally woken up to what is happening. They see another Carthage in the making, just as Titus has been warning.'

I said, 'Do these cities not fight?'

'They are too weak, too disunited. He picks them off, one after the other: Elaious, Alopekonnesos, Kallipolis, Madytos have all opened their gates to him. But – and that is why I am here – the city of Abydos has refused.'

The name stirred in my memory. But before I could place it, he went on, 'I have been discussing all this with Pomponius. I will show you the map later. But now, let me tell you what we should like you to do . . .'

He talked for some time. When he had finished, he stood and said, 'But come, Marcus, let us take a turn in the garden, and I will tell you all my private news, such as it is.' And to Pomponius, 'Will you excuse us?'

When we were outside he cast his eyes around the wide court, taking in the ornate flowerbeds, the fashionable painted sculptures, and the liveried slaves who came and went along the far colonnade. 'I see,' he said with a quick smile, 'that our ambassador does not spare himself the necessities.'

We walked to one side, where there was a little bronze figure of Pan, and beside it a stone bench and a tinkling wall-fountain. Here we sat.

'Forgive me for that little subterfuge,' he said. 'In truth I have no private news that would interest you. But I could hardly say what I want to say with Pomponius present. Tell me, how well have you got to know this ambassador of ours?'

'Well enough,' I answered, giving him a look.

He laughed and nodded. 'Then you will understand why we feel he is not the man to undertake this mission. He has caused enough trouble already. First he tells everyone who cares to listen that Rome will not stand up to Philip. Then, at the wrong time, when we are not ready, he loses his temper and threatens war. Well, he has forced us to advance our plans. Our agents in Macedonia tell us Philip believes we lack the will to stand up to him. But be careful on this mission, Marcus. Philip is dangerous and hard to predict. Stick to what I have told you. It is no time to play the hero.'

Menexenos was waiting back at the house. 'What did Pomponius want this time?' he asked with raised brows. Pomponius had become something of a joke in Athens.

I said, 'Philip is besieging Abydos. The consuls want me to go there and warn him off.'

He stared at me. 'Abydos? Are you sure?'

'Of course.' I relayed to him what I had been told, about Philip's progress through Greece, and the cities that had fallen. 'But Abydos,' I said, 'is refusing to surrender like the others, and Philip is laying siege . . . What is it? What is wrong?'

'But don't you remember?' he cried. 'Pasithea is in Abydos!'

I looked at him, realizing now why the name had caught in my mind. Then I said, 'What will Philip do if it falls?'

'It *will* fall,' he said. 'It cannot stand alone, not against the whole Macedonian army. And when it does he will sack the city and enslave the citizens, for daring to resist him.'

I sat down on the bench and frowned at the flagstones under my feet, trying to think. Then I looked up. Menexenos's eyes were upon me still.

'We cannot leave her to that,' I said.

'No, we cannot. Nor can you go marching in to rescue her alone. So I am coming with you.'

Just as it is impossible to sail from the Middle Sea to the Atlantic Ocean without passing the Pillars of Herakles, so it is impossible to enter or leave the Black Sea without passing the city of Abydos. A distance of only two stades separates Abydos on one side of the Hellespont from Sestos on the other: a distance a man could swim. Indeed, if the old story is true, Leandros swam the strait each night to visit his woman, the priestess of Aphrodite on the other side, until one night a storm blew up that drowned him.

These facts, and this story, I heard from our captain, who was a regular on the Black Sea route, and knew every port and inlet and stream like the palm of his hand. Abydos, he said, had an excellent harbour, sheltered from the dangerous currents that ran through the narrows of the Hellespont, and it would be easy to get us inside.

But when we arrived, we saw that Philip had sunk huge wooden piles in the harbour mouth, and linked them with iron chains, blocking all shipping in and out.

The captain frowned and gave the order to put about. We turned south, and made landfall at a small inlet concealed by rising ground. Disembarking here, we climbed to the top of the grassy ridge, and looked out over the plain.

Twilight was coming on. Abydos lay in the distance, with torches burning on the walls. All about, scattered over the flat ground between, the Macedonian cooking fires flickered like evening stars, and the siege-engines stood like monstrous slumbering beasts along the line of the encircling trenches.

I turned to the captain. 'Is there any way you can get us in?'

He rubbed his beard and frowned at the sunset. 'Not through those entrenchments, I can't. And you saw the harbour for yourself.'

He paused and paced along the ridge, considering. Then he turned and said, 'The tender would be small enough. But there is no way at all it could outrun the Macedonian patrols.'

We all looked seawards. Out in the bay the Macedonian triremes were sitting at anchor, dark silhouettes against the last glimmer of the day, like hunting dogs waiting at a rabbit's burrow.

I turned back to the captain. 'But first,' I said, 'they would have to see us. What time does the moon rise tonight?'

We set out as soon as night had fallen.

The tender was a small, oared boat, used for carrying stores, and for running passengers to and from the quay. It was hard work against the strong opposing current; and without light we were in constant danger of being drawn onto hidden rocks.

But the Macedonian warships were not looking for something so small, and we slipped past them unseen.

The current dropped as we passed into the shelter of the bay. We eased ourselves under the great linking chains that blocked the harbour and rowed in. As we passed the sea-wall, two Abydean night-guards who had been watching at the end of the mole shouted down a challenge, directing their spears at us. But we were ready with our answers, and they let us through.

We tied up at the waterfront. The city was deep in fear; which was no surprise, once we discovered what had happened there.

Eventually we were brought to the house of one of the city magistrates, and stood waiting in the unlit courtyard while the slave went inside to call him.

The night was drawing on. We paced on the flagstones; but soon he stepped out, an elderly white-bearded man, still dressed in his day-clothes.

Even in the moonless night his eyes were like dark shadows, and I wondered when the last time was that he had slept. But he greeted us civilly, saying his name was Iphiades and sending the slave for refreshments.

He sat down, and listened in silence while I told him why I had come. When I had finished he said wearily, 'It would have been better if you had come to tell me the Roman army was on its way. That is the only thing Philip will heed.'

Then he told us his dreadful story.

Although, he said, Philip's army was many times stronger, the Abydeans had managed at first to fend off his attacks. He had brought up great war-engines, mounted on ships; but against these the Abydeans had launched boulders from catapults, and had set fire to the ships with burning arrows.

Then, thwarted in this first assault, Philip mounted an attack from the landward side. The walls of Abydos were strong and well maintained; but over time his sappers had undermined them with tunnels and trenches; and at the same time he had blockaded the port, cutting the food supply.

When the outer wall began to crumble, the Abydeans had built up a second wall within the first. 'But,' said Iphiades, 'by then everyone knew the end could not long be postponed. The people were beginning to starve. The Macedonians were undermining the walls faster than we could shore them up. The Council met, and I was sent to speak to Philip.'

He stared into the shadows and drew a long breath. In the brief pause, from somewhere in the town, a solitary dog bayed into the night. It sounded hungry.

I said, 'Yet you remain. Would Philip not come to terms?'

He gave a dry laugh. 'We hardly demanded terms. We offered surrender. We told him he might have the city – the buildings, the treasury, everything. We asked only that he let us go, to seek exile where we could. As you have guessed, he refused. He made a joke of it, saying we would make useful slaves in Macedon, and bedfellows for his troops. We could either fight to the death, or we could submit to slavery; he would leave the choice to us.'

He paused, and pressed the flats of his hands against his closed eyes. Gently Menexenos said, 'You are tired, sir. Let us speak again in the morning.'

'No,' he said, pulling himself up. 'The city may fall at any time, and you need to know this, so that you may tell the world what happened here.'

A siege is a siege, full of horrors. And yet I sensed something else, some deeper horror, which he had not yet spoken of. I felt the beginnings of dread creep in my hair.

He rose from the stool and walked the few steps down to the lower terrace, and paused among the flower-urns, absently touching them with the ends of his fingers – rosemary, bushing lavender; a flowering shrub climbing up a trellis. Then he turned and looked back at us.

'To choose the time and manner of his own death is the noble act of a free man,' he said. 'But to choose it for another . . .' He shook his head. 'There is impiety in it somewhere; but they will not listen.'

'But what do you mean, sir?' I said. 'What has happened?'

He drew in his breath, and let out a long sigh. 'Forgive me; I am telling the end at the beginning. The assembly has decreed that everything of value that the citizens own – their money, their silverware and gold, their necklaces, rings, amulets and every precious thing – shall be deposited in the agora. When that is done the womenfolk shall be taken to the temple of Artemis – there, up on the hill; you can see the cresset burning – and the children to the gymnasion.'

I looked at him. 'But why, sir?' Yet, even as I spoke I felt my hands go cold.

'When the inner wall falls,' he continued, 'a troop of soldiers, specially chosen for the task, will proceed to the temple, and to the gymnasion, and there they will slaughter the women and children. No one shall survive: the men were made to swear it on the altars of the gods. Then, when that is done, they will cast the gold and silver into the sea, and fight the Macedonians until the last man is dead.'

'Great God,' whispered Menexenos.

Iphiades nodded. 'That was yesterday. I opposed the motion, but I was outvoted. Since then our troops have ceased to shore up the walls. The defence is over. The walls will not hold much longer. We wait for the end.'

There was a silence.

I said, 'Does Philip know of this?'

'Not yet, or he would be inside the city already.'

'Then I must go to him before he finds out. Can you persuade the Council to delay – to shore up the walls, at least?'

He spread his hands in a gesture of hopelessness. 'I shall do what I can. They are determined.'

Menexenos said, 'Have the women been taken to the temple yet? A friend of ours is here.'

'Might I know her?'

'I think not, sir. She is visiting, but her home is Korinth now. Her name is Pasithea.'

Iphiades seemed to me no more likely to know a woman like Pasithea than old austere Kleinias. So much for appearances. His head went up immediately. 'You know Pasithea?' he cried.

'Why yes, sir,' replied Menexenos, somewhat taken aback.

'Then I can tell you exactly where she is . . . Better still' – gesturing to the slave who was waiting by the pillar – 'Gyrtias will take you there.' A glimmer of a smile appeared on his tired face – the first since we had met him – and he added, 'When she was ordered up to the temple with the other women, she told the man to give her his sword and she would take her chances on the walls. She can be quite an Amazon when she chooses.' He glanced at the sky. 'But you had better make haste.'

I followed his gaze. I had been so taken up in his tale I had forgotten. The moon was up, a cold shining half-disk in a cloudless sky. It would illuminate the harbour like a beacon.

We hurried out. As soon as we were in the street Menexenos said, 'Marcus, you must leave *now*.'

'But Pasithea —'

'I'll go to her. The captain is waiting. There is no time. If you delay, you will be seen. Come back tomorrow after dark and collect us. If you cannot, I shall find another way out.'

'No, Menexenos, wait! You heard the old man. I will not leave you here —'

But I was talking to the night air. Already he was hurrying off up the street with the slave-boy. He turned and made a quick gesture of affection that we had between us. 'Go!' he called, 'before the whole Macedonian squadron sees you sailing out.'

I found the captain pacing beside the tender.

As we rowed out I gazed back at the town. Up on the ridge, in the porch of the temple of Artemis, a great basket-cresset flared, sending sparks scattering in the breeze. I turned and shuddered, and pulled harder on the oar.

By the time we arrived back at the ship, the first hint of dawn was showing in the east. I went off to sit on the shore alone, and watched the shooting stars, and the lapping water of the Hellespont.

At first light I stirred myself. I stripped and washed, and prepared to be conducted through the Macedonian lines.

King Philip was waiting with a group of courtiers and military men in front of a great square blue-dyed pavilion, painted on its side with the golden sunburst emblem of the Macedonian royal house.

He affected not to notice as I approached with the escort, though he had been warned I was coming. But when the captain of the guard announced me he turned with raised brows and gleaming eyes and said, 'Greetings, Roman. Have you come to witness the end of Abydos?'

I had seen him from far off at Athens. Now for the first time I saw him close. He had a short-trimmed black beard, and shining curling hair tied with the royal diadem. His eyes were the colour of old bronze, like a wolf's.

I recalled the stories of how he had had many lovers in his youth, both men and women. One saw the attraction still. He had animal good looks, like a smell, and an insolent half-amused expression, as if to say: 'What I want, I take.'

But there was something chilling about him too, something feral and destructive. He had too many lines around his eyes, like a man who has slept too little, or drunk too much.

I knew what I had been told to say, and had spent the dawn thinking carefully how to say it. I began now, neither submissive nor vaunting, informing him that I had come on behalf of the Senate, asking him to hold in mind the common peace, and to cease to make war on the cities of the Hellespont. The Senate, I told him, did not wish for war between Rome and Macedon, but was resolved to fight him unless he drew back. I urged him to end his siege of Abydos.

As I spoke he kept glancing over my shoulder at whatever was going on in the plain. I realized this rudeness was deliberate, and ignored it, and carried on with what I had to say.

But then, as I was speaking, there came a coughing and stirring from behind the leather flap that was the doorway of Philip's pavilion. The flap parted, and a man emerged, blinking and pushing his fingers sleepily through his hair.

Except for a towel around his waist he was naked. His chest and legs were shaggy with curling blond hair; his body was scored with white marks from old sword-wounds. I stuttered and gaped, and my head emptied of all the words I had carefully prepared. It was Dikaiarchos.

Philip's eyes slewed to my face. 'Have you finished already? Is that all?'

'No, sir,' I stammered, struggling to pull myself together.

'Well go on then.'

Behind him, Dikaiarchos was splashing his face and upper body at a water-trough. I tore my eyes away, thinking of the Abydeans. But it was too late. I had been wrong-footed, and I began to hesitate and stumble in my words.

Philip sensed it at once. He fixed his keen wolf-eyes on me, suddenly intent, and when next I hesitated he broke in with, 'No, Roman, you are wrong. It was the Rhodians who made war on me, not I on them. So too with that old fool Attalos. They attacked me first, and I have outwitted them. And now, like children running to their mother, they have gone to Rome for help.'

He was playing with me.

Realizing this, and feeling angry with myself, I retorted sharply, 'And what of the Abydeans? Did they attack you first as well?'

The murmur of voices around me fell suddenly quiet. The courtiers and generals and clerks and slaves turned and stared. Dikaiarchos, who had been slouching against the stone horse-trough scratching himself, came up and stood at Philip's side.

As for Philip, for a moment, before he concealed it, I saw in his face that it had been some time since he had been addressed bluntly by anyone.

Smoothly he said, 'You are too outspoken, Roman. You are speaking to a king.'

I glared at him, and felt the colour rising in my face.

Seeing this Philip laughed and turned to Dikaiarchos. 'A good-looking youth, wouldn't you say? Did you see his strong thighs and buttocks? What do you think?'

I tried to continue, reminding him of the Abydeans, whose lives hung in the balance while he joked. But it was no good. He and Dikaiarchos were standing with their heads cocked to one side, considering my body as if I were a bull at market. I could see the mark on the back of Dikaiarchos's hand, where my javelin had pierced him. Yet, for all his staring, he did not seem to know me.

Meanwhile, Philip's dark, amused eye stripped me of my clothes. I knew my face had reddened to the ears; and the more I tried to stop it, the worse it became.

I stumbled to a close. Philip smiled, then broke into a grin. 'Well I have heard you out, and now I have a city to take. But it won't take long. Why don't you wait in my tent? The bed is big enough for two, and I'll soon be back.'

He looked round with bright amused eyes at his

generals and officers and clerks, and, dutifully, they joined in his laughter.

'Do you mean to kill every Abydean then?' I cried, furious at being mocked.

The laugher stopped. In a different voice he said, 'If the Abydeans want to end the siege, let them open their gates.'

'They have already offered you their city and their gold.'

'Why should I stop at half, when I can have all? I shall kill their men, and take their women and children as slaves and playthings.'

'They will kill themselves first.'

He tutted. 'Will they? Then they had better make haste.'

'Is this your answer to the Senate, sir?'

At this he paused. His eyes became fierce and dangerous, and for the first time I knew the stories of how he had murdered his family were true.

'It is time,' he said slowly, 'that you western barbarians were put in your place. You may tell your Senate they rouse me at their peril. And if they do, they will find Macedon is more than a match for Rome.'

I returned to our ship, and for the rest of that day, I watched as the Macedonians attacked the city. War-engines, lined up in rows, fired massive bolts of stone and bronze into the crumbling walls. Troops with scaling-ladders surged forward, scrambling over the fallen masonry.

I could see the Abydeans fighting them off. But each hour the defenders were fewer, and each hour the Macedonians advanced. It was the longest day of my life.

By the time night came finally on, the Hellespont was bright with reflected fire, and through the orange glow we set out once more for Abydos. The captain eyed the Macedonian triremes clustered at the harbour entrance and shook his head. But we made it past them, and when we reached the town the fighting on the walls had ceased for the night, and an uneasy silence had descended.

I returned to the house of Iphiades. As the slave led me inside, I heard the unmistakable sound of Pasithea's voice in the courtyard.

All the way there, along the coast and through the Macedonian blockade, when I was not thinking about Menexenos, I had wondered how she would be. I pictured her half starved, or broken like the city, with all her dignity gone.

But when I saw her, it was as if nothing had changed since Tarentum. She was sitting poised on the edge of the garden-seat, with Menexenos on one side and Iphiades on the other, deep in conversation. She was wearing a dark Ionian robe, and her hair was bound up just as I remembered it.

'My dear, dear Marcus,' she cried when I appeared. 'How kind of you to come.'

Then from the porch two other men stepped forward, whom I did not know. Iphiades said, 'This is Glaukides, and this is Theognetos. They are members of the Council.'

They greeted me somewhat coldly, and I sensed a

wariness or tension in them. Iphiades asked about my meeting with Philip, and when I told him the one called Glaukides said, 'Then it is as we expected. Who can be surprised? The man is a barbarian.'

He spoke with an air of finality, as if there were no more to be said, and beside him the man called Theognetos nodded solemnly in agreement.

Iphiades slowly shook his head. He looked crushed and exhausted. But it was Pasithea who spoke.

'By the gods, Glaukides,' she said, 'will you not reconsider?'

Glaukides gave an impatient sigh, like one who is forced to repeat his words to a child or a fool. 'This is the home of our forefathers. What should we be elsewhere but slaves and wanderers with no place of our own, for ever strangers? No. A man may not choose the time of his coming; but it is in his power to choose his end; and we have chosen.'

Pasithea said, 'You set yourself too high. It is not your place to make that choice for another. Such things cannot be decided by a vote in the assembly.'

'She is right,' said Iphiades.

'It is done. The question is closed.'

'Then reopen it,' retorted Pasithea, 'while there is still time.'

'Time for what?' Glaukides flared back at her. 'You heard our Roman friend.'

'Sir,' I said, stepping forward, 'the city is not only a parcel of land, not only stone and marble. It dwells in your hearts too. Is it not better to let the people live?

Cities have been refounded before, and surely it can happen again. But if every Abydean dies it is finished for ever.'

'You have tried to help us,' said Glaukides, 'and I thank you for it. But you have seen now for yourself what kind of man Philip is. This is not merely a defeat where one can wake the next morning and think, "So what now?" This is annihilation, an end to all, the destruction of our city, our home, the temples of our gods, our place in the world, the community of our people. Forgive me, but you are young still. Have you witnessed a city taken? Children torn from their mothers' arms and butchered before them? The mothers themselves raped in front of their daughters, knowing their husbands are already dead? And if one should survive the massacre, it is to nothing but a life of inhuman servitude, all dignity gone, the thrall to some brutish master.'

He turned to Iphiades and Pasithea, and raising his voice went on, 'Do you think I do not know what choice we face? Do you think I order lightly the deaths of those we love? I do it to spare them the agony, the moment of decision when the dagger hangs heavy in the hand, and the final cut is too hard to make. We are powerless before Philip's force. But this is a victory of sorts, a victory over fear of death, and over his greed and malice. Future generations of men will come to this place; they will walk upon the grassy ruins and they will say, "Remember Abydos!" '

He fell silent. The lamp in the wall-sconce spluttered in a sudden breeze that blew up from the harbour. From somewhere far off, I heard a baby crying.

Pasithea said quietly, 'You have let your fine words blind you, Glaukides, to what is real.'

He rounded on her angrily. 'So you say, woman; you who have chosen to make another place your home.'

'Yes,' she replied. 'That is true. Sometimes it takes distance to see a thing for what it is.'

I said, 'Rome will come.'

'But not soon enough.'

Before I could speak again there was a din in the street outside: men calling, the running of feet, and then a loud hammering on the outer door. The slave hurried off, returning moments later with two soldiers. Their uniforms were ragged. They were filthy with dust and old blood.

'What now?' asked Glaukides, turning to them.

'A night attack, sir. The Macedonians are massing at the crosswall.'

I said, 'I will come with you and fight.'

The soldier in front began to say something, but Iphiades, who had been sitting with his head in his hands, broke in. 'No, Marcus, that is not what we need you for. You must leave us now. Go and speak for us at Rome. Tell them what happened here.'

He got to his feet and from the deep shadow within the colonnade brought out a sword in its scabbard, and began buckling it on around his waist. The old slave ran forward, and cried out in a voice torn with emotion, 'Oh no, sir!'

'Come, come now, Antiphon,' said Iphiades, turning to him. 'You have been a good friend; but now you are free to go. Save yourself. The Macedonians will let you through the lines.' Then, turning to Glaukides and Theognetos, 'Will you be joining me, gentlemen?'

Before they could answer there was a great crash, followed by the sound of falling masonry. The catapults had started up. Iphiades shook my hand, and then Menexenos's. 'Farewell. Go with God.'

We left him standing in his courtyard, an old man clad in his old armour, noble in defeat, on his way to meet his death.

Down at the harbour, the captain was almost frantic. He had half put out already; the tender was held to the quay only by its thin bow-lanyard.

'Hurry!' he cried as soon as he saw us, 'the triremes are closing on the harbour-mouth; we shall never get out.'

Then he saw Pasithea. He took one look at her long dress, scowled, and said, 'We are not going to a banquet, madam.'

'No, we are not,' she replied. 'But I may be going to my death; and if I must travel to the underworld tonight, then I wish to arrive looking my best.'

He raised his eyes at the sky and muttered. She walked past him, stepped into the tender, and took a seat.

We set out and sped across the still water of the inner harbour, towards the line of sunken piles at the harbour mouth, and the Macedonian triremes waiting like wolves in the open water beyond.

The moon was up, almost at its zenith; but we passed through the barrier of chain-linked piles unseen. The triremes were so close I could hear the voices of the

Macedonians on their decks. They stood lining the rail, their eyes were on the spectacle unfolding in the town.

The captain at the helm-oar steered a course between the warships on one side and the rocky coast on the other. It was a narrow channel with strong, dangerous currents. From Abydos the noise of battle carried in the air, mingled with the thuds and crashes of artillery. We pressed onwards, the captain intent on his steering; the rest of us at the oars, or watching the rushing water.

Just as it seemed we were almost through, a lone Macedonian trooper on the nearest trireme ambled across the deck. He paused, fumbled with his clothing, and began to relieve himself over the rail.

As he did so he looked up absently. I saw his face change. He started back from the rail; then began yelling out at the top of his voice.

His comrades came running. We were so close I could hear the beat of their feet across the trireme's deck. At the helm-oar the captain cursed, and shouted, 'Pull for all you're worth.' There was no more need for silence.

On the trireme the thud-thud-thud of the drumbeat began, and from within came the sound of shouted orders and men running to their stations. The banks of oars creaked, and stirred into life.

In the tender the captain fixed a judging eye on the current, frowned, looked again at the jagged coastline, then decisively swung the steering-oar, taking us in towards the rocks. The tender shuddered. The crewman on the bench beside me called out, 'There are rock-shoals there, sir.'

'I know; I know,' snapped the captain, without taking his eyes from the dark water ahead.

The nearest trireme was gathering way. There was a commotion on deck, and some sort of rigging appeared.

'What is that thing?' I cried, pointing.

'A ship's catapult,' replied the crewman next to me. 'Can you swim?'

The trireme was turning, its banked oars sweeping the water like some heavy bird labouring into flight. On the deck, archers took up positions and began firing arrows of burning pitch. They scythed through the air around us, trailing tails of light in the blackness, hissing as they struck the water.

One fell an arm's length from me. The pitch floated and burned. Then, in its light, I saw a great round-backed swelling mass.

'Rocks!' I shouted.

Immediately the captain threw the helm around. We heaved in the starboard oars, just in time to save them from being snapped off by the protruding boulder.

There was a loud crack. The whole tender juddered and groaned as the reef scraped beneath us. The crewman next to me began muttering some sort of a charm. Then, with a dull bass twang of taut leather, the trireme's catapult fired.

It was the rocks that saved us. If it had not been for the smooth mossy shoal, bulging up beside us like a turtle's back, we should have been smashed to pieces. But the catapult-ball glanced off the rock, skimmed and bounced, then shattered. Even so, the tender leapt and heeled over, and a great wave broke upon the stern, throwing me forward and sending me sprawling across the deck.

All about me the crew were shouting and struggling with the oars. The captain fought with the helm. Then, as I scrambled back to my place, I heard Menexenos cry out, 'Where is Pasithea?'

I jerked my head round to where she had been. There was nothing but empty space there.

Already Menexenos was up, pulling off his clothes.

'Have you lost your senses?' yelled the captain. 'The current is too strong; it will drag you down.'

Menexenos ignored him, and, naked now, prepared to leap.

'Wait!' I cried. 'Menexenos, look!'

Hearing my voice he turned. Just behind the stern, in the swirling water, Pasithea's head broke surface. She was swimming strongly, her hair flowing out around her like a spreading lily.

We ran aft and threw out a line, and stretched out our arms to her. She reached us, and with an agility I had not thought her capable of she leapt up the side and over the bulwark.

'Hold fast!' shouted the captain as another missile flashed through the air.

This time the bolt from the catapult fell further off. The warship was at full battle-stations now, its black-and-white striped oars striking the water in unison, the crew and soldiers at fighting positions on the deck.

But now I saw the sense in the captain's steering us onto the rocks. The steady beat of the drum on the trireme's deck slowed. It faltered. Then it broke off.

I heard urgent shouted orders. The banks of oars paused in their motion, hesitated, and then planted themselves in the water, breaking the ship in its progress.

The crewman beside me broke into laughter. From the helm the captain said, 'They won't risk these shallows, and by the time they work out another route we'll be gone.' And then, turning to Pasithea with a broad grin on his face, 'You swim like an oyster-boy, madam.'

She laughed. 'Little wonder. It was they who taught me. I used to dive off these rocks when the other girls were preening themselves in front of their mirrors, dreaming of marriage.'

'Well,' said the captain, nodding and regarding her with new respect, 'then you are a woman of many skills indeed.'

She smiled and answered, 'You are not the first man to tell me that.'

Then she pulled out a comb from her dripping robe, and began to arrange her hair.

TEN

THAT AUTUMN I SAILED for Italy, for the Senate
had summoned me to Rome.

Pomponius, with a great deal of solemnity and portentous self-consequence, had relayed the message that I was
to brief the senators on Philip and Abydos. On a fresh,
clear autumn morning, when the high-city shone like a
chryselephantine jewel against an immense blue sky, and
the painted hulls of the little fishing skiffs bobbed in the
shining water, I boarded a fast Rhodian cutter bound for
Brundisium.

I had written ahead from Athens, to tell Caecilius I
was coming; but no reply had reached me, and there was
none waiting when I reached Brundisium.

I pressed on by the official transport that was waiting,
and when at length I arrived at Rome I took a room at
an inn on the slopes of the Aventine, in a busy street of
shops and taverns. I sent off a note to Titus, to say I had
arrived, then ate at one of the taverns, and spent the rest
of the day looking round the Forum and the other public

places, for this was my first visit to the city my father had so disliked.

After Athens, Rome seemed austere and colourless. I had supposed I should feel at home: instead I felt like a foreigner. I had lived in Greek Tarentum, and then in Greece itself. I had grown used to seeing traders and visitors from every city and race that dwelt about the Middle Sea, each with his own language and dress and custom. Compared with this, Rome seemed like an army barracks, a place without trade and without beauty. Even the food in the tavern was dull, served by an innkeeper whose manner seemed to say: this is what I have cooked today; take it or leave it, it's all the same to me.

I returned from my explorations to a note from Titus, saying he would send a slave next morning to fetch me.

His house lay a short distance beyond the city walls, close to the Tiber, on the edge of a grassy marsh where cattle grazed.

It was a low, spreading, red-roofed place set on its own beside an oak wood, surrounded by a high wall. It looked more like some old rural farmstead than a town house, and no doubt that was what it once had been, before the city had begun to spread.

I wondered, as I walked beside the slave he had sent to fetch me, how much Titus had changed. Pomponius, who followed every nuance in the political life of Rome like a gambler with his eyes on the dice-table, had said he was now a political force to be reckoned with, and might soon be consul. I knew myself that this had been his hope; but I had not realized he had advanced so fast.

Before I left Athens, Pomponius had spent a good deal

of time assuring me he had always been a supporter and great admirer of Titus, whatever false impression I might have drawn from his hasty and humorous words in the past. He hoped I would not forget to mention his name; indeed it would be a kindness if I could remember to make a point of it. I smiled to myself. After having lived so long with my stepfather, I knew sycophancy when I saw it. But still, I thought, as the grazing cows absently swung their heads and eyed me without interest, and I eyed them back, power changes men, and so does success. I hoped Titus would still be the friend I remembered.

But I need not have worried. As soon as the servant announced me he hurried across the room and greeted me with genuine warmth, and sent the servant off to fetch a flask of the best wine in the house.

He was dressed more soberly than I remembered him, in the purple-bordered toga of a Roman senator. His light-brown beard, which had been fair and wispy in Tarentum, was darker and denser now; and he had taken more care with his hair. But his eyes were the same: blue as a springtime sky, full of vitality and dreams.

The servant returned, and while he was busy setting out the refreshments Titus asked how I was finding Rome.

'I think,' I said, 'I must be seeing it with Greek eyes.'

At this he laughed. 'Dull and provincial, you mean? Well you have seen what you have seen, and one cannot unlearn knowledge. But philosophers and artists are starting to come, more each year; and one day, when enough Romans have seen beyond the confines of their narrow world, they will begin to make changes. A man must first perceive what he lacks, and form a vision of what he wants to make himself. For now, they know only the rough rustic Italian villages, against which Rome is a sparkling cosmopolis.'

He went on to tell me of his political affairs. The land commission had been a success, and this had helped his reputation greatly. The consular elections were coming, and he had been persuaded by a number of Rome's leading men to stand, in spite of his young age.

'Will you win?' I asked.

He dipped his finger in the wine-cup and made the sign on the table the Greeks make against bad luck. 'I have opponents still. But after what has happened in Greece, they are fewer than they were.' He paused and looked at me. 'And here, Marcus, is where you can help.'

I laughed. 'But what do I know of Rome?'

'You know what happened at Abydos, and you can tell the senators for me. They know it from dispatches, of course; but they have not heard it from one who was there, who saw it all. Tell them the truth, nothing more or less.'

'Well the truth is bad enough,' I said, remembering.

We talked for a while of Philip and of Greece, and all that had happened since last we met. In the midst of this a servant tapped on the door and came in with a note on a piece of folded sealed papyrus.

'Forgive me,' said Titus, taking the paper and breaking the seal. I turned away, leaving him to read in private, and glanced idly around the room.

There was a large oaken sideboard by the window, solid old-fashioned work, the kind of thing we had at home in Praeneste. Upon it stood a few vessels of polished bronze – a casket with a lock, a table-lamp, a tray with a stand worked into the shape of stag's feet. Beside it, light and delicate next to the solid old bronzework, was a Greek wine-cup, white on black, perfectly made, with smooth shining sides and a leaping Tarentine dolphin painted inside.

It was a beautiful piece, but it made me think immediately of Lucius. Titus had not mentioned him. But when the servant had finished and gone off once more, I asked him how his brother was – making sure to avert my eyes from the wine-cup.

'Oh, Lucius is well enough,' he said, assuming a bright expression. 'He was chosen for the aedileship last year, and—' He broke off and glanced at me. 'Well, I shall not pretend, Marcus, not to you. He has not changed as much as I had hoped . . . Yet he is family, for all that, and I must help him where I can.'

Next morning, back at the inn, I was woken early by the noises from the street, which seemed never to cease except in the deepest hours of the night.

I rose with the first glimmer of dawn. I bought a raisin-cake at a food stall, and taking it with me went to sit alone on the steps of the Rostra in the Forum.

The leaden cloud of yesterday had lifted. Crimson streaks shafted across a dappled sky. As I chewed on my breakfast, I gathered my thoughts for the day to come, like a man preparing for battle.

I had gone to bed early, determined to be as fresh and alert as I could for this day; but in the end, with the din from the street, and my own thoughts, I had slept badly, turning over and over in my mind what I should say to the Senate. As the night-hours passed, each version I ran through in my head seemed worse than the last, until even the simplest words seemed wrong, and I felt myself falling into a vortex of doubt and indecision. Eventually, in the silent early hours, I had drifted into sleep, and dreamed bad dreams of Abydos.

Rome is a city built on seven hills. That day, the Senate was holding its meeting in the temple of Good Faith, one of the temples on the hill known as the Capitol, which rises steeply up behind the Forum.

I finished my breakfast and made my way there.

The temple was on one side of the open ground on the summit. After the buildings of Athens, it seemed squat and plain – old, weathered red brick, faced here and there with grey stone, and, on the eaves, little crude statues in painted terracotta. A drab-looking priest was busy sweeping the open area beneath the porch.

I was much too early for the Senate meeting. But that was as I had intended. After my failed interview with Philip, which had upset me greatly, I wanted no surprises.

For a while I wandered about among the shrines and altars and statues, pausing to look at the piled-up victory trophies – a clutter of old shields weathered almost to nothing; ancient spears, swords turned to rust and verdigris, rough-cut votive figures: all of them mementoes of battles long forgotten and heroes turned to dust.

I stood on the steps of the shrine of mighty Jupiter, and gazed up at the image of the god, frowning and all-powerful, rigid and austere, like the city he watched over.

Soon the sky lightened to a cloud-studded blue and, seeing the senators begin to arrive, I made my way to the porch of the temple, and looked in at the open bronze doors.

The chamber was cold with the morning chill. Sunlight lanced down from tiny high window-slits, casting thin bars of brightness across the wooden benches. At the far end, beneath a wood-pillared baldachin, the statue of the goddess stood on a plinth of black granite. Before her, twigs of fragrant juniper smouldered in an open censer.

The senators were taking their places. They were old men mostly, lean and grave-faced, like veteran warriors or country squires.

At first their age, and their grim unsmiling solemnity, made me uneasy. But then I thought of the Athenian Demos, who in their ignorance were swayed by the honeyed words of every clever speaker who wished to bend them to his will. Better, I thought to myself, to be governed by these stern, serious old men, who knew of battle first-hand, and could weigh up an argument without emotion. They were here, I thought, to deliberate on peace or war; on life or death. It was no place for levity.

Just then Titus arrived with a group of younger senators. He greeted me briefly. I suppose he saw the uneasiness in my face, for he said, 'Don't worry. Tell it as it was. They are decent men, even the ones who don't agree with me, and they know truth when they hear it.' And then, with a quick smile, '—And thank you, Marcus. There is no one I had rather address the Senate today than you.'

Then he went off to take his place; and I waited to be called, and looked out at the far-off Alban hills. Here and there, feathers of smoke were rising. It was the end of the harvest, and the farmers would be burning the old wood from the vineyards. The sight of it made me think of home. I would go there, when my business in Rome was done. But now the usher spoke my name, and I turned and followed him into the chamber, and focused all my mind on the task before me.

My words came out well, for all my night-time fears. I told myself later that it was the shades of the people of Abydos, coming to my aid, and I made a silent promise to offer something to Mars the Avenger, since it seemed this was his business most of all.

The senators heard me out in silence. Afterwards, there was some discussion and questions. Much of it I had heard before, from Titus. I recall one old senator who objected, and Titus answered him saying, 'How much longer will you delay? Must we wait till Philip lands in Italy, like Hannibal and Pyrrhos?'

The old senator dismissed his comments with a wave of his arm, as if he had heard it too often before.

'Now is not then,' he said. 'The situation is different.'

'Are you so sure?' returned Titus. 'Philip already dominates Greece; our spies report he is in secret talks with Antiochos; Egypt is weak and prostrate. Must we wait until the whole of the East is united against us?'

He turned to the others and continued, 'No city has the divine right to exist, not even Rome. We survive by our virtue, for so long as we possess it, and by our strength, for so long as we maintain it. We have staked our authority on ordering Philip to stop, and he has ignored us. If we do nothing now, why should he believe us next time? He will think us weak, and lacking in resolve. Let everyone remember, an idle threat is worse than no threat at all!'

From around the chamber there came murmurs of assent. These men were men of honour, and a man's word was his bond.

After this I felt a subtle shift, a change in the mood, like the first air of spring in winter. And when, at length, the time came to vote, I knew what the choice would be, and I was glad.

As the hands went up in support of Titus, I recalled Philip's words to me, that we threatened him at our peril.

Then I thought of the people of Abydos.

I had not failed them a second time.

I took the familiar ascending track, up through the oak forest.

The air was still; the sky showed deep and cloudless, and up on the high rocks, where I had played as a boy, came the familiar clanking sound of goat-clappers.

I drew the air into my lungs, and felt a longing for I know not what: for simplicity; for lost childhood.

Presently I came to the long avenue of poplars that marked the beginning of our own land, and immediately I began to notice signs of change. The brook that trickled down between the terraces, its natural course formed by time and the contours of the mountains, had been hollowed out, widened and dammed. The surrounding woodland had been felled and ploughed, and there were new cattle-pens behind the white-painted block where the farmhands lived.

I arrived unannounced. I smiled to myself, thinking of the surprise. What I had not been prepared for was my mother's tears.

I found her in her private room. She turned, then started.

'Mother,' I said, and crossed the floor to kiss her.

It took me a moment to realize what was different. The room seemed somehow empty and stark, though I could see nothing missing. Then, lifting my head, I realized that the old spreading rowan outside the window had gone.

'You took away the tree,' I said. 'You always liked it.'

'Your father decided we needed more light.'

I went to the window. There was a sawn-off stump where the rowan tree had once been. I thought again of the scarred land outside, needlessly changed in conformity with some ill-considered plan. A sudden bitterness filled my heart, and before I could stop myself I said sharply, 'Is there nothing at all he can leave alone? He is not my father, curse him. He will never be that.'

I had spoken harshly, and in anger. Immediately I felt ashamed, for it was no fault of hers. I turned from the window, my face full of regret.

She sat unmoving, staring at the little piece of sewing-work in her lap. Her hair was as it always was, tied back, with careless wisps at the side. But the last traces of fair had gone, replaced by grey.

For the first time, I thought, she looked old. I felt a falling within me, as if the foundations upon which I had built my life were crumbling. It came to me what she had sacrificed to keep the farm. She had never spoken of it. It filled me with a dull, bleak, impotent sadness.

She turned then, and it tore my heart to see the moisture welling in her eyes.

'My dear, precious Marcus,' she said softly, 'how glad I am to see you. What a shock you gave me.'

She blinked, and touched at her face, and in a firmer voice went on, 'We received your letters from Athens. You have done so much, and I am proud of you. Your father – your true father – would be proud of you too. And look how broad and manly you have become.'

I looked away, lest she see my eyes. But my voice cracked when I said, 'But I am still me, Mother. Still the same Marcus.'

I heard her catch her breath.

'Well he – Caecilius – is not here,' she said. 'He is in Patrai; he has business with some king or ruler there.'

I nodded.

There was a painful silence. Then she said in a small quiet voice, 'The farm was important. Understand that. I would not see it lost.'

It seemed then that all my pent-up grief broke out. I had wanted her to speak to me, to open the closed door, to drop the mask of duty just for a moment. And now that she did so, my emotion swept over me like a wave.

I let out a sob, for her loss, and my own, and for the deep unending brutality of the world, which even the shading rowan tree could not withstand.

I hurried across the room and knelt, and took her hand in mine. 'I know, Mother,' I whispered. 'I know.'

She touched my hair and cheek. After a short while she released her hand and stood, and went to gaze out of the window.

'Your sister has missed you,' she said. 'She loves you dearly. Did you know? Perhaps some god brought her here, knowing what she needed most. She has found a brother in you. Scarcely a day goes by that she does not speak of it.'

'I have brought books for her.'

'She will like that. Go then and see her. You will find her down on the lower terrace, where the old oak grows above the summer pasture. It used to be a favourite place of yours. Do you remember?'

She swung round startled when I called. She had a heavy winter cloak wrapped around her, and a book spread open on her lap.

'Marcus!' she cried.

She set her book aside and came running.

'Why didn't you send word? I thought you were in Greece.'

I explained, and she listened with her wide intelligent eyes on me.

When I had finished she said, 'Another war. Well, there has been talk of it long enough.' She paused and looked at me. 'Will you have to fight?'

'Perhaps. I have fought before . . . Oh, I almost forgot, there's a big parcel for you up at the house. I went shopping at the bookshops in Athens before I left.'

She caught her breath with joy. 'Oh, Marcus,' she cried, and kissed me on the cheek.

'But first,' I said laughing, 'you must tell me how you've been.'

'Oh, I have been happy,' she said. 'I treasure each day. I have your mother with me, the people from the farm, and your father's books.'

'Then I'm glad.'

I paused for a moment and met her eye. 'And how is *he*?'

Neither of us needed to say whom I meant.

'He is in Greece,' she said with a shrug.

'I know. Mother told me.'

'You ask how he is. Well he is richer, of course, and he makes sure everyone knows it. He is fatter. He listens less.' She glanced out over the sloping pasture towards the far hills. 'Did you ever look down into the valley from here, and notice the farm houses, and the animals, and the men working in the fields, all tiny and distant, as a bird might see?'

'All the time,' I said. 'I used to sit in this very place.'

'Far away you can see it all; the cart on the track; the stallion with the mare; the boys swimming in the river; the servants about their work. Not one of them can see the other; yet from here I can see it all, as, surely, a god must see it, all of a oneness, in its true proportion. And so it is with him. Before, I thought of him as my father: that was all I knew, it was the limit of my world. But when he comes here now, after his long absences, I see not the father, but the man.'

'Has he changed so much?'

She shook her head. 'No, Marcus. I have changed. I see what I did not see. Riches are no longer enough for him, though he talks of them often enough. Now there is something else: he has caught the scent of power, enough to know that he wants more. But he does not understand it, or how to win it, or what it can do to a man. Have you seen his study yet?'

I said I had not.

'Then go and look, if you have the stomach for it. You can learn a lot about a man by seeing what he desires, and what he regards as beautiful. He has filled the room with every fashionable vulgar trinket he has set eyes on. Bronzes of kissing naked boys; satyrs on nymphs; goddesses reaching at their privates; it is a mirror to his secret soul.'

I considered her serious, intent face. Yes, I thought, she had changed indeed. She had looked into the dark places, and from there she had drawn a calm wisdom, born of knowledge, and of pain.

Then I asked, 'Does he bring women here?'

'Not here, thank God. He knows your mother would not stand for it. He has sense enough for that, at least.'

I nodded, and we said no more about him. For a while we talked of matters of no consequence. But presently she said, 'You are different. Something has happened to you.'

I smiled.

'Well I am older, I suppose. And I have seen things I had not seen before, not all of them good.'

'Yes,' she said. She paused for a moment. 'Yet there is

something else; I can see it in your eyes.' Then she said, 'Are you in love?'

I laughed out loud. 'You see a lot, little sister.'

'Sorry. I should not have asked. You need not tell me.'

'No, I want to.'

And so I told her about Menexenos.

I went on far too long, as lovers do. When I had finished she said, 'I thought it was something like that. It must be a wonderful thing to have such a friend. Is he like a brother to you?'

'A brother?' I shrugged and smiled. 'Why, I cannot say; I have never had one.'

'Nor I.' And with a shy sideways glance she added, 'Until now.'

I remembered my mother's words. Turning to face her on the bench I said, 'And I have a sister. I could not hope for a better one in all the world.'

Her serious face brightened, and then she smiled her rare, round-faced smile. 'I hope you'll bring him here one day. I should like to meet him.'

I imagined with happiness bringing Menexenos to Praeneste and showing him my childhood world.

'I shall,' I said. 'One day soon. You and he would be friends, I am sure of it.'

One day that winter, while I was out on the land, I saw a horseman making his way up the long track. It was a special messenger from Rome, and he brought a letter from Titus.

I sent the man round to the stable house at the back, where he could get a meal for himself and his horse. Then I broke the seal and read.

The letter said, 'Titus to his friend Marcus, greetings. In ten days the elections take place. All is in the balance. Come if you can.'

I went round to the kitchens at the back, and found the messenger over a steaming dish of bacon and beans, with the house slaves clustered round, listening to his news. When he looked up I said, 'Tell him I shall see him in Rome.'

Standing against Titus that year was an old senator put forward by the faction opposed to war with Philip, or to any foreign venture. Titus's own father, I had heard from others, was part of this faction. Titus feared the vote would go against him; but in the event he was elected comfortably, aided by the votes of the veteran colonists he had helped settle in new lands. To celebrate, Titus held a banquet. It was almost like the old days in Tarentum. He had hired a Greek kitharist, and a renowned cook from Neapolis. But now, of course, everybody wanted to be his friend, and I was only one of many guests.

There was one notable absence, however. His own father did not come, claiming, so I heard, that he had other commitments.

The consuls, though they are elected in the winter, do not take up office until the Ides of March of the following year. While he waited, Titus made his arrangements; and of these, one in particular came as a shock to me. The

Senate, on Titus's advice, had appointed Lucius his brother to the command of the fleet.

I do not know if they expressed misgivings. If they did, Titus did not tell me; and, as you may suppose, whatever I thought of this appointment I kept to myself. Titus, who usually saw so clearly, had a deep loyalty to his brother, which I knew better than to question.

At the time, Lucius was away, on some army business in Gaul. I gave the matter little thought. But then, one day that winter, Titus said, 'Philip is pressing hard on Attalos and the Athenians; we must do what we can to relieve them. I've written to Lucius asking him to sail to Athens as soon as the sea routes are open. You know the Greeks better than he does: I want you to go with him. Your advice will be useful, and besides, it is time you had a formal command of your own.'

I thanked him, wondering if he had forgotten about Lucius's quarrel with me in Tarentum. Titus was too greathearted to think of such things. Lucius, I sensed, was not.

That winter, as I got to know Rome better, I liked it more.

I spent time with Villius and his friend Terentius, and, with them as my guides, I began to discover the secret places behind the drab exterior.

As Titus had said, at that time teachers, actors and artists of every sort were being drawn to Rome. One heard them in the little backstreet taverns, and found their workshops in secluded courtyards in the unfashionable quarters where one would not think to go. Quietly they practised their trades, and passed their skills on from old to young, master to apprentice, as they had done since time began and men had first gathered together to live in cities, and civilize themselves. There were potters working in the Greek style; there were vase-painters; there were silver- and goldsmiths; sculptors, painters and architects. In time the loaf would be leavened. They would beautify Rome, and they would spread their knowledge like rays of dawn light to the furthest reaches of the world, where barbarians wandered naked and beasts roamed untamed.

One day, Villius and Terentius took me to hear a visiting philosopher from Rhodes, who had come to deliver a series of lectures.

He began by praising the Good, in words of such polish and beauty that my very soul seemed to soar from my body. But then, afterwards, deliberately, and with equal skill, he demolished everything he had said, leaving my head reeling.

When the lecture was over, and we were walking down the street towards the Forum, Villius asked me what I thought. I answered that after such a performance I no longer knew even whether I walked on solid earth or not, and at this he laughed.

'It is for such reasons as this,' he said, 'that some men want to drive the philosophers out of the city. They serve strong wine; they force men to look at how they think, and how they act; and there are some who do not care for that. Tell me, have you met Titus's father yet?'

I said I had not.

'He calls them over-educated babble-mouths, who talk and talk and settle nothing. If he had his way, every philosopher and artist, rhetor and rhapsode would be expelled at the point of a spear . . . Once you know the father, you will begin to understand the sons.'

This surprised me, and I said, 'What, *both* sons, Titus *and* Lucius? Yet they seem so different.'

'So they do, yet they are different plants from the same garden. Their father is a man who thinks you can beat virtue into a boy with a stick. Half-rations. Food not fit for a dog to eat. No music. No books. And, of course, never – *never* – anything Greek. They both bear the scars, in different ways.'

I walked on beside him, considering this with a frown. 'Yet Titus seems so . . .' – I hesitated, scarcely daring to use the word after the lecture I had heard – 'so *good*. He must have got it from somewhere.'

'Oh, he did. And this is the great joke of it; this is what his father cannot bear. One day, quite by chance, he happened to hear some streetside rhapsode reciting Homer. It can't have been much good, but after that he was captivated. Whatever he has made himself, he got from the Greeks. He has fashioned himself from his dream. And his father, knowing the source, cannot for give him.'

'But Villius,' I cried, 'that's terrible!'

He smiled at my indignation.

'I've heard worse. Scratch around in any family, and you'll find something.'

We said no more, for just then Villius saw a group of his friends advancing up the hill, and we went to greet them.

But it was not long after this, one day when I called on Titus, that I met his father for myself.

303

The winter had turned suddenly cold. Smoke from a thousand household fires hung in the chill morning air. As the steward was taking my cloak Titus emerged from his workroom, looking grave and preoccupied.

Seeing me he almost started. I think he had forgotten I was coming. But he hid this, and said, 'Ah, Marcus!' And then, in a low bleak voice, 'My father is here. He will be gone in a moment, but you had better come and meet him. He already complains I keep my friends from him.'

Titus's father was standing between the desk and the window, looking out at the grey winter garden. He turned sharply when Titus entered, and immediately I had the sense that my arrival had interrupted some dispute between them.

Titus presented me, mentioning a little of what I had done. As he spoke, his father regarded me with an immobile face. It was thinner than his son's, and there were long lines around his mouth, emphasizing his scowl. But what one noticed were his eyes. Where Titus's seemed to shine light, his father's quenched it.

He glanced at my tunic and sniffed. It was one I had bought for myself in Athens; nothing showy, just a narrow border of red oak-leaves touched with blue. But he himself wore drab homespun, the sort of thing some country farmer might wear about the stables.

There was something about his cold appraising look that made me want to feel ashamed. But I knew I had nothing to be ashamed of. So I looked him back in the eye and told him I was glad to meet him at last.

He grunted an acknowledgement. 'Well I am on my way out, as soon as that foot-dragging steward brings

my cloak. Are you not the boy from Praeneste, whose
father died in Epeiros?'

'Yes, sir.'

I supposed he was going to say he was sorry for it, but
he went on, 'Well Epeiros is a dangerous place. It would
have been wiser if he had not gone . . . How old are you?'

'Twenty, sir.'

He laughed. 'Twenty, and you are rushing off on this
wild foreign venture.' And then he said, 'So you were the
one at Abydos?'

'Yes, sir. I was there when it fell.'

'Well the Greeks have brought this trouble upon themselves, and now they expect us to go and rescue them.
But I am wasting my breath. I don't suppose you will
listen to me any more than he does' – jabbing his thumb
at Titus. 'In my opinion a young man would better spend
his time tending his father's farm, and honouring the
example of his ancestors. *They* did not take themselves
off overseas, to fight other people's wars.'

Behind me Titus sighed. '*They* did not have to.'

'And nor do you. What is it to us if they all kill one
another? Let them get on with it.'

'Sir,' said Titus patiently, 'we talked of this before. It
is not for the sake of the Greeks alone that we must fight
Philip. It is for ourselves.'

'I do not believe it.'

'I know you don't.'

'Once we begin this, there will be no turning back.
The Greeks will corrupt us. Don't shake your head.
Have you looked about the city lately? The youth are all
scented fops, dressed up like actors, filling their heads with

305

nonsense – Greek nonsense. They look more like women than men. I suspect they do not know themselves whether they are girl or boy.'

Wearily Titus said, 'Yes, Father.'

'Too much learning is no good. It makes men dissatisfied. Look at that drunken wastrel Lucius. I said he would come to nothing, and I was right. My own father would have beaten it out of me. Well I blame myself; I have been too soft . . . Spare the rod . . .'

Titus looked down, his cheeks reddening under his light-brown beard.

His father went on, 'Look at you! You are not yet thirty. Your head is full of dreams, and now you have persuaded the people to make you consul. Consul! At twenty-nine! I have never come across such public folly.'

'Scipio did it.'

'Scipio is another fool. Only yesterday I was talking to Cato. He agrees with me. Now there is a young man who shows promise. You could learn something from him.'

'Cato!' cried Titus, rolling his eyes to the ceiling. 'If Cato had his way we'd still be living in mud huts, and washing once each half-year in the Tiber. I do what I do for Rome.'

'You deceive yourself. What you do, you do for yourself . . . Sextus! Where is my cloak?'

He made for the door, intending, I suppose, to go searching for the slave. Then, remembering me, he turned.

'Goodbye,' he said. 'Mind you do not get yourself killed like your father.'

Then he walked out.

Titus met my eye. 'Cato!' he said bitterly. 'He holds

Cato up as an example! Have you met him? He is a heartless young prig who affects poverty and thinks there is no one in Rome more virtuous than he. There is nothing more distasteful than a rich man who pretends to be poor. But the old die-hard senators, and my father, take his vain posturing for old-time virtue and adore him.'

He threw himself down at the desk. 'No matter what I do, it is never enough. He sneers at the Greeks, because they know more than he does. To him, virtue is to act without question, like a slave. Why is it always those who need it most who despise philosophy?'

I searched for something to say. He looked utterly crushed. But what did one say about fathers? I realized I did not know. Feeling embarrassed, and at a loss, I eventually said, 'I suppose he means well.'

Titus looked up. 'Do you, Marcus? That is because you do not know him. He is like the Gorgon, turning everything he gazes upon to stone.' Unconsciously, as he spoke, his hand had been toying with the marble paper-weight, tapping and rocking it on the tabletop. The fidgeting reminded me of Lucius, and I remembered Villius's words, that the two brothers were plants from the same garden. Yet, even with such poor soil, one had grown to the light, while the other had languished. It seemed a mystery to me.

Presently he grew conscious of the tapping and stopped, stilling the weight with his hand. He stared at the dark veins in the stone, and then impatiently set it aside.

In a quiet, taut, final voice, he murmured, half to himself, 'So much for my family.'

That was all. It was as if the furnace door had closed, shutting the raging fire within.

He shook his head, then rousing himself said, 'But come, Marcus, let us send for some warmed, spiced wine, and talk of the future.'

I never met his father again. But ever since, when I hear some important politician extolling the family as a self-evident good, I think of him.

Eleven

WE HAD BEEN DELAYED. Lucius had held a praetor-
ship in Gaul during the previous year, and although Titus
had urged him to make haste as soon as he was able to
relinquish his office, telling him the fleet was waiting for
him at the Roman base on Kerkyra, still I had to wait
almost to month-end, kicking my heels at Brundisium
with the other officers, the pilots and sailors, and a small
detachment of troops.

Finally he arrived, not on horseback, or in a swift
one-horse gig, but in a ponderous four-wheeled carriage drawn by a train of languid oxen, with another
carriage following on behind, laden with his personal effects.

Once, in Tarentum, I had mistaken Lucius for his
brother. There was no chance of that now. It was like
seeing some ruin of Titus, an apparition of how he might
have been. His brown hair, which on Titus curled about
his neck and brow, was flaccid and dull. He was expen-
sively dressed in a fine purple-striped long tunic, and over
it he wore a heavy winter cloak, dyed peacock blue, the

kind of thing certain rich men had begun importing from Greece.

His body was concealed under all these folds of finery, but one could see even from his face that he had gone to fat. There had once been a dissolute handsomeness about him; now his eyes were sunken, his face was drawn and irritable, premature jowls hung around his mouth, and his brooding sulkiness had transformed into something permanent, and dangerous.

The others standing beside me had seen it too. Eyes were averted. No one wanted to be the first to meet his challenging gaze.

All except mine. And so, fool that I am when it comes to such things, his roving hostile eye fell on me first of all.

'What are *you* doing here?' he cried.

His voice had deepened since I had last seen him in Tarentum. Then there had been a hint of unsureness about it, a lack of confidence. Now he spoke like a man who has grown used to ordering others around.

My comrades beside me shuffled and allowed themselves to look up, now that I was singled out and the danger averted. I made some answer to Lucius; I knew full well that Titus had written and told him I should be there, and my uniform and insignia of a military tribune would have told him the rest, even if he had not inspected the list he had been sent by Titus, which, I saw, he held rolled up in his hand, slapping it against his palm.

But it did not matter much what I said, I could see from his face he was not listening.

'Well, since you are here, you can see to it that my things are properly stowed,' he said, waving his arm at

310

the bulging wagon behind, as if I were some deckhand. Then, to the quinquereme commander, who had stepped forward, 'I will see my ship now. There is no time to lose.'

We arrived in Kerkyra to find the fleet had sailed on without us. Lucius was incandescent with fury. He sent for the military officer whose job it was to oversee the movement of Roman warships, and demanded an explanation.

I stood watching from the deck as he railed at the man. Beside me stood the pilot, a black-haired youth from Ostia called Lamyros, who had a cheeky, smiling face and a good nose for fools.

As Lucius blustered on, Lamyros shaded his mouth with his hand and murmured, 'Just as I tried to tell him, Marcus; the fleet commander had orders to wait for no one, not even him.'

We exchanged a look and allowed ourselves a private smile. On the quay the military harbour-master was explaining, in between Lucius's snapping interruptions, that the fleet had moved on to Kephallania, where it was taking on stores, prior to sailing round the Gulf of Malea and onwards to Piraeus.

Lucius heard him out with grunts of anger and impatient snorts. Then the harbour-master paused, clearly uncomfortable with what he had to say next. But he set his face firm, and pressed on, like a man treading on the lintel of his house after an earthquake has struck, not knowing which movement will bring the roof down on top of him.

'I have been asked, sir – that is, ordered – to convey to

you that you are to proceed with all haste to Kephallania as soon as you arrive; and that, although the fleet will be there for some days, the—'

'*Ordered?*' burst out Lucius. 'Who dares to order me? Who gave that order? I want the man's name. I want him brought here.'

The harbour-master stared at him appalled.

'Well?' cried Lucius, glaring.

'Why it was the consul, sir. Titus the consul. I have the order here.'

It was as well Lucius had his back to the quinquereme, or he would have seen the grins and flashing eyes that passed among the crew behind him. Even the pilot had to draw his hand to his mouth and pretend to cough.

On the quayside there was a long, unpleasant pause.

'Very well,' said Lucius eventually. 'It is no great matter; we can catch up with the fleet on Kephallania, just as you say . . . I was delayed, and the fleet has gone on, that is all.' He let out a sudden sharp laugh. It sounded like a dog choking. 'Still, now we are here, we may as well eat and amuse ourselves a little . . . Which tavern is best? And which house has the best girls?'

The poor harbour-master, a lean, serious-looking man of middle age who was, no doubt, an excellent organizer of ship movements and such things, assumed a stricken expression, suspecting, I think, that Lucius was trying to catch him out in some lapse of military discipline.

'Why I cannot say, sir,' he stuttered. 'I eat at the mess generally; though I hear there are good dining houses up on the hill . . . For the rest, I do not know.'

Lucius gave him a careful sidelong look, trying to

gauge whether he was being mocked. He must have decided, in the end, that the man meant no more than he had said, for with a dismissive toss of his hand he cried, 'Oh leave me alone then,' and went marching off up the quayside.

We busied ourselves with what little there was to do.

Lucius returned soon after, having regained a degree of composure, and announced that, with the fleet already sailed, there was no need for haste. He was going into the town for the night, and the rest of us could do as we wished.

I had already noticed, from the moment our quinque-reme passed through the harbour wall, the grand white-painted mansion up on the ridge, where I had first met my stepfather. The sight of it revived all my bad memories. I had not even troubled to find out whether Caecilius still owned the place; I did not care, for I had no intention of going there; and when we had finished with the business on the quay, I put up with the rest of the ship's men in a boisterous sailors' inn in the street behind the harbour.

I was in my room, arranging my few things, when one of the crew tapped on the door and said a man was asking for me below. He had declined to come in, and was waiting in the street.

'Did he give his name?' I asked, wondering who in Kerkyra might know me.

'He would not say,' said the crewman. 'But he told me he was a friend of yours.'

Curious now, I left my things half-unpacked on the bed and went downstairs. By then evening was coming on. The westering sun had already sunk behind the hills, leaving the street in shadow. A figure was waiting under the porch, leaning against the pillar with his back to me. As soon as I stepped through the door he swung round.

'Marcus, sir, so it is you after all . . . Well, what can I say?' – with a show of admiring my uniform – 'you have certainly made something of yourself since Tarentum, but of course I always knew you would, in fact . . .'

He talked on, pouring out a stream of babbling empty compliments while I stared at him.

It was fat Florus, much thinner now, who had done his best to make my life in Tarentum miserable, and had ridden off when I was in danger.

Clearly he wanted something. For a while I listened to his unctuous insincere protests of affection and respect. When at last he paused I asked if he was still working for Caecilius.

'Ah!' he said, sucking his breath through his teeth, 'you see Marcus sir, that is the very thing. I am here when needed, always available . . . though your father is in Greece at present, as you must know.'

'My *step*father. Yes, I heard.'

'Yes, yes,' he said, nodding vigorously and wringing his hands, 'but if you see him – I suppose you *will* see him – perhaps you would tell him, Marcus sir, that you met me, and that I am here, and that I await his instructions.'

I gave him a careful look. 'Yes, if you wish. If I see him. Is that what you wanted to speak to me about?'

'Yes . . . Well no, not only. Since you are so important' – with another flourish at my uniform – 'maybe you will speak to the garrison commander for me, just put a word in . . . any work will do – anything equal to my dignity, that is – you will find me at—' He hesitated, then stepping up went on in a lowered voice, 'Well, to be honest with you, Marcus, I am between lodgings just at present; but ask the under-clerk at the harbour-master's office – his name is Amplicius – and he will know how to reach me.'

Up close, his breath and body smelled bad. He had done his best with his clothing, but I saw his cloak was dirty, and worn threadbare where the hem caught on the ground. His feet were grey with dust, and the overstraps of his sandals had been botched together with rivets. He was trying to look like a successful man of business; it was pathetic; anyone could see it was a sham, and for a moment I felt sorry for him.

'I'll put a word in at the garrison,' I said, thinking they might find something for him there. Then, for no particular reason, I asked, 'How is your friend Virilis, the one who was in Tarentum with you. Is he here too?'

Immediately his face changed. He leapt back and cried, 'That snake! Why do you mention him? Has Caecilius told you then?'

'Told me what?'

He seemed not to hear, but went on, 'Virilis is no friend of *mine*, that ditch-born son of a whore – may the gods rot him, the weasel! It was an oversight, no more than that—'

'What was?'

He regarded me suspiciously. 'You *know*. You knew all along, and you are making fun of me. Caecilius must have told you. I was not stealing the land-rents, as that informing snake told Caecilius; it was no more than a misunderstanding. I had the money for safe keeping in my room; I meant to bring it but must have forgotten, that's all; an oversight, anyone could have done it.'

I began to understand. Perhaps Florus saw it in my face. Suddenly ingratiating again, he clutched at my tunic as I stepped towards the door. 'Tell him so, Marcus sir. Don't forget. A mistake. That's all. A mistake.'

Just then, from somewhere down the street, a voice shouted out, 'Hey, you!'

Florus's head jerked round. He gasped, bit his knuckles, hitched up his grubby old mantle, then hurried off along the side-alley without another word.

I watched him go, then turned. The man who had shouted was racing up the street.

I stepped out, and extended my arm to block him.

He halted, looked angrily at my face, then glanced down at my uniform.

'He owes me,' he said.

I said, 'He has nothing.'

'Pah!' said the man. 'He should have thought of that.' But by now Florus had made his escape.

Seeing this, the man gave a contemptuous shrug, spat in the gutter, then turned and sloped off the way he had come.

So much for Florus. I don't know what trouble he had got himself into; but I did no more for him than put this man off his track for a while.

I shook my head and returned inside. I had concerns enough of my own, for it had become clear, on the crossing from Brundisium, that Lucius had neither forgiven nor forgotten. With that, and his fractious mood, I was not looking forward to the rest of the journey to Athens.

We departed next day, steering south for the island of Kephallania. I stood with Lamyros the pilot at the stern, and watched the rocky sinuous coast of Epeiros recede in the east.

I was thinking of Titus. Already he was there, somewhere among the steep wooded ravines and high peaks, and with him were the crack troops he had taken from Italy: the best of Scipio's veterans, men who had defeated Hannibal in Africa, and who knew the taste of victory.

All through the winter he had been holed up with the military planners, working on dispositions, appointments, troop transports, intelligence reports and all the business that moving an army required. But commands are only formally assigned to the new consuls when they take up office, when each consul's province is chosen by lot – unless the Senate consents to some other arrangement. And so, until that day, nothing was certain.

That year, his co-consul was a man named Paetus. On the Ides of March, on the day they took up office, he and Titus convened the Senate and sought permission to allocate that year's commands not by lot, as was customary, but by arrangement; telling the Senate that he and Paetus had agreed between them that Paetus would remain to administer Italy, while Titus would go to Epeiros, to conduct the war against Philip.

The Senate had agreed, and next day Titus had set out for Brundisium, where his ship was waiting.

From somewhere behind me, Lucius's voice broke into

my thoughts. He was complaining to Lamyros. I scarcely listened; he had found reason to complain of something or other ever since Brundisium. At least, for a brief while, I was not the target of his anger.

He had been abrupt and hostile from the moment he set eyes on me. On a ship, such things are quickly noticed. Even before we reached Kerkyra the rest of the crew, having got the measure of Lucius for themselves, were throwing me discreet sympathetic looks – and adding, when they could be sure Lucius would not see, a mocking gesture of the fingers, or a roll of the eyes and tongue, parodying sea-sickness, or hilarious imitations of Lucius's awkward pot-bellied way of walking along the deck.

It would have been the easiest thing in the world to play on this to my own advantage, and to Lucius's detriment. But, I reflected, I should only be feeding my own vanity, and doing no good to Titus, or the cause of Rome, or to the shades of the innocent people of Abydos.

I resolved, therefore, that, whatever the provocation, I should give Lucius no cause, nor undermine his command. And so, when, scarcely two hours out of Kerkyra, Lucius went to the stern-house and called for a flask of wine, I refused to meet the crew's knowing nods and winks, and instead leant on the rail, watching the long line of the coast in the distance, keeping my thoughts to myself and reflecting on the battles to come.

On the second day we rounded the sheer, white cliffs of Cape Leukatas, with its temple of Apollo perched on top. Ahead, beyond the headland, lay Kephallania, pine-clad, rising from a glittering sea; and next to it, close by, the island of Ithaka.

The sail was hauled down. The pilot gave the order for oars, and we passed through the channel which separates the two islands, emerging shortly before sunset into a wide, sheltered bay.

On the far side, spreading up the hillside, was the town of Sami, white-painted, shining orange and golden in the late sunlight; and all around us, on still water like burnished bronze, sat the triremes and quinqueremes and storeships of the Roman fleet, lying peacefully at anchor.

I should not have cause to mention our stay at Sami, but for the fact that it was here that Lucius met the love of his life.

I do not know where he first found the boy, but by the second day they were inseparable. His name was Doron. He was more than ten years younger than Lucius – sixteen or seventeen – though his slender body and girlish manner made him seem younger still.

He had flawless olive-coloured skin; pretty, fluttering hands, and shrewd black eyes like a money-lender's. His father, as I later learnt, had run off some years before with a woman from Syracuse, leaving him to be brought up by his doting embittered mother. She had allowed him to do as he pleased, which is not the best way to bring up a son or daughter in a busy harbour town. He had little money, but at some point he discovered the one thing he possessed that gave him power over others: his epicene looks.

These looks he exploited to the full, gaining for himself, along with a hoard of petty love-gifts, enough money to keep himself in bright, fashionable clothes. Anyone who has walked down the streets behind a port could guess what he gave in exchange.

For all my dislike of Lucius, yet it was painful to see how he was put upon. Doron played on the strings of his heart as an expert musician plays the kithara. He was all tenderness and smiles whenever Lucius was within sight. When he was not, he was sulky, sharp-tongued, long-faced and petulant. He could change his features as an actor changes his mask.

During those few days at Sami, Lucius fell completely for the boy's siren song. He thought he had found the perfect love, though even the roughest deckhand or wharfside trollop could see he was deceived. He was a slave to Doron's every whim.

But if Lucius was blinded, Doron was not. With all the skill of a master angler he had Lucius caught.

It was a catch he did not intend to lose.

Before long, the provisioning of the fleet was done, and it was time to depart.

The bulbous, heavily laden transports would need to be towed around the Gulf of Malea, a slow and tedious journey, with many halts. Lucius had no patience for this. He announced he intended to sail ahead to Athens in a convoy of three fast quinqueremes. The rest of the fleet could proceed at its own pace and meet him there.

Next day we prepared to put to sea. All about the wide bay, tenders were rowing between the ships, or from ship to shore, and on the decks the crews were making final preparations – loosening the furled sails, preparing the ropes, stowing the last baskets of provisions and casks of water.

All of a sudden there was a commotion at the far end of the waterfront. I glanced up from what I was doing and saw Doron, striding onto the quayside from under the archway, wearing a sunhat garlanded with a ribbon, and sumptuously dressed in a sky-blue travelling cloak with ruby buttons.

On the deck everyone turned to look, just as Lucius appeared at his side, beaming like a bridegroom, followed by three porters struggling with a vast cedarwood clothes-chest.

'By God!' muttered Lamyros beside me. 'Surely he's not bringing the boy with him?'

The rugged old marines, veterans from the war with Hannibal, were sitting about on the quay, busying themselves with their gear, or lounging in the sunlight while they waited to board. One turned and said something. Then all their heads swung round.

They were solid, hard-living, country men who knew how to fight and kill; I do not think they had ever set eyes on the likes of Doron before. They stared open-mouthed, gaping like chicks in a nest, totally absorbed in the sight, oblivious to everything else.

Lucius, ignoring them, swept past and up the gang-board. But Doron paused, rolled his dark eyes, gave them a broad smile, and flourished the embroidered hem of his new cloak, as if to say: Are you not envious? For see what a pretty coat he has bought me.

We sailed shortly after, a swift-moving convoy of three

sleek quinqueremes, painted black and gold, with white-tipped oars. On the third day we rounded the point of Aigina; and then, gleaming like a pearl in a bed of green, the high-city of Athens showed in the distance.

The sky was cloudless and blue as sapphire, and on the plateau the Virgin's temple shone clear and sharp. Someone came up beside me at the rail. It was Lamyros.

He whistled slowly through his teeth and said, 'I have seen Africa and Spain and Gaul, and I have even sailed beyond the Pillars of Herakles, out to the encircling ocean, where twice each day the sea recedes from the land. But never have I seen anything like this. It is like a thing built by gods. And Philip wants to destroy it? Then truly he must be as mad as people say.'

'He *is* mad,' I replied, 'and there is an insane kind of glory in being remembered as the man who destroyed a thing of irreplaceable beauty. But I don't think even he wants to destroy it. He wants it for himself, like every tyrant. But if he cannot, then he would rather see it burn.'

I glanced back over my shoulder. The marines, who liked to make out the world had nothing new to show them, had fallen silent and were staring. It seemed everyone – the helmsman, the men at the rigging, the pilot's mate – had paused to look. But then I heard Doron's sudden bright laughter coming from the deck-house, and saw that I was wrong. He and Lucius were reclining on a heap of cushions, shaded by the awning, talking softly and drinking in turns from one silver wine-cup which they shared, intent on nothing but each other.

By the time we rounded the harbour entrance at Piraeus a crowd had gathered.

I looked about for Menexenos and saw him straight away, up under the great cresset-beacon on the harbour wall, in the place he knew I would look first.

I raised my arm in greeting, and, seeing me, he grinned and raised his in return.

Standing there on the low steps, apart from the crowd, in his simple white tunic, with his hair falling about his brow, he looked like the image of some god, and for the second time that morning I found that beauty had taken my breath away.

As I looked, someone moved up beside him, a woman in green and saffron and scarlet, looking like some exotic flower. I laughed and waved. It was Pasithea.

Presently, when the ship had docked, and we were standing on the quayside talking, Menexenos motioned along the wharf and said, 'Who is that youth, the one making all the fuss?'

'That,' I said, 'is Doron. Lucius found him at Sami.'

He looked again. Doron had commandeered a team of stevedores who had been busy unloading a neighbouring ship. They had brought a crane, and he was directing from the quay as they lifted his clothes-chest from the hold. He had spoken to them with a good deal of arrogance – never a wise idea with Athenian workmen – which had set them against him from the start. Now his frequent cries of 'Stop!' and 'Wait!' and 'No, you fools!' had unnerved them, or annoyed them, and the chest hung suspended over the water, swaying in its cradle of ropes, while they argued about how to proceed.

'He looks very young,' said Menexenos, turning back to me.

'He *is* young. Sixteen, so he says.'

'He looks nearer fourteen.'

'I know he does. He has a child's build, or a girl's. I don't suppose he's ever set foot inside a gymnasion in his life.'

'Then what is he doing here? He's not a soldier, surely.'

I laughed out loud. 'No. Certainly not that. Just at the moment he has Lucius dancing like a trained monkey.' I told him about Sami.

Menexenos frowned.

'I wonder what he expects from Lucius. Does he suppose he will teach him virtue?'

'To tell you the truth,' I said smiling, 'I don't think he cares much about virtue. But he likes the expensive gifts Lucius buys him. That clothes-chest is stuffed with treasures from just a week together. As for Lucius, he is in love, besotted.'

'Really?' said Menexenos, gazing up at the chest suspended over the water. 'I wonder what he sees in the boy. It cannot be a meeting of minds, or a care for the Good . . . But what, Marcus? What is so funny?'

I shook my head. Then, seeing the sincere, puzzled look on his face I broke into a laugh. He looked questioningly at Pasithea, and at this she laughed too.

'Sometimes, Menexenos,' she said, 'you really are an innocent.'

'What, I, Pasithea?' he said, looking put out. 'Not so. It is Lucius who is the innocent, if he can really be such a fool.'

324

Laughing I said, 'Well you already know he's a fool. Actually I can't help feeling sorry for him, seeing him taken in by that sly trickster. But who will tell him? Certainly not I.'

I grinned and laughed with Pasithea. And in my heart I thanked the gods that, out of so many, I had found Menexenos.

The quayside was full of crowds and noise and bustle – people jostling and calling for their friends, porters touting for business or pushing handcarts, stevedores chanting as they worked; water-sellers, wine-sellers, food-sellers, and, sitting on the wall behind, dockside whores of both sexes, making eyes at the sailors.

Amidst all this I became aware of a stirring behind me. I thought nothing of it, until I saw Menexenos's eyes suddenly go up.

Then I glanced round, just as a large red-faced man emerged, elbowing his way through the crowd, saying irritably in a Latin accent, 'Let me pass; let me pass.'

It was Caecilius.

I looked at him in amazement.

'What?' he said crossly. 'Do you not know me?'

'Sir,' I said, finding my voice. 'I had no idea . . . I thought you were in Patrai.'

'I was. Now I am here, on business for your friend Lucius Flamininus. Did he not tell you, though you have sailed so far together? You surprise me.'

Then his glance was caught by Pasithea and he paused.

'Greetings, Caecilius,' she said, 'I trust I find you well.'

'Hello madam,' he said, unsurely, and I saw his brow

move in a frown as he wondered to himself how she knew his name, and whether he had met her before, and whether he should admit it.

Eventually he coughed and looked away. 'Well, anyway,' he said, turning to me, 'you will find me at the house of Tuchon the Phoenician shipowner, in the street behind the arsenal. Anyone knows his house, it is the one painted red and blue, with the gilded statues outside. Come when you have finished with your friends, if you can find time.'

Just then, from behind, Doron's high-pitched, nasal voice suddenly rose above the din like some shrill birdcall, crying out indignantly, 'No, leave it there I tell you! Oh, where is Lucius?'

Caecilius turned, craning his neck.

'Who is *that*?' he said, a sneer forming on his lips.

'A particular friend of Lucius's, sir.'

'Ah! A friend of Lucius's. I see. Of course. Well I must be getting along. I am a busy man.'

He gave Menexenos a brief nod, frowned once more at Pasithea, turned, and pushed off through the crowd.

Later I went to him. He grumbled at me for a while, as if somehow I should have known he was in Athens. But I could see he was eager to get onto his own affairs, and before long he said, 'Well, anyway, you will be pleased to hear my friend Tuchon has included me in a nice deal, supplying munitions from workshops on the islands, for which there is quite a need at present. War breeds opportunity, as I have told you before.'

He paused and waited for me to nod. I nodded, and considered Tuchon.

I had met him on my way in. He was a Phoenician

from Sidon with sleek black oiled hair, who reeked of some pungent Asiatic scent and flaunted his wealth in his clothes and jewellery. He was, in short, a man in my stepfather's mould – all except the scent, which in those days no Roman would dare to venture out in.

Caecilius, meanwhile, was talking on, explaining how he had secured from some associate of Lucius's a contract to supply the fleet and marines, and, since the need was urgent and unexpected, he had been able to push up his price. Lucius, he said, was eager to make his mark while Titus was still busy in Epeiros: he was planning an attack on Eretria in Euboia – 'a secret still; mind who you tell'– a city held by Philip, which was causing great disruption to allied shipping. 'I knew my friendship with Titus would prove useful,' he said, raising a plump didactic finger. 'Always look to the long term, Marcus. Remember that. A useful lesson.'

'Yes, sir. I see.'

He leaned back into the soft cushions, folded his hands across his belly, and peered at my uniform, seeming to see it for the first time.

'What has Titus promoted you to? A captain?'

'A tribune.'

'Ah, a tribune.' He nodded. 'I suppose, then, you will be going off with the army, and leaving me to handle business alone?'

'Of course, sir,' I said carefully, 'business comes first, that is clear, and I thank you for reminding me. I am sure Lucius will excuse me from my duty, if I tell him you require my help. He will not be pleased, and we are short of men, but—'

'What are you thinking?' he cried, lurching forward. 'You must not displease Lucius at any cost. Have you not been listening to anything I've told you?'

'You are right, sir,' I said, nodding thoughtfully. 'I shall go and fight. That would be best.'

'Quite so; quite so.' And then, '*Can* you fight? Who taught you? I hope you are better at war than you are at business.'

News came from Epeiros. Philip had asked for a meeting with Titus, supposing he could persuade the new young consul to come to easy terms, or, failing that, waste his time in drawn-out negotiations.

He soon discovered that Titus was not another vacillating Roman general, to be pushed back and forth across Epeiros until his consulship was over. At the meeting, Titus told him that if he wanted peace with Rome he must abandon his strongholds in Thessaly, Euboia and Korinth. These cities – Demetrias in Thessaly, Chalkis in Euboia, and the great towering fortress of Akrokorinth – the Greeks called the Fetters of Greece, because whoever held them held effective control of Greece.

If Philip withdrew from these cities, Titus told him, and pulled back his armies from Greece, he could have peace. Otherwise Rome would fight. He had come to free Greece, not conquer Macedon. That was what he intended to do.

But Philip, when he heard this, flew into a rage. He did not fear Rome. He would not be dictated to by some

Roman upstart. He vowed to drive Titus and his army back into the sea.

Pomponius sent for me as soon as he heard I was back in Athens.

When I arrived at his residence, he sent for wine, and, when it arrived, actually poured it for me himself and handed me the cup.

Then he said, 'What are we to do? I imagine you have heard the news from the East?'

I told him I had only just arrived, and had heard nothing.

'Oh dear,' he said, shaking his head and looking grave. 'While Attalos has been occupied in Greece, Antiochos has taken advantage of his absence to attack Pergamon.' He gave me a bleak look, shook his head again, and went on, 'It is all going wrong. Antiochos is closing on us from Asia, and Philip bears down on Greece. And now Titus is trapped in the passes of Epeiros . . . I fear, to be quite frank with you, Marcus, that we have taken on more than we knew.'

He looked at me hopelessly and waited.

'Well, sir,' I said, setting down my cup, 'it is war, and now we must fight it.'

'But think, Marcus, what will happen if we lose. They will not stop at driving us from Greece, you know. They will be in Italy within a year.'

'Then,' I said, 'we must not lose. Titus knows what he is doing.'

'I hope you are right.'

I looked him in the eye and answered, 'I am sure of it.'

What I did not tell him, however, was how little confidence I had in Lucius.

I had seen Lucius that morning. After what I had heard, I was starting to fear he would bring down disaster on us all.

I did not tell Pomponius; but, that night, I confided in Menexenos.

I was sitting naked on the edge of the bed, absently dabbing my finger through the single lamp-flame as I talked. Menexenos lay in a tangle of sheets beside me, propped on one elbow, listening.

I was telling him how I had been summoned to Lucius's quarters in Piraeus, and, arriving at the outer office, had found the clerks rushing about in a great state, while, from beyond the door, Lucius's angry voice barked out.

I had paused in the antechamber, and asked the officer at the desk what the matter was.

Word had come, he told me in a hushed tone – for Lucius terrified them all – that the combined fleets of Attalos and the Rhodians were already at sea, making for Euboia. As soon as Lucius had heard, he had flown into a fury.

'Well he can't sail without the fleet,' I said.

He blinked at me. 'Tell him that yourself, if you dare. Everyone else has tried. What do you think all this fuss is about?'

Just then the door flew open and a harried clerk rushed out. The man at the desk said, 'You'd better go in.'

I went through to the map-room.

As soon as I saw him I realized that Lucius was beyond heeding advice from anyone. He was blustering, cursing, red-faced. He had already commandeered the transport ships that happened to be in Piraeus. He would sail for Euboia next day at first light. The fleet – 'cursed, slow and useless' – was ordered to follow as soon as it arrived.

'And so,' I said, turning to Menexenos, 'we are to go rushing off to Euboia before we are ready. This is how wars are lost.'

He threw out his arm, resting his hand on my thigh.

'What is it with that man?' he said. 'Surely it makes no difference to wait for the fleet.'

'It does to him. He is afraid Attalos will take Eretria without him. He doesn't want anyone to steal his glory.'

Menexenos fell back on the pillow and let out a long breath. When it came to Lucius, neither of us had need for words.

Our small flotilla sailed next day.

Off Andros we met as arranged with the fleets of Pergamon and Rhodes, and together proceeded up the sea-strait north towards Eretria. What Lucius did there would be remembered for a long time by the Greeks.

Eretria is a port-city, on the west side of the long island of Euboia, overlooking the gulf of water that separates it from the mainland. To the north is the great stronghold of Chalkis, one of the Fetters of Greece, where Philip had posted Philokles his general and a force of Macedonians, for he had no intention of losing it. The

Eretrians too were allied to Philip. He had left a Macedonian garrison in their city, to make sure of their loyalty,
in case they thought to question it.

Everyone had assumed, in as much as we had thought
of him at all, that Doron would be staying behind in
Athens. But on the morning of our departure he had
appeared on the quayside, dressed up in a parody of
military clothing – soldier's scarlet embroidered with blue
prancing warriors – and declared in front of the astonished marines that he had come to fight at Lucius's side.

Lucius had come hurrying down the gangboard and,
speaking in the cooing love-talk they used in private
together, had pleaded that the mission was too dangerous.

At this, Doron cried out that he would rather die in
Lucius's arms beneath the walls of Eretria, than live his
life without him.

The poets and philosophers say that a man's lover
helps him to be brave, and to remember his own virtue.
No doubt Doron had picked up some of this from the
hack-rhapsodes and cheap entertainers in the dockside
taverns of Sami. He had a quick mind, like all tricksters;
and now he came out with a long, embarrassing monody
to love.

Lucius listened with tears welling in his eyes, as if he
were hearing the words of the divine Muses themselves.
When the boy had finished he declared, after a short
unconvincing protest, that he had lain awake half the
night, hoping Doron would come. 'We shall live or die
together!' he cried. 'Like the great heroes of old.'

The dockhands, his audience for this pitiful scene,
looked on astonished.

In due course, we made landfall close to Eretria.

Though we ourselves were few, Attalos had brought his army and a fleet of twenty-four quinqueremes, and the Rhodians had brought twenty warships of their own fleet, under the command of their general Akesimbrotos.

I had expected to be given my own company to command. But Lucius, I soon found out, had other plans, and shortly after we arrived he summoned me to his tent and said that since I spoke Greek so well I should act as liaison between Attalos, Akesimbrotos and him.

It was little more than a messenger's work, and he knew it. But it would have been futile to protest. Besides, I was soon glad of this assignment, for I was always one of the first to hear what was going on, and it was through this work that I came to know King Attalos.

At the start, the Eretrians defended the city with vigour. But then, one morning, Attalos said, 'Marcus, come and listen to this.'

He led me across his encampment towards the guard-house, explaining as we walked. The night before, he said, his scouts had captured two shepherds who had crept out of the city under cover of darkness, to see what they could retrieve of their flocks. He wanted me to hear what they had to say.

The shepherds were scarcely more than boys. They were being kept in a disused stable, but they had not been tied, and had been given food and drink. They were clearly overawed by old Attalos in his purple-hemmed uniform and royal diadem; but he had told them they had nothing to fear, and during the night they had talked. Now Attalos told them to repeat to me what they had told him.

The walls, they said, had been weakened by our artillery. Food stocks were running low, and it was clear the city could not hold out. The magistrates had said they wished to sue for terms, but the commander of the Macedonian garrison would not permit it. When the magistrates had objected, the Macedonians threatened them. The Eretrians had had enough of it.

We learnt, too, that Philip had sent urgent messages ordering the Eretrians to hold out at all costs, saying he was sending a force to relieve the city. We doubled the watch on the northern coastal approaches, with scouts keeping watch from the forested high ground, and a few days later an advance party of Macedonians appeared on the road.

We were ready for them, and surprising them with a charge from the hills we drove them back. Old Attalos, though he was then in his seventieth year, rode in the vanguard, on a splendid white horse caparisoned in red. Lucius rode at his side.

But Doron, in spite of all he had said, was not there, for when the alarm had come, and the camp was abuzz with all the hum and rattle of an army preparing to march, he had developed a sudden stomach cramp. I heard him whining and simpering in Lucius's tent. He suspected last night's supper.

Lucius, grief-stricken, was sure the supper was the cause – though no one else had fallen ill – and ordered the camp surgeon to have a healing posset prepared and to sit with the boy. He would have remained behind himself, he said, except he would not leave all the glory to Attalos.

After that day the Macedonians remained at Chalkis and did not venture out again. Attalos, a shrewd old bird, made sure the Eretrians got to hear of it, and, soon after, the townspeople sent envoys to negotiate.

That same night, Attalos called us together. The city, he said, was ready to come over to our side. The only obstacle was the Macedonian garrison. 'But the garrison is small, and the citizens are many. If we are wise, Eretria will fall into our hands without a fight.'

I shall not relate all that was said. In the end the common view was that we should give the magistrates of Eretria the assurances they asked for, and wait for them to admit us secretly to the city. In the meantime, we should do our best to spare the citizens, and not mount a full-scale assault on the walls.

I glanced at Lucius. He was not a listener by nature. Usually he was the first to make his views known, but tonight he was quiet. He stood biting his lip, as he did when his mind was working.

In the days that followed there was a slackening in the city's defence. It was nothing sudden, nothing the Macedonian garrison might notice. I was sharing my tent with Lamyros the ship-pilot. One night, past midnight, something woke me. I opened my eyes and listened, staring into the darkness.

Outside, near the tent, men were stealthily moving. I reached for my sword beside the bed.

'Lamyros,' I said in an urgent whisper.

He stirred in his bed, then jolted up. I silenced him

with a gesture. We listened, then grabbing our weapons we rushed out, thinking the enemy had found a way into the camp.

But instead I saw our own men, a line of marines passing in the shadows along the outer path of the camp, carrying scaling-ladders and dressed for battle.

I found one I knew by name, and asked him what was happening.

'Why, has no one told you, Marcus sir? We are going to take the city – a surprise attack . . . But what is it? Is something wrong?'

'No, Tertius. Nothing's wrong.'

I left them, hurriedly pulled on my clothes, then went looking for Lucius.

I found him standing outside his tent, dressed in his best parade-armour: a sculpted, gleaming, muscled cuirass; shining strap-buckles; a gold-studded sword-belt; and a crested helmet of combed red and white horsehair. Doron was at his side, got up in his strange uniform, trying to look like a soldier.

The night was dark almost to blackness. Lucius did not notice me till I stepped into the circle of light thrown by the cresset. Then, seeing who it was, he broke off from whatever he was saying to the boy and glared. He was trying to look fierce and challenging, but he had the look of a schoolboy caught stealing his neighbour's apples. It was at that moment I knew for sure he had intended to deceive me.

'Yes, tribune?' he said coldly.

I asked him what was happening.

'Is it not clear? We are taking the city.'

I glanced out across the plain, towards the camps of Attalos and the Rhodians. But I had already guessed what I should see. Here and there watchfires burnt, but otherwise all was still.

'Sir,' I said, 'the city is ready to open its gates to us. It will be any day now. There is no need for this battle.'

'Do not presume to tell me what is needed,' he snapped. 'If the city is ready to fall, then I shall take it.'

I lowered my eyes, lest he see the flaring anger in them. I was beginning to understand, and with that understanding came a dull, sick feeling in the pit of my stomach. It was no oversight that I had not been told: he had kept his plans from me deliberately, thinking I would warn Attalos. He wanted the glory of taking Eretria for himself alone, whatever the cost in the citizens' blood. The Eretrians had been led to believe we were their friends, ready to assist them against the Macedonian garrison. Because of that they had lowered their guard. Now all Lucius needed to do was pluck the ripe fruit from the tree. No wonder, I thought, he had put on his dress-armour. It would be as easy as taking a rattle from a baby.

Before the night was out Eretria had fallen. The terrified citizens, fearing they were about to be slaughtered, fled with their wives and children to their akropolis, where the temples were, and threw themselves upon the mercy of the gods. The Macedonian garrison, seeing they were surrounded and cut off even from the rest of the city, quickly gave themselves up.

But still Lucius was not content. At first light he went to the treasury, which the Eretrians keep in the temple of Apollo, and, finding it empty, demanded to know of the leading magistrate where he had hidden the gold and silver.

The terrified man answered that there was none, for Philip had taken it 'for safe keeping' to Chalkis.

'You lie!' shouted Lucius. He pushed the man roughly aside and went searching through the inner rooms of the temple, banging about among the jars and tripods and other sacred vessels. Then he began tapping the flagstones and walls, searching for a concealed vault.

As this proceeded, the rest of us stood outside in the porch, scarcely daring to look at one another, while from within we listened to Lucius's curses and frustrated grunts.

Then suddenly, without warning, Doron, who was with us, rushed forward and gave the old white-bearded magistrate a vicious kick, yelling in his high-pitched voice, 'You are a liar! Where have you hidden it?'

The poor man, who must have been four times Doron's age, wrung his hands and pleaded he had told the truth. 'Please, sir,' he cried, abasing himself, 'just ask anyone. We all saw the Macedonians take it away.'

I think he feared Doron was about to run him through with his showy new jewel-encrusted sword. In truth, I doubt he could have managed it. But before it came to this, I stepped up and put myself between them, and turning to the old magistrate, who was trembling and clearly expecting to die at any moment, I said, 'Come sir, you have had a long night of it. I shall take you home.'

Needless to say, the man was telling the truth and Lucius found no treasure. But in his fury at being thwarted he ordered his quinquereme to be rowed into the city harbour, and I watched with the citizens and our allies as he set his men to loot every valuable thing that could be carried away.

The shrines and temples and galleries were stripped. Antique pictures were torn down from the walls of the public buildings and dragged along the streets. Bronze sculptures were sawn from their pedestals and piled up on the quayside like corpses. Tripods were taken from the temples; gilded wreaths from the altars. Even the houses of the citizens were ransacked, and their silver plate and precious cups piled up in barrows, and carted down to the waiting ship.

At one point, in the midst of this plunder, Attalos, standing some distance off with his generals, caught my eye and gave me a questioning, reproachful look. I shook my head, full of shame, hoping he would understand I had no part in it.

The worst, however, came from someone I did not know at all, an old Eretrian citizen who happened to be standing on a street corner. Thinking I did not understand his Greek, he said to the man beside him, 'You see, they are nothing but barbarians, just as Philip warned. So much for our liberation. We have exchanged one tyrant for another.'

The Macedonian garrison was ransomed. The troops were stripped of their arms and allowed to depart for Boiotia.

That day, Lucius had gone off hunting in the forest with Doron, leaving me to oversee the embarkation of the men onto the transports.

The Macedonians were filing down the landing-pier, a long line of them, unwashed, dishonoured, sullen in defeat, with their heads bowed.

Beside me the captain of one of the transport ships was complaining, talking on and on, grumbling of the low fee Lucius had required him to accept.

Eventually I turned impatiently to him, and was drawing my breath to tell him for the third time there was nothing I could do, when in the corner of my eye I caught a sudden movement.

I looked round. Halfway down the pier one of the Macedonians, a hard-faced squad-captain with a grizzled beard and a deep rutted scar on his cheek, had turned seawards and was signalling discreetly to a comrade further down the line. Then he saw me, and quickly looked away. But it was enough to make me follow his gaze.

Out in the bay, in the middle distance, perhaps two furlongs off, a cutter had struck out from the shore, emerging from behind a low wooded promontory and rowing furiously. A man was standing in the bow.

I stared. Even from this distance I knew him. I should have known him anywhere.

'Where did he come from?' I shouted, rounding on the Macedonian captain.

But he merely glared at me, and shut his mouth firm.

I stared up and down the mole, to see what vessel I might commandeer. But the only ships were the great hulking transports, tied one to another and to the quay in a tangled net of lines and rigging, their gangboards down, their sails furled and bound.

Reading my thoughts in my face the Macedonian laughed and said, 'You will not catch him now, Roman.' And all along the line the prisoners raised their heads and smiled, enjoying, in the midst of their defeat, this brief moment of triumph.

He was right. There was nothing I could do. I turned and stared helplessly out across the water. The prow of the cutter was beginning to pitch now, as it moved beyond the shelter of the bay. But Dikaiarchos remained where he was, right out in front, letting the spray wash over him, his feet set firm, the wind ruffling his scarlet tunic and blowing back his wild flaxen hair.

Fury burned in my heart. Even from so far away I knew that he was laughing.

TWELVE

WE LEFT EUBOIA, AND returned south, rounding Cape Sounion and setting a course for Korinth.

During the voyage Doron praised Lucius's bravery as if he had won a great battle. He admired too the looted treasures, and eventually as a keepsake got a filigree casket inlaid with malachite and lapis; and, to put in it, a heavy onyx signet-ring with the octopus symbol of Eretria carved on top in chalcedony.

He showed it to me triumphantly, saying, 'You see, he loves me.'

With the sack of Eretria, Lucius had become rich overnight. He had sent home to Italy a transport-ship stuffed with treasure. He said little of it, sensing, perhaps, that there was something shameful in it.

But Doron was not so reticent: he boasted of the luxurious villa they would buy, which would be furnished with the looted statues, paintings, gilded lampstands and silverware. It would be the envy of Rome.

Meanwhile, news had come of Titus. While Lucius

was busy in Euboia, he had finally broken out of Epeiros into the broad plains of Thessaly and was laying siege to the cities held by Philip.

As he advanced, Philip retreated, drawing our legions onwards, refusing to engage in battle.

It did not take long for his strategy to become clear. Each city that Titus came to had been abandoned and put to the torch. The fields had been destroyed, the water supplies fouled, and Philip had taken off the citizens of fighting age, abandoning the rest – the women, the old, or the infirm. Titus's progress was slowed. He had expected to feed the army from the lush fields of Thessaly. Instead he had to send the men foraging far and wide over the countryside, or wait for supplies to arrive through the passes from Epeiros. Autumn was drawing on. Nothing had been achieved.

It was from Lucius that I heard this. By now he had allowed himself to be persuaded by Doron, and by his own vanity, that his shameful sack of Eretria had been a marvellous victory; and he could not resist crowing about it even to me.

And worse, he began to set his own great victory against Titus's difficulties, saying, as Doron smiled and nodded beside him, 'If I were leading the army, I should be in Macedonia by now.' Or, at another time, 'He has lost his touch. He is too timid.'

This was what he said openly. What he said in private, I could only guess at. But as I heard these constant sneering remarks, it came to me that in spite of all Titus's efforts to help his brother, Lucius resented him bitterly. He wanted nothing more than to outshine him, even if it meant defeat and humiliation for Titus. He delighted in every new piece of bad news, retelling it eagerly to whoever would listen.

That year, Titus had been sending envoys to the cities of Greece, trying to persuade them to come over to his side. Most had agreed. But Korinth, with its impregnable mountain fortress of Akrokorinth, refused. Greece would never be free while Philip held it. Everyone's eyes were upon us. We could not afford another setback.

And so, while Titus was still holed up in the north, we brought our forces to Korinth.

I was billeted once more with Lamyros. One morning, while we were washing, he said to me, 'I was down at the waterfront taverns last night.'

'Oh?' I said with a laugh, splashing my face as I talked, 'and who was the lucky girl this time?'

Lamyros had a roving eye, and Korinth-port was well known for its attractions.

'I don't recall,' he said, flicking the water across the trough at me. 'But guess who was there? It was that pretty-boy of Lucius's.'

'Is that so?' I said, looking up. 'Well I suppose dock-side taverns are where he feels at home. Was he selling, or buying? . . . And where was Lucius?'

'I don't know. But he was not there, anyway. The boy was drunk. He can do quite a turn at bawdy songs, you know. And when he was not singing, he was holding forth about the war, boasting how Lucius was going to take Korinth and win the war himself.'

I shook my head. 'Easy to brag, when someone else must do the fighting. But let us worry about today's work today. Has no one told him it is unwise to tempt the gods?'

The previous night, while Lamyros was listening to Doron in the tavern, I had been to supper with Akesimbrotos the Rhodian commander, and a group of Attalos's generals. It had been clear they were uneasy, and eventually, before the night was out, they told me why.

It did not look good, they said, to besiege a great and ancient city like Korinth, with the eyes of all of Greece upon us. They had come to free Greece, not conquer it.

'But surely,' I had said, 'everyone knows the Korinthians are little more than hostages of Philip's garrison.'

'That is not what Philip is putting about,' said Akesimbrotos. 'He is saying the garrison is there to protect them.'

'And is he believed?'

'If you say a thing often enough, somebody will believe you.'

At this one of Attalos's men said, 'Well either way, Korinth must be taken.'

'Yes,' said Akesimbrotos. 'But let it be quick, and done with justice.' He glanced towards me. 'We do not want another Eretria.'

The siege began. Not for nothing did Philip call Korinth one of the Fetters of Greece. Attalos's men told me it had been contested by opposing armies time out of mind. Seeing it, with its mountain fortress of Akrokorinth dominating the whole plain of the isthmus, I could understand why. Whoever held it held Greece by the throat.

345

Our strategy at first was to give a show of force. King Attalos had insisted that the fewer citizens that were harmed, the better for our cause. If we could drive a wedge between the Korinthians and the Macedonian garrison, they might throw the garrison out, or invite us into the city without a fight.

But before long it became clear that this was not to be. The defence was fiercer than we expected. The heavy siege-engines, and ramps, and scaling-ladders and catapults were brought forward; and that evening Attalos convened a council of war in his quarters. When the dispositions had been discussed and agreed, he stood back from the map-table and said, 'Well, it is unfortunate that news of what happened to Eretria has spread all over Greece.'

'Unfortunate?' snapped Lucius. 'How so?'

Attalos looked at him. He was an experienced politician and a king; but for a brief moment the contempt showed in his face. 'Because,' he replied in an even tone, 'the Korinthians might otherwise have been persuaded to open their gates.'

Lucius gave him a chill smile.

'Then too bad for the Korinthians. I shall take the city anyway. And when I do, they will wish they had not resisted.'

'I remind you, sir, this is not a war of conquest. We are here to free the Greeks from Philip's yoke. If ever they begin to think otherwise, they will close their cities against us, and Macedon will have won. You would do well, sir, to remember that. Or must I send to Titus and discuss the matter with him?'

Lucius jutted his chin forward and glared, as he did when he wanted to terrify the clerks and junior officers. But Attalos kept his steady eye on him.

'It was I, not you, who took Eretria!' he cried. He turned and swept out of the door, before anyone could answer him.

Attalos watched him go with one brow raised. There was an appalled silence. For a moment our eyes met. Then he turned back to the map-table, and continued in a wry tone. 'Well, gentlemen, I believe that concludes our discussions for tonight.'

Later, when I returned to my quarters, Lamyros said, 'Oh, Marcus, a messenger was just here looking for you; you must have passed him in the street. Lucius wants to see you. But haven't you just left him?'

I thought, 'Now what?' and walked out again.

Lucius had requisitioned a large villa near the port, casting out the owner and telling him to seek lodgings elsewhere. I found him in the marbled dining room beyond the peristyle courtyard, just starting his supper, with Doron at his side, sharing one couch.

'Ah, tribune, there you are.'

He set down his heavy gilded wine-cup. It was the kind of vessel the priests use to pour libations to the gods; and, as the lamplight caught it, I noticed the octopus symbol of Eretria embossed on the side.

'I suppose,' he went on, 'you have been gossiping with that timid old fool Attalos.'

Doron tittered. Lucius smiled at him. There was an unpleasant air of conspiracy between them. I wondered what was coming.

'In any case, I have not called you here to talk about Attalos. He may choose to preen himself outside the walls, waiting for the citizens to invite him in; but I am here to take Korinth and finish this war, and that is what I intend to do.'

'Yes, sir.'

'Let the Korinthians complain all they want: tomorrow I mean to mount a full assault and take them by surprise. I did it at Eretria; I can do it at Korinth . . . with or without old man Attalos.'

He sat forward, regarding me. A sudden chill of dread crept up my spine. There was a side of Lucius that was terrifying, a part of him that had never learned boundaries, like a madman, or some fearsome monstrous child.

There was a pause. Then he said slowly, 'I am told you fight well with a sword.'

'Yes, sir, I fight well enough.'

For a moment his eyes moved to Doron, and I saw a quick, conniving look pass between them. I thought to myself: it is coming, whatever they have planned between them.

'Then tomorrow,' he continued, fixing me once more with his eye, 'you can prove it. You shall fight in the vanguard, with the veteran infantry. I want you at the front. At the very front. Do you understand me?'

He peered at me. I think he was hoping I should flinch, for he knew as well as I what these words meant.

There was a brief silence. I could hear the spluttering of the lamp, and Lucius's heavy breathing.

I said, 'Yes, sir. I understand you perfectly.'

348

'Good. Then the captain outside will give you your orders.'

He reached to the table, plucked up a slice of suckling kid, dipped it in a dish of sauce, and dropped it into his mouth. Beside him Doron gave me one of his pouting doe-eyed smiles.

I said, 'Will that be all, sir?'

'Yes. Go away.'

He gave me a chill smile, then added, with his mouth still full of meat and sauce, 'If I were you I'd get some sleep. You'll need it . . . Goodbye, Marcus.'

Lamyros was lying on his bed when I returned, with his arms folded behind his head. As soon as I walked in he began, 'Something's afoot; while you were gone, the order went out to mobilize . . .' And then he saw my face and sat upright. 'But what has happened? You look as if you have just seen a demon.'

I shrugged. 'I saw Lucius. He means to attack at dawn.'

'Then I hope he knows what he's doing.'

'He doesn't.'

I sat down wearily on the bed opposite him and took up my sword – the sword which had once belonged to Antikles, my teacher. After some moments looking at it I drew it from its sheath and twisted it in the lamplight. I had kept it sharp and oiled. I always did.

'He's put me in front,' I said eventually, 'with the veterans.'

Lamyros looked at me. He drew his breath to speak, but in the end said nothing.

There was a pause. I set the sword down.

'I have a friend in Athens,' I said. 'If I die, will you make sure he gets a message?'

As soon as I saw the company I had been assigned to I detected Lucius's hand in it. They were not merely veterans, they were the hardest of the battle-hardened veterans; dangerous, violent men twice my age who had fought in Africa under Scipio and were proud of it. They knew their job; they despised rank; and they resented having a youthful stranger like me thrust upon them, and made no effort to hide it. I could hardly blame them: no soldier likes to go into battle with a man he does not know.

But already the artillery barrage had begun. There was no time for talk, even if they had wanted to talk to me – and I could see from their faces they were not the talking type. I had to make the best of it. I daresay they were thinking the same thing.

The sun rose in shafts of red over the sea. The air shook with the deep twang and thud of the catapults. The trumpets blared, and the order went out to advance: first the crack veterans; then the light-armed troops, auxiliaries and javelineers.

The approach to Korinth from the eastern side is uneven and difficult, with ditches and other obstacles to hinder a rapid assault. For this reason Lucius had concluded the defences here would be lightest. But even as we went forward at the double, carrying between us a great oaken battering ram on leather slings, the rain of arrows and missiles began, and it was clear that the defenders were prepared.

We raised our shields over our heads, to deflect the arrows. I was at the front, on the left, the most dangerous position. I had taken it deliberately. I knew, with men like these, there was no other way to win their trust.

Naturally enough, they had assumed I was some favourite of Lucius's, thrust upon them at the last moment for some purpose that had not been explained to them. But, I calculated, such men respected bravery. I had to show them quickly I was not a coward.

At first we advanced rapidly. Then, as we drew close, we were forced down a steep grassy cutting – a deliberate earthwork to slow an enemy's advance.

The veterans cursed as we laboured up the far side. The heavy beam of the battering ram slowed us.

Up ahead I saw the part of the wall we were aiming for. It was a place where a catapult bolt had struck. The high crenellated walkway was staved inwards, and there was a huge crack in the brickwork.

'Here!' I cried, and we veered left, to where the stonework looked weakest. We sprinted up the incline, levelled the beam, and struck the wall with a resounding blow.

From somewhere above, the defenders were firing down arrows and javelins and stones; they clattered on our shields. The battering ram juddered in its sling; the cracked wall splintered, and from above I heard voices cry out in alarm. They were Macedonian voices, not Korinthians. Lucius had been wrong. The defences here were not poorly defended: we were up against crack men from the garrison.

'Again!' the veterans cried, swinging the great oak beam a second time.

Once again it crashed into the wall. The masonry crumbled and split. From above came shouts and the sound of running feet. Already the missile blows had grown fewer, as the men above cleared the walkways.

There was a brief lull. I glanced about me. Half a stade away there was a tower in the wall. Korinthian archers were crowded on its upper rampart, firing at us. I looked back for our own light-armed troops. They were supposed to be drawing away their fire. But they were nowhere to be seen.

I raised my shield again as a volley of arrows came my way. By the time they reached us their force was half spent. They clattered off our shields and fell about our feet. But they could still kill a man, if he was unlucky.

We drew back, and advancing at a run we struck the wall a third time. Mortar rained down upon our heads. The battering ram vibrated and sang. There was a pause, and then, like a falling tree, the wall creaked and rasped and collapsed inwards in a cloud of dust.

We dropped the ram and rushed forward, even before we could see our way. I knew then I was with good men, for all their grim, unsmiling hostility. They did not hesitate, or pause for another to go first. Without a backward look they surged after me into the breach. The gap was no wider than a farm-cart. This was the most dangerous time, when the defenders knew they had their last chance to cut us off.

We spread out, left and right, filling the gap, stumbling on the fallen masonry, our swords drawn. The dust swirled around us. Then, from the side nearest to me, the Macedonians charged forward, yelling out their paean.

I killed the first of them even before he finished his battle-cry. The trooper beside me took the second. This gave our attackers pause, and for a short moment they hung back. I glanced behind me and shouted once again for the reinforcements Lucius had promised. It was now we needed them, before the enemy formations could regroup and close around us.

Suddenly the veteran beside let out a cry. I swung round. A long javelin shaft was sticking out of his thigh, just below the protecting leather of his kilt. He hesitated, looking down at it with frowning contempt. Then he gripped the ashwood shaft with his broad hand; paused, as if taking its measure, and with a roar through gritted teeth yanked it out. Blood streamed down his leg and over his greaves.

'Get back,' I yelled at him.

He grimaced at me through his beard. 'Later,' he shouted. 'There's a job to do . . . watch out!'

We both ducked, deflecting with our shields another volley of spears. A new wave of defenders was coming at us from the other side.

I cursed out loud and shouted, 'Where are the backup troops?'

There was no more time to look about. I had three men in front of me, each one advancing with a sword. We stood perhaps ten wide, fighting off thirty, and fighting still on the uneven ground of the fallen masonry. But the men of my company knew what they were doing; they fought with a calm, deadly skill, moving with the automatic reflexes that come from years of practice. We were holding our own against superior numbers, but we could not last long without support. We had to break through, or retreat.

Behind me, from the breach in the wall, I heard the approach of men. Their voices rose in the battle-cry, and I realized with a start they were not our troops, whom I had been calling for. They were Greeks. For a moment, with the small part of my mind which attended to this, I was confused. Had the enemy somehow come behind us? But then one of our company, who must have been thinking the same, cried, 'It's Attalos's men!'

'Then where are ours?' shouted another.

'Go and ask Lucius,' said the first bitterly.

But it was help – from whatever quarter, and there was no time to consider it. They came crowding up, filling the breach beside us.

Finally, we began to drive the defenders back, fighting hard for every foot of ground. The gap widened as we advanced: enough for ten men, then fifteen, then twenty. As we moved beyond the rubble I saw a long shattered building with its roof crashed in, a storehouse or an animal-shed that had been struck by our catapults. A fresh wave of defenders was surging from behind it. These new men were not Macedonian troops; they wore mismatched scraps of armour and had a rough, unkempt look. Yet they were not townsfolk drafted in to defend the city: they fought too well for that. One of them cried out an order to those around him. At first I could not tell what had struck me as so strange. Then it came to me: he had not spoken in Greek, or Macedonian, which is a kind of Greek. He had spoken Latin.

My comrades exchanged frowning looks.

The man beside me, the one who had got the javelin in his thigh, cursed and nodded, and said, 'So that's it.'

Then they were upon us, like a pack of dogs.

Our line wavered. The far flank, where Attalos's Greeks were fighting, buckled and broke. The men next to them, suddenly exposed, were forced to drop back, to protect their undefended side; and moments later the whole line was collapsing. A man appeared in front of me through the rising dust. His hair was cropped to his skull; he was heavy-shouldered with a broad upper body, like a rower from the fleet; and in his hand, in place of a sword, he was brandishing some kind of two-headed axe on a short chain, which he tossed expertly from one hand to the other, grinning.

I lunged at him. He stepped deftly back, twitched the strange weapon with a snap of his wrist, and in the chain of it caught the point of my sword.

I tried to pull free, but he moved with my own movement, drawing closer, holding my sword locked in the loop of the chain. With his free hand he snatched a long curving dagger from a sheath; he lunged, and the blade of the dagger flashed like a mirror under my eyes. I shied back; something yielding caught my foot – a man's body – and I stumbled. He had aimed to slice my throat; if I had not tripped he would have done it.

With a laughing cry he leapt over me. I looked up, and saw my own death reflected in his black eye. I shouted and thrust upwards, but he twisted, and my sword glanced harmlessly off his corselet. Then he brought down the axe; I swerved and fell, and the blade hissed beside my ear, catching my armour.

I realized, as I tried to stand, that he had hooked my cuirass with the edge of the axe-blade. He yanked me towards him, as a fisherman reels in a fish. But then, with a sound like a cough, his eyes widened and he ceased. Protruding through his breast, red and glinting in the sunlight, like some hideous blood-stained brooch, was a sword-point. He stared at it in surprise, retched once, spewing blood, dropped the axe from his hand, and fell.

My comrade, the one with the javelin wound, had run him through from behind. He drew out his sword from the body, nodded at me, and said, 'You could have finished him off yourself, but there is no time. Come on, lad. This battle is lost. We're falling back to the wall.'

Later, when we had withdrawn to safety, and I was sitting with the men of my company, dressing our wounds, I thanked him for killing the axe-man. He looked at me and grunted, as if my thanks embarrassed him. Then he said, 'Did you think we were going to leave you there to be killed by that rabble?'

The others murmured agreement. I knew then that things had changed between us, and I confess I felt a glow of triumph, for all our defeat. I was no longer on the outside. They had accepted me.

'Who *were* those men?' I said. 'They weren't Greeks . . . I heard them speaking Latin, or something like it.'

At this they all spoke up, cursing, and saying, 'traitors', and, 'scum', and 'bastards'.

The first one said, 'Since Zama, every deserter, out-of-work mercenary and itinerant cut-throat has been heading this way. We saw their sort in Africa, fighting for Carthage. Chaos draws such people. They will fight for anyone, so long as he pays them. And Philip's as good a paymaster as any other.'

'. . . Or Antiochos, or Ptolemy,' said the man beside him. 'But they're not being paid now, if I'm any judge.'

'Then what?' I said.

'Some fled to Philip after Zama, to avoid being captured. The rest are just looking for work, or fleeing justice of one sort or another.' He tossed his head contemptuously in the direction of the walls, now lined with jeering defenders. 'Korinth is the right place for that; and the right place to find a job in someone else's army.'

I thought of the wild-eyed man with the axe and said, 'Yet you'd think they were fighting for their very lives.'

'They are. They know what happens to deserters.' He made a death-sign with his hand.

A man came striding up, in the uniform of Attalos's army.

'Which one is Marcus?' he said.

'I am.'

'The king asks to speak to you.' He paused, just long enough for me to feel his disapproval, then added, 'Sir.'

Attalos, as I had already guessed, was furious. He was the kind of man who goes calm when he is in a rage. Not like Lucius, who was all bluster. Seeing me he gestured his lieutenants away and said, 'Come and walk with me, Marcus. Are you hurt?'

'Scratches, sir. Nothing more.'

'Then I thank the gods.'

We walked down the slope until we came to a ruined stone-built barn, and here he halted and turned to me. He was as brisk as any soldier, in spite of his great age.

'Now tell me,' he said, 'what that idiot thinks he is doing. Does he want to lose the war single-handed? If so, then let him have the courtesy to tell us, and we can sail back to Pergamon.'

I met his eye, and made a hopeless gesture, and he continued, 'If I had not come, you would have been killed in there.'

'I know, sir,' I said.

'And where was that *fool*? You do not know? Then I shall tell you. He had taken the men who were supposed to back you up and was making a try on the Kenchreai Gate. He intended to throw your lives away. He thought he could force his way into Korinth while you distracted the defenders. By Zeus, Marcus! If my runner hadn't had the sense to find me, they'd have poured out of that breach and overwhelmed your camp.' He paused, and drew a long breath. 'And there's more. I haven't told Lucius yet because I can't find him. So I'll tell you.'

I looked at him. I expect my fury at Lucius showed in my face. 'What more?' I said.

'Philip's general, Philokles, who unlike that buffoon Lucius knows something of the conduct of war, has taken advantage of our confusion and has landed fifteen hundred Macedonians on the western shore of the isthmus. We might have stopped them, if we had not been busy here. But now we have the enemy on both sides. In short,

Marcus, we cannot now maintain this siege. I suggest you try to find Lucius, for if he were not a Roman general who, presumably, knows something of dignity and how to behave, I should tell you that he appears to be hiding from me. His actions today have cost us Korinth; they may indeed have cost us the war. He needs to understand that.'

The siege was broken off. What we could not ship, we burnt, and from the walls the defenders – the Korinthians, the Macedonians, and the rabble of deserters and cutthroats and hired killers – cheered. It was a humiliation and a defeat, one which all of Philip's allies in Greece would soon hear of.

But before we departed, a messenger arrived from the north, bringing news that Titus had finally broken through in Phokis.

I was with Lucius and a group of ship-pilots on the quay when the messenger arrived. A change had come over Lucius. His overbearing confidence had dissolved. His face was grey and puffy, and he would fall into long silences, broken by violent tantrums.

The messenger, a fresh-faced young tribune, knew none of this. He had come from Titus, from an army which had at last won a victory. His eyes were bright with hope and enthusiasm, and the joy of being the bearer of good news. Little did he know that his every smile and bright-eyed look was a barb to Lucius, and as he reported how the Macedonian garrisons in Phokis had surrendered, and the citizens had welcomed Titus through the streets as a liberator, cheering and clapping and casting down wreaths and flower petals in his path, he failed to notice the signs of danger – the chewing lip, the rising colour in the grey face, the nervous fidgeting of the fingers. He talked on, taking Lucius's silence for interest; and when, at last, Lucius burst into a frenzied rage, the poor youth almost fell over with shock.

Of course he could not be seen to complain directly of Titus's success; he railed instead at the young tribune for disturbing him when any fool could see he was over-laden with cares of his own. 'Do you think I have time to listen to all this?' he spluttered. 'Just give your cursed dispatches to the clerk and get out of my sight.'

We were standing a little way back from the harbour, in a grove of oak and cypresses behind the temple of Hermes. As it happened, Doron was present. He had arrived just before the messenger. Even he could see that Lucius was making a fool of himself, and with hissing whispers and tugs at his cloak he tried to calm him. For once, I think, everyone was glad he was there. But then, all of a sudden, Lucius rounded on him and at the top of his voice shouted, 'Stop pawing me like some dog-bitch, can't you see I'm busy!'

Silence fell like a lead weight. The pilots and captains and clerks exchanged appalled glances. The young tribune stared and swallowed.

Then Doron began to wail – a high-pitched keening sound – crying out between his sobs that Lucius did not love him, that he was all alone far from his mother and without a friend in the world.

He had made an art of such things; Lucius was like

soft potter's clay in his hands. He rushed to him and flung his arms around the boy's heaving shoulders, and led him off into the grove, saying as he went, 'Come, my little bird; Lucius is sorry; here, dry your tears,' leaving the messenger staring after them as if he had seen some dread apparition.

That winter I spent in Athens.

A nervous air hung over the city. People were asking what had become of the hoped-for victory. The fate of Abydos was in everyone's mind.

Menexenos's father welcomed me back to his home almost as a son. It touched my heart. But it grieved me to see the change in him.

In the months since I had last seen him he had become suddenly old. He walked with a stoop. His grey hair had turned to white, and when I spoke to him his attention drifted.

I asked Menexenos whether he was ill.

'He is weary to his soul,' he said, 'and perhaps that is a kind of sickness. He has not been the same since the loss of the farm.'

'The crops will grow again,' I said, 'and we can rebuild the farm.'

'That's what I tell him. But he says that when a man grows old enough, he begins to see everything for a second time: he says he has seen too much.'

I was about to give some easy answer, but in the end I said nothing. Kleinias was old and had seen much. It was not for me to explain away his sadness.

We had gone walking out to the gardens of the Akademy, and had paused near Plato's tomb.

The grass and shrubs had begun to grow again in the places where they had been burnt; but the old marble still bore the scorch-marks of Philip's ravaging, and it would be many years before the planes and tall cypresses and shading myrtle groves were as I had first seen them.

I dabbed with my foot at a little clump of autumn flowers and said, 'A man can never go back to anything, can he Menexenos? There is only ever onwards.' I shook my head. It seemed a cold, empty vision.

Menexenos stepped up and touched my cheek, so that I turned and looked at him.

'Remember that?' he said, nodding across the scrub.

I looked. The landscape had changed so much I had almost forgotten. Not far off stood the little altar to Eros, like a standing stone in a burnt field.

'Of course I do,' I said, smiling, suddenly filled with love, and the memory of love.

'Only the gods do not change,' he said, 'which is why I honour them. A man must have solid ground upon which to build his home. Otherwise what are we? Wind-blown chaff, carried along by every chance eddy and current. No, there is no going back. But what would that be, but a return to ignorance? The task of each day is to strive for what is real, a constant return to the light.'

We walked along the path to the altar. The shadows were lengthening; the sun had already dropped below the western spurs of Parnes, sending shafts of light fanning out and upwards. Bats darted among the broken walls that had been the gymnasion and Plato's school, and somewhere a solitary bird was singing, its call unanswered.

At the altar we paused, each of us resting his palm on the cool, golden marble, our hands close. I looked out towards the river.

'Eros,' I said. 'Love. Yet love is not a god.'

'He is a daimon – a spirit; he leads us out of ourselves, and towards what is true.'

I smiled. 'He led me to you.'

'And me to you. But it is only a beginning, not an end. What we have, we have because of that perfect place that is always beyond. That is where Eros leads, if we are wise.'

I nodded, and not for the first time reflected that he saw so much further than I. His vision fed and sustained me, and sometimes, in moments when my mind was clear – on a mountain top, or beholding some thing of beauty – I caught a glimpse of what he saw.

A shadow of grief touched my heart. The gods may be for ever, I thought, but for men time is short, and time for love shortest of all.

I had already noted that we were alone. I took his hand and drew him to me, and before he could speak again I closed his mouth with a kiss.

Only my stepfather Caecilius seemed untouched by the general air of gloom. At the house where he was staying in Piraeus there was a constant traffic of merchants and their agents; men with suspicious eyes, who would fall suddenly silent when I passed. They came from Ionia, from Sidon and Antioch, from Sicily, and from vaguely mentioned cities in the north that bordered Macedon, cities that were allies, or near-allies, of Philip.

They were the sort who wait to see which way the wind is blowing before deciding where they are headed. I have always despised such men. I perceived, on my visits to that house, that while we fought to free Greece from tyranny, a whole community of men throve in the shadows, feeding on corruption, and the sufferings of others.

One, a rich merchant from Thebes called Tyrtaios, was my stepfather's favourite at that time, and they spent long hours together working on some secret business. In general, nowadays, he and I kept a safe distance between us. But one day he announced he was holding a banquet for his friends, and said he wished me to attend.

I was minded to refuse, but Menexenos said it would seem churlish, after I had been away for so long. And so, reluctantly, I went.

Tuchon the Phoenician was there, whose house it was, reeking of Lydian oils and laden with heavy jewellery; there was a trader from Lesbos, and another from Byzantion. But it was Tyrtaios the Theban who was the guest of honour, and I guessed that whatever deal they had been working on had been concluded. I steeled myself for an evening of heavy drinking and gross amusements. These I was prepared for. In the end, though, it was the conversation itself which took me by surprise.

Tyrtaios was a man of about forty-five, with shrewd cold eyes and the demeanour of one for whom concealment had become a habit. Unlike showy Tuchon with his garish jewels and odious scents, Tyrtaios did not dress up. This was not, I sensed, through poverty, but because it suited him not to draw attention to himself.

The wine began to flow even while the first course was still being carried in, each raising his cup to the other with conniving nods and looks of triumph.

At first, the conversation was as dull as I had expected, all talk of trade and property and possessions. The evening dragged on. I wished I were with Menexenos. The main dishes were served. When the slaves had finished and withdrawn, Tyrtaios observed smoothly, 'Well I think we all agree that Titus has overreached himself this time.'

There were nods and a general rolling of eyes. 'Pride before a fall,' intoned the Byzantine.

'And, in between,' said my stepfather, 'there is business to be done.' He winked at Tyrtaios and added, 'Fortune favours the brave.'

'Quite so, Caecilius, quite so. And from what I hear in the street, it is not only we who now see the folly of supporting him and his stooge Attalos. The Athenians have backed a lame horse, yet again, as indeed your own fine son here can testify.'

At this, the man from Byzantion said, 'Well they are not to be trusted. When the Romans crossed to Sicily, they said it was to drive out the Carthaginians . . .'

'Exactly,' nodded Tyrtaios. 'And now the Carthaginians are gone, but the Romans are still there. Where is the Sicilians' liberty now?' He gave a light, sophisticated laugh, and over the rim of his wine-cup he cast his eyes among the guests, making sure they had taken his point.

I looked away. Could Caecilius have misjudged me so

badly that he supposed I would to listen to this? I forced myself to bite my tongue. But then Tyrtaios said, 'But I sense, Marcus, you do not agree.'

'No, sir,' I said turning, 'since you ask me. I do not agree.'

Caecilius gave me a warning look. Tyrtaios arched his eyebrow in overplayed surprise. 'Do you deny, then, that the Romans are still in Sicily?'

'We went to Sicily because Hannibal was there. It was the Sicilians who chose to become our enemies, not we theirs.'

'Of course it is natural for you to feel for your own.' He gave a patient smile, the kind a teacher might give a dullard pupil. 'But if the people of Sicily decided to support Hannibal, who is Rome to tell them they may not? And now look at Korinth. Rome cannot expect to march on every free city it chooses.'

'The Korinthians are not free. They are hostages to a band of cut-throats and pirates, with Philip as paymaster.'

He inclined his head. 'So you say. Certainly it suits Rome to have it believed.'

Caecilius coughed loudly. 'The boy is young and naïve.'

'Yet there is charm in youth, even if there is folly. So let the boy have his say. Freedom for each man to speak his mind is the Athenian way, I am told. And since we are in Athens . . .' The others joined in his laughter. 'But perhaps,' he went on, 'you have no more to say on the matter. I understand. I hear from Caecilius that you are a friend of Titus, and I am sure no one would blame you for supporting your benefactor, especially when he has made you a tribune. Perhaps, though, when you are able to consider these matters with a more dispassionate eye' – casting an amused look around the room – 'you will begin to see that I am right.'

'You were not at Korinth, sir, and you were not at Abydos. But you are here. So walk beyond the walls and look with your own eyes at the desecrated shrines and burnt-out farms, for that is the kind of freedom Philip offers the Greeks: obey or die.'

Tyrtaios flinched. For an instant I caught a glimpse of the real man behind the mask. Caecilius saw it too. Sharply he said, 'Marcus, you will apologize.'

But now my anger was up. I cast my eye over the silken hangings and damask cushions and dishes of expensive food, and I thought of the good men who had laid down their lives so that these rich merchants might sit here and sneer, safe in the knowledge that they would never be called upon to fight. I thought of Priscus's son, who had died at Trasimene. I thought of Abydos, and of the men who had fought at my side at Korinth.

'Apologize?' I said. 'Surely Tyrtaios hopes for Philip's defeat as much as you or I, or why is he in Athens, which is, after all, at war with Macedon. But forgive me, sir, if I do not stay. All of a sudden I feel sick. It must be something in the food.'

So much for Tyrtaios. Soon I had more serious matters to concern me. A summons came from Lucius. He had taken a house for the winter in the expensive quarter of Athens, in the same neighbourhood as Pomponius, near the gardens of the precinct of Zeus.

He gave me a cold look when I was shown in to his workroom; there had been few pretences between us since the day at the walls of Korinth. He pushed a scroll across the table at me, as a man might push away a dish of food that disgusted him. 'That is for you,' he said.

I took up the scroll and glanced at its outer cover, and recognized Titus's broad hand. Then I looked again and frowned.

'What?' said Lucius, as if he had been expecting this.

I said, 'The seal is broken.'

'I know.'

There was a tense silence. We both stood regarding one another.

But then the quiet was broken by the sound of Doron's voice, coming from somewhere within the house, shouting angrily at the slave, demanding to know where his boots had been left – the red calfskin ones, his favourites. Distracted by this shrieking, Lucius blinked and looked away.

'It was I who broke the seal,' he snapped. 'I read the letter. I am your commander, and I have every right.'

Doron's voice once again echoed down the passageway. I said, 'Shall I read the letter now; or do you prefer to tell me what it says, since you have read it?'

He gave me a sharp narrow-eyed look, sensing insubordination. But I had been careful with my tone, and after a moment he huffed and said, 'It seems my brother wants you to go to Nikaia. Philip has asked for a conference, and, since you have met Philip, he thinks your presence there will be useful.'

Nikaia is a little fishing town on the Malian gulf. I went by sea, in a fast military cutter. Titus met me at the jetty, and introduced me to the delegates from our allies who had gathered there. There was a representative from King Attalos called Dionysodoros; there was the admiral of the Rhodian fleet, Akesimbrotos, who had fought with us at Eretria and Korinth; and there were two men who had been sent by the League of Achaian cities. They greeted me with well-bred military courtesy. The final delegate, however, a discontented-looking, overdressed man, whom Titus introduced as Phaineas, the leader of the Aitolians, stared at me so intently that it bordered on rudeness, and I was left wondering whether he had somehow heard ill of me, or held some grudge. Later, when we were alone, Titus enquired whether I had brought a letter from Lucius. He looked crestfallen when I told him I had not.

'What, nothing at all?' he asked.

I looked down and frowned, and rather than hurt him with the truth, said I was sure Lucius would have written if there had been time; he had been much occupied with the withdrawal from Korinth, and seeing to winter quarters.

Titus nodded. 'Of course. I expect he has much on his mind.' We were walking in the pleasant walled garden of one of Nikaia's leading men, where he was staying as a guest. There was an ancient vine growing up over the walkway, and orange trees, and, further off, a row of stately cypresses, with the mountains of Phokis rising up behind. 'Well, anyway, it is good to see you, Marcus,' he said after a short pause. 'Tell me, what did you make of Phaineas?'

I thought again of the staring Aitolian. He had been wearing a heavy dark-blue cloak festooned with ornament: encrusted brooches; rings; pendants on thick chains that hung one on top of the other around his neck.

'He looked like a pirate,' I said. 'And why was he staring at me?'

Titus laughed. 'He does that to everyone; you'll get used to it. It's his eyes: he can't see unless things are close up.'

'A strange choice for a general then.'

'Yes indeed, though I am told he leaves the fighting to others. But you're right, he looks like a brigand, and that is what he is. All the Aitolians are, just as men say. They're good horsemen, and tough as old vinestock, and they know the passes between Epeiros and Macedon better than anyone else. But they can't be trusted. They're barbarians at heart, and whatever vows and promises they make, they keep them only so long as it suits them.'

'As bad as that?'

He shrugged. 'They need to be watched. As for Phaineas, he was Philip's ally until last year. Then he decided he had more to gain by switching sides.'

'A man of honour then?' I said dryly.

'Indeed. Well, the Greeks are not suspicious of their

Aitolian cousins for nothing. But they have been useful, and in war one cannot always choose one's allies.'

Two days later, Philip arrived, by sea, accompanied by a small fleet of warships.

Everyone looked on from the shore. But it was not Philip I was staring at as the cutter drew in to the shallows; for Dikaiarchos was standing next to him, dressed in a thick quilted coat studded with bronze, his wild, blond hair bleached from a summer of campaigning, his quick amused fox's eyes taking in the scene around him, and his mouth under his fair beard twisted in a wry grin.

The sight of him kindled all the rage that lay buried in my heart. I filled my lungs with the cool autumn air and tried to calm myself. I told myself I should have guessed he would be here. But in my rush from Athens I had not considered it.

The cutter slowed. I saw Philip incline his head towards the shore and say something. Dikaiarchos grinned his rakish broad-toothed grin, and placing a hand on Philip's shoulder said something in answer, at which they both laughed merrily, like two boys out on a fishing trip, without a care in the world.

I realized Titus had spoken to me and looked round.

'Who is the one with the fair hair?' he said again. 'Do you know him?'

'That is Dikaiarchos,' I said.

Titus turned and looked. As for me, I realized as his

name issued from my lips that I had uttered it no more than a handful of times in my whole life, this man who filled my bad dreams, who burned my very soul.

'So that is the man,' said Titus, considering him. And after that there was no time for talking. The cutter drew up till it was some fifteen paces from the shore, leaving the warships standing at anchor further out in the bay. Philip dropped his arm, and at this signal the rowers backed their oars and brought the craft to a halt.

There was a silence, broken only by the lapping of the ripples on the shore, and the calling sea-birds.

'Will you not come ashore?' called Titus after a few moments. His voice echoed off the face of the surrounding rocks.

Philip said something to Dikaiarchos, then turned and called, 'I think not.'

There was murmuring from those around me.

Titus spread his arms. 'There are no troops here, as you can see, so who are you afraid of?'

Philip took a step forward. He was wearing a short horseman's riding-tunic, and around his head a gold fillet, sign of kingship. 'I am afraid of no one,' he declared. 'But I do not trust those men standing with you.' He jabbed his finger at Phaineas, adding, 'Especially *him*. He is probably hiding a dagger in his cloak. He is an Aitolian, after all.'

Phaineas let out a hiss of indignation. Titus called out across the water, 'But surely, King Philip, this danger is the same for all.'

'Not so,' replied Philip. 'For if I killed Phaineas, there

are a thousand Aitolians to take his place; but if he killed me, there is no one to take mine.'

'This is outrageous!' cried Phaineas. 'I will not stand here and listen to these insults!'

Philip grinned at him. 'Leave then.'

Titus took a step forward. 'King Philip, you have asked for this conference. Now I have come as you requested. What is it you wish to discuss?'

'I am here to listen to you,' said Philip.

'How so?'

'Rome claims it wants peace. Very well. Let there be peace. What are your terms?'

'You know my terms.'

Philip cocked his head.

'He is wasting our time,' muttered Phaineas.

Titus gestured for him to be quiet, then called out across the water, 'Very well, the terms are these: withdraw your armies from Thessaly and Epeiros; remove your garrisons from Korinth and Argos and the other Greek cities. All this you know. For the rest, you have made war also on our allies, and they must notify you what reparations they seek.'

The delegates began to chatter, like women at the well. Dionysodoros, Attalos's man, demanded the return of stolen warships and their crews, and the restoration of the sacred groves Philip had destroyed at Pergamon. Akesimbrotos called for Philip to hand over the Rhodian sea-ports occupied by Macedon, and for the freeing of Abydos. Then Phaineas came shoving up between them and cried, 'Look at him! He smiles! He plays with us.'

Philip raised his brows. 'Do you know my private mind now, Phaineas? Have you suddenly developed insight?' He laughed and threw a grin at Dikaiarchos.

'You are trying to divide us!' Phaineas yelled back, furious.

'Yet,' said Philip, drawing down his black brows in mock-puzzlement, 'so far it is only you and your friends who have spoken. Could it be that you are already divided?'

Phaineas, momentarily lost for words, glared blinking at the water. Then he cried, 'You are not man enough to face us in open battle, so you hide behind city walls and sell civilians into slavery. Behold! You are too afraid even to step onto the shore.'

Philip turned to Dikaiarchos. 'Why, listen,' he said dryly, 'an Aitolian accuses me of dishonour! Some historian should write it down, so that our grandchildren may hear of it and marvel.'

He snapped his fingers at the rowers. They took up their oars and brought the cutter closer to the shore. 'I am the King of Macedon. It is for me to determine how the Macedonians wage war, not some Aitolian turncoat.'

'Why do we waste our time here?' cried Phaineas. Then, jabbing at Philip, 'I can see what you are trying to do!'

'Oh,' said Philip with a broad grin. 'It seems to me you can't *see* anything at all. Are you pointing at me, or at that clump of myrtle?'

'Please, gentlemen,' said Titus.

'You should watch yourself,' said Philip with a nod.

'Aitolians have difficulty understanding what friendship means. They say they are your allies, and then, when you turn your back, they plant the knife. So beware, Titus. Phaineas is standing behind you.' He laughed, and continued, 'Nevertheless, since you ask it, here is what I will do. I shall return the warships you demand, and I shall give the Rhodians their trading ports. As for the damage done to your sacred groves, even I cannot cause trees to spring up full-grown overnight, but I shall send choice plants from Macedon, and my best gardeners to plant them, if that will satisfy Attalos.' He pulled a face, then smiled, and behind him Dikaiarchos and all the rowers grinned broadly at his joking, mocking tone.

'Gardeners!' spluttered Phaineas. 'Do you hear him?'

'As for Argos, I care nothing for it. Have it back, if you want it.'

'And Korinth?' cried Phaineas. 'Have you forgotten Korinth?'

'Don't trouble yourself, Phaineas, about Korinth. It is too far from Aitolia to be a concern of yours. I shall discuss Korinth with Titus, not you.'

At this there was uproar. Philip waited, with a look of amused patience on his face like a comic actor. He turned and said something to Dikaiarchos and the rowers which made them laugh.

Presently he called, 'It is getting late, gentlemen, and I have a pretty Thessalian girl waiting for me in my bed. Clearly you still have a good deal to discuss, so here is what I suggest. When you have agreed what your terms for peace are, I recommend you set them down in writing, so that you don't forget.' He paused and grinned, then turning he nodded at the rowers, and the cutter drew away.

For the rest of the day, and well into the night, the delegates put their various claims in writing. Titus did his best to contain his impatience with this, but in the end said to me, 'Come, Marcus, let us get some air.'

We walked out along the beach. It was a clear, cool night. The stars shone like crystal, and from the wooded slopes the moonlight silhouetted the forest of maple and oak and tall poplars.

'No wonder Philip despises them,' said Titus, after a long silence. 'He asks them what they want, and they cannot even tell him.'

I nodded. We had left them bickering like midden-dogs about who had rights to which city and which strip of land. I said, 'Do you think Philip is serious in wanting peace?'

'No. I realized that this afternoon.'

I asked him why, and he said, 'Oh, it was nothing Philip said. It was them.' He gestured back the way we had come. 'He knows them. He knew that as soon as he offered them something they would squabble over it.'

'Then what is he doing?'

'He wants to show me what they're like. He wants me to see them through his eyes.'

We walked on. Presently I said, 'You like him, don't you?'

He gave a quick laugh. 'Not quite. He is like a wolf in the mountains, wild and dangerous. He kills at will. He goes where he pleases, and does what he likes . . . No, I don't like him. He has let his passions rule his reason.'

He paused, frowning, and walked on for a few paces. Then he said, 'And yet there is something impressive about him; like fire, or like a god, careless of what he is.'

Next day, at the appointed time, we gathered once more on the beach and waited, scanning the sunlit sea. There was no sign of Philip.

'You see,' said Phaineas, staring pointlessly out at the empty water. 'He will not come. He has had his fun.'

'He will come,' said Titus. And when the sun had passed its zenith and was sinking towards the mountain ranges of Phokis, Philip's black warships with their sunburst sails finally appeared.

'Forgive me,' called Philip, without a hint of contrition, 'I have been puzzling over your demands.' He gestured for his rowers to draw nearer. 'I wish to speak to Titus Quinctius alone.'

Titus refused, saying the allies could not be excluded. But when Philip insisted, the others agreed to withdraw a little up the beach, leaving only me with Titus. Philip's cutter drew in. He jumped down into the shallows, and strode up the shingle.

'Do you never tire of those bickering fools?' he said.

'They are my allies.'

Philip shrugged.

'Will you accept our terms?'

'Yes,' said Philip. '. . . Mostly.'

'But not all?'

'I will give those cur-dogs the bones they want. Attalos may have his ships; the Rhodians may have their strips of land; the Achaians may have Argos, and' – he pulled a face – 'Korinth.'

Titus nodded.

'But not,' Philip continued, 'Chalkis in Euboia, or Demetrias.'

'Then you intend to keep hold of two fetters out of three?'

'Well you gain one, which is better than none. Remember, Titus, you are losing this war. Do you reject my offer?'

'It is not for me to accept or reject. It is for the Senate in Rome.'

Philip sighed and winked at me. 'It is so tiresome,' he said, 'having to deal with servants instead of masters.'

'We all serve, King,' said Titus, stung by this.

Philip grinned, showing his perfect white teeth. 'Not I,' he said.

Up on the beach the delegates stood just beyond the range of hearing, staring curiously. All of a sudden Philip waved his arms up in the air and cried, 'Boo!' at them. They looked away in disgust. Philip laughed.

'You joke,' said Titus.

'Why not? Life is fun.'

'. . . And you play for high stakes.'

Philip laughed. 'Always.'

Titus nodded. I could see in his eyes that he would have liked to smile. He said, 'I must confer with the others.'

'Again?' He glanced at me, casting his eyes over my legs with a lascivious leer. Then he turned back to the water and splashed out, like bearded Poseidon returning to the depths.

No one was content, Phaineas least of all. Eventually the delegates agreed to follow Titus's suggestion, and refer the matter to the arbitration of the Senate in Rome. Each side would send ambassadors to put its case. In the meantime, there would be a truce of two months.

'A truce?' complained Phaineas. 'Only a fool would agree to a truce with that madman.'

'Either way, I must seek the Senate's agreement. So let it be now, in winter, when we cannot fight.'

Thirteen

I RETURNED TO ATHENS to the news that Menexenos's father was dying. The winter had turned suddenly
cold, with a biting, dry wind blowing down off the
mountains. Kleinias had caught a chill, and it had gone
to his chest.

By the time I returned, the house-slaves had brought
his bed into his downstairs study. He was lying on his
back, unmoving, already like a corpse. In the corner a
bronze stove warmed the room.

But when I went up beside him he stirred and regarded
me with watery eyes, and made an effort to pull himself
up from his pillow.

'Marcus,' he whispered, and reached out his hand for
me to take.

I sat down on the stool beside the bed, and took
his hand. There was a silence. The only sound was his
shallow breathing, and the gentle splutter of the charcoal
in the brazier.

Presently he said, 'I am glad I have lived to see my son

find a lover such as you. You do this house honour. You have brought me joy.'

My eyes filled with sudden tears. I swallowed. A ball of grief had lodged in my throat, and for a long time I could not answer. But eventually I said, 'It will pass, sir. You will be up again soon.'

He squeezed my hand. 'Nonsense,' he said. 'You know it and I know it.'

His body might be weak, but he had not grown stupid, and would not be talked to as a child. He closed his eyes to rest, but I could tell from his grip on my hand that he was not sleeping. So I waited, and after some little while he turned his head across the pillow to Menexenos.

'See to the farm, my boy. There is much to do.'

'Yes, Father.'

He paused, and attempted to smile. 'And there is something else . . .'

'Father?'

'Win the foot-race at the Isthmia for me. You know you can do it.'

He died that night, in the chill hour before dawn. Next day, while the women were busy with the body, Menexenos and I went out onto the slopes below the high-city.

The wind had ceased, and the air was still and cloudless. Frost clung to the pines, and as we walked our breath plumed in the early morning air.

We came to the grove behind the Areopagos hill, and here we sat, on an outcrop of grey rock. Menexenos pushed his broad hand through his hair, pausing when he came to the place where he had shorn the locks at the back, as an offering to the dead. For a long time we were silent.

I have often thought, when faced with the hard necessity of death, that words dissolve of meaning, like mist before a gale. But presently, for the silence was beginning to weigh on me, I murmured, 'So suddenly.'

He let out his breath. The vapour dispersed in the chill air.

'He was ready,' he said.

I thought of the burnt-out farm, and the war, and Menexenos's lost brother Autolykos. It seemed that everything Kleinias had worked to build had been swept away by madness, and the hard hand of unforgiving fate.

We sat, he with his thoughts I know not where, and I with my thoughts on him. He was staring out at the sky, where it was streaked with crimson dawn behind Hymettos. In the cold I could feel the heat from his body.

He sighed, then turned and looked into my face. 'I was going to tell you yesterday. While you were away I went to the office of the Strategos. I have enlisted in the hoplite corps.'

I knew of this corps. It was a company of volunteers that were going north to join the allies against Philip. For all the brave war talk of the Athenians, few had put their names forward when the call went out.

At another time I might have said that there was no need. But now I merely nodded. But for Philip, and the vainglorious folly of the Athenian Demos, Kleinias might still be living. It was an offering of sorts.

'In that case,' I said, 'we'll be fighting together . . .

Titus has asked me to join him in Phokis. He does not expect the Senate will agree to Philip's terms.'

He nodded at the sky. 'Some god had a hand in it then.'

'Perhaps.'

'Did you tell Titus about Lucius?'

I shook my head. 'No. He can find out about Lucius from others . . . if he cares to know. Either way, I don't intend to come between them.' I frowned out at the dun hills. For all Titus's good sense and judgement, when it came to Lucius he could not, or would not, see.

'This year will be the end,' I continued after a moment. 'Philip knows it. So does Titus. And whoever wins, the world will not be the same afterwards.'

We returned home, and next day we travelled out with a cart to the farm, to bury Kleinias there, in the little plot beneath the vine-terraces in the lee of Mount Paneion, where his father and father's father lay, and his ancestors before that, time out of mind.

Among the ancient faded gravestones I saw there was one still bright and new. It showed a naked youth beside a colt, with a wreath lying at his feet. The name was obscured by ivy. I did not need to ask who it was.

The envoys from Philip, and from the allies, went to Rome to address the Senate. It was Pomponius who told me what happened there.

The Senate, he said, had heard the representatives of the allies first. They had spent most of their address bickering with one another, or heaping insults upon Philip. For a while the senators had listened to this, but quickly they had grown bored with details they did not understand, and irritably questioned the delegates on where the various cities and strips of territory they spoke of lay.

The allied delegates explained: whoever held Demetrias, Chalkis and the heights of Akrokorinth – the Fetters of Greece – held Greece in his fist.

'And who holds them now?' the senators asked.

They answered that Philip did.

'Thank you,' said the senators. 'That will be all.'

Next, the envoys from Philip were brought in. They began on a lengthy argument, but the senators, who by this time were in no mood for long-winded Greek rhetoric, cut them off in mid-speech with the blunt question, 'Does Philip intend to evacuate Demetrias, Chalkis and Akrokorinth?'

The Macedonian envoys looked at one another. They were not used to Roman directness. As far as these cities were concerned, they said, stalling, they had not received, as yet, precise instructions from the King.

'In that case,' came the reply, 'there is nothing to discuss.'

'And so,' said Pomponius, looking pleased, 'Philip has come away with nothing at all. But tell me, when will you see Titus?'

I told him I should shortly be leaving for Elateia in Phokis, where Titus was wintering.

'You will not be staying with the fleet then?'

'No.'

He paused for a moment, looking at me through the corner of his eye. 'The word is,' he said with a faint smile, 'it will suit you to get away from Lucius.'

I shrugged. He was fishing for gossip. I did not intend to be his catch.

'I go where I am told,' I said.

'Yes, of course. Quite right. I expect, now, Titus will march up to Macedon and slaughter the wolf in his lair?'

'I cannot say. If he can persuade Philip to withdraw from Greece, there will be no need for war. That is his aim.'

'Well, yes,' said Pomponius nodding. And then, with a laugh, 'I wish I could go and fight myself; but, well . . .' He gestured at his slack, overweight body by way of explanation.

'I understand, sir,' I said.

I stood, and thanked him for his news, and we walked out to the terrace.

Out in the garden, his usual clients were waiting in the cold of the morning – Greeks seeking permits; Roman traders; junior officials of the Athenian government. I smiled inwardly, amused at how I had suddenly become the honoured guest, since Titus had become consul. Pomponius had been telling everyone who was likely to mention it to me that he had seen my potential from long ago.

'Oh, Marcus,' he said, pausing at the top of the step before we parted. 'Do please remember me to Titus when you see him.'

'Yes, sir. Of course.'

'You might mention, if the opportunity arises, that I

have been recalled to Rome. He may care to put in a word on my behalf . . .'

I bade him goodbye.

As I passed out beneath the gate, I heard his voice, returning to its usual self-important tone, cry out at the waiting clients, 'Who's first?'

Soon after, I travelled north.

I found Titus distant and preoccupied, and looking tired. It took me until the second day to find out what was troubling him.

We had eaten a dinner with the military commanders who were gathered there. They were Romans mostly, but among them were a few Greeks, including short-sighted Phaineas the Aitolian. Titus's friend Villius had come from Rome. I was glad to see him again, and it might have been a pleasant evening but for the Aitolians.

Phaineas and his entourage were in the mood to celebrate. They had got what they wanted from the Senate, and as the evening wore on, they grew loud and vaunting, declaring with drunken sweeps of their arms and great belly-laughs that they would utterly destroy Macedon, enslave the people and display Philip's head on a spit.

The new Roman officers listened with disapproving restraint. Their Greek was poor, but they understood enough to realize that there was something excessive and gross about such talk. War was war: unpleasant but necessary. The Aitolians' blood-lust disgusted them.

I suppose Phaineas's company sensed their disapproval, and, with the odd sensitivity of such men, they objected. They began to wonder in loud voices why these new officers had not stayed at home in Italy, for clearly they had no stomach for the fight.

They were not the first – or the last – to take Roman restraint for Roman weakness. The officers were men who had battled against the marshalled ranks of Carthage for a generation, and they did not need drunken Aitolian bandits to teach them courage. In pointed asides in Latin, they began to say so, and their meaning would have been clear in any language.

Eventually Titus threw his men a warning look and they fell into a bristling silence. Afterwards, Villius and I joined him in his private rooms. Titus sat down heavily in the armchair and called for wine. 'Remind me of this night,' he said, 'if I ever pick Aitolians as allies again.'

He sighed, and pressed his fingers to his eyes. There was a tap on the door, and a dark-haired Phokian slave-boy came in with wine in a bronze flask. Titus absently watched him as he filled the cups.

I said, 'Is that what's been troubling you – the Aitolians?'

He took up his wine-cup, looked at it, then set it down again without drinking. 'No, not that. I can manage the Aitolians ... I have not had the chance to tell you, Marcus, but—' He broke off, and turned to the slave-boy. 'Thank you, Damoitas. I shan't be needing you any further. You can go off to bed now.'

He waited until the boy had closed the door behind him and his footfalls had disappeared along the passage before he went on.

'Ten days ago,' he said, 'I had a visit from Zeuxippos of Thebes. He travelled at night, and came in disguise. He told me the Thebans have appointed that rabble-rouser Brachylles as leader, and he has been stirring up the common people against us, telling them we mean to enslave them.'

I sat forward. 'What will they do then? Will Thebes declare for Philip?'

He shook his head. He looked strained. One saw it in his eyes, and the corners of his mouth. 'Not while we are so close – according to Zeuxippos. No; like cowards, they will wait until we are halfway to Macedon and otherwise engaged. Then they will turn against us.'

He pulled himself up from the chair and crossed to the window. The court outside was lit by a flaring cresset, mounted on the gateway. Under the arch stood two guards in Roman uniform. He looked out for a moment, then turned back to me and Villius. 'We need Thebes on our side, or at least neutral. I cannot move against Philip with the threat of a hostile Boiotia behind us.'

'Then take Thebes,' said Villius.

Titus smiled. 'I wish it were so easy. A siege of Thebes could take half a year, and all that time Philip will be strengthening his forces. Already our spies in Macedon have reported he is calling up the old men and the youths of sixteen, and has been sending to Asia for supplies and mercenaries. But even if we could take Thebes in a week, it is not what we are here to do. We must persuade them, not conquer them.'

'Then how?' said Villius. 'Will you go and persuade them yourself?'

He had been joking. But after a pause Titus answered, 'Why not? Yes. I shall go to them myself, and they can decide once and for all who to support.' He nodded to himself, then suddenly grinned. 'Yes indeed. That is the last thing they will expect.'

We set out soon after, taking a small force through Phokis and into Boiotia. It was the last thing Brachylles and the Theban demagogues had expected. They had taken Philip's gold; but they were not prepared to pay for it with their blood. Titus addressed the Theban assembly. He did not refer to our army, or the strength of the allies. Nor did he insult Philip. He merely said that he had come to restore freedom to the Greek cities, which Philip had taken from them. He was fighting for all Greeks, including Thebes, and he hoped they would find it in their hearts to support him. If they would not, he merely asked them not to stand in his way.

When he had finished, the presiding magistrate asked if anyone else wished to speak. No one stood. No one raised his hand. All eyes slewed towards Brachylles, who was sitting with a face like stone. Like all demagogues, he knew a crowd, and Titus had shamed them by reminding them of their honour. There was nothing Brachylles could say.

With Thebes won over, the stage was set for the final battle, and at the time of the spring equinox our spies reported that Philip was massing his forces at Dion.

We marched north to meet him, through the passes of Phokis, taking the coast road past Thermopylai, and up into the high ranges above Thessaly.

Near Lake Xyniai we made camp, and there we waited for our allies to join us.

The highland air was fresh and clear and luminous. There had been a settlement once beside the lake, until the Aitolians had sacked it earlier in the war; now the only inhabitants were the wildfowl that nested in the reeds beside the water, and rose up in great resentful clouds as we passed. The troops had been penned up all winter: they were impatient for the campaign to begin. Expectation hung in the air, and everywhere was the sense that the final decision was at hand. The camp sounded with the scrape of whetstones on javelins and swords; and when the men were not busy with their kit and weapons, they swam in the lake's chill crystal waters, or sat gossiping and gaming outside their tents.

One afternoon, during these days of waiting, I was out walking in the heights above the settlement when I saw a figure standing alone, gazing out along the passes.

As I drew near I saw it was Titus. He had cropped his hair short for the season's campaigning, losing his curls and leaving a short light-brown fuzz. It made him look like a young trooper. We had joked about it.

He glanced round as I approached, to see who it was, then raised his hand in greeting.

'Still they do not come,' he said, turning back to look out along the valley. 'How much longer? We have come all this way to defend them; they promise troops; and now, when we need them, they are not here. They talk and talk about freedom, but when the time comes, they think someone else will do the fighting.'

I drew my breath and looked out across the high

pastures and the empty road. In the distance, over the still water of the lake, a lone eagle soared, turning in a great arc. The air was sharp and clean, like mountain water. I said, 'Are we strong enough to defeat Philip, if they do not come?'

He frowned. Out across the lake, the hovering eagle suddenly plunged, then rose with beating wings from the water. In its talons a fish was struggling. I tried to see an omen in it.

Titus nodded and smiled, guessing my thought. 'It is not a matter of numbers only; it is like a battle between two creatures of different elements, each the master of its own.'

I asked him what he meant.

'So far we have fought only garrison troops. We have not faced the Macedonian massed phalanx, row upon row of dense-packed men, each bearing against the enemy a pike fourteen cubits long. It is said they are invincible.'

'How then do we defeat this phalanx?'

He turned, and I saw the light in his blue eyes. 'The phalanx has one great weakness. In time of war, a general cannot always pick the place of battle; and yet the phalanx fights at its best only on level ground, where there are no ditches and ridges and trees to obstruct it. If the Macedonians could always pick their place, they would be unbeatable. But they cannot. Their strength lies in their formation, and if once their lines are broken they are exposed. They cannot turn, they cannot retreat; they must go forward or stay where they are.'

'Then,' I said, 'we must not let Philip choose his ground.'

He nodded. 'But Philip knows that too. He will do everything in his power to ensure we fight at a place of his choosing.'

He shrugged, and took one more look at the empty valley. 'Too much depends on chance. Let the allies come; then at least our forces will be even . . . Tell me, have you decided yet which company you will command?'

I said I had. He had sent a tribune to me the day before, offering me whichever company I chose. It was a great honour, and a sign of his trust, and I guessed he must have heard something of what had happened between me and Lucius.

'I did not even have to think about it,' I said. 'The veterans who fought with me at Korinth arrived yesterday. I will fight with them.'

He nodded. 'Then you have chosen well. They were in Africa, with Scipio at Zama. They are good men.'

'I know,' I said. 'They saved my life.'

Two days later the contingent of Athenian hoplites arrived, and with them Menexenos, dusty from the road, with his owl-emblazoned shield slung on his back, and his broad soldier's sun-hat on his head.

He too was leading his own company. I recognized some of them from my time in Athens: there was young dark-haired Lysandros, who had fought with me in the burning barn outside the gates of Athens; there was Ismenios, marching beside his lover Theodoros; and there was strong, broad-shouldered Pandion the pankratiast.

It was the first time I had seen Menexenos leading men. He made no pretence at being anything other than what he was. I have seen those who think the way to lead is to assume a vulgarity they do not possess, hoping to be liked. So they spit and swagger and slap, and all the time the men know they are being talked down to, and despise them for it. It would never have occurred to Menexenos to treat them that way. He looked for excellence in everything, and finding it in his men, helped them to find it in themselves. And all this he achieved by the simplest gestures and words, because it lay at the core of his being.

As I stood considering this, I found myself recalling the day he had won at the games; and the pot-bellied stone-cutter afterwards, who set so much store by doing as he pleased, and claimed that all were equal. There were no such men here. Nor would this small band of proud hoplites, who stood straight-backed and bright-eyed as the Roman troops looked curiously on, have tolerated a man like that among them. They had come to face death, and they knew, with the wise instinct that lies within each man's soul, that there is a truth in such hard reality that causes a man to see things in true proportion.

That night we lay beneath the open window of my room in the old settlement, talking quietly of what was to come. The room smelt of mountain heather, and cedar-wood, and sex. Now that the heat of Eros had passed, I felt a stillness, and the melancholy that always touches my soul at such times.

As I lay in the darkness, listening to his steady breathing beside me, feeling his warmth against the night-time chill, it seemed that I saw the pattern of our love written in the very stars themselves, and in every thing that was.

It filled my heart, and I wanted to say that we should turn away from the battle ahead, and go to a place where time and danger would not touch us.

But, I knew, there was no such refuge, for it would be a refuge from life itself. So I said nothing; turning on my side I drew him close, and pulled up the blanket around us against the night chill.

On the afternoon of the next day, Phaineas arrived at last with his Aitolians.

Menexenos and I had gone out walking along the shore of the lake. Seeing the army approach, we climbed up the goat-track rising up the hillside, the better to see.

Phaineas and his generals led; then came mounted warriors on prancing Thessalian horses, decked out in gaudy finery; and, behind them, a meandering raggle-taggle line of infantry.

In the days that followed others came too: men from the cities of Epeiros and Thessaly which Philip had ravaged; a troop of Kretans; contingents from the Helles-pont, and from Pergamon and Rhodes.

And then, after too long waiting, we finally struck north, to meet Philip and his army.

We advanced to Pherai, which lay on the main route south from Macedonia. Here we made camp, and next day at daybreak Menexenos and I rode out northwards with two Aitolian scouts who knew that country, looking for signs of Philip.

We rode for most of the day, halting often, scanning

from the high ground, questioning the peasants we came across on the land.

But when we asked they shook their heads and looked grave. They had not seen the Macedonians, they said.

Then, towards evening, we paused beside a pine wood, to relieve ourselves and rest the horses. We were on the edge of the rising ground, following a track in the foothills of Mount Chalkedonion. I crossed to the far side of the wood, where a bare rocky promontory jutted out, and, shading my eyes with my hand, scanned the plain below one last time before turning home.

The plain was empty, and deep in shadow now, as the sun dropped below the distant heights of Pelion. Far off, to the north and east, a bank of cloud was gathering, lit from behind so that it glowed red and purple. A breeze had picked up. It stirred the pine branches, and I thought to myself that soon there would be rain.

Just as I was about to turn back, I heard the sound of scree on rock. It was no more than a few light tumbling stones, but I paused and looked up, thinking to see a goat or coney.

The slope was empty. But then, on the high hillside track above, half hidden by pine and ash and thickets of arbutus, a troop of Macedonians appeared on horseback.

I hurried back to the others. Menexenos had seen them too. He was crouching down with the scouts, peering warily up from behind the tree cover.

'Have they seen us?' I whispered.

'I don't think so. Not yet. But they will, when we move.'

Silently we made our way back to the horses. The Macedonians were little more than a javelin's throw away. We could hear them talking among themselves in their broad, flat accents. It was hard to tell exactly how many they were; perhaps ten, perhaps fifteen. The track they were following was obscured by trees. I asked one of the scouts where it led. He shrugged. It was not a route he knew. He supposed it ran somewhere up over the ridge.

We crouched down and waited, expecting at any moment that one of the Macedonians would spot our tethered horses and sound the alarm. But no one shouted out, and when they passed momentarily behind an obscuring screen of pine we edged out into the open ground, and eased the horses back along the mountain track.

Moments later the cry went up behind us.

'Go!' I cried.

We flicked the horses to a canter – we could move no faster on the uneven stony path. A javelin clattered somewhere on the rocks behind us. But I could tell from the sound that it had fallen far short. After that, the Macedonians, realizing we were beyond their range, saved their weapons. I heard them crying out challenges and frustrated insults; and when the track levelled I turned back to look.

They were silhouetted against the twilit sky, a row of mounted horsemen staring furiously down. I smiled to myself, and then allowed myself to laugh. For I could see, now, that the track they were on doubled back up the hillside, leading them away from us. They could get to us only by returning the long way they had come, and by then we would be gone.

Next day, in the hour before dawn, Titus sent out a troop of men into the hills above Pherai, to take possession of the high ground and see what they could find.

Later one of them returned, bringing news that they had run into a similar advance party of Macedonians, scouting the high pass. Both sides, he said, had stood off, awaiting orders, neither attacking nor retreating.

Titus considered for a few moments. Then he said, 'Order the men back.'

'What?' cried Phaineas, who was with him. 'We have found them at last. Now you say we should not engage.'

'No, Phaineas; here is not the place.' He looked out from the terrace towards the distant wooded slopes of Pelion. The cloud-bank I had seen earlier had moved inland, hiding the high peaks, casting pools of shadow over the plain. 'What are the Macedonians doing up there in the hills?' he said, frowning. 'No, I don't like it. Philip is up to something, and I don't know what it is.'

'He is slipping away from us,' complained Phaineas. 'That much I know.'

But Titus seemed not to hear. He cast his eyes over the plain – a peaceful vista of neat well-tended fields, paddocks, smallholdings and fruit orchards – as if the answer lay there, if only he could see it.

Phaineas blinked and shrugged, and said to the rest of us, 'We could have fought them.'

'I have not come here to skirmish,' said Titus. He

rubbed the brown stubble on his chin. 'And nor,' he said after a moment, 'has Philip.'

He turned and gestured at the plain.

'He doesn't like the terrain. It doesn't suit him. He is trying to draw us west, into the open spaces of Thessaly, where he can crush us with his phalanxes.' He nodded to himself. 'Marcus, send word for the camp prefect. Tomorrow we march south.'

'South?' cried Phaineas in disbelief.

'Yes, south. Either he has retreated, which I do not believe, or he is moving behind us. That is why we cannot find him.' He looked up at Mount Chalkedonion and said, 'This high ground is hiding him. He is somewhere behind it.'

We struck camp, and returned by the way we had come, crossing the tributary streams of the Enipeus, which runs down into the Thessalian lowlands. That night we camped on the south side of Chalkedonion, where the sanctuary of Thetis is, below the little hillside town of Skotoussa.

Menexenos sniffed the air and looked at the sky. The last of the sunset seared the thickening cloud with grey and purple. 'The rain is coming at last,' he said.

That night a violent storm came rolling in from the east, first distant grumbling thunder and flickering backlit clouds; then a crashing din like the onset of some Titan army as it moved overhead. With it came wind, then sudden, torrential rain. The men sheltered under their hide tents, trying to keep dry, and talking of omens.

Sometime in the black night the rain stopped. But

with the first light of dawn we saw that the cloud had descended from the hills, shrouding everything in a chill, pallid mist. I went to Titus, and found Phaineas already there.

'. . . And now how will you find him?' he was saying. 'You should have attacked while you could. He will march right past you, and you won't even know.'

'He could, but he will not,' answered Titus.

'You are so sure? How do you know?'

'I knew when I met him. He wants this fight. He wants this fight with *me*.'

'Pah!' Phaineas switched his hand in front of his face to show his contempt. 'I don't trust him.'

'Nor do I,' answered Titus. 'But I think I understand him.' He looked out into the murk. 'You know this country. What is up in the hills behind us?'

Phaineas turned and blinked at the mist. 'Nothing much. Uneven terrain. Sheep and goat pasture. A few terraces of barley near Skotoussa. They call these hills Kynoskephalai.'

'The Dogs' Heads,' repeated Titus, saying the word in Latin.

'Yes,' said Phaineas. He frowned under his thick black beard. Then he said, 'But why? You don't think he's hiding up there, do you?'

'I don't know where he is. But I don't want him holding the high ground above our camp. Marcus, how ready are your men?'

'Ready,' I said.

'Then go and see what's up there, will you? I don't

want this cursed mist to lift and find him bearing down on us.'

I gathered my men, and we set out, up into the mist, ascending into rolling, grassy upland wet with long tracts of collected storm water.

No birds sang. In the mist there was no echo. Every sound was muffled and died around us.

As dawn turned to morning the sun appeared only as a cold white blur in the east. The men marched in silence, serious-faced and uneasy, scanning the muddy goat-tracks and turf for traces of the enemy.

I tried to ascertain the nature of the terrain around us. It was difficult, when I could not see even to the end of our line of men. Sometimes the land rose and fell in rolling, grassy undulations; at others it flattened out into open ground. But how wide these clearings were I could not tell.

We trudged on, keeping to one side of a low valley.

I heard footsteps. One of the men came up at the double through the mist. Keeping his voice low he said, 'Sir, Decimus says he heard something, over there.'

He pointed to a ridge on the opposite side of the valley. Its higher part was lost in the mist.

I looked but could see nothing. 'What did he hear?' I asked.

'He wasn't sure. Maybe a bird cry. Maybe a man's call.'

'Did you hear it?'

'No.'

I looked again, and listened.

The only sounds were the footfalls of the men in the mud, and the rustling of their equipment.

'Pass the order to halt,' I said. 'Battle formation. We'll go and look.'

We spread into a defensive line, and mounted the far slope. The mist encircled us, sometimes thinning, so that it seemed to be lifting; then, with a stirring of the breeze, it would close once again around us.

The man beside me – the one who had got the thigh-wound at Korinth – cursed under his breath and spat.

'What do you think?' I said.

He wiped his nose on the back of his hand and scanned the terrain.

'Something's there.'

I nodded. I sensed it too, like distant heat through a chill, though still I had seen and heard nothing.

I fingered the hand-grip of my sword and walked on.

Presently the ground flattened into a broad grass-covered plateau, the edges of which I could not see.

At the limit of my vision, on a piece of higher ground, a clump of tall pines stirred the fog. All of a sudden something caught my eye, a flash in the gloom; and then, a cubit in front of me, a spear sliced into the sodden turf.

I started back, and stared at the quivering ashwood shaft. Then I yelled, 'Shields up!' and all along the line the men's shields snapped up, just as the first volley rained down upon us out of the mist.

Then they came, surging out from the tree cover, crying out the paean.

We locked in battle. They were peltasts – light-armed

infantry; they must have spied us as we entered the valley below, and lain in wait.

Around us the mist stirred and tore and momentarily cleared, and I saw that what I had taken for a plateau was no more than a step, with higher ground around it. The Macedonians had caught us in a basin, and were coming at us from three sides.

I dispatched a runner to summon help. We were forced back into the low ground, where the damp, sucking earth hindered us.

The mist was thinning at last, but what I saw brought no comfort. Macedonians were streaming along the up-land flats. All along the hump-backed ridge that Phaineas had called The Dogs' Heads their battle-lines were form-ing. I realized that this was no mere skirmish.

'Sir,' cried a youth beside me. It was the messenger back from the camp, saying that Titus was bringing up the whole army, and we must hold till he arrived.

'Tell him we'll be here waiting for him,' I cried, and sent him off.

Beside me the old veteran grinned, showing his black teeth.

'They are twice as many,' he said.

Another said, 'More than that.'

'And we,' I said, 'are Romans.'

He laughed. 'Then we'd better set to work.'

And after that there was no time for laughing, for the front line of the Macedonian peltasts was upon us, and the battle was joined in earnest.

We were pushed back, but the Macedonians were not

yet ready to bring all their force to bear, and our line held.

Then, at last, the reinforcements began to arrive – first the Aitolian cavalry, then cohorts of the allied infantry. Through the breaking cloud low sunlight shafted through the mist, glinting on the approaching standards. All along the valley trumpets sounded.

The ground mist parted and dispersed, and I saw then, on the top of the hill, a figure appear, a rider in a gilded sunburst breastplate and purple cloak, mounted on a splendid white horse trimmed with gold.

I could not see his face. I did not need to. As he came into view, a cheer rose up from the Macedonian line. He acknowledged it with a high salute; then, urging his horse, he took up position at the front.

The battle-pikes descended. From his horse, in a clear, steady voice, Philip sounded the note of the paean, and it was taken up by the whole line, a clamour like rolling thunder that echoed down the valley. The king raised his arm, then let it fall, and with a roar of men's voices the whole phalanx began to advance.

Our forces met. I saw, in the distance, our left wing falter and buckle. Then, from the right, the men opposite us charged, and I had to concern myself with my own business, as the Macedonian infantry crashed into our line.

Our company fought in a close-knit band. What we had suffered at Korinth, fighting at bay in the breached wall while Lucius deserted us, had forged a bond between us, and now we fought with one mind. The Macedonians were trying to drive us down the ridge, into the low ground where they could overwhelm us. We did not give way. For a long time, as it seemed, we fought, neither advancing nor retreating.

Presently, as happens in battle, there was a brief lull around us as the heat of the battle moved elsewhere. We paused to get our breath.

The veteran beside me said, 'Isn't your lover fighting with the Athenians?'

I looked at him. He had used the crude army term he was familiar with; but I saw he meant no offence by it.

'Yes,' I said. 'Why?'

But by then I had followed his gaze, and could see the answer for myself.

The right wing of our line had driven the enemy from the high ground. But at the same time our left wing had fallen back. Everywhere men were locked in close fighting, and in the midst of it I saw the Athenian colours surging forward, falling into a trap they were unaware of, which was closing about them even as I watched.

I looked back at the veteran. I do not know what my face must have told him, but my voice said, 'They need help.'

He nodded. 'Yes they do. Then what are we waiting for?'

He shoved his fingers in his mouth and gave a sharp whistle, and like a pack of hunting dogs the whole company looked up. I turned and looked again across the battlefield. The Macedonians had closed on the Athenian hoplites and I could no longer make them out among the general mêlée of fighting men. I called on Mars to give me sight. I looked again. And then I saw what I needed to see.

The Macedonians, in their blind eagerness to pursue our flank, had failed to notice we still held the high ground on the right, and as they advanced a gap had opened in their line.

'See there?' I cried to our company, pointing. They nodded, and their eyes flashed at me through their helmet-slits. And then we charged, slicing through the breach in the Macedonian phalanx.

I recalled what Titus had said, and now I saw it for myself. The phalanx was locked in formation, and could not turn to face us. And so they did what any man would do. They threw down their long pikes and scattered before our charge, and as they did so the rest of their line buckled and collapsed behind them.

From his vantage point on the ridge, I saw Philip on his white horse, surveying the field. Then our hard-pressed left wing regrouped and charged, and before them the Macedonians took flight. Philip paused, one man alone against the cloud-clearing sky. Then, with a switch of his gilded reins, he turned his horse and was gone, and from all along our lines a cheer went up.

And yet, during all this time, there was only one thing on my mind: Menexenos. What prevented me from breaking off and going in search of him I do not know. Perhaps it was no more than pride and shame, which holds a man together when much else has deserted him. That, and the men around me, to whom I owed a warrior's loyalty.

But now I began to look about at the fallen bodies.

Halfway down the ridge the Athenian standard lay

fallen. I picked my way through the dead and dying –
Macedonians, Romans, Aitolians, and Greeks from other
cities. Then, at last, I came among the Athenians.

I saw Ismenios first. He was lying on his back, with a
spear lodged in his throat. It had cut through his neck
from front to back, pinning him to the earth as he fell.
Close by, face down, was Theodoros his lover, his arm
stretched out before him. I wondered which had died first.

I walked on, my mind frozen with just one thought.
And then I saw him.

His hair was matted with blood and sweat, and his
helmet lay tumbled on the ground beside him. He was
crouching down beside young Lysandros, cradling the
boy's head in his lap. As I drew near he looked up. His
cheeks were glistening.

'He fought bravely,' he said.

The boy lay staring up at the sky. His eyes were open
still; but his soul had fled.

I nodded and knelt beside him, and as I wiped the
tears from my eyes, I smeared my face with the blood of
the men I had killed that day.

When Philip had left the field, everyone thought the
Aitolians had gone in pursuit of him.

But when, later that day, we reached the enemy camp,
we found them there.

The Macedonians had fled north with Philip. The
Aitolians had let them slip through their fingers; they
were more interested in reaching the camp before anyone
else, to have first pick of the plunder.

By the time we arrived, the camp was a smoking upturned ruin of burnt-out tents and charred wooden outhouses. Scattered among them, struck down as they ran, were the bodies of the innocent camp-followers: old men, women and children. Those the Aitolians had not murdered had been corralled into the horse-pens, to be sold as slaves. They crouched cowering, half naked, having been stripped of everything that was of value.

The Aitolians had discovered the wine-store – long before, judging by the state they were in. They were drinking out of whatever containers they came across – looted cups, an unwieldy silver krater, food dishes, even shards of smashed amphoras. As we made our way along the camp's central avenue they staggered around us, calling out and singing, vaunting and red-eyed, waving their swords in the air, bellowing out to the disciplined Roman troopers how they had vanquished the greatest power in Greece.

Menexenos, who was walking beside me, regarded them with cold distaste. 'The only victory here,' he said, 'is that of passion over reason.'

Just then we reached the remains of Philip's great square pavilion. It had been looted and burned like everything else, but I recognized it from its position, and from a scrap of blue-dyed fabric on the ground, painted with the golden sunburst emblem of the royal house of Macedon. The bodies of serving-slaves lay all about, their throats cut.

Titus arrived, his blue eyes aflame with anger.

'Curse them!' he said. 'Philip has not yet conceded, and they have let him get away.'

In front of us an Aitolian captain came staggering past, cradling in his arms a bulging sack from which a silver lampstand protruded.

'You!' Titus shouted at him. 'Set that down, and bring Phaineas to me.'

The man paused. He glanced around him, and then at his bag of loot, and one could see the workings of his mind in his face.

His mouth twisted into a smirk. 'Set it down?' he sneered. 'So you can take it from me? I found it first, and so it's mine. You must think I was born with the day's dawn.'

Titus took a step forward, and the Aitolian stumbled off.

'This,' said Titus, turning back to me and Menexenos, 'is what mankind becomes when law and decency and order are taken away. The price of war is more than blood. We should do well to remember it.'

FOURTEEN

WE PURSUED PHILIP NORTH through Thessaly. At Larissa we were met by a herald seeking terms, saying the king desired a final settlement. The peace conference met at Tempe; Philip, who had no choice now, agreed to withdraw from Greece, and provide sureties against his future conduct. Everyone agreed, except the Aitolians, who wanted to crush Philip into the ground.

Menexenos had travelled up with the Athenian delegation. When the conference was over we rode out along the banks of the Peneios, finding a secluded glade under the high cliffs, where flat rocks extended into the cool water, and here we stripped off our clothes and swam. Afterwards, drying off in the hot afternoon sun, we talked, while all around the cicadas sang among the laurels. The air smelled of summer flowers and the dampness of the rocks.

The conference had left me with a bad taste, like tainted water. I had had enough of Phaineas and the Aitolians. 'I cannot understand him,' I said. 'Does he really suppose Titus is taking Philip's gold?' For in the end, seeing himself outvoted, Phaineas had rounded on Titus, saying he had been bought off.

Menexenos was sitting on the edge of the rock, beside where I lay, with his well-formed runner's feet trailing in the bright clear water. He had got a sword-cut on his right arm at Kynoskephalai, and a wound on his shoulder, where a javelin had caught him.

'Phaineas is like most men,' he said. 'He does not see beyond what he is, because he lacks philosophy. His words are a mirror of his soul. He would have taken a bribe himself; and so he cannot conceive that Titus would not do the same. He does not know what it is to be noble, and so, when he encounters nobility in others, he does not understand. He looks for low motives, hypocrisy, corruption and self-interest behind every act of greatness, and is not content until he finds it.'

He frowned up at the slopes of Ossa and Olympos, and I saw in his face, like hidden light, the sadness that was always there.

We had had little time together since Kynoskephalai. He had lost good friends that day, young men who felt it was their duty to answer the call of the city, and risk their lives in its defence.

I knew he grieved for the youth Lysandros, who had looked up to him, and would not have volunteered to fight except that he wanted to be alongside Menexenos.

The battle, the war, the death of his father, had all left their mark.

Lately I had been having unsettling dreams; not of the battle, as one might expect, but of my father, as I once did at home in Praeneste. In them he was trying to speak to me, to tell me something important. But his words were faint and distant, and I could not make them out.

I had kept this to myself, for it seemed pointless to burden Menexenos with something I could not explain, when he had troubles of his own. But as I looked at him now I remembered that some kind god had preserved him for me, when so many others had died. Though it was warm, I shivered. I could not conceive of losing him. It was like the place where the world ends, and ocean falls into chaos. I averted my mind from it, seeing only madness there.

For a while we sat with our thoughts; but presently he said, 'Did you notice, today, how quiet the allies were when Phaineas spoke?'

'Yes,' I said. 'It was as though there was something they would not say.'

He nodded. 'Phaineas does not mention it, but he knows it as well as anyone, and that is why he is so angry. If Macedon is destroyed, it will leave the Aitolians masters of Greece. No one said so, but we have not fought in order to exchange Philip for Phaineas.'

Two days later, Philip came to Tempe to seal the treaty, at the shrine of Apollo, in its setting of laurels, beside the Peneios.

'Behold,' he said, arriving with his entourage, 'I am a wolf brought down by cur-dogs.'

The conditions were read out. Philip listened without comment. When Titus said that his son Demetrios was to be handed over to Rome as surety, he merely said, 'It must be as you wish.'

The allies exchanged glances. The envoy from Pergamon said, 'You do not object?'

'Of course I object. But I agree. You may have your cities; you may seize my fleet. And you may take my son away. I shall even send my gardeners to Pergamon ... What more? Is there more?'

Phaineas, vaunting and in triumph, said, 'It would be better, King Philip, if you showed more humility, now you are defeated.'

'Humility?' said Philip, his voice rising. 'I do not know the word. Are you fool enough to suppose there is anything you could do that would make me grovel in the dirt? Then, Phaineas, you do not know me. Look at you, puffed up in all your finery, festooned like a Lydian whore. Even if you possessed the whole world, and were as rich as Xerxes or Kroisos, you would still be no more than a sightless fool. But if I lost everything, I should remain a king. That is the difference between you and me, Phaineas. You will never understand.'

That autumn, when the leaves on the trees were starting to turn from green to gold, and the grapes stood purple on the vine-terraces, we travelled south, and for the rest of that year Titus was occupied with the commissioners who had been sent from Rome to settle the peace.

I returned with Menexenos to Athens. At home, a summons was waiting for him. He had been selected for the Isthmian games, and was to present himself to the gymnasiarch for the trials, which would take place that winter.

When he informed me of this he seemed so unmoved that in the end I asked him if he was not pleased.

'I'm pleased enough,' he answered with a shrug. And then, because I had my eyes on him, he added, 'I'll go to my old trainer at the Lykeion. He's still the best in Athens.'

Yet I sensed there was something else, which he was not telling me. I was minded to ask him again, but just then, as we passed the colonnade of the Stoa of Zeus, on our way back from the Council House, someone called from the shadows and Pandion the pankratiast stepped out, with two of his young friends.

Neither of us had seen Pandion since Kynoskephalai, and we were eager to catch up on our news. He had heard that Menexenos was going to the games, and insisted on taking us to celebrate, to a wine-shop he knew up on the hill. And after that Menexenos seemed in better cheer.

That night, when we were alone, he said, 'Well it's going to be a winter of hard practice.'

'Then I'll practise with you,' I said. I stretched out on the bed and reached out to him. 'We have been too long apart.'

He laughed and took my arm.

Later, as we lay quiet, he said, 'Let us go to the farm until it's time for the running trials. There's work to do there, and I'm not in the mood for the city. I expect it's the war, but I've had my fill of people for a while.'

I propped myself up on my elbow, and smiling said, 'But not, I hope, of me.'

His serious eyes looked into mine. 'Not you, Marcus. Never you. It is a sacred thing between us.'

Next day, since I could put it off no longer, I made my way down to Piraeus to call on Caecilius.

As usual he was full of his own concerns: the Theban Tyrtaios had disappeared, taking with him a large sum of Caecilius's money. I was not surprised, and told him so, adding that I had never liked the man.

'No?' said Caecilius. 'Then why didn't you think to tell me? You might have saved me a great loss. Really, Marcus, I wonder what you spend your time thinking about, when you forget matters of such importance. A quiet word might have saved me a case of gold.'

This was a path I did not wish to go down, so I answered, 'I don't think you ever told me, sir, quite what business it was you had with Tyrtaios.'

'Oh, it's not important now,' he said, suddenly developing an interest in the papers on his desk. 'Ah, see here.'

He pulled out a half-open scroll that lay under his wine-cup, and flourishing it said, 'Your mother writes. She is well. The farm prospers. She says I must not hurry back to Italy for her sake, if there is business to do in Greece . . . It is admirable in a woman, don't you think, to show such a grasp of the priorities?'

I agreed, imagining my mother and Mouse at peace in Praeneste without him; and in case he saw the light of irony in my eyes I quickly asked what his plans were now. 'For surely, sir, there is nothing more that keeps you in Athens.'

'You are wrong. While you have been off fighting I have been busy.' He paused, and gave one of his significant looks. I felt a sinking feeling in my gut. 'No doubt you would like to know all about it, but, Marcus, in my experience, the fewer who know the better, and so I shall keep the details to myself . . . for now. But I can tell you I plan a trip to Asia.'

'Asia?' I said, eyeing him suspiciously. 'Not King Antiochos, sir, I hope; no good will come from him.'

'Don't pry. I shall tell you when I'm ready. Besides, I know what I'm doing . . . I suppose you heard about old Attalos, by the way?'

'He was taken ill at Thebes.'

'Oh, more than that. News came from Pergamon this morning, brought by a Chian trader. He is dead. It seems he never recovered from his illness, and now he is gone.'

He stretched back in his chair and laid his hands on his protruding belly, like a glutton who has enjoyed a good meal. 'Still,' he went on, 'he died a rich man; one can hope for no more than that.'

I remembered Attalos's various kindnesses to me, and his decency, and how he had used the last of his strength fighting for the freedom of Greece.

'He was a good man,' I said.

'Was he? I daresay he was. His son Eumenes succeeds him. We should keep our ears open. There are always opportunities at such a time.'

I looked at him, and he looked back at me with his small sandstone eyes. His face had fattened since last I had seen him; the weight sat ill on him, for he was not a big-framed man.

There was a scratching on the door.

'Come!' boomed Caecilius.

Florus stepped timidly in, like an ill-used mongrel, unsure of its welcome.

'Ah, there you are; I was just about to summon you ... Marcus, you remember Florus, don't you? I have decided to engage him once more. He was in Kerkyra, you know.'

Florus gave me a quick, weak smile, and avoided my eyes. No doubt he did not wish to recall our last meeting.

'Now is there anything else?' said Caecilius, already shuffling impatiently at his papers as if I were delaying him. 'If not, Florus and I have business to attend to.'

Shortly after, Menexenos and I went to the farm.

We hired help, and gathered the little of the olive and grape harvest the Macedonians had left us. We cleared the hillside terraces, retrained the vines, and set to work on repairing the house and animal-enclosures.

To begin with, it was sombre work – shifting charred beams; clearing burnt-out rooms; being reminded of how the farm had once been, and what was lost. But soon we had built something new out of the ruin, and, stone by stone, we set the past behind us.

Each morning we went out running, side by side, in the cool of the dawn, following the track out past Paneion and along the coast-path. Sometimes we saw a farmer, or a traveller on foot or muleback, but mostly we were alone, our footfalls matched, breathing in unison, a curiosity for the goats and sheep.

We talked of the games. Nowadays I expect every Roman with an education knows it, for we have become familiar with Greece. But then Greek things were less well known, and when I asked, Menexenos explained that the games at the Isthmos were held every two years, in honour of Poseidon, who had a temple there. The footrace, he told me, was a race particular to the Isthmian games: it was neither a short sprint nor a long-race, but something in between.

I asked him what he thought his chances were; but he only shrugged and said he could not tell.

All winter we trained together, and worked on the land, and lay together beside the fire in the old house. When the solstice had passed, and it was time to leave, we could look back on a job done well: the vines had been trimmed, the withy enclosures remade, and the house stood once more with its roof and doors.

We returned to Athens shortly before the running trials were due. Then, for the first time, I saw the other youths who were being sent from Athens for the games.

Most of the runners had bodies lean to the point of ugliness or sickness, except for their legs, which were a knot of muscles and sinews, as if they had done nothing in their lives but spend each day from dawn to dusk on the sand-track. As they practised, their trainers watched from the terraces, biting their lips; and as soon as each race was done they came rushing forward, clucking and fussing, swaddling their charges in cloaks and warmed towels, and hurrying them off to the bath-house to be rubbed down with aromatic oil.

I looked to see if anyone I knew was there. I had

expected to see some of Menexenos's friends, who had competed in the Athenian games. But there was no one I recognized.

As I was considering this, I saw Pandion amble in under the entrance-arch. He paused, glanced at the runners, then seeing me, came to where I was sitting on the terraces. 'Hello, Marcus. Isn't Menexenos with you? I thought he'd be here.'

I told him Menexenos had just gone off to the bath-house. Just then an umpire's voice sounded as a new race started – a short sprint. We paused to watch. When it was finished Pandion nodded at the scrawny runners and said flatly, 'And Menexenos is up against such creatures as these.'

I nodded. 'I know, Pandion. He stands out like a lion among goats.'

We both paused. And then, saying what had been on my mind, I asked him why none of his friends were competing, for they had done well enough in the Panathenaic games. 'And indeed, Pandion, as I recall, you won the prize for the pankration.'

He frowned. 'Yes, Marcus,' he said, 'but that was just a local affair.'

'Yet surely one contest is as good as another? But now you only watch from the sides, like the old men.'

After this he paused for so long that I began to wonder whether I had offended him. I was about to tell him that it was of no great importance when he said, 'Surely you've seen for yourself, Marcus? There's no proportion in it any longer. The games should exist for man; not man for the games. At home we compete with one another out of tradition, and love of physicality, and to try ourselves against our peers. But nowadays, at the great games of Isthmia, or Olympia, or Delphi, there is no place any longer for a gentleman. It is a thing of shame to devote oneself to one thing only, like a slave. A free man should strive for balance and proportion, in the body as well as the soul. The games were about the whole man once: just look at the old statues of Pheidias, or Lysippos, where the soul and the body are in harmony; and now,' he said, with a nod at the track, 'look at *them*.'

He sat down on the stone terrace, and crossly waved a dismissing hand, as if he had said more than he intended.

He must have guessed what I would ask next, for when I said, 'But Menexenos is competing,' he answered straight away. 'Yes, yes, I know he is. And Menexenos sees it more than any of us. Who do you think I got all this from? Sometimes I think that, but for him, I should not love excellence at all.'

He paused, and glanced at me, as if considering whether to tell me a private confidence. 'You know, I only became a pankratiast because of Menexenos. At school they thought I was no good; but he saw something in me, and made me feel it, and gave me a goal to strive for.'

He sat forward frowning, his chin in the ball of his hand, gazing out across the track. I believe he was even blushing a little.

'Then why does he compete at all?' I said. 'Why did he not tell the gymnasiarch no? He has reason enough.'

He shrugged. 'Because of his father? His brother? He does not talk of these things. Or maybe,' he said, shaking his head, 'because, even now, there is still some honour in it, if you can win without sacrificing those things which make one a man.'

I did not mention this conversation to Menexenos. Some god signalled against it. Or perhaps it was that I knew, with a knowledge that is beyond mere words, that whatever drew him to compete was something buried deep in his being, something from the same well of goodness that caused him to fight for the city, and to honour the gods, and to love me.

There are, after all is said, certain doors one does not seek to open, and certain things that love does not question.

That winter, Titus's friend Villius called at Athens on his way south. Titus, he said, was having difficulties with the commissioners from Rome; and with the Aitolians.

The commissioners were opposing the withdrawal of Roman forces from Greece, arguing that, with the question of Antiochos in Asia not settled, and the disturbing news that Hannibal was at large, neither the security of Greece nor the safety of Rome would be achieved by such a move, irrespective of what had been promised before.

'And what does Titus say?' I asked him.

'He says he has given his word, and must keep it. The Greeks will not settle for less. But in the end, Marcus, the decision is with the commissioners, and the Senate, not with Titus . . . And then,' he added, with an exasperated gesture, 'there are the Aitolians.'

Each time, he said, we thought a question was settled,

the Aitolians came forward and reopened it, making unexpected claims to territory to which they had no right. 'Everyone is tired of them. Their only aim is to snatch as much as they can.'

He was on his way to Korinth, he said, where the final negotiations would be completed. It was Titus's hope that he could announce a final agreement at the Isthmian games. 'Provided that rogue Phaineas doesn't poison the water first. He is putting it about that we intended all along to keep the Fetters for ourselves.'

Spring came. In the courtyard pink buds showed on the climbing jasmine, and in the temple precincts the almonds and narcissus bloomed.

On a blowy April morning, I went down with Menexenos to Piraeus, and from the waterfront I cheered with the rest as the state galley, decorated with garlands and bunting, pulled out beyond the sea-wall, and raised its owl-painted sail, bearing him and the other athletes to Isthmia.

Then, when the ship was lost in the morning haze, and the crowds began to disperse, I turned my mind to my own journey.

Villius had said a Roman quinquereme would be sailing there in time for the games. But in the end I decided to make my own way, by the land route, past Eleusis and Megara.

It seemed all Greece was travelling to the games that year: a steady stream of men and women, mules and horses, carts and traps and litters.

To begin with I walked alone, enjoying the solitude; but near Megara I fell in with a rugged-faced, middle-aged farmer from Phokis, leading a pack-mule loaded with empty baskets, which, he said, he intended to fill with the kind of well-priced luxuries that could be got in the markets at Korinth.

By now my Greek was polished enough that, if I wished, I could pass for a Greek anywhere, and so when he assumed I was from Athens, I did not tell him otherwise.

He told me as we walked that he farmed a few acres of land not far from Elateia, and, since there was peace at last, he was going to the games to watch the boxing, which he liked best of all. He raised his fist and con-torted his face, parodying the stance of a boxer. He was that sort of man. Later he confided, with a knowing leer, that after the games he planned to spend some time visiting the backstreets of Korinth, enjoying its particular pleasures.

He was a man who liked to talk about himself, and as we made our way along the road I heard about his farm, his livestock, the condition of his fields, and his wife – who was an unfortunate put-upon drab, judging from how he described her.

At one point, when he fell momentarily silent, I com-mented that it must be a relief to him that his city was free at last, after having been under the rule of the Macedonians for so long.

At this he snorted derisively. 'Why,' he said, 'all we have done is swap one slave-master for another.'

I looked at him surprised. 'Oh, sir? Yet Titus promised. Soon you will have your freedom once again, to do with as you please.'

He laughed at me. 'Mark my words. What the Romans have taken, they will keep. That is how men are. Rome has unshackled the feet of Greece, only to bind her at the neck.'

I said no more. It was clear he had already made his mind up.

For a while after this we walked without speaking, and I thought to myself that the Aitolians had done their work well, if men who had so recently been freed from tyranny thought as this man did.

But presently, as if the silence irked him, he said to me, 'So what do *you* suppose the Romans will do?'

I shrugged. 'I have heard it said that Titus is determined to leave Greece free. Everything he has promised, he has done. Why doubt him now?'

'Because,' said the farmer, 'I have seen what men are.'

'I too,' I said. 'And I have seen good as well as bad.'

He cast me an amused look, as if someone my age could not have seen anything in life. Then he cleared his throat and spat in the grass. 'Let me tell you, youth, there is nothing in the world but cruelty and baseness and self-seeking; and if a man is wise, he will snatch what he can, like a jackal at a carcass, before some other man takes it.'

He smiled to himself, seemingly satisfied with his words. But after a moment he cursed for no reason, and gave the mule a vicious yank on its tether. The mule gave a resentful grunt, but otherwise took no notice.

He turned, muttering; then looked ahead, narrowing his eyes irritably against the light, and said, 'Ha! See there!'

I followed his gaze. Half a mile ahead, a bright-painted carriage stood pulled up at the side of the road. Two mules stood by, chewing at the grass, and beside them a man was staring blankly at the wheel.

The farmer laughed. 'Some rich aristocrat broken down,' he said. 'Serves him right; that will teach him to travel in style; let him go on foot like the rest of us.'

As we drew nearer the man noticed us and began casting forlorn entreating looks.

'Fool,' muttered the farmer, chuckling to himself. But I said, 'I'm going to help.'

'Are you? Do as you please; but you'll be stuck here half the day, and I want to reach Isthmia before dark.'

I told him he must go on ahead then. And bidding him goodbye I turned off into the short grass.

I saw, as I drew close, that the man beside the carriage was a slave. He watched me approach with a sullen face. I wondered where his master was.

I was about to ask, when from the far side a woman's voice called out, 'Well come along, don't just stand there. It won't fix itself. Here, take this strap and bind it round the axle as I told you; or must I do it all myself?'

I crouched down on my haunches and peered under the carriage. Then, seeing who was there, I laughed.

'Pasithea! What are you doing?'

Her elaborate chestnut hair darted from behind the wheel.

424

'Marcus? Here, take this.' She passed me a broad leather binding-strap.

I crawled under the vehicle and took the strap, and called the slave to help me.

When, presently, the repairs were done I stood dusting off my hands and looked at her.

'Never in my life,' I said, 'have I met a woman like you.'

She sat down on a towel on the grass, and eased her feet into a pair of dainty calfskin slippers. 'In that case,' she said, giving me a wink, 'you should meet more women. Besides, I have learnt that if something matters to you, then teach yourself; otherwise a time will come when you'll wish you had.'

She told the slave to re-hitch the mules. Then she noticed the farmer, who had paused in the road to stare.

'Who is he?' she said, returning his look, upon which he quickly turned away. 'Has he never seen a women mend an axle before?'

'I doubt it,' I said, grinning. 'Where are you going? The games?'

'Where else? I would not miss them for anything.'

'Well, everyone wants to find out what Titus is going to say.'

'Oh, I'm not going for *that*,' she said, in a tone that told me she too had heard enough of the rumours and gossip. 'No, it's time I reopened my house in Korinth . . . and what better time than now, so that I shall have somewhere to entertain the beautiful Menexenos, when he takes the victor's crown in the foot-race?'

I laughed, then made a sign in the air against ill-luck.

'First,' I said, 'he must win it . . . and everyone seems to think he has a hard task on his hands, not having been bred to it from birth.'

'Then I shall say no more.' She fluttered her heavy lashes at me, then glanced over my shoulder towards the road. 'Is your friend not waiting?'

The farmer was finally moving off.

I told her he was no more than a road-acquaintance. In truth I was glad to have left him.

'Then good,' she said. 'In that case, we shall travel together.'

We set off, with the slave sitting in the back. On the way she told me she had spent the winter with friends in Megara. 'A dull, dull place, full of merchants. Have you been? You wouldn't like it . . . How is Caecilius, by the way? I heard he was still in Athens.'

'He was, until a few days ago.' I told her about his new venture in Asia.

'I hope,' she said, 'that he knows what he's doing.'

'I doubt it. I tried to warn him, but he would not listen.'

'No,' she said, unsurprised.

She told me she had sent her young black slave, Niko, ahead to the house in Korinth. 'He likes it there. He will be glad to be back home at last . . . Now *he* would have known how to fix an axle.'

She intended, she said, to pay a visit to the grave of Laïs, to whom she owed an offering.

'Laïs?' I said.

'Why, Marcus. Have you not heard of her? In her time she was the most famous courtesan in all Greece.'

'Did you know her?'

She smiled and tapped my knee. 'Oh no, my dear. Not even I am that old: she has been dead three generations at least. And yet, in a way, she has been my greatest friend. Laïs was beautiful, successful, graceful, loved by everyone. Even we courtesans need someone to look up to, you know, though many men would not pause to think it. And when I was a girl, and the pinch-faced wives of Abydos looked down their noses at me, I remembered Laïs and smiled back at them.'

And thus we rode on, chatting as we went.

Towards evening we came out into the broad coastal plain, and ahead lay Isthmia, with the red roof of Poseidon's temple showing among the pines; and, beside it, the marble-faced stadium, shining mellow gold in the late sunlight.

Presently we halted. The visitors' tents and makeshift awnings extended in all directions over the slopes. The cooking-fires were being kindled. Dogs barked and squabbled. Men sat around in groups, exchanging news. The air smelled of woodsmoke, and animals, and humankind.

Pasithea, casting a cool eye over the crowd, said, 'I fear I have grown too used to my comforts for all this. Are you sure you don't want to come on to Korinth with me, and sleep on silk sheets, with a servant to take care of you?'

'Don't worry, Pasithea,' I said laughing. 'Anyway, I'm meeting Menexenos here in the morning.' He would be barracked with the other athletes.

'Well send him my love,' she said, leaning across and kissing me on the cheek.

At this an old man passing in the crowd tutted up in disapproval; assuming, I suppose, I had begun early to indulge myself in the pleasures for which Korinth is renowned. From her high seat on the carriage Pasithea gave him a sweet smile. He hurried off grumbling.

We laughed. Then, with promises to meet soon, we parted.

I met Menexenos at the place we had arranged, at the plinth of the bronze Poseidon, in front of the temple.

People paused and stared, as they do at an athlete at the games. He was tanned from days of running on the practice-track; in his short white tunic his arms and thighs showed golden-bronze. Little wonder, I thought, that everyone's eyes were upon him.

He was too well bred to wear his emotions on his sleeve, but I knew him well enough by now to read his mood. Presently he frowned at the little crowd that had gathered and said, 'Let's go somewhere else.'

We left the temple sanctuary and passed along the street between the long colonnades. All about, traders had set up their stalls: sellers of fine Egyptian linen, glittering Koan silks, Persian tapestries, Indian pearls, trinkets to hang around the neck or wrist, crude carved votaries to offer at the temples, and charms for luck. As we walked I caught the conversation of those we passed, and each time I heard the same thing: Titus's name, the Aitolians, and the freedom of Greece.

Soon, however, we left the crowds behind us, and came to a garden on a slope, shady with pines and olive orchards. 'It will be quieter here,' said Menexenos. 'The grove is sacred to Demeter.'

We found a grassy bank and sat. Here and there people were walking along the paths between the trees. Further off, near the road, the stadium with its banners and garlands shone brilliant white under the noon sun. We talked of my journey, and Pasithea, and such things; and then I asked him what he made of the competitors from the other cities.

He made a balancing gesture with his hand. 'I have the measure of most of them. There are two I don't like the look of – though no one else seems to have realized.'

I asked him what he meant.

One, he said, was called Thorax, an Aitolian. 'He's a great boaster, like all Aitolians. But behind all the bluster he's fast as well.'

'Will he win?'

He shrugged. 'Perhaps. But I have been watching him. If he has a weakness it is this: he was born with speed, and has never had to trouble to make himself better. He's probably come first in every race he has ever run. It has come too easy to him. He has never had to pause, and look inside himself.'

'And the other?' I said.

He gave a quick laugh. 'His name is Damindas. He's a spoiled rich man's son from Aigina, and if you saw him clothed in a crowd, you would scarcely believe he was an athlete at all. No one has ever taught him manners, or posture. But someone has taught him how to run.'

That evening I saw them for myself.

We had been up to the sanctuary, and at the little round shrine of Palaimon had offered a pinch of incense at the fire. It was a warm, clear evening. The stars shone in a great arc over the Isthmos and the sea. Returning through the town, Menexenos touched my arm as we passed one of the crowded streetside taverns and said, 'There they are.'

A row of youths were seated at a long table of scrubbed pinewood, surrounded by wine-pitchers, dishes of half-eaten food, and the wide, flat cups that tavern-keepers use because they are hard to break.

'See the thin-faced one with the girl,' said Menexenos. 'That's Damindas.'

I looked through the crowd. He was a sandy-haired youth, surprisingly pale, with round shoulders and pro-truding eyes. He might have been a merchant's clerk. He had one hand on the table, holding his cup. But the other, I saw, was wedged between the girl's legs, and it was clear she did not like it.

'Who's his friend?' I said.

'Oh, some flute-girl he's hired for the night. He treats them all like that, as if he hated them and wanted to shame them. I don't know what he does to them later, but you never see the same one twice.'

I looked again. Just then there was a great laugh from the far end of the long table, from a group crowded around a flat-faced, grinning, black-haired youth. He was nodding and smiling, and judging from the reaction of the others had just told a joke.

'That one,' said Menexenos, 'is Thorax. He makes

430

jokes about everyone. But Damindas thinks he only jokes about him, and hates him for it.'

'Then why doesn't he go somewhere else?'

He shrugged. 'He doesn't want to miss anything.'

Just then Thorax turned and noticed us, and began calling for Menexenos to join the table and drink a cup of wine with him.

'Well you may as well meet them,' said Menexenos grimly. We stepped forward, and threaded towards them among the busy tables.

Thorax shoved his neighbours along and Menexenos sat beside him. I took the only other place, which was at the far end of the long bench, beside the flute-girl.

She turned as I sat, and flashed me a quick smile. I smiled back and said hello. It was no more than a kindly greeting, but beside her Damindas seemed to object. He gave her a sharp tug, and made her turn away.

Being at the end of the table, I was somewhat outside the ambit of the various conversations that were going on, and for a while I sat in silence, listening to the others and sipping at my cup of wine. For all the noisy merriment, I had picked up an undertone of hostility, like a bad note at a concert. Damindas seemed tense, and was sitting with a long face. I could not suppose it was merely because I had spoken to the girl.

As I was turning this in my mind, Thorax shouted down from the top of the table. 'Hey, so you fought at Dogs' Heads, did you?'

I looked up. Like all Aitolians, he said everything at the top of his voice, like a goatherd bawling across a field.

431

'Yes I did,' I answered warily. I looked away. I had not come here to get into an argument about the war.

I heard him shout out across the tavern for the boy to bring a fresh pitcher of wine. When it came he refilled his cup and drank it. Then he seized the pitcher, stood, and came striding down towards me.

I kept half an eye on him. When he reached where I was sitting he halted, and banged down the pitcher on the tabletop beside me. It was an old bronze one. It sang like a bell, and dark wine slopped out.

By now half the tavern had paused in their conversations and were watching curiously. A silence fell.

Then, with a great clap, he slapped his hand on my shoulder, and with the other took the pitcher by its handle and slopped wine into my cup, till it overflowed and began dribbling off the edge of the table onto my thigh. He filled another cup, then raised it. 'To you, then!' he cried, 'I honour you.'

He drank, then tossed the empty cup at the startled onlookers.

I was so surprised that for a moment I just looked at him. Then I took my own cup and drank down the rough wine, and even threw it off into the dark behind me afterwards.

Thorax laughed. 'We showed those Macedonians,' he cried. And then, realizing with a frown that his cup was gone, he took a great swig from the pitcher, and thrust it in front of me for me to do the same.

Around us people began to laugh and bang the tables with their fists. Thorax turned and gave them a mock bow. 'To the defeated Macedonians!' he cried. 'Death to our enemies!'

There were cheers all around. But beside me Damindas hissed, 'You disgust me, Thorax. You're drunk as a muleteer. Why don't you shut up?'

He had spoken quietly, but I knew Thorax had heard. I do not think he was much bothered by the words, but he had sensed the intent. He turned to Damindas with an amused look, and before he spoke he winked at the girl. Then he said, 'Yes, I am drunk, Damindas. What of it? Come the day of the race, I shall still beat you, and what will your rich daddy have to say about that?'

The flute-girl – who, though pretty, was clearly not bright – giggled, failing to see that this was deadly.

'Curse you, Thorax,' hissed Damindas. 'Shut your stupid mouth.'

'A loser,' nodded Thorax at me. 'Take no notice of him. No one else does.' And then, slapping the flat of his hand on my back, he pointed at Menexenos and asked at the top of his voice, 'Is it true that he's your lover?'

I saw Menexenos bristle. He did not care to have our private love cheapened, passed around by vulgar hands and inspected like some curiosity. But, of course, by now everyone was looking, and to appear cowardly or ashamed was worse. So I replied with equal force, 'Yes, it is true.'

For some reason Damindas, who had been sitting silent with a face the colour of oxblood, found this funny, and let out a sudden guffaw. At this Thorax swung round and looked at him.

'Do you laugh at love, Damindas? Then beware, for one day love will laugh at you. And, whatever you think of my friend here, at least he does not have to pay for it.'

And then, turning his back on Damindas's appalled face, he sat down beside me. 'Let us drink, Roman. Any friend of Menexenos is a friend of mine, even though he's going to lose the foot-race.'

At this the tense silence broke once more into laughter and talk. All except Damindas, who stood abruptly, dragging the flute-girl to her feet. 'Get up,' he said to her. 'We're leaving. I don't like the stench around here.'

FIFTEEN

AFTER THAT NIGHT THE athletes were confined to
their barracks until after the games, as the custom was.
It was still two days before the first contests began,
but I did not have to kick my heels, for next day early,
shortly after I had risen, and was washing my body at the
fountain, Villius arrived.

He tossed a towel at me. I caught it. 'What news?'
I asked. 'Will Titus still attend the games?'

He glanced around the stark walled courtyard of the
little guest house I was staying at before he answered.
Curiosity about the course of the negotiations had
reached fever-pitch. Any rumour would be seized upon,
and any listener would carry it.

But I was alone. Seeing this he turned back and said,
'Get dressed, and you can ask him yourself. He's down at
the port, locked in talks with the commissioners.'

'Still?' I said, pausing from rubbing my hair and
looking at him.

He lowered his voice. 'The commissioners will not agree.'

He stood by while I pulled on my clothes. And then we set out together.

We arrived to find Titus slumped in his chair, his head propped on his hand, peering at a great open scroll weighed down with stones. 'Villius; Marcus,' he said, greeting us in a flat, tired voice.

I asked him how the talks were going, though his face told me all I needed to know. He sat back and made a contemptuous swipe at the great scroll. 'May the gods save me from bureaucrats: small men who have never had one vision of greatness in all their lives. Everything is 'but this' and 'but that' as if a man could provide for every shift of chance and fortune.' He let out a long sigh, and rubbed his eyes with his fingers. 'I did not come here to be remembered as the man who betrayed the Greeks.'

His hair had grown again since Kynoskephalai, and was as it had been when first I had met him, all boyishly unkempt and curling at his brow. I thought of the youth he had once been, whom I had met in Tarentum, sitting in the library gardens there, with fire in his blue eyes, full of hope and ambition, who had dreamed the dream of Greece.

I said, 'The games have not yet begun. There is still time.'

'Yes, Marcus. There is still time . . . Forgive me, how is Menexenos?'

I made some quick answer, as one does when a question is asked only from politeness, for I could see his mind was elsewhere, and as soon as I had spoken he said, his eyes straying back to the scroll, 'Now, if ever, while the whole world is watching, is the time for a grand

436

gesture, something that will ring through the ages. But the commissioners see only detail and difficulty. I tell you, nothing great was ever done by a committee.'

There was a tap at the door and a tribune put his head in. 'Sorry, sir, but the commissioners have returned.'

'I am coming,' said Titus wearily.

He stood, and gathered up the scroll. But at the door he paused and looked back. 'I know what people are saying. They say I am not a man of honour; they say I am a Roman barbarian who cannot keep his word. But I will show them a Roman's word counts for something; and, by the gods, I will prove the Aitolians wrong.'

The games began. By now every spare piece of ground from the temple to the stadium and beyond was taken up with tents and pavilions. Everyone who wished to see or be seen was there: politicians with their entourages; rich merchants with wives or courtesans or boys; off-duty soldiers up from Korinth; sailors from the port; painters and sculptors touting for a commission; rhapsodes and public entertainers, and among them all the itinerant traders who are present at any such gathering, selling wine and fruit and honey-cakes.

On the first morning, all the athletes were called together in the sanctuary. They stood in line, dressed in their white tunics, while the priests intoned the prayers, performed the sacrifices, and filled the air with blue curling incense. On the temple steps a boy-choir sang a hymn to horse-loving Poseidon, and then the games were declared open.

It seemed to me that the whole world had come to the Isthmos. There were Achaians and Arkadians from the south; Phokians and Thessalians and Aitolians from the north; Ionians from the eastern islands; and, among them all, non-Greeks as well: Lydians and bearded Persians; Egyptians with painted eyes dressed in white muslin; shining Nubians; gaudy Phoenicians; tall, broad-shouldered Galatians with their fair plaited hair and strange language; dark Sikels from Sicily; rich Etruscans; and wealthy merchants from Roman Italy, speaking loudly in Latin as if no one else could understand it, while their wives stood beside them, frumpy and self-important and overdressed.

I watched the boys' running events and the pentathlon, and went with Villius to see the chariot- and horseback-races out on the plain. Titus had wanted to be there, but he was still busy with the commissioners.

On the third day I went to the Odeion, to listen to the music contests and watch the dancing. And then came the day of the foot-race.

I was awake before the first cock crew, and, rising in the half-light, I went alone to a little ruined shrine of Demeter I had discovered up among the pine groves. There, as the sun rose over the sea in a great spread of light, I spoke my own prayer to the mother goddess.

It was early still when I arrived at the stadium. With the dawn an inshore breeze had picked up. The air smelled fresh, of pine and sea; and high on their poles above the terraces the great coloured banners flapped and billowed in the wind.

I took a place I had already spied out. It was on the

stone terrace at the far end, opposite the judges' seats, by the turning-post with its bronze sculpture of a leaping dolphin. I sat and waited, watching as the first spectators began to drift in. Down on the track a lone boy was making a final check for stones or windfall. From somewhere, carried on the breeze, came the faint tang of athlete's oil.

Before long the crowds arrived, talking loudly, waving and calling to friends, clutching cushions to sit on, and baskets of food and drink. Among them I saw Villius enter alone. We had arranged to meet. He paused and looked about; then, seeing me, strode up between the terraces to join me.

'What news of Titus?' I said.

He shook his head and said, 'Nothing.'

We turned to look as, to an excited buzz from the crowd, the judges entered in procession, garlanded, and robed in white and purple. They took their seats at the front. An official gave a signal; and then, through the athletes' arch, the runners filed in.

Now, for the first time, I saw all the competitors for the foot-race side by side. Broad-shouldered black-haired Thorax was there, his tanned body shining with oil. Further along the line was Damindas. His thin face was tense with nerves, so that he looked almost angry. Seeing him naked, one could see he had powerful runner's thighs, and the strong girdle-like muscle round his pelvis. But, like most of the others, his arms and upper body were neglected, so that he looked like two ill-matched pieces of some sculpted bronze, cobbled together where they did not belong.

'There is Menexenos,' said Villius pointing. I leaned to look. He was half hidden by the post.

The sun was in his upturned face. He looked like a god set down among men.

I remembered Pandion's words, at the practice-track at Athens, when he had spoken of the sculptors of old, who strove to show the perfect body as a mirror of the perfect soul. It seemed to me that what they had fashioned in bronze and stone, Menexenos had wrought out of the very stuff of his being. And the vision they shared, which no man may touch or point to, was the same.

My surroundings broke into my thoughts, and glancing along the stadium I saw other heads had turned to look as well. Here was an image of perfection, and somewhere deep in their souls they knew it and were touched by it, like plants that turn to light.

'He is ready,' nodded Villius.

'Yes,' I said. 'He is ready.' And for an instant tears welled in my eyes, for that beauty which is always beyond the reach of men.

The herald stepped up and proclaimed the name of each runner.

When I heard, 'Menexenos, son of Kleinias, of the deme of Zoster, of Athens,' I yelled out with the rest.

The judges spoke some words; the athletes, turning as one, advanced to the line. They crouched, seeking the scored stone with their toes. There was a pause. The crowd waited.

I remembered what Menexenos had explained to me. This race – which was neither the long-race, nor the short one-stade race – attracted both sprinters and distance-runners. Some had trained for stamina and strength, others for sprinting speed. Each youth's body displayed his own trainer's belief in what quality would win.

Then, sharp and clear, the umpire barked out 'Go!' and they leapt forward, like hounds unleashed.

The crowd roared. Immediately the sprinters surged ahead. But Menexenos fell back, letting the others pass him. His mind was on the end, not the beginning.

I saw that others too – including Thorax and Damindas – had allowed themselves to drop behind, pacing themselves, unworried by the sprinters.

Of the three, Thorax led by a few paces. Damindas was just behind him, his eyes fixed on the back of Thorax's head, his face a mask of furious concentration.

The front runners reached the turning-post with its bronze leaping dolphin, below where I sat. They closed around it, their bare feet throwing up the sand as they sharply turned.

In the lead was a thin, olive-skinned youth, a Kretan herd-boy from Herakleion, so Menexenos had told me, who had trained in the high mountain passes. He had put all his strength into the start, and if he had been running the short-race he would have won. But I could see from his face he was realizing his mistake.

'He is catching up,' cried Villius.

I looked. As the sprinters began to drop back, Menexenos edged forward. Ahead of him, Damindas closed on Thorax, then passed him. As he passed, he turned his head and threw a look of haughty triumph. It spurred

Thorax on as if someone had prodded him in the back with a spear-point. He caught up again, but Damindas would not let him pass, and they ran side by side.

By the third lap the sprinters were clearly struggling. All around on the terraces, the crowd was bellowing and chanting. Thorax and Damindas were still neck and neck, neither one of them willing to let the other pass, as if they were bound by some invisible chain.

Beside me Villius said, 'What is it about those two? You'd think they were the only runners on the track.'

He was right. Damindas had eyes only for Thorax. Whatever had caused the hatred between them must have cut deep. One could see in his face his determination. It had an ugly quality to it, as one sometimes sees on the battlefield. He would not lose the race to Thorax, whatever it took.

But I could see now what Menexenos had meant when he said Damindas knew what he was about. Though he still had not broken ahead of Thorax, he was beginning to set the pace. The two of them struggled like two opposing principles of nature: Thorax running with a power that did not know itself; Damindas burning like a closed furnace, angry, driven, each sinew of his body bent to his will.

Once again they rounded the dolphin in a cloud of sand, and by the fourth lap they were surging past the others. But Menexenos was catching up too. The last of the sprinters dropped back, and now there were only the three of them, with Menexenos half a lap behind.

Finally now Damindas began to push ahead, his

powerful oversized legs pounding the ground. Thorax resisted, refusing to let him open the gap between them. I saw the look of surprise on his face, that out of all the others the despised Damindas should be the one to over-reach him. And I saw the searching too, as he sought within the depths of his being for the speed he needed, like a man searching desperately for hidden gold in a riverbed.

But Damindas was not one for such mysteries. He had other plans.

For the first part of the fifth lap the two leaders vied with each other. At one moment Damindas would seem to be opening the gap; but then, just when it looked as though Thorax had expended his strength, he drew on some new reserve that pushed him forward once more.

All the time, though they had not seen it, Menexenos was closing on both of them; but he was still far behind. The crowd were urging him on, calling his name, calling the name of Athens. His body gleamed with sweat and oil. His eyes shone.

Below me, Thorax and Damindas were at the turning-post again. Menexenos was not far behind, closing faster now. But then something at the post caught my eye: something not quite right, a faltering, the miss of a beat, like a flat note in the intervals of a harmony. It made me look down; but before I could think further I felt Villius's hand grip my arm.

He was not, as a rule, the kind of man to touch other men, or shout out, or make much of little. But now he stared ahead into the rising dust, standing half out of his seat, his fingers locked around my forearm. 'Did you see that, Marcus? Did you see? That thin pale youth did something, I swear it.'

There were mumblings from those around us. They too had seen, or sensed, it. But the judges, seated at the far end of the track, on their stately marble thrones, had not.

Menexenos had once said that we know good from before we are born, which is why we recognize it when we see it. Perhaps we know baseness too. But it came to me in a flash that Damindas had picked his spot with forethought, precisely at the place where the dolphin statue and its stone base momentarily obscured the runners from the judges' eyes. Whatever had happened – a kick? a blow? no one, in the rising dust, could tell – it had thrown Thorax off his beat, just when he was summoning the last of his strength.

Now, as the two of them pressed into the final lap, I could see he had lost his stride. Damindas was opening a gap between them he could never close. Thorax must have known it. Even as I watched I saw the fight go out of him. He dropped back, first by a handspan, then a cubit, then a pace or two. Damindas's supporters were bellowing out, standing and waving their fists and urging him on.

And then, like a golden dart, came Menexenos.

The cheering changed. Different people got to their feet, rising up from the terraces like windblown corn, drowning out Damindas's supporters.

First he swept past Thorax, who was falling rapidly back, his spirit broken. But it seemed too late. Already

444

Damindas was on the final stretch. His eyes were upon the line. His face glowed with the certainty of victory.

When Menexenos surged up behind him he briefly turned his head. But he need not have turned, for in an instant Menexenos was in front, moving with a calm steady power, like wind across the sea.

And then he was at the line, and the whole stadium surged to its feet, shouting and cheering and punching the air.

He turned and saluted them with his raised fist, and broke into a broad smile; and the crowd roared back at him. And then he caught my eye, and gave a slight nod, as if to say: After all, then, it is well done.

The judges crowned him with the celery crown. The other runners, though they were downcast, wished him joy. All except Damindas, who looked away, and would not take his hand. It was while these closing ceremonies were taking place that I noticed a stir in the crowd.

At first I thought nothing of it – often there are small altercations, or someone is taken ill in the heat. But then, from the direction of the archway, people began craning their necks to see, and moments later a trumpet sounded and a herald stepped forward into the open ground. I knew the herald. He had been with us at Kynoskephalai. He was one of the Greeks employed by Titus.

A spreading murmur had begun, moving through the stadium and growing louder, like the first swarming of a hive of bees. All around us men were asking what was happening; and, after the wild excitement of the race, there was suddenly fear in their voices. But as they spoke, others hushed them, for the herald had begun to speak.

Over the noise I heard the name of the Roman Senate, and Titus's name. Then, as each man quietened his neighbour, silence finally descended, and I heard the rest.

Now that King Philip and the Macedonians had at last been vanquished, the herald said, Titus Quinctius and the Senate and People of Rome hereby restored to the peoples of Greece their ancient freedoms. They were to live without foreign garrisons and be subject to no tribute, and would henceforth be governed by their own laws, in the manner of their own choosing, Korinthians, Phokians, Euboians, Achaians, Thessalians . . .

And after that the long list of names was lost in the cheering.

Each man was asking the man next to him what had been said. Beside me, shouting into my ear over the din and slapping me on the back, Villius cried, 'By all the gods, Marcus, he's done it!'

The herald, meanwhile, urged by the crowd, began repeating what he had said, and everyone fell silent, even those who had heard the first time, so that they could hear once more.

Then, when he had finished, a mighty burst of cheering arose, louder even than the first, spreading out beyond the stadium, all through Isthmia, echoing across the valley, a mighty sound like the paean – except that this was not the onset of war, but its end.

From somewhere in the crowd a chant began, spreading like fire in tinder until it was taken up by every man who heard it, and the words they spoke were, 'Titus! Titus! Titus!' And it came to me then that he must be there himself, somewhere in the surging crowd. How not?

He would not have missed this for the world. But not even he could have expected such overwhelming joy.

'Come on!' cried Villius, rising to his feet.

I glanced round for Menexenos, but he was lost from view. We were swept along with the rest, like twigs in a torrent, down the steps and out through the archway, and into the even greater crowds beyond.

Then I caught sight of Titus. He was standing on a low incline, in the open ground near the road. The Greeks were crowding all around him, calling his name, reaching for his hand, touching his cloak, raining down garlands and coloured ribbons upon him.

He was smiling. But the few guards who attended him were starting to look alarmed, as the crowd overwhelmed them.

Villius and I pushed our way forward. As we moved through the press of people, Menexenos arrived, accompanied by Thorax and some others, and together we cleared a path and formed a cordon.

All around us people were cheering and laughing. Somewhere nearby I heard a voice I recognized, and turning I saw the farmer from Phokis, who had walked with me on the road.

He must have heard the words of the proclamation himself, for he was recounting them at the top of his voice, to a group who stood around him. He was praising Rome, wagging his finger at the others and declaring that there really was a nation on this earth prepared to fight for the freedom of other men, a nation that would cross the seas to put down tyranny, and spill its own blood so that right and justice should prevail. 'It has taken a foreign general to remind us,' he cried, raising his hand in a flourish, 'that man is still capable of noble deeds!'

I do not know where he picked up these fine words. From some play he had once heard, no doubt. But the people around him broke into a loud cheer.

He nodded and bowed to them. So taken up was he with his speech that he had not noticed me. I smiled to myself and turned away.

When the games were over, I went with Menexenos to the little supper-party Pasithea had called in his honour.

Her house was everything I had come to expect, a modest dwelling on the edge of town with a terrace of coloured mosaics beneath a vine-trellis, which looked out onto a walled garden planted with rose-trees and trailing herbs.

Niko the Nubian slave-boy, whom I had not seen since Tarentum, welcomed me like an old friend. He had dressed in his best for the occasion, and wore his big golden earrings, and a long tunic of gossamer through which you could see the lithe contours of his body.

He was, indeed, more a part of Pasithea's idiosyncratic family than a servant, and he talked of her with fond affection, and pointed out with broad smiles, as he led us through to the garden, the garlands he had woven round the columns, of violet and dark hyacinth, in honour of Menexenos's victory.

The supper-couches had been set out on the terrace, and Pasithea was waiting there. She kissed Menexenos on the cheek, saying, 'At last, the victor! This evening, my dear, you shall share a couch with me.' She was dressed exquisitely as always, in a dark, shimmering robe of silk and taffeta, and on her breast a necklace of woven gold, inlaid with red cornelian.

I was seated with one of the other guests, one of Pasithea's female friends from Korinth, a cultured young courtesan who had recently come back from Alexandria in Egypt, and was full of its marvels. In the corner a single musician sat under the arbour, picking out a tune on a lyre, and, all about the garden, lights glimmered from tiny shaded lamps.

I looked towards Pasithea and Menexenos. Already they were deep in conversation. I smiled to myself. Truly, I thought, she had made an art of pleasure.

Presently, when Niko had served the wine, she raised her cup and toasted Menexenos, saying, 'You won, my dear. I knew you would. And now I want to hear all about it.'

So he told her of the race, adding at the end, 'But I knew the Aiginetian was faster. He only lost because he hated Thorax more than he cared about winning.'

'Well maybe he *was* faster,' she replied. 'But what of it? Whatever it takes to win the race, clearly it is not speed alone.'

She let out a happy sigh and smiled, and in the silence the music sounded gently. Everything – the setting, the delicate food, the cool wine – was perfectly balanced, designed to heighten the senses, not overwhelm them.

'What now, Pasithea?' asked Menexenos. 'Will you stay in Korinth?'

She cast her eyes around the shadowy walled garden

with its flickering lights and dark climbing shrubs. 'Yes,'
she said. 'For now I shall stay. I shall enjoy my garden,
which I have missed; I shall entertain my friends, and I
shall improve my mind. What more could I ask? I thank
the gods for such a life . . . And you, Menexenos, what
will you do?'

He turned and met my eyes. 'Marcus wants me to go
to Italy, to meet his mother and sister.'

She nodded and smiled, and said, 'Is that so? Well it is
about time.'

They talked on, and, with happiness in my heart, I
watched them. He sat with his broad, muscular hand
unconsciously upon the hem of her robe. His eyes were
bright with wine and pleasure. They might almost have
been lovers.

He had dressed that night in his best white tunic, the
one with a border of meandering squares; and in his thick
bronze hair he wore a spray of myrtle. I thought how he
had changed me, with his example, and with his gentle,
constant love, which was like a rock upon which I could
build my life. A sadness touched me. I shook my head,
and took up my wine-cup. For me the world held nothing
so dear. Somewhere on the high wall, beyond the pool of
light, a bird suddenly cried out, crow-like, harsh and
discordant. No one seemed to notice. The girl beside me
was talking on about her visit to Alexandria; but before I
turned to answer her I made a quick private sign against
the gods of night, who lie in wait for the unwary. The
crow-call had reminded me, lest ever I should forget.

Later, shortly before we left, Pasithea touched my arm
and said, 'Where is Titus tonight, Marcus?'

450

'Titus?' I answered. 'Why, I don't know. I expect he's celebrating somewhere, since that is what all of Korinth is doing.'

'Do you think so?' she said quietly. 'Why don't you call in and see him? Something tells me he will be at home.'

I made some light answer, saying the last place he would be was his own quarters, when there must be a thousand parties he had been invited to. But there was something – a momentary look – that fixed these words in my mind; and after, walking back with Menexenos and the link-boy, I told them to go on ahead, saying I would catch up later, and turned off to the house where Titus was staying.

At the gate I greeted the guard – a man I knew – and took some time to ask after his comrades. Then, eventually, I drew the air of the warm night into my lungs, looked around, and said, 'Is Titus back from celebrating yet? I wanted to wish him well.'

'Why no, Marcus sir. He never went out.'

'Then he has friends here?'

'Not that either. He is alone.'

I found him in his workroom. The only light came from a single lamp, glimmering in the corner. He turned upon hearing the door, to see who it was.

'Why there you are!' I said brightly – I had drunk more than usual that night, and was in the sort of mood where the whole world is beautiful. 'Are you ill, or what is it? Tonight you are the toast of all Greece, and yet you sit in the dark alone.'

As I spoke I walked across the marbled floor to where

he sat. He looked up at me, and then the lamplight caught his face.

'But what has happened?' I cried, staring at him.

He looked away, and passed his hand across his eyes. Without a thought of waiting to be asked, I sat down beside him on the couch. A pitcher stood on the low table, and a cup, half full of wine. I cast about with my eyes, in case whatever disaster had befallen him lay there among the shadows. But there was nothing.

Then, in a voice of infinite sadness, he said, 'It is over. I have nothing more to reach for.'

I stared at him, not understanding; but for a long while he stayed silent, with his head propped on his hands, looking down at the floor. From somewhere far off, through the open window, came dance-music and men's laughter. It sounded suddenly harsh and unpleasant.

Eventually he drew a heavy breath and said, 'I had a dream. It sustained me through my youth. It fed me when nothing else could. It was the light that drew me on.'

He shook his head. 'Listen to them. They have their freedom, but they do not understand how to keep it. It is no more than a word to them. They will squabble and bicker and make petty wars on one another just as before, until once again they find themselves enslaved. And yet I dreamt of this day, I lived to make this happen. And what is it, Marcus? No more than an illusion, a lie, a child's fantasy.'

'A dream is not a lie,' I said. 'It made you what you are, and because of your dream, many men have followed you, and believed in you. Perhaps you are right and the

Greeks will not use their freedom wisely. Yet they have it, and you gave it to them. Because of you, men who have not yet been born will climb higher than they thought possible; and when they grow weary, and feel they cannot go on, they will say to themselves, "Yet there was another, who took this path before me." '

He turned his face to me, and I went on, 'There are times, in our dreams, or on the mountaintop, or in the moment of love, when we are touched by the hand of God, and we see the whole world as it should be seen, in its true proportion. It is in such moments that we know what is real. A shoot in springtime does not know why it grows to the light, and yet it grows; and so it is with men. There is no nobler task than to lead where others might follow, if only they would strive for it. You had a childhood dream, and tonight, because you dreamt that dream, and refused to let fools tell you it was not, Greece once more has her freedom. A man is not a god. But let him strive to be more than he is, and in doing so he will find himself.'

I finished, and afterwards Titus sat for a long time silent. Finally he leant forward and reached for the pitcher.

'Here, drink with me,' he said. 'We have been a long way together, you and I.'

We drank, and did not speak. And as I sat there in the shadows, the thought came to me like the touch of loneliness that for all my wishing it otherwise, my words had not reached him. I thought of the day, long ago, when as a boy I had first set out from Praeneste at my father's side, when he told me it was time I saw something of the world. That boy was gone, and in his place sat the man I had become. Did Titus not see what I saw, he who had given me part of his dream? I cannot say. But when he looked away I saw the brightness fall from his face, and his stricken look returned.

I thought, next morning, it was the sunlight streaming through the shutters that had woken me. Then I heard once again the rapping on the courtyard door.

I listened for the slave, but he must have gone out for provisions, or be sleeping still. Taking care not to wake Menexenos, I twisted off the edge of the bed, grabbed a towel, and walked out across the inner court to the door.

'Oh, Marcus sir, thank God I have found you!'

I looked at the man. Though I knew his face, my sleep-hazed mind could not work out what he was doing here at the Isthmos.

'Florus,' I said eventually, blinking at him. 'What is it? Why are you here?'

He stood in the doorway, staring at me. His face and travelling cloak were dusty. He looked as though he had ridden all the way from Athens.

'What is it?' I said again.

'Why, anyone could have told him. I hardly need explain the danger to you, sir.'

He could not keep his plump hands still. He kept pressing one into the other, as if he were grinding wheat in his palms. Sharply I said, 'Calm yourself, Florus. Sit down here. You have found me. Now tell me what has happened.'

'It is your father, sir. Your stepfather, I mean. I did not know what else to do. I have been on the road since yesterday, and looking for you since the dawn. They have taken him, and I don't know what to do, if only I had—'

'*Who* has taken him, Florus?'

'Why, pirates. Did I not say? The pirates have taken him.'

I sat him down, and managed to calm him somewhat, and eventually, bit by bit, I got it out of him. The previous day – or the day before, he could not remember – a ship had docked at Piraeus carrying a sailor from my step-father's ship. The sailor had been freed by the pirates – so he claimed – in order to bring back to Athens the ransom demand. Most of those on board had been killed. But not Caecilius. The pirates, seeing he was a rich man who would command a high price, had spared him; they would let him live until the next moon. After that, if there was no gold, they would cut him up and feed him to the fishes.

'Curse him!' I cried. 'I told him to keep out of Asia; I told him no good would come of it.' But then, as if a god had touched me on the shoulder, I shivered, and my hands went cold, and looking him in the face I said, 'What pirate, Florus, was this? What was his name?'

But even then I knew.

He shifted, biting his lip, and looked down at the pattern in the tiles at his feet, avoiding my eyes. I remember that pattern. It was of Herakles, wrestling with the Kretan bull.

'You know how it is,' he said, making a helpless

gesture, 'everyone talks of him, but in truth it could be any pirate—'

But then, looking up, he saw my face and said, 'It was Dikaiarchos.'

In my mind the past came crowding in – the Libyan with the gold hoop earring, the girl stepping to her death, and my father's headless corpse. I shivered as if from fever, and felt a clenching in my stomach. I remembered Mars the Avenger, and my cry to heaven, sealed with blood on the altar of my ancestors. Such bonds could not be broken; they were part of the deep structure of the world, and now Dikaiarchos was part of me.

My head was ringing. I pressed my palms to my eyes, and saw blackness and images of death. Through it I became aware of Florus, babbling on about gold and payments. Angrily I shouted, 'Shut up Florus! There will be no gold!'

He looked at me in horror. 'But sir, but Marcus sir, if you don't pay they will kill him. He is your *father*!'

'No; curse you! He is not. I told him not to go. Let him answer for his actions!'

He drew his breath to speak again, but then I saw his eyes move. I looked round. It was Menexenos, standing in the doorway to our room. He was naked still. His hair was tousled from sleep.

'Good day, sir,' said Florus, switching from Latin into his bad Greek.

I do not know how long Menexenos had been listening; but he must have understood enough. Quietly he said, 'You must go; you know that.'

Our eyes met and locked; but I could not speak.

He said, 'You must end it, or he will consume you.'

'No, Menexenos. I can leave it. It is past. Caecilius brought this on himself.'

His eyes studied my face. After a pause he said, 'This has nothing to do with Caecilius. You know that. If not now, then it will be some other time. You cannot turn away.'

I shook my head. But in my heart I knew he was right. And as my mind raced, crowding with the shades of the dead, beside me Florus talked on, words I no longer recall.

We sailed from Korinth. Titus said, 'Take whatever you need.' I took a skilled crew and a small fighting force. And Menexenos.

We sailed under an immense cloudless springtime sky, over a lapis-blue sea between rocky, wooded islands. A strangeness had descended on me, like the still before a tempest, and for long periods I sat silent in the bow of the ship, reflecting on how my father, and inexorable fate, had first brought me to Dikaiarchos; and now my step-father, in his blindness and his greed, was bringing me back. The time had come to repay blood with blood, to avenge my father's shade: it was what I had prayed for; it was the dark anger that had fashioned my life and made me different from other men. And yet, on the threshold of what my soul had burned for, I felt cold and reluctant and full of foreboding. I frowned down at the light-flecked water dancing below the bow, as if, beneath the shining surface of the sea, there lay concealed some answer to the mystery of my life. But all I saw was reflected sunlight and dancing spray, and the shadow of my own form moving on the water.

Eventually I put these brooding thoughts from my mind, still unresolved, and prepared for battle, sitting with Menexenos and the others on the deck, waxing the straps of my armour, oiling my sword.

We came at length to a small island close to Paros, where Florus had said the ransom must be sent. As we drew close, the captain pointed to the land and said, 'What's that?'

Everyone looked. On the white sand of a long curving bay stood two crude structures, fashioned from rocks and driftwood.

'They are altars to Lawlessness and Impiety,' I said, remembering. 'He sets them up wherever he goes. It amuses him.'

'Does he not fear the gods?'

'He laughs at them. He says there are no gods.'

The captain, a pious Roman, shook his head and said no more.

The island was covered with a forest of pine, a pale-green canopy with, here and there, white marble outcrops showing through. We looked carefully, but saw no sign of movement; but we knew there would be spies, concealed and watching, from somewhere among the wooded high-points. We sailed deliberately on, as if we were passing by, taking care to look like a merchant-trader; then, in the last of the dusk, we turned about and made landfall on the far side, in a small inlet concealed from view by rising cliffs.

We set no fire that night, but rested by the ship, beneath the waxing moon; and next morning, with the first glimmer of dawn, we set off on foot along the track which led inland between the pines.

The pirates had made their encampment below a low treeless promontory that commanded views of the eastern and southern approaches. The place had once been someone's farm; there was a courtyard and a well, and a low-roofed red-tiled house, and terraces of vine and olive, neglected and overgrown.

We crept up through the scrub to the stone gateway of the enclosure. It was early still. They had not even posted sentries, so confident were they of their security.

'You would think they owned the whole island,' muttered the Roman captain beside me.

'They do,' said Menexenos. 'They will have enslaved or driven off the inhabitants long ago. No one challenges them; they think they have nothing to fear.'

We found them at their food. There were about thirty of them, outnumbering us three to one, deserters from foreign armies, common criminals, urban rabble, clad in mismatched stolen clothes, the kind of men I had seen before at Korinth and in Epeiros.

They were used to scoring victories over defenceless civilians: they were no match for a well-disciplined force of Roman troops, few though we were. I fought with hard, cold determination, and all the time I was searching for only one man – and nowhere did I see him.

When the fighting was over and the few prisoners were kneeling in submission, I grabbed one of them by the matted strands of his filthy hair, and jerking his head back held my sword-point to his throat. 'Where is he?' I shouted, 'Where is Dikaiarchos?'

At first he tried to pretend he did not know what I was talking about. But when he realized I would kill him, he spat on the ground, and sneered, 'You will never catch him. You cannot defeat him.'

I cast him forward into the dirt, and leaving the others scrambled up the path between the stepped terraces. Below me, on the far side, down a steep track, the pirate ship lay beached and unattended. I cast my eyes about in frustration. The bay – an inland bay – stretched in a long curve northwards, enclosed by a sandy peninsula ending at a headland, which gave onto the open sea. The distance was, I guessed, about two miles; and halfway between me and the open sea, moving with almost serene purpose on the sheltered water, was a small sailing cutter, with one man at the helm, evading me once again.

For a moment I stared in silence. The captain came up, with Menexenos.

'Can we catch him?' I asked. 'Can we bring the ship round?'

But I knew, even before he answered, that it would take too long.

I stared out at the small receding craft. Even before I knew clearly what I intended, my hands were at the straps of my armour.

'Here, take my sword.'

I began pulling off my cuirass and boots.

'I'll come with you.'

'No,' I said, staying his hand, which had already moved to his own armour-straps.

His eyes met mine.

'It must be alone, him and me . . . If I can catch him.'

I gave him a final press on the arm, then turned and bounded down the steep path; and when I reached the beach I began to run.

He was at the helm of the cutter, looking ahead to the place between the rocks where the lagoon let out into the sea. His wild blond mane of hair stirred in the breeze. Here in the open I could feel it, warm and dry, blowing up from the southwest; it favoured him, but not quite, so that, as he advanced, he was forced to tack and attend to the sail.

My bare feet struck on the hard white sand. I paced myself, preserving my breath and strength. At the nearest point, where my running could bring me no closer, I halted, pulled off the rest of my clothes, all except my belt and dagger, and went crashing into the water.

I think he turned then, but with the glare, I could not be sure. I ploughed through the shallows, then began to swim, making for the point ahead of the cutter where the wind was taking it. Even then I had no clear idea of what I should do; yet I felt the unfolding of my destiny, as if some powerful hand were drawing me on.

The cutter was nearing the headland and the open sea; wind filled the sail; a bow-wave appeared as it picked up speed. I raised my head as I swam, gauging the distance between us. Dikaiarchos was making one final change of course to take him through the rocky strait; the cutter would cross my path: but only once, and it was moving faster than I could swim. I knew, if I missed him, there would be no second chance.

461

The black hull bore down on me like some skimming sea-creature, closer and closer, until I could make out the fine detail of the painted eye etched in white on the bow. And then, when it was almost upon me, its direction changed, only slightly, but enough to pass me by. I ducked down and swam, but even as I swam I sensed its passing, and when I looked again it was the receding stern I saw.

I threw myself after it, but I knew it was useless: I could not match its speed. Then I saw something moving and splashing beside me in the craft's wake about a spear-length away; I screwed up my eyes against the glare, thinking at first it was a fish or bird. Then I saw. It was the mooring lanyard, trailing in the water, which, in his haste, Dikaiarchos had not pulled aboard. The knot in it was snagging on the surface. I lunged forward and grabbed at it.

The lanyard, slimy with weed, slipped through my hands; but then, near the end of its length, my hand found the knot which had been hopping and dancing on the water. The line jerked tight, my body surged forward, and in the cutter, Dikaiarchos, feeling the movement, looked round.

I pulled myself along the rope and hooked my arm over the bulwark, and at the same time he sprang from his place by the helm. A knife flashed in his hand, and he brought it down hard at the place where, an instant before, I had been clinging on. The blade lodged in the wood with a shudder. He had struck with such force that he needed both hands to pull it free, and this gave me a moment to regain my hold – but only a moment, before, once again, he brought down the blade, aiming for my hands and forearms where I was trying to hold on. Each time he struck out I was forced to let go, first with one hand, then the other, as I tried to avoid him. My hands slipped and slid on the varnished wood. Then suddenly, in the midst of this, the cutter gave a violent lurch as a wind-flaw caught the sail and the untended helm swung round. Dikaiarchos staggered back; and I, with a shout of frustration, lost my grip altogether and fell crashing back into the water.

I watched bitterly as the black hull raced away from me. I could see him fighting with the sail-rope and the helm, and glancing urgently ahead. And then I saw why. In his struggle to dislodge me he had missed his course: he was no longer heading for the gap of open sea, but for the jagged grey rocks that rose up on one side of the headland. With an angry swipe he threw the helm hard over. The cutter veered sharply round, avoided the rocks, and ran skimming up onto the sand of the long beach.

He leapt out, but he did not run. He stood waiting, watching with narrowed eyes while I swam to shore and climbed naked from the water.

'I can see,' he called out, when I was near enough to hail, 'that I shall have to kill you.'

I advanced along the sea-strand, brandishing my dagger in my fist.

'Fight me!' I yelled. 'And kill me if you can.'

He laughed. 'What am I to you, Roman? Do you want gold? Is that it?'

I threw his laughter harshly back at him.

'Even now, do you not know me?'

He regarded me, slitting his eyes against the glare of the white sand.

'Remember Epeiros!' I cried. 'You killed my father there.'

He shrugged.

'I have killed many men.'

He did not remember, any more than a man, years later, might recall what he ate one day for his dinner.

Something broke in me then. My eyes burned, my feelings bled, and I felt the power of the god within me, like fire surging through tinder. And it seemed to me he said: I have brought you here, this is your destiny; blood must answer blood, and even gods yield to necessity.

And then we closed, one on the other, and fought. I remembered Antikles and his lessons, and knew then, for the first time fully, what he had sought to teach me. I was nothing and everything. I knew each motion of his body, and the intention of his muscles, even before he moved, as if we were united in one being; I released myself from fear and death, existing in one timeless moment that was like a high drawn-out note of music. His knife cut me – across the chest, the forearm, the thigh – but I felt no pain, or no more pain than I had always felt, and as we locked and struggled and kicked and swerved and fought I moved with his motion, breathed with his breathing, and danced to his own deadly dance. At one point, when we were locked together each brandishing his knife, each wet with mingled sweat and blood, he said again, 'Who are you?' but this time with no laughter in his voice. I was warding him off. His wrist slipped from my grip, and his knife came down at my throat. I evaded it like a cat, twisting and curling, and the blade sliced into the sand at my ear. In that instant his eyes locked on mine, and, knowing what must follow, some deep knowledge passed between us. I struck, and pierced him with the mortal blow, and for a moment he held my gaze and smiled, before, with an exhalation of breath, his soul left him.

For a long time after that I sat in silence, on a low rock at the edge of the water, searching my mind for feeling, trying to regain the person I had been. After a while I knelt down beside the body. I touched his hand, and felt with my fingers the contours of his palm, and the bones beneath his skin. He was warm still, and his skin was soft. I knew he was dead; and yet I could not comprehend it. I took my hand away, and saw it was wet with his blood. For a long time I stared; then I touched it to my lips, and tasted it with my tongue, and on the far side of the rock a lizard sat watching me, judging me with its basilisk eye. I became aware of sounds, and realized that my comrades were calling. I got to my feet, and took up my knife, and walked away.

Caecilius had been locked in an outhouse, a foul stone-built hovel behind a latrine-pit, beside the muddy sty where pigs were kept.

He must have heard the distant sounds of battle. Now, hearing the approach of men, and unable to see who they were, he supposed we had come to kill him, and from behind the locked door began wailing out for the gods to take pity on his plight.

He came stumbling out stupid with fear, dressed still

in the expensive clothes he had been taken in. His hair, and the fine wool of his clothing, were caked in filth and mire.

We seated him on a log, and told him it was all right, that he was safe, and need not fear. As we spoke he sat muttering to himself, angrily snapping his hand at the flies that buzzed around him, and blinking at the light.

The others, shamed perhaps at the sight of a man who had lost so much of his dignity, left him to recover himself. But when I turned to go he snatched at my arm and said, 'Why are you here?'

'We came to find you, sir, as I told you. I have come to take you home.'

'Look at me! Look at my clothes!'

'I will find you something clean to wear. But rest now. You have had a shock.'

He gaped at me. Menexenos had cleaned my wounds, and bound the deep cut in my thigh, and helped me dress because my arm was stiffening. But no doubt I was a fearsome sight.

'What have you been doing?' he said sharply, in a tone closer to his usual voice.

'I was in a fight; but it is over now.'

'Have you found my money? There were at least ten talents, in a casket. Go and search, will you? It must be somewhere hereabouts. Go on, go now, before someone takes it. No one can be trusted, you know, and I cannot afford to lose it.'

I looked at him, and looked away. My throat tightened, and I was overcome by a sudden urge to weep, filled with a grief I had no name for. My wounds were starting to hurt. I felt changed, and new, and vulnerable. I had believed, in the deep place in my heart where instinct dwells, that somehow the whole world must be changed with me. But this vain and foolish man, who had so nearly lost his life, and a moment ago had been calling upon the gods to save him, was just the same, fretting on about his petty concerns while all about him were blood and death.

He began speaking again, but I no longer listened. Without another word I turned and left him, and behind me, as if I were still there, I could hear him chattering on, cataloguing his troubles.

Menexenos found me sitting alone beside the sea. He sat down beside me and looked out. The sun was sinking to the west. The air was clear, and clean, and filled with light.

'They have found his money,' he said. 'He is counting it. He seems much better now.'

'Nothing changes him,' I said.

'No one changes unless he wills it. To little men the gods send little things. It is always so.'

I smiled, and picking up a fistful of white sand, watched as it fell between my fingers.

'But you have changed,' he said, after a pause.

I cast away the remains of the sand. The tiny grains scattered in a cloud over the water.

'Yes. I feel different . . . empty, as if something within me has died.'

'You killed what needed to be killed. The god knew

that. Everything has to be paid for, Marcus; and it is the price we pay that makes us men.'

I nodded at his words, and let out my breath. And together, in silence, we looked out at the setting sun.

HISTORICAL NOTE

MARCUS AND MENEXENOS ARE invented charac-
ters. Titus is the historical figure Titus Quinctius Flamininus
(229–174 BC), and the story covers the period between
207 BC and 196 BC when Titus rose to prominence and
led Rome's fight against Philip.

Philip is the historical figure Philip the Fifth, king of
Macedon (238–179 BC), and at this time he dominated
Greece as described in the story, and threatened, or was
perceived to threaten, Rome. He should not be confused
with the more famous Philip the Second of Macedon
(382–336 BC), who was the father of Alexander the
Great.

At the time the novel is set, Rome's territory was
largely confined to Italy; it was not the great empire it
later became. There was no emperor: its political arrangements were still those of a republic, ruled by the Senate
and people, and headed by two elected consuls who
held office jointly for one year. The rise of Philip co-
incided with the final victory of Rome against its old

enemy Carthage. Carthage, led by Hannibal, had nearly destroyed Rome. There were many at Rome who feared that Philip was another Hannibal: they were not prepared to wait until a Macedonian army was at the gates of Rome, as Hannibal had once been. It remains an open question whether Philip did in fact pose the threat Rome feared. Certainly he was vaunting, dangerous and unpredictable; and he had been caught out helping Carthage against Rome.

At this period in Rome's history, two important changes were under way: first, there was a great flowering of interest in Greek culture, with Greek teachers, artists and ideas flowing into Rome and Italy; second, the merchant class was on the rise, taking advantage of Rome's growing political dominance and the accompanying opportunities for trade and profit. In the story, the tensions between the old and the new are reflected and explored in Marcus's relationship with his stepfather, and Titus's with his father.

Titus was a philhellene, a lover of Greek culture, and his time spent in the Italian–Greek city of Tarentum (modern Taranto) is in the historical record. There is no reason to suppose that his wish to free Greece from tyranny was not genuine, except among those who look for baseness in any noble motive.

Lucius, Titus's brother, is a historical figure, and mention is made in the sources that he was removed from the Senate for dissolute behaviour. The sources also mention Lucius's boyfriend, though no name is given. He appears to have been equally dissolute.

Dikaiarchos is a historical figure, though to suit the

purposes of the story, I have merged part of his character with another historical figure, Demetrios of Pharos.

It should perhaps be noted that bisexuality was ubiquitous in the ancient world, and well attested in the sources. Such behaviour was not, in itself, an object of censure, and this remained true until the end of the classical period when the Church, wielding its growing political power, began to impose its own uniform blueprint on human relations.